THE SEVEN

AN ODYSSEY OF SEVEN HORSES AND SEVEN SOULS

ALISON GIESCHEN

DEFIANCE PRESS & PUBLISHING, LLC

The Seven: An Odyssey of Seven Horses and Seven Souls
By Alison Gieschen
© 2024 All rights reserved.

This is a work of fiction. Names, characters, businesses, places, events, and incidents are either the products of the author's imagination or used in a fictitious manner. Any resemblance to actual persons, living or dead, or actual events is purely coincidental

Published by:
Defiance Press & Publishing, LLC
www.defiancepress.com

ISBN:
eBook: 978-1-966625-02-5
Paperback: 978-1-966625-03-2
Printed in the United States of America

For permission requests or inquiries, contact Defiance Press & Publishing at:
publishing@defiancepress.com

The Father and Son

"THEY HAVE STRAYED SO far," the Father said to his Son.

"You knew they would. That is why You sent me," the Son replied.

The Father nodded. "There is the matter of free will. I gave them the will to choose. It's always been about choice. That is why I implemented the backup plan. I was hoping it would never come to this."

The Father continued, "Fifty million years ago, I placed horses on this planet. Horses began as man's quiet counterparts. As beasts of burden, these animals evolved alongside man. They provided the support that allowed man to build civilizations. They carried man to explore new boundaries, enabling him to travel further and faster than he could on his own. Horses helped man cultivate crops. They were trained to pull equipment and plow fields. Man taught them to pull wagons and carry goods, leading to the development of trade.

"Next came expansion and wars. Man elevated horses from beasts of burden to the keys to new kingdoms. He began selecting the largest and fiercest equines. Specific breeds were developed—some for speed, others for size and agility. The most revered were the warhorses, which allowed troops to move en masse. They pulled wagons filled with weapons, ammunition, and food for the soldiers. Mounted warriors were more likely to claim victory in battle.

"The world seemed smaller because horses opened the doors to new horizons. Men looked to conquer new continents, packing horses on ships as explorers sailed to new lands. They could now cover vast expanses of territory and claim that land as their own. Once they claimed this land, it was horses that carried families, supplies, and troops needed to protect it. Horses were in the background of all human civilization.

"Over the centuries, the essence of the horse and its importance has dwindled. For many people, they have become vanity items, bought and sold for profit and sport. The sperm of a renowned stallion can sell for millions of dollars. Horses are often bred to run the fastest, skillfully separate a cow from a herd, and jump the tallest fences. Most are kept by the elite as status symbols, rather than for their contribution to mankind.

"Sadly, the shift has begun. While there are people who love and value them, the majority feel no connection to horses. Before cars, buses, and trains, there were only horses. In a hundred years, man evolved from relying on horses to believing it's more natural to drive a machine. This is proof of man's separation from the gifts of the Earth.

"It's only in the poorest countries that man still use horses to travel and carry their wares. Humanity has lost touch with the one animal that has remained obedient to man through all the centuries of his existence. Equines are the reason man achieved his level of sophistication, and yet, most humans fear rather than respect them. Thousands of years of innate knowledge about these great beasts have evaporated in a single century.

"Seven attributes of mankind dictate whether he is living by the Holy Spirit: love, joy, peace, patience, kindness, goodness, and faithfulness. To honor these attributes, to decide if man has progressed to a point of no return, and to determine if there is enough good left in this world, I will let the beasts who carried men to this point decide. Seven equines will choose. With seven, there can be no tie."

"It will be done," the Son said. "Seven equines will determine the fate of humanity."

"May they choose wisely," the Father replied. "They may be animals, but they know better than most what lies in the hearts of men."

Reginald Dupuis

Paris, France
CEO Omega Drug Company

9.3 BILLION. THE NUMBERS were in for the latest dividends on the sale of the Omega vaccines. Reginald sat back in the first-class train car and let his head recline against the padded seat. His eyes glanced lazily out the window at the countryside of south-central France. The train was bound for Paris. It would be about a five-and-a-half-hour ride, plenty of time for Reginald to pull out his laptop and review the presentation he would be making to the board of directors.

The train departed at 5:30 AM. It would arrive in Paris in plenty of time to make the 1:00 PM board meeting being held in the conference room at the most prestigious hotel in Paris, the Ritz. A stretch limo would be waiting at the train station to pick up Reginald; a man in a crisp uniform holding up the sign "REGINALD DUPUIS - OMEGA CEO" would greet him as he entered the lobby.

Reginald learned early in life to leave nothing to chance. He had watched the toll physical labor had taken on his father.

Although he had his father's intense brown, heavily lidded eyes and his thick, rustic head of unruly auburn hair, the similarities ended there. Reginald decided to use his brain rather than his body to find success. When Reginald was 17, his father held his young, strong, vibrant hands in his gnarled, arthritic hands. He looked his son in the eye. He spoke to him about the merits of hard work and dedication as Reginald prepared to leave their small hometown and attend a university in Paris.

For the men who worked in the Thiers knife factory, their labor preserved the craft and heritage of the historic town. Thiers became known early in the 18th century for its artisanal savoir-faire and unrivaled quality of its cutlery items. The craftsmanship of the knives from this small factory was discovered by King Louis XIV. La Victoire knives grew in popularity first in France, then throughout the world. Over the centuries, the fame spawned 80 companies with nearly 1,300 employees, thanks to men like his father, bent, withered, and arthritic from the effects of the physical labor needed to preserve this craft.

Reginald smiled. He thought fondly of his father. He wished his father were still alive to see his success. Five years ago, his father passed; his mother shortly later from her broken heart. Reginald inherited the family home in Thiers, France. He held onto it as a weekend retreat, a reminder of his parents and his childhood. The past two years had changed his perspective on keeping the house, which overlooked the village famous for its knife factory, his piece of legacy from the town's rich history.

His father, a humble man, valued his job at the knife factory. When Reginald was little, his mom would take him to the factory to bring his papa a warm lunch. A cold stream ran through the building. The workers had to lie on their bellies on cold slabs of concrete and reach into the stream that powered the grinding stones used to sharpen the knives.

The job was hard on his father's body, soul-sucking. The chill ran deep from the water, especially in the winter. The family dog, Jacque, accompanied his father to work each day. All of the men brought their dogs. The dogs faithfully lay on the backs of their masters as they worked, sharing the warmth of their large, hairy bodies. The extra heat was beneficial, but not enough to prevent arthritis from crippling many of the workers.

Looking at his own hands, Reginald saw the difference between his father's hands at his age and his own. Reginald's were flawless. His nails were professionally manicured. His hands were strong, but not beefy. When he shook hands with his counterparts, there was strength in his grip, but not hardness. Reginald had been fortunate to discover the merits of building strength from within during his first year at the International School of Management (ISM) in Paris. By the time Reginald earned his Ph.D., he had studied in New York, São Paulo, and Shanghai. His skills in research, marketing, and as an international modern business leader launched his career in the pharmaceutical industry. On the eve of his 48th birthday, he became one of the youngest CEOs in the Omega drug company's history.

Time aboard the train was precious. It was rare downtime for Reginald. He usually traveled by private jet. He didn't get away to Thiers often, but when he did, it was therapeutic. He purposely took the train rather than fly or drive. It was his time to relax, shut the world out, and study the gorgeous scenery of the wine country in which he grew up. His one regret was not having married and raised a family. There wasn't time in his journey up the corporate ladder to woo a woman or focus on a relationship.

Financially, he was set for life. Developing and marketing vaccines for the last two years during a worldwide pandemic had launched an immense campaign that far exceeded the goals and expectations of any pharmaceutical company in history. He had been instrumental in achieving that. Yes, the road had not been paved smoothly in front of him. He had to ask more of his employees than he had intended. He worked tirelessly, sometimes staying awake for 48-hour stretches to meet crucial deadlines. Sure, he had to fudge some numbers, statistics, and reports to make things happen. But that's how he accomplished the impossible, exacted results that seemed inconceivable to others. The work ethic he inherited from his father was channeled in an opposite direction, but one that reaped the rewards of hard work on a global level.

Glancing down the aisle of the train in the first-class car gave him chills to know he was, without a doubt, the most successful man in the car. If people knew who he was, they would probably stand up, walk over, and shake his hand. In a few short hours, he would be delivering a presentation to the board of directors outlining his success. It was a good feeling to have spent the prior weekend in his father's home. It took him back to his roots, his foundation, but he also had his suspicions that he had outgrown the small home in his village. Without a wife or children to pass on the legacy, it was a warm memory, but it was time to move on. Since his time was so valuable, he would rather spend it at one of his other properties: one of his many elaborate city suites, his mountain chalet in the Swiss Alps, or the incredible lodge he had recently purchased in Lake Tahoe.

It was time. He had honored his past. He loved the familiar rise of the vine-covered hills of the French countryside. These were his roots, but they could stay planted here—a fond memory. He nodded to no one in particular as the train barreled silently across the floor of the valley. The tracks meandered along the banks of the Loire River, the longest river in France. The view was breathtaking. However, this would be his last visit to Thiers. As soon as he had time, he would have his house in Thiers put on the market. He had taken away the sentimental items from the home when his father died. It was time to move on. The world had changed, and if Reginald knew one thing about himself, it was that he would adapt.

*****

An unexpected lurch in the smooth stride of the train jolted Reginald from his relaxing introspection. The steady chug of the train decreased in cadence, began slowing rapidly, then came to a halt punctuated by a hiss from the brakes. There were no scheduled stops on this express train.

At half capacity, the members of the first-class car remained calm. Heads leaned into the aisle, looking for some explanation with questioning expressions and looks of mild irritation, but no one seemed to be panicking. Those traveling with a companion talked animatedly amongst themselves. Reginald glanced at his watch. It was only an hour and a half into the journey. As long as there was intervention within the next hour, he would still be able to make his meeting on time. He had to smile at the irony. Arguably the most important meeting of his life, one he had spent a solid week in the seclusion and privacy of his childhood home preparing for, and the train taking him to his meeting had to break down.

Reginald rolled his eyes and pushed his head into the neck rest. He waited for the announcement to give an update on the unfortunate turn of events. He was glad he had thought ahead and sent his Stuart Hughes Diamond Edition$700,000 suit, purchased just for this meeting, to the suite he had reserved at the Ritz. All he had with him was a weekend bag of casual clothes. He planned to stop in his room before the meeting, change into the power suit, and have a shot or two from the bottle of Uísque Single Malt Glenrothes whiskey that he had purchased as a celebration gift to himself. It cost over 10,000 euros. Then he would be ready for his meeting.

This delay was irritating, but one of Reginald's best attributes was overcoming obstacles, finding ways around roadblocks, and thinking outside the box to get things done. He was confident that after a successful meeting, he would be back in his hotel room by midnight, sitting with his prized bottle of whiskey, telling the story to his counterparts with whom he would choose selectively to share his whiskey and the story of his day's accomplishments.

The Father and Son

"Do you think it is a bit extreme to challenge the most important day in this man's life while he is dealing with a battle for the existence of mankind?" the Son asked.

"No man is given more than he can bear," the Father replied. "I have chosen to remove us from the equation and leave the decision to the equines. Therefore, I have chosen not to know the outcome."

"Yet You chose this particular man for a reason," the Son pressed.

"There are over 7.9 billion people on the planet Earth," the Father said. "Many are not good candidates to represent humanity. While My choice was random to an extent, it was made from a specific pool.

"The pool was created by the strength of the human spirit. To be worthy to represent mankind, I thought it important that each individual achieved a level of competence worthy of respect. Each candidate is a person who displays great passion for life."

"Yet, if we judge humanity by this qualification," the Son countered, "did You not teach us that even Your Son is not above washing the feet of His disciples? How did You decide who is worthy? Did You not say that all men are created in Your likeness to receive glory and honor and power? You created all things, and by Your will, they exist. Does this not make all men worthy?"

"All men have the potential to be worthy," the Father said. "Not all have embraced their worthiness and used it to achieve what is possible. Whether it is washing feet or climbing Mount Everest, what they have chosen, they must do with their whole heart, to the best of their ability."

*****

After five minutes of silence, the speakers crackled to life, and the conductor began his announcement. All eyes raised in anticipation to where they were mounted in the front of each car.

"Ladies and gentlemen," the announcement commenced in French, in brief sections, followed by a repeat of the information in English.

"It is with regret that we are informing you that we are having technical difficulties with our train's power system. Our engineers are currently assessing the situation. We have also been in communication with the station in Paris. They have been informed of the delay. The schedule will be updated and made public."

Groans sounded from several of the passengers. Reginald took a deep breath. He crossed his arms, glanced down at his watch, and began preparing a mental list of contingency plans.

Ten minutes later, an update was provided by the conductor. "Ladies and gentlemen, we thank you for your patience and understanding. We have an update on our situation. Please be advised of the following schedule change."

By the second announcement, Reginald had already calculated exactly how much flex time he had in his schedule. The train departed that morning at 5:30 AM. It was due to arrive at the station in Paris at 11:00 AM. That gave him 2 hours to take the ten-minute drive to the hotel, shower, dress, have his whiskey, and show up for the board meeting. That was plenty of time.

His assistants had the presentation loaded and ready to play. Leaving nothing to chance, Reginald made the entire tech team show up at the conference room on Sunday night. He spent Sunday evening on the phone with his technical crew, making sure all the equipment was in place and ready to go. The software was loaded and ready to play with the click of a mouse.

Reginald was highly conscious of security. He had learned to trust no one. The software was loaded, and the newest file had been uploaded. The slide show could not be presented unless it was unlocked with a password. That series of numbers, letters, and symbols was safely stored on his computer. Espionage was common in his industry, and he could not take the chance that his data could be tampered with. He could call in the password if needed. The COO could make the presentation, but he knew it wouldn't come to that.

It had been a struggle for him to decide whether to arrive Sunday evening or Monday at noon back at the Ritz in Paris. In the back of his mind, he knew this trip might be his last to Thiers. Sentiment overtook logic. He decided to spend Sunday night in his childhood home before his big presentation on Monday to have a clear head and no distractions. He knew what would happen if he ended up spending the evening with some of his buddies. It was a decision he was now regretting.

Unlike air travel, train delays were not common. They usually ran like clockwork. He was looking forward to the comfort and quiet of the long ride, the opportunity for introspection and reflection, and to mentally prepare for his big presentation. There was no way he could have predicted a train delay. Reginald looked up and hoped for some good news.

"A vital system on our train's engine has stopped functioning. Repairs cannot be made here. There is a replacement component on its way. The estimated time of arrival is 10:30."

Reginald looked at his watch. It was a little after 7:00 AM. That meant the engine would not be ready for over 3 hours. They still had 3 ½ hours to go to reach Paris. That scenario was not going to work for him. He waited for the conductor to continue.

"We apologize for any inconvenience. During the wait, feel free to walk about the train, use the toilets, and visit the dining cars. We will open the doors for ventilation. We will inform you when the coupling of the pilot engine is complete. Be prepared to return to your seats when you hear the announcement. Ladies and gentlemen, we ask that you remain onboard the train as there is a danger of serious injury if you try to disembark. Thank you for your cooperation, and again, we apologize for the inconvenience."

A collective moan rose from those in the first-class car. More than one day had been ruined. Reginald felt quite sure his disruption was the most serious, barring a brain surgeon who was on his way to perform a medical miracle, or perhaps the delay of a vital organ being transported in a cooler for an emergency transplant. He didn't see anyone grabbing a cooler and racing off the train.

He peered out the window. The terrain included rolling hills, some covered with shrubs and trees, and others with symmetrical rows of grapevines. There were no towns as far as he could see, no major roads, and little hope of finding someone to pick him up in this remote location in time to make his meeting. Way off in the distance was the hint of an orange-tiled roof. He could almost make out what looked like an outbuilding. His best guess was that the dwelling was an old homestead. It was the only sign of civilization in his periphery.

The train was equipped with Wi-Fi. If he left the train, he would have no cell signal in these remote parts. An unfamiliar feeling started creeping its way into the fringes of Reginald's mind. Was it uncertainty? It wasn't fear yet. Fear was something he had never dealt with and didn't plan to in the foreseeable future. There were only obstacles. With the right resources, all obstacles could be overcome.

Pushing aside extraneous emotions, Reginald laid out his options and formed a semblance of a plan. First, he had to text his assistants and apprise them of the situation. His instructions were clear. He was currently delayed on the train and was looking into alternative transportation. If, for some reason, he was delayed in arriving at the conference at 1:00, his assistants were to order the champagne reserved for after the meeting. A series of toasts and brief talks by his business partners could be used as a stall tactic until his arrival.

If his delay was more than an hour, the COO, Mary Farnsworth, would have to give the presentation. All she had to do was read the slides. The board of directors would have to be apprised of the situation. The most important factor was that the information was disseminated on the profit margin and how this company had made more on these vaccines than on any new product in the company's history.

It wouldn't look good if he was not there to make the presentation, but damage control would be implemented, and he would move past this setback. It's what he did. He didn't plan on missing the meeting. He still had a five-hour window. He Googled the nearest major town to his present location, which turned out to be Dijon, just a few miles away. The nearest airport to Dijon was 31 kilometers away. If he could make it to Dijon, he could take a bus or taxi to the airport. He could jump on a flight; hell, he could even charter an emergency flight to Paris. The cost was no object. Omega would foot the bill.

With a plan in place, Reginald set his sights on implementation. His communications had been sent. The next phase of the plan was to disembark the train. Reginald grabbed his briefcase with his laptop and his duffle bag. He made his way down the aisle to the junction between the cars. The doors were open, and the fresh breeze from the French countryside circulated through the entryway. A few Frenchmen stood in the open air smoking cigarettes.

A man in uniform stood in the doorway of the first-class car. He was eyeing Reginald as Reginald made his way down the aisle with purpose, carrying his briefcase and duffle.

"Excusez-moi, monsieur," he politely addressed Reginald.

Quite directly, Reginald didn't hesitate in stating his intent. He addressed the worker in French. "I have an important meeting to make in Paris. I can't wait for the engine. I'm going to get to Dijon, which is just a few miles away, and then to the airport. Believe me, 'mon ami', this is my only option."

"One moment, please, sir," the worker replied. "I need to contact my superior."

After a brief conversation with his boss, the worker nodded. "I can't detain you from exiting the train, sir. I do have to warn you that you are exiting the train at your own risk. There is a chance of injury leaving the train."

"I acknowledge, understand, and accept that risk."

"May I have your name, please, sir?" the worker asked.

"Reginald Dupuis."

"Mr. Dupuis, I will assist you as best I can in departing from the train car. The descent down the embankment can also be dangerous. Please proceed with the utmost caution. I'm not sure where you will be going. We are not near any major roads."

"I am heading to the house I can see from here," he said, pointing to the distant orange roof. "I'm hoping to find someone home, or maybe another house nearby that can drive me into town."

In a few minutes, the worker had dropped down the four feet to the level of the track. He took the briefcase and duffle from Reginald and placed them on the ground. He had Reginald sit on the edge of the platform and took his arm. Reginald jumped the span with ease and landed cat-like on the balls of his feet.

Once safely on the ground, Reginald assisted the worker by giving him a boost back up to the platform between the cars. He gave a quick salute to the man, grabbed his duffle and briefcase, and began the slippery descent down the rocking outcropping that led to ground level.

Reginald reached the base and turned to look back at the train. Faces lined the windows of the train and open doorways, staring in disbelief. No one followed. He knew they all thought he was crazy, heading off into the remote countryside on foot. It wasn't being crazy; it was thinking outside the box. He had a timeline that had to be met. He felt confident he could accomplish his task, work around this obstacle, and make it to his meeting. His victory over this obstruction would be legendary. It would escalate his status in the company, proving once again that his resources were unlimited and nothing could stand in his way. He waved to the faces peering at him, turned, and set off with determined strides toward the small farm in the distance.

*****

It took almost an hour to cover the stretch of land between the train tracks and the orange roof on the horizon. Reginald walked briskly, breaking into a jog when the terrain allowed. He had to trailblaze across fields. It was further away than it looked from the train. When the ground became uneven, he had to slow his pace.

Exercise had not been at the top of Reginald's list of priorities during the past two years as his time was immersed in developing vaccines to fight a global pandemic. He was not as fit as he used to be. He had gained a few pounds from late-night meals and consuming one too many cocktails at the end of each exhausting day. The duffle and briefcase slowed him down. He considered ditching the duffle to make better time but decided, in the end, to carry the extra weight rather than give in to his physical discomfort.

If all went well, he would reach the tiny farm in the next 30 minutes. If he could get to Dijon within the next hour, he would be back on track to arrive in Paris by 1:00. Panting hard, he glanced at his watch and took note of the time. He set the goal of arriving at the farm within his 30-minute deadline and then finding a ride to Dijon within the hour. It was doable. He randomly checked his cell phone. As predicted, there were no bars illuminated and no chance of cell service.

With his heart pounding past the point of comfort, Reginald pushed the limits of his physical strength. He arrived at the perimeter of the homestead a few minutes before his 30-minute deadline. He knew he had reached the boundaries of the small farm. There was a distinct change between the unkempt fields and the maintained look of the property surrounding the small house.

Distinctly old-style French architecture, the one-story stucco house was missing a few of the orange roof shingles. The unsymmetrical wooden door and window frames were adorned with faded and peeling blue paint. A long driveway wound its way away from the house and disappeared over a small hill. Two stony dirt tracks comprised the driveway, with a strip of green grass dividing the lanes. It seemed to be used infrequently as small flowers and tall grass grew relatively undisturbed within the grassy strip. It did appear the house was inhabited, which gave Reginald hope that someone was home or might be soon.

Reginald strode up to the front door and knocked loudly. He waited impatiently for sounds of movement inside, willing a human being to come to the door. No one answered. He put his duffle and briefcase next to the door, against the stucco. Hesitantly, he tried to open the door. When it didn't budge, he rattled the knob in frustration. The door was locked.

"Shit! Ok, let's assess what we have here to work with," he said, verbalizing his next attack strategy as he glanced at the yard around him. "We might not have a car, but maybe there is a bike, tractor, or a goddamn all-terrain vehicle in the barn? Would that be too much to ask?" he questioned the universe as he turned to make his way to explore the outbuilding.

Constructed with stone, the barn appeared to be more ancient than the home. It could have been a remnant of the very first settlers on this property. Some of the barns in the older French villages dated back hundreds of years. The roof was not in good shape. The thatched roof showed indents and other signs of structural weakness.

Reaching the main door of the barn, Reginald peered hopefully into its dark midst. He felt inside the doorway, hoping for a light switch to illuminate the interior. There was none. He stood for a moment and let his eyes adjust. He could see the details fairly well as he stepped inside.

There was one main aisle centered under the low wooden ceiling. Cobwebs draped every inch of the rafters. Four stalls lined the right side. There was a doorway on the outside of each stall leading to a pasture behind the barn. Farm animals could access the stalls or leave as desired and as weather permitted. The left side was open and used for storage of farm tools. Wheelbarrows, axes, shovels, hoes, and a variety of tools were placed haphazardly in this area. At the very end of the barn on the left side was an enclosed room with a door. Reginald hoped this was where the owners kept their power tools or a nice bike, and with any luck, something motorized.

Reginald grasped the handle and took a deep breath as he opened the door. The dim light shone into the room, revealing horse equipment. No tractor, no bike, and nothing helpful in providing transportation was visible. Then, he spotted a saddle and bridle.

"Hmm," he thought out loud. "Now this might be something I can work with. I bet there's a horse in that pasture. I have no idea how to put these things on a horse, but how hard can it be? If I can get down that driveway and close enough to town to spot a car, this day might just yet be saved."

*****

Recalling his college spring-break vacation to Mexico when he was attending school in NYC, Reginald tried to remember his only experience on a horse. Other than pony rides in his village as a child, his only adult encounter with a horse had been in Cancun. The horses were ready when the group arrived, all saddled and bridled. He climbed up onto the Western saddle, put his feet in the stirrups, grabbed the reins, and off they went. He pulled the reins left; the horse went left. He pulled them right; the horse went right. He pulled them back; the horse stopped. It certainly wasn't rocket science.

He remembered bouncing uncomfortably when the horse broke into a trot. The guide promised that if he kicked the horse to make it canter, the gait was faster but a lot smoother. When the horse cantered, there was a more rhythmical cadence. It was faster but much easier to find the rhythm and keep his ass in the saddle. The group of college students laughed and had a great time cantering down the sandy beach. One girl did fall off, but she had also been drinking too much. She didn't get hurt landing on the soft sand. The guide boosted her back on the horse, and the group continued the ride at a walk.

The mere thought that Reginald had to resort to this archaic form of transportation to make it to the most important meeting of his life and then present his historical modern medical breakthrough to the board of directors was irony at its finest. What were the odds? He looked up toward the heavens for a brief moment, paused reflectively with his hand under his chin. He contemplated the odds of divine intervention—then shook his head and said, "Nah..."

Reginald sprang into action. He hoped his assumption was correct. Why else would the owners keep the horse's equipment safely in a room, away from the dust and cobwebs, if there wasn't a horse outside? Reginald grabbed the bridle that was hanging on a hook and a strange-looking saddle that sat perched on a post protruding waist-high from the back wall. It was much different than the Western saddle with a horn he had used in Mexico. Lastly, he found a rope in a box on the floor with some brushes and other items, which he ignored. He knew he needed a rope to catch the horse.

Carrying the equipment into the hallway, he laid it on the floor. There was a steel ring attached to one of the support posts in the aisle of the barn. Reginald assumed this was where the owners tied the horse up. His most important task at this moment was to find the horse. He opened a stall door and walked through to the door leading outside and into the pasture. At first glance, the signs were good that a horse was occupying the field. There was a pile of hay in a round metal feeder and lots of horse manure on the ground. Reginald put his hand to his forehead to block the sun, now almost directly above him. He scanned the field.

There, under a tree along the fence line, was a horse. It seemed an average size, dark brown with a black mane and tail. It had a small white star in the middle of its forehead, mostly covered by a shaggy forelock. Intense brown eyes peering through the forelock studied Reginald. There was a metal water basin also under the tree. The horse had been dipping its nose into the water, taking deep slurping sips of the cold, fresh water when Reginald interrupted it. The horse remained frozen in place, water dripping from its hairy chin.

Time was of the essence; Reginald quickly approached the horse, slowing down as he neared so as not to spook the animal. He wasn't sure, but he assumed the horse was smart enough to know the difference between its owner and a stranger. He guessed they were like dogs; they knew their owners and might be suspicious of strangers. When he got close, Reginald reached down and pulled up a handful of grass. He held it out toward the horse as a peace offering. He knew horses liked grass.

The horse seemed less than impressed with the offering. "Well, it's the only thing I have. If I had an apple or a carrot, I would give you one, but I don't. Time is of the essence here, buddy. You have the most important job of your entire life to do today. I'm calling you into service. I'm coming over there and putting this rope around your neck. I'm taking you back to the barn, and we are going on a little ride. A fast ride."

Throwing the grass on the ground, Reginald approached the horse's head with the rope in both hands, ready to throw it around its neck. Inches from his target, the horse spun around. The horse's large behind now faced Reginald. The tail switched angrily from side to side. The horse's ears were pinned back against its neck. Reginald knew nothing about horses, but he assumed this was not a friendly greeting.

"Whoa there, buddy," Reginald said in a consoling voice, raising his hands in a peaceful gesture as he backed up a few steps. "Maybe we got off to a bad start here. I just need you to come with me peacefully. I'm going to try this again. Slowly."

In the back of his mind, Reginald knew he didn't have time for this crap. He glanced at his watch and saw that he was 10 minutes away from his goal of leaving the farm and being on his way to the town of Dijon. He could still do this. He had to think smart and fast. After all, this was just a stupid horse. His high level of intelligence could certainly figure out a solution to capturing this horse. *Think, think,* Reginald prodded his brain. *What do all animals respond to? Food. Food is going to be the answer.*

Reginald bolted back toward the barn. He entered the stall and ran into the barn aisle, then turned right toward the room with the horse's equipment. As soon as he entered the room, he noticed metal trash cans with lids in one corner. Instinct told him he would find horse food in those bins. The lids would be used to keep out the mice. As soon as he pulled the lid off one of the cans, he was greeted with the aroma of oats and molasses. Paydirt.

Unwilling to be outsmarted a second time, Reginald made sure he thought things through before his next attempt to capture the horse. He shut the stall door leading into the aisle of the barn and then walked out the back door. He held the grain in a bucket and shook it, calling to the horse. At the sound of grain rattling around in the bucket, the horse raised his head in interest. He was still under the tree, but at least Reginald had his interest. Reginald shook the bucket and called, but the horse, although tempted, remained trans-fixed.

"Shit, shit, shit. This stupid animal is wasting my damn time," Reginald spat as he made his way with the bucket back into the field. Five precious minutes later, Reginald was walking backward, shaking the bucket, the horse taking agonizingly slow steps to follow. His goal was to lure the horse into the stall, pour the grain into the bucket inside the stall, then he would have the horse trapped.

Finally, arriving back at the barn, Reginald backed into the stall ahead of the horse and made lots of noise pouring the grain into the food bucket. "There you go. Come and get your delicious food," Reginald prompted sarcastically as he eased carefully away from the bucket. He slid himself along the wall toward the back of the stall. The horse entered the stall without hesitation, without even a sideways glance at

Reginald. He walked straight to the bucket and dove into eating the sweet feed.

"Well, that was anticlimactic," Reginald mused. The horse raised his head to chew a mouthful of grain, then lowered his head back into the bucket. Reginald approached cautiously as the horse seemed completely occupied, unconcerned with his presence. When he reached the horse's neck, he slid the rope slowly and carefully over his neck. He reached under, grasping the tail end, making a loop around the horse's neck. He tied a knot close to the throat, just below his thick jowls. Thinking ahead, he kept the end long to lead the horse out of the stall and have enough rope left to tie the horse to the metal ring in the aisle. Reginald smiled, mentally patting himself on the back for his resourcefulness and quick thinking. He took a deep breath. "One task down, and one to go. Let's get you saddled and get the hell out of here."

Careful to keep hold of the rope, Reginald opened the stall door. He had to get the horse out the stall door, around the corner, and tie him to the ring. One step at a time. The horse was chewing the grain with agonizing slowness. He would dip his head into the bucket, take a few small nibbles of the grain, then spend an eternity chewing it. "What? Did your mother tell you that you had to chew every bite a hundred times? That's a fallacy, you know," Reginald chided, seriously beginning to lose his patience.

The horse had eaten enough; Reginald tugged on the rope to pull the horse away from the bucket. The horse didn't even budge. He lowered his head back into the bucket, more determined than ever to finish every last morsel. Reginald tugged harder. The horse didn't even flinch. This was the straw that broke the camel's back. The clock was ticking; too much was riding on the outcome of this situation to be patient any longer. If the horse refused to respond to a direct request, Reginald was going to have to be more forceful. He glanced around the stall for something to hit the horse with, just to get his attention, but there was nothing. Reginald shrugged. "Sorry, horse, you leave me no other choice."

Finally running out of patience, Reginald kicked the horse as hard as he could in the belly. While the blow did little to hurt the horse, it did take him by surprise. The horse backed away from the bucket, the whites of his eyes showing clearly; he was not expecting a physical attack from the human. "Ready to talk now? Let's go!"

Reginald pulled the rope, keeping tension on it. The horse followed. He didn't look at the horse. He simply walked through the stall door. The horse followed warily. He walked directly to the pile of tack on the floor and stopped at the post with the iron ring. He took the end of the rope and tied a strong knot, tethering the horse securely. "This can go the easy way or the hard way from here," Reginald explained to the horse. "We can get this done, and you can be back in your pasture in no time, or things can get ugly. It's your choice."

Inspecting the pile of tack, Reginald picked up the saddle first. He had a vague suspicion there was supposed to be a pad or something under the saddle. He remembered watching Westerns as a kid. The first thing a cowboy did before putting a saddle on was to throw on a blanket. He didn't have time to look for one. One ride without one probably wouldn't do any harm.

Forgoing the pad, Reginald grasped the saddle, one hand in front, the other on the back. There was a long strap hanging down. He figured the strap was tightened under the horse's belly to keep the saddle on. He folded it over the top of the saddle, confident the worst of this day was behind him. Things would go smoothly from here. He almost paused in reflection on this pivotal and defining moment. He wanted to remember this second for the rest of his life; the story of how the train broke down, how he forged alone into the remote countryside, found a horse, captured that horse, and then saddled him and rode the beast to defeat his obstacle. There would be books written about this.

In one swift motion, Reginald tossed the saddle onto the horse's back. Reginald had been correct that the moments that followed would be pivotal and defining. Reginald failed to consider that there was more than his will factoring into the outcome of events. Had there only been his will, things might have gone smoothly. However, the instincts of animals, especially horses, are strong. Those who do not understand those instincts cannot predict the cause and effect of their actions. Reginald, not knowing that horses are "fight or flight" animals, could not have predicted that after he kicked the horse violently in the belly, the horse instinctively viewed him as a possible threat. When the horse felt he was being attacked with the saddle while being tied to a post, there was only one option: flight. The horse freaked out.

In a matter of seconds, Reginald's plans went from a series of calculated actions to uncontrolled chaos. The horse pulled back in an attempt to escape what he perceived as a threat. As the horse pulled with 1,000 pounds of body weight, the rope tightened around his windpipe. Bracing himself for a pull to freedom, the horse's back end sank low to the ground, and his front legs straightened. He became locked in a death struggle.

Horrified, Reginald stood back and watched the horse, eyes wide with fright, strangled breathing coming from flared nostrils. Every muscle in the horse's body clenched tighter than a steel drum. For the first time in Reginald's life, he had no idea what to do.

It was clear that if he didn't free the horse quickly, the horse was going to die. He was cutting off his oxygen supply by pulling so hard. All his chances of getting to Dijon would die with this stupid beast. "Stop, stop," Reginald pleaded, holding his hands up and walking slowly toward the horse. "Just stop pulling, and you'll be fine!"

The horse renewed his efforts, pulling even harder, back feet slipping and sliding on the floor as he tried to find purchase. His breathing came in rasping gasps as the knot continued to tighten.

Reginald ran up to the post and tried to untie the knot. With so much weight on the rope, it only took a second for him to realize there was no hope of getting the knot untied from the post or from under the horse's chin. Reginald scanned the room for something that might help. He didn't see any shears or saws to cut the rope. He spotted a shovel, a big square shovel. He ran to it and grabbed it from the pile of gardening tools.

Grasping the shovel by the handle, Reginald angled the flat side of the shovel directly behind the horse. He figured if he could scare the horse into moving forward, he might be able to get the rope untied. He swung the shovel and made an impact directly on the large hindquarters of the horse. There was a loud thud, but not a single reaction from the horse. It remained locked in battle with its own demons. Frustrated, Reginald swung again, harder this time. The horse didn't even flinch. Reginald dropped the shovel, his wrists stinging from the impact. He kicked it off to the side, ready to scream.

"You stupid animal!" he yelled in desperation. "You wouldn't even be here if it weren't for humans. We bred you, trained you, and pulled you out of the wilderness so you could evolve into something useful! This is the best you can do? Hang yourself? Thank God we got rid of you for modern transportation!" he spat, turning red with rage. "Now I have to figure out how to save your ass."

Reginald ran down the barn aisle toward the tack room. He quickly searched for a knife, scissors, or anything sharp he could cut the rope with. He found nothing. Finding something in the house seemed like the only option. Reginald sprinted back down the barn aisle, hoping as he passed the horse that it would give up pulling. Instead, he could see the horse beginning to falter; his breathing had become even more ragged.

Back at the door of the house, Reginald didn't even pause. He took his foot and, just like he had seen policemen do on television, kicked just below the handle with all his might. The door shattered inward. Reginald bolted down the hallway but suddenly skidded to a stop when he realized he was passing the kitchen, the first doorway to his right. As he attempted a U-turn, the rug underneath his feet slipped, causing him to come crashing down onto the hardwood floor. He landed hard on his hip and elbow. Shooting pains radiated from the impact with the floor. "GOD DAMN IT!" he screamed as he clutched the door frame to the kitchen and pulled himself to his feet.

In the center of the small kitchen was a wooden butcher block-style table with four stools neatly tucked underneath. Above the table, cast iron pots and pans hung neatly from hooks suspended from the ceiling. The countertop next to a large ceramic sink instantly drew Reginald's attention. A wooden block holding a variety of knives contained the key to resolving the crisis. Reginald dashed to the block and pulled out the largest of the knives.

Time seemed to stop as Reginald stared at the words emblazoned on the blade of the knife: La Victoire. This was a knife made in his hometown of Thiers. Thoughts of his father came flooding into his mind: his father's strong hands, the sound of his father's voice, the love that he felt for the man who inspired him to be who he was, to strive for only the best.

Reginald began to cry. It was the second time in his adult life, the first being the day his father died. No matter how he steeled himself against anything life could throw at him, nothing could prepare him for how he was feeling at this moment. He had been so confident that he could control every aspect of his destiny. There had been no problem too big for him to tackle. If he used his intellect, there was nothing that could stop him from reaching his goals. Until now. True, it was only the life of a horse at stake, but for the first time in his life, he felt he had failed.

Racing back out the shattered door, past his duffle and briefcase leaning against the house, Reginald knew he had to fix this. Sunshine glinted off the blade as he ran back to the barn, as if his dad was sending him strength from heaven. He burst down the aisle, hoping he wasn't too late. He cut the rope, and the horse collapsed to the floor. Reginald's fingers worked the knot under the horse's throat, loosening the knot and stretching the rope away from the horse's neck. The horse's eyes were closed.

Just then, the silence was broken by the sound of car tires on the gravel next to the barn. The owners had arrived home and had seen their barn door open.

Reginald looked past the horse in disbelief. The bright sun silhouetted two figures exiting the car. One was a man, the other possibly his son. Reginald couldn't make out any details of the figures as the sun illuminated them from behind.

Then, someone asked, "Qu'avez-vous fait à mon cheval?" What have you done to my horse? It was a boy's voice.

"I had him tied and he pulled back. I couldn't get him to stop. I ran to get a knife to cut him free," Reginald explained as best he could.

The strangers approached. The man knelt by the horse's head, the boy put his ear to the belly of the horse. "Pappa, I can hear a heartbeat. I hear his breath!"

"Talk to him, Pierre. Tell him it's going to be okay. He needs to hear your voice," the father instructed.

"Jacque," the boy whispered close to his ear. "Please, don't give up! You will be okay. Just breathe, Jacque. Just breathe."

The man and his son massaged the horse, murmuring soft words of encouragement. Within moments, the horse coughed. He lifted his head and sneezed. The boy smiled. He kissed his horse on the nose and stood, giving him room. The father moved away also.

The horse stretched his front legs forward and, with a great heave of his hindquarters, managed to get back into a standing position. The horse shook with all his might, sending a shower of dust motes flying into the sunbeams reaching their way down the barn aisle. He coughed again, sending air flowing back into his gigantic lungs. The man and the boy hugged.

Sofia Santiago

Olhão, Portugal
Marathon Runner

NO ONE IN HER family understood her desire to run. Since she was six years old, Sofia's passion was running. Sofia developed her ability to run as a self-defense mechanism against her two older brothers. They chased her relentlessly. Her best defense was to be faster than them. Two and four years older, they had size on their side. She had speed and determination. She was a gazelle; they were lions. One-on-one, over a short distance, she could outrun them every time.

Sofia learned about determination from her father. He was a fisherman. He had attended school until he was 11, until her grandfather took him out of school to help support the family. Her father could read and write, but the knowledge he had of the ocean and how to catch fish was what put food on their family's table and kept a roof over their heads.

He was a kind and loving father. When Sofia would climb into his lap with tears in her big, brown eyes, complaining that her brothers were being mean to her, her father would whisper in her ear: "Every morning in Africa, a gazelle wakes up. It knows it must run faster than the slowest gazelle or it will be eaten by a lion."

The repetition of this phrase instilled two ideas in her young, impressionable mind. The first was that she must learn to run like a gazelle. Second, she developed a fascination for life in Africa. The Dark Continent seemed wild, mystical, and steeped in the survival of the fittest. She knew that someday she would visit Africa and run like the fastest gazelle. When, as a teenager, she learned about the Comrades Ultramarathon held once a year in South Africa, it became her obsession.

Her brothers were expected to carry on the family business of fishing. Her father owned several boats. He had plenty of men working for him, so he didn't need to take his sons out of school to learn the family trade. They enjoyed fishing with their father on the weekends. It was never expected that Sofia would join them. Women in Portugal were the housekeepers, cooks, and mothers, and her mother's generation still held the idea that all women should be wives and mothers. Sofia had not yet developed maternal instincts. She would rather take any job in the world than cook, clean, and have babies.

Sofia's olive skin and her long, dark, curly hair were inherited from her mother. Apart from that, they were as different as night and day. Her mother kept a tightly run household, as well as attending to her primary job, mending nets. This was her passion, the focus of her life. The work was overwhelming at times, which resulted in Sofia having to spend most of her afternoons after school fending for herself.

Growing up in the tiny fishing village of Olhão, activities for a young girl were limited. Settled by fishermen, Olhão was important in the Algarve as it served as an important trade route between Portugal and North Africa. Fishing and tourism were the town's main sources of income. Because Sophia was a loner, she wasn't quick to develop friendships. Sophia quickly outgrew playing the traditional Portuguese games after school with other children from the town. With her speed and agility, she dominated the games of Cat and Mouse, Blind Goat, and Elastic Jumping. By the time she reached her 12th birthday, she had no interest in joining the organized school sports of soccer, swimming, or gymnastics. All she wanted to do was run.

Fortunately for Sophia, along the coast of the Algarve runs the Via Algarviana. The Via Algarviana is a long-distance trail beginning at the Cape of St. Vincent and ending 300 kilometers away at the spectacular cliffs of Alcoutim. The trail was perfect for cycling, especially mountain biking; however, it became instrumental in helping her train for long-distance running. The trail wanders into the interior of Portugal for a bit. It has steep hills and varied terrain, and it is perfect for training for someone whose only goal in life was to attend the Comrades Ultramarathon in the hilly terrain of South Africa.

Sophia's dream of running in the Comrades Marathon was known to her family. No one ever talked about it, considering it only a pipe dream. Sophia's parents suggested that she train for the Olympics and use her God-given talents for the glory of her country. Sophia knew that the funding, sponsorships, and backing she would need to go to the Olympics were nearly impossible for a girl from a fishing village in

Portugal. There were no coaches in her town to guide and train her. There wasn't even a track team in her high school to help her travel and make a name for herself.

Besides, she wasn't running for glory. She was training for a contest that only the strongest and bravest runners ever even considered. It wasn't a race; it was a passion. It was a seed that somehow got planted inside you and grew roots in your soul. The sprouts wound into your very existence. It was more than an obsession. It was as if you were chosen, and if you didn't compete, you would be denying your essence, the very reason for being born. How did Sophia know this? She studied the history and competitors of the Comrades Marathon. Their obsession told the story.

The Comrades Marathon, considered an ultramarathon of approximately 89 kilometers or 55 miles in length, is run every year in the KwaZulu-Natal province of South Africa. It spans the distance between the cities of Durban and Pieter-maritzburg. It is the world's largest and oldest ultramarathon race. Competitors must be over the age of 20 to run the race. They must qualify by completing a recognized marathon, 26 miles, in under five hours.

What sets the Comrades apart from regular marathons is that there are additional requirements beyond simply completing the race. Five cut-off points must be reached within a designated time frame. Unlike a regular marathon, there is a spiritual aspect. The runners of the Comrades are required to acknowledge and embrace the attributes of dedication, camaraderie, selflessness, perseverance, and ubuntu. The term ubuntu, in Zulu, means "humanity." It can be translated as "I am because we are" or "humanity towards others." In

Xhosa, there is a more philosophical translation: "the belief in a universal bond of sharing that connects all humanity." It was this definition that drove the passion for Sophia. She felt it was her destiny to run this race and connect with humanity. She would find the connection she had been searching for her entire life, one that she was never able to find in her small fishing village in Portugal.

Comrades was established on May 24th, 1921. It has been run annually with two exceptions: World War II and the 2020 COVID-19 pandemic. Over 300,000 runners have completed the race. It was created by World War I veteran Vic Clapham to honor the South African soldiers who lost their lives during that war. To Sophia, this race had meaning. It was created to honor those soldiers who endured a 2,700-kilometer, or 1,700-mile, march through sweltering conditions in German East Africa. The race was meant to be a test of human endurance and to celebrate mankind's spirit over adversity. It was for those who had the spirit of a gazelle, and that was Sophia.

The Father and Son

"This woman seems an odd choice for Your judgment of humanity," the Son said.

"Why is that, My Son?" the Father asked.

"She does have great strength of spirit," the Son replied. "Unlike our first human, she seems to cherish humanity and is driven by her love for it. Can she be used as a litmus test, as a true representation of the common man?"

"A valid observation," the Father said, "yet she is myopic with her passion. She has chosen to pursue her dream without regard to anything or anyone else in her life. What happens if her dream is challenged? What is she willing to sacrifice to see her dream fulfilled? Will there be weakness when one only focuses on a single strength?"

"No human is perfect," the Son pointed out. "You have said that it is not through strength that one prevails. If You intend to take away her life's dream, her passion, is that not asking more of a human than she might be able to bear?"

"This test is to determine if there is any compassion over strength left in mankind," the Father answered. "Does man only have love for himself? Has he lost his connection to the world around him?"

*****

Sophia's nineteenth birthday was a pivotal moment in her life. This was the year she would attempt to qualify for a recognized marathon. If she succeeded, she would enter the Comrades Marathon the following year, after she turned 20, and achieve her life's dream. Her mother asked her what she would do when she finished. Sophia didn't have a clue. Training for and entering this race was as far as she had planned. She was young and would figure out the rest when it was all said and done.

Fortunately for Sophia, Lisbon, Portugal, holds one of the world's most prestigious marathons every October. The EDP Lisbon Marathon has one of the most scenic courses among the big marathons in the world. Starting in Cascais, the popular resort city with sandy beaches, well-preserved architecture, and iconic tiled streets, the route leads up the coastline and finishes in downtown Lisbon. It was a no-brainer that Sophia would enter this home-field marathon as her qualifying event for the Comrades.

Sophia wished there were more hills and changes in terrain in the EDP Marathon. She could have chosen to travel to another country where the terrain was more challenging, but her funds were quite limited. She had been working as a waitress at a café in town since she was 16. This was the only source of money for her training. Her parents had encouraged her to go to university and get a degree, but she set her sights on training for the Comrades with the promise of considering going to a university when her dream was completed.

When October finally arrived, seemingly arriving slower than molasses drips on a cold day in December, Sophia had been training relentlessly on the Via Algarviana trail. Without any professional training, Sophia had to rely on finding research regarding the ultimate training for running a marathon. Thanks to the internet, she felt she had followed the most successful training regimen.

Adhering to the National Strength and Conditioning Association's plan, seven weeks before the marathon, Sophia ran five days a week. The training contained varied lengths of trails, with one day dedicated to short runs and hill sprints. In weeks eight through 11, she did three days of shorter runs, one day of hill sprints, and one 12-mile run. From weeks 12 to 15, she followed the same schedule with a 20-mile run. Finally, the week before the marathon, she did shorter runs so her body was not sore or taxed for the big race. Interspersed with her running, Sophia swam in the ocean every morning. She also had weights in her bedroom and trained by doing squats with the weights to build up her leg strength. She also stretched and did yoga. Sophia focused on her mind, body, and spirit. She felt ready for her first marathon.

Her entire family boarded the train to Cascais with Sophia. They were supportive of her, eager to see her complete her first marathon. Sophia had resisted the urge to attend a marathon before this date. Her only goal in competing in a marathon was to qualify for the Comrades, the only race that mattered to her.

When the train arrived in Cascais, Sophia looked out the window as the train pulled into the station. Groups of runners were gathered. She knew they were runners by the clothing they wore, by their footwear, and by the shape of their bodies. There were few humans as lean and fit as marathon runners. Many of them had already signed into the event and carried backpacks emblazoned with EDP MARATHON. During the trip, Sophia had spotted athletes on the train whom she suspected were also on their way to the marathon. Outside, friends waited at the station to greet the newcomers. Runners were grouped around their coaches, who had tracksuits with their nations' names and flags. Sophia could feel the excitement in the air even before the 'swoosh' when the train doors opened.

The family disembarked and headed into the main square along the beachfront, where they would be spending two nights at the Hotel Baia. It was an extravagance for their family to be spending the weekend in such luxury. The Baia was not the most expensive hotel in town by any stretch, but it was a far cry above the hotels where they usually stayed. In fact, they rarely took family vacations. However, her parents knew how important this race was to their daughter, and they wanted to contribute. They knew how hard she had been working, how intensely focused and dedicated she had been toward achieving her goals. Her two brothers, Miguel and Antonio, now 21 and 24, wanted to be there also. They were professional fishermen now, learning to run their father's legacy, but they also wanted to be there for their sister.

It was a short walk from the train into town and easy to find the registration tent. It was centered in the town along the beachfront. Huge banners flapped in the ocean breeze, welcoming runners to the event and pointing the way for the competitors to sign in and register. This was a world-class event. No expense was spared. A band was playing on one end of the venue. Tables selling t-shirts, souvenirs, and local wares lined the streets. Olá ice cream stands with their red and white roofs offered tantalizing ice cream treats for the onlookers.

The backdrop for the race was the cerulean blue ocean lined with a heavenly host of gigantic, white, fluffy clouds. Hundreds of sailboats bobbed at anchor in the center of the harbor. Closer to shore, fishing boats were moored to orange buoys. A dock along the edge of the harbor was strewn with fishing nets, traps, and the equipment needed for those who reaped the bounty of the sea. The town buzzed with excitement.

After their long day of travel, the family turned in early. Sophia had carb-loaded at an all-you-can-eat pasta buffet hosted by the marathon for the competitors. Her family had wandered into the heart of Cascais for a traditional Portuguese dinner of sardines. Sophia had to laugh at the fact that her fishing family was eating fish, rather than a rack of lamb at the Irish pub or having a lasagna dinner at the Italian restaurant. Cascais was filled with international restaurants and cuisines from every corner of the globe. You could take the family away from the fish, but you couldn't take the fish away from the family.

Sophia mingled and chatted with a few of the Portuguese competitors at the competitors' buffet. She had little in common with any of them. All were seasoned marathon runners. All were there with the hopes of breaking previous records. While it was never spoken, it was implied that each runner had their sights set on the prestigious honor of crossing the finish line first in their division. Sophia didn't care about finishing first. She only needed to complete the course in under five hours to qualify for the Comrades.

It was like a dream for Sophia, waking up early on the morning of the race. She donned her shorts, tank top, sneakers, and competitor's bib. Her family rose, dressed, and accompanied her to the start of the course. Sophia was slightly nervous. She had practiced this morning in her mind a hundred times. She remained calm, focused, and thought only about the run. She had trained on hills and rough terrain. This course was completely flat. She trained in high winds generated along the high coastal cliffs. Today, there was only a light breeze. The sun was shining, but the air was still cool, though not cold. The temperature and weather were perfect.

Thousands of runners mingled around the starting area. Special runners, those with invitations to the event, were placed at the front of the pack. These were the runners at the forefront of the running world, the ones with the highest probability of winning the event. Jostling for a good position was no longer such an issue for marathon runners; it was more of a status symbol. Timing chips encased in a hard plastic ring had been given to each runner in their race packet before the event.

On the morning of the race, the marathoners tied the chips into their shoelaces. Antennas sheathed in wide rubber mats had been positioned along the course. When the runners stepped on the rubber mat across the starting line, the chip activated, and the runners' times were recorded. Likewise, when the runners crossed the finish line, their official times were recorded and transmitted instantly to gigantic screens.

Sophia jostled for a position as close to the group of starters as she could get. She strained to see the sidelines over the heads of the runners to where she knew her family would be watching. They would take the train into Lisbon after the start of the race and find a place to watch Sophia cross the finish line.

There were almost a dozen water and refreshment stations along the way where spectators could catch a glimpse of the runners as they passed, but the family voted to be at the finish line to celebrate Sophia's crossing. She spotted her family and waved, then glanced at her watch, knowing the starting gun would be going off in mere minutes. Her heart rate remained steady; she remained calm and confident. She had been training for this moment for most of her life. She knew she would have no problem finishing this race in far less than five hours.

In what sounded like a clap of cosmic thunder, a small cannon was used to signal the start of the race. The contestants surged like a wave, breaking into one giant swell of energy. The force caused several people to collide. Sophia tripped over a woman who sprawled unexpectedly in front of her. One twisted ankle at the beginning of the race would end things quickly for Sophia. She jumped with all her might to clear the woman's body. She not only cleared her but landed with a foot to spare before sprinting off. She knew medics would attend to the injured. She remained focused, like a gazelle, running to be faster than the lions, the fastest gazelle in the herd.

While the goal was five hours, Sophia wanted to test her limits. This was her first race. She had no idea how she compared to other athletes. This was her trial by fire, and she was going to give it all she had. This race would not translate to the Comrades, but it would be a measure of how she held her own against professional runners. She kept her speed at a strong but steady pace, knowing that there were no steep hills to climb, no downward slopes to threaten her footing. She vowed not to look at her watch. She only wanted to focus on her breathing, her heart rate, and willing every toned muscle in her body to work in unison to provide the ultimate amount of power for her level of exertion.

She didn't stop at the first few stations. When she guessed she was halfway through, she veered over to a station and grabbed a cup of water. She downed it and threw the cup to the side where volunteers yelled encouraging words and retrieved her cup. That's when she noticed the runners in front of her had thinned considerably. Most of the runners in front of her were men. There was a smattering of women. She had earned her way into the hardcore group, spurring her desire to be competitive. Sophia decided, with half the race under her belt, to turn it up a notch. She was feeling fantastic.

Finally, Sophia couldn't resist glancing at her watch. She knew by the stations she was at least three-quarters of the way through the race. The timer on her watch indicated she had been running for two hours. She was far ahead of meeting her goal of finishing in five hours. An involuntary smile creased her face. Grabbing one more cup of water from a station she was passing, she threw the cup with gusto and turned on the afterburners. The road in front of her began to straighten as she realized she was nearing the city of Lisbon. The iconic buildings climbing the hill above the city loomed closer.

About ten minutes later, she could see the forerunners of the pack in the distance. As she focused on placing one foot in front of the other, she saw half a mile ahead the first runner across the finish line. His arms went up, the tape curled around him, and the photographers and reporters jostled to get close to him. Runners filtered in behind him. Sophia didn't waver; her feet rhythmically pounded the pavement as she struggled to eke out as much speed as her dwindling energy could manage.

Two hours and twenty-eight minutes after Sophia crossed the start line, the chip in her sneaker touched the finish line mat and recorded her time. She had no idea where her family was, but she raised her arms to the sky and high-fived the air. She managed to rein in her stride, taking deep cleansing breaths and slowing to a walk. She was exhausted, completely depleted, but she felt euphoric. She guessed if this feeling could be attained with a drug, she might just become a drug addict. She couldn't imagine feeling any more elated than she did at this moment, even though her body was screaming at her, threatening to cramp if she didn't keep moving forward. She began walking, willing herself to recover as she searched the crowd for her family.

As her heart rate finally slowed and her breathing began to return to normal, Sophia approached the tents with the refreshments, physicians, and waiting press. Immediately, she became swarmed by reporters sticking microphones in her face. She was stunned for a moment, not believing the cacophony of voices shouting at her.

"Sophia Santiago! How do you feel?... Sophia, who is your trainer? Sophia, what does it feel like to win the Lisbon Marathon?"

Not believing her ears, she gaped at the reporters. "What do you mean, how does it feel to win the Lisbon Marathon?" Completely incredulous and still breathing heavily, her body tried to suck in as much oxygen as possible.

Moving beside her as she walked, a reporter stuck a microphone next to her face. "Sophia, you were the fastest woman to finish the race with a time of two hours and 28 minutes. The fastest record is two hours and 24 minutes. You only missed the fastest time by four minutes! How does that feel?" In the span of one sentence, Sophia's world was rocked.

*****

Winning an international marathon had several major impacts on Sophia. The most poignant moment was when she was reunited with her family. Her parents were crying. Tears of pride and joy consumed them to the point that all they could do was hug their daughter. Her brothers picked her up and spun her around, hoisting her like a hero. And a hero she was. The Portuguesa media was having a field day. "Local girl defies all odds and wins the Lisbon Marathon."

Sophia was a quiet and shy girl. She was not ready for the barrage of microphones in her face as reporters barked questions, the television cameras capturing every word she spoke, tailing every movement she made. As soon as she was able, she begged her family to get back on the train and head back to her quiet fishing village. It was all overwhelming since her goal was simply to finish in under five hours, not to take home an international title.

Another major impact was that Sophia became flooded with sponsorship opportunities and invitations to join professional running associations. They all wanted Sophia to join their team. Of all the solicitations she received by letter, phone, and email, there was only one that interested her. A Portuguese athletic wear company was looking for the face of their new spokesperson. Sophia had the perfect runner's body, luscious long curly hair, seductive brown eyes with thick lashes, and with her recent marathon win, she was the perfect candidate to be the Compentensia Deportes spokesperson. When they asked if she had an agent willing to negotiate a contract with the company, Sophia told them she didn't. But she would agree to represent them if they would pay all her expenses for the 2023 Comrades Ultramarathon in South Africa.

Sophia's oldest brother, Antonio, was the most book-smart of the family. He attended a local university and got a degree in business so he could help manage and invest the money made from the family fishing business. Sophia's father insisted that Antonio bargain with Compentensia to make sure Sophia was getting a good deal. Antonio and Sophia met with the company representatives. They came home with a signed agreement that, in return for paying for all Sophia's expenses to travel and compete in the 2023 Comrades Ultramarathon, Sophia would wear their brand and do a series of photoshoots for the company. Sophia was not thrilled with the idea of being a model, but she loved that she would be able to focus on her training full-time and even give up her waitressing job. It was a dream come true for a young athlete born in a fishing village.

With money no longer an issue, Sophia immersed herself in training for the grueling 55-mile race. It was almost twice the distance of a regular marathon, which had been difficult, with the added challenge of hills and rough terrain. There was one small spark of contention between her and her parents regarding her decisions. They had done their homework, and they knew the physical toll long-distance running had on the human body. They loved their daughter and knew that she was on a path of self-destruction if she continued her running obsession beyond the Comrades.

Her parents begged her to promise them that once she completed this marathon, she would put running behind her as a career, go to college, and find a passion that would not have such a toll on her physical health. Sophia reluctantly agreed.

They weren't wrong. As Sophia trained and began increasing the distances she ran, she had the luxury of lots of time to think. She didn't listen to music as she ran for hours at a time. She listened to the sound of the wind and the crunch of gravel beneath her sneakers. As she climbed the cliffside trails along the rugged Portuguese coastline, she listened to the sound of the waves crashing against the cliffs and the seabirds calling as they drifted like kites on strings on the updrafts of the sea breeze.

There was time to reflect on what she had learned. Sophia spent a lot of time researching long-distance running. There was evidence to support that ultra-endurance exercise caused adaptations that made runners more prone to certain diseases. These could include functional and structural changes in the heart and blood vessels. It could cause electrical changes in the cardiac nerves and possibly permanent damage to heart tissue.

Besides the muscle damage and superficial damage long-distance running could cause, it also increased the chance of a generalized global inflammatory response within the body. This could trigger the suppression of the body's immune system. The collateral damage was an increased chance of upper respiratory infections. This is well documented, as many runners develop a cough, runny nose, and sore throat after a long-distance marathon. In addition to the physical risks, there are other concerns, like sleep deprivation and chronic fatigue issues.

Sophia did have an increasing fear, especially now that she was under a contract to run, that she would suffer an injury that would prevent her from being able to compete. This added to her mental stress. She found herself not sleeping as well at night. She had nightmares about stumbling over a rock and breaking her leg. She developed a fear of running down the hills.

As she trained, when the terrain became uneven on a steep downhill, Sophia understood this was where there was the greatest risk of suffering an injury. As she fought to slow her descent against gravity, her muscle fibers lengthened under the increased load. This caused microscopic tears in her muscle fibers. These small tears initiated markers of cellular damage that accumulated in her blood—creating a paradox of peripheral fatigue. She found herself looking forward to running up hills.

In the quiet times between the distractions of the wind, birds, and fears, Maria thought about the phenomenon that drove runners to compete in the Comrades race. This race demanded more than most humans were willing to endure. To enter the Comrades, one had to be a bit obsessed. It was a calling of sorts, a siren wail heard only by a few select individuals. Once that siren held you in its grip, it was impossible to ignore. The proof was hidden in the history of its competitors.

Russian identical twins Olesya and Elna Nurgalieva were the ultimate examples of this obsession. While most were happy to endure the rigors of a single Comrades race, these sisters won ten titles between the two of them from 2003 to 2013. Two individual men, Bruce Fordyce and Stephen Muzhingi, each won three races in three consecutive years. Bruce won from 1981 to 1983, and Stephen from 2009 to 2011. Sophia wondered how these individuals could afford, physically, mentally, and financially, to achieve that level of success.

Other facts about the race flitted randomly through Sophia's mind as the minutes ticked by during her runs. It amazed her that Gerda Steyn held the fastest women's record of 5 hours and 58 minutes. Sophia would have to run all 55 miles at the speed she ran for 25 miles at the Lisbon Marathon. She didn't think that was humanly possible.

She thought about the fact that there was more than one set of twins that ran the race. When the siren called, apparently both twins could hear it. In 1999, the Motsoeneng brothers from Bethlehem, Free State, were so intent on winning that they attempted to cheat. They exchanged places at toilet stops and used a car to catch up to one another. They were caught when television footage revealed they were wearing watches on different arms. In addition, a time pad reading confirmed that one of the brothers was not winning the race at the crucial Botha's Hill, and the winner of the race, Nick Bester, didn't recall anyone passing him between Botha and the finish line. Even though they were caught cheating, they continued to compete in later years. The brothers performed well in later years, although Sergio tested positive for a banned substance after finishing third in 2010 and was disqualified.

Everything about this race was an enigma. Sophia agreed with her parents that it was in her best interest to give it her all, compete in the race, and fulfill her obsession. Then, it was time to move on and find another purpose in life, one that was less destructive to her physical and mental well-being.

*****

One month remained until October 28th and the 95th running of the world's biggest, oldest, and most famous ultra-marathon. Sophia had to pinch herself. She was entered and representing Compentensia Deportes, the rapidly growing sports activewear company. She would be one of the "invited" elite, beginning the race in the front of the pack. She had officially become one of the fastest gazelles, and she wore that honor with pride.

In her best interest, she had taken advice from the sports trainers in her company. While they were not officially coaching her, they had been providing tips for her training. They monitored her closely and gave her regular check-ups by the company's sports physician. They had her best interest in mind but knew they would benefit greatly from her success if she won the Comrades. In one of the training guides they provided to her, they listed the most common injuries for marathon runners. They highly advised Sophia to consider each one and take preventative measures. They also provided her with a timeline and distances to practice as race day approached.

On this day, the one-month marker, Sophia was preparing for a 40-mile or 64-kilometer practice run. She was starting in the town of Parizes and running along an inland route of the Via Algarviana to the town Corte de Seda, where she had parked her car. The route had lots of hills, was very remote, and was a good cross-section of the actual route in South Africa.

Her mother had followed her to drop her car off at the ending point, then drove her back to where her run began. Sophia promised to call her mom the moment she arrived at the finish line. Her mom kissed her on the cheek, said a brief prayer on her behalf, and, with tears in her eyes, drove off. Sophia smiled at how cute her mom had become, now her biggest fan and supporter. Who would have thought?

The major difference between the real run and this practice was that she had to carry her own water, snacks, and first aid kit. Fortunately, her sponsors equipped her with a lightweight water bladder that she carried as a backpack. It even had a tube clipped to the front of her shirt. She could take sips as she needed without any disruption to her run. She had the best energy bars on the market and a small first aid kit in a Kevlar pouch that clipped around her waist. It was so lightweight she barely knew it was there. She chose her watch as her only technology. She didn't want the extra weight of carrying a cell phone. She even left her car keys behind the tire of her car, not wanting to carry an ounce of extra weight.

With butterflies dancing in her stomach, Sofia stretched one last time and took a deep breath. She noted the time on her watch, clicked the timer, and launched herself down the trail, picturing in her mind the starting line of the Comrades. Finding an easy stride, Sofia fell into a steady rhythm. She took the inclines with less speed than the flat, but downhill, she remained cautious. She anticipated every footfall, ensuring every step had a smooth landing surface.

As was her routine, she made a mental note running down the list of the most common ailments for marathon runners and noted what preventative measures she had taken. First on the list was preventing blisters. Sofia had the best running socks available thanks to her sponsors, and her running shoes were nicely broken in. She had even applied petroleum jelly as a precautionary measure to her heels to make sure they were well lubricated.

The list was long. She thought herself lucky she hadn't been prone to shin splints. She attributed this to her stretching routine and yoga, which kept her lower legs supple. She also never skimped on quality running shoes, which reduced the chance of inflammation that caused the splints. Fractures and sprains were preventable if you ran carefully. Sore nipples, another irritating hazard, occurred with constant rubbing and chafing from the impact of running. Thanks to the nipple guards for runners, she didn't have to worry about that discomfort.

Going item by item down her mental list helped the time pass for Sofia. She was happy to not have experienced the worst items on the list: cramping, vomiting, diarrhea, or chest pains. She glanced at her watch and saw that three hours had passed already. She had hoped to complete the course in 4 1/2 hours, but she was curious to see if she could complete it in less time. Her watch's GPS tracker verified she was past the halfway mark.

The terrain was varied. There was a nice combination of hills and flat areas. There were very few people on this part of the trail. An occasional duo of mountain bikers would pass, along with a few hikers, usually Europeans with large backpacks. There was a growing trend of young Europeans who hiked their way down the coast from their country of origin, usually to Lagos. There, they would try to hitch a ride on a sailboat to get to the Canary Islands. It had become a popular pilgrimage for young adventurers.

Rolling hills dotted the horizon. There were often herds of sheep and goats grazing on the hillsides. Sometimes, a shepherd was with the herd; mostly, they seemed to be on their own, wandering the familiar hills. Sophia loved watching nature during her runs, whether it was birds, the small mammals that flitted across the path, or the nomadic herds. She embraced it all.

Finally, the eventuality she knew would happen did arrive. She needed to pee. She had to hydrate to prevent dehydration and cramping. Even though she was perspiring at a solid rate, she had fluid in her bladder that she needed to evacuate. Unlike organized races, there were no porta-potties along the way. Sophia searched her periphery for a quick deviation off her course that would give her some privacy but not take her too far off the trail.

She spotted an area ahead and to her right. There seemed to be a ravine surrounded by large shrubs. Slowing down slightly to make a visual check, she evaluated the ground and saw there were not too many boulders. She could dash to the bushes and be back on the trail in no time. She would also use this opportunity to eat a protein bar. Her body was screaming for fuel.

Sophia slowed to a walk and approached the bushes lining the ravine. She took a few deep breaths to try and slow her breathing down, took a big sip of water, and ducked behind a bush. When she finished relieving herself, she pulled up her pants but was startled when she saw movement in the ravine out of the corner of her eye. It was something large and white.

Unable to contain her curiosity, Sophia finished her business quickly, then wandered closer to the ravine, cautiously peering at the white form at the bottom. Even though she was still breathing heavily, she sucked in her breath when she realized what she was seeing. It was a horse. It seemed to have fallen into the ravine and appeared to be injured. Sophia raised her hands to her face and looked down in horror. The horse appeared to be injured as it lay at the bottom of the ravine on its side. It was thrashing in pain.

The Father and Son

"You certainly are not making this easy for the humans," the Son said.

"Do you think any of this has been easy for the horses?" the Father asked.

"Were they not put on Earth to be our beasts of burden?" the Son replied. "Horses are no strangers to hard work, physical pain, and endurance."

"Man does have a distinct advantage," the Father said. "Horses know and accept their fate. For those who believe, man has the assurance of My written word. In Isaiah, man is told, 'So do not fear, for I am with you; do not be dismayed, for I am your God. I will strengthen you and help you; I will uphold you with My righteous right hand.' For those who have faith, they will find strength."

"It is difficult to watch our children struggle," the Son said softly.

"Struggle is a part of life," the Father replied. "By overcoming difficulties, humans grow stronger and wiser. It is more difficult for Me to watch their struggles over the choices they have to make. They know not how their decisions will change the course of their lives. I know, but I can't influence them one way or the other. My pain in watching them struggle with their decisions is real.

"This is why I am confirming that humanity has made enough of the right choices that mankind should continue."

*****

Her first instinct was to run back to the trail and look for help. Sophia sprinted back to the trail. She could see for quite a distance in each direction from the top of the hill. There was no sign of another human being anywhere. She cursed that she didn't carry her cell phone. But how could she have predicted this emergency?

Okay, so there is no one in sight. Sophia possessed the ability to think things through logically. She thought now about her choices. She could turn back down the trail and continue to run. The thought that she was leaving an animal in trouble would haunt her forever. She could never describe to anyone when she got back exactly where she was, where this horse was, to form some type of rescue. Would anyone even care?

She could return and assess the situation. She could try to determine how badly the horse was injured. If the situation seemed hopeless, she could return to her run without too much guilt, knowing the horse could not be saved. But what if it could? What could she do? She had one tiny human first aid kit with her. Assessment seemed like the best option. Sophia turned and jogged back to the ravine.

The slope down was steep. She could see the horse lying still now. It seemed it was still alive; she could see the horse's sides heaving. There were no obvious wounds. The legs didn't seem broken from her view from above. Sophia took one last glance behind her, hoping someone would magically appear and take over the rescue task. No one was in sight. Sophia looked to the heavens. "God, please help me," she prayed as she began her descent down the steep ravine.

Rocks and scree tumbled down the hill next to her as Sophia slid down the slope. Her shorts did nothing to prevent the rocks from scratching her legs. She tried not to regret her decision as she descended, making her way toward the horse at the bottom. Suddenly, the horse lifted its head. It watched Sophia as she slid to the bottom, then dropped its head back to the ground.

Sophia stood and brushed the dirt off her legs. She had several scratches that were bleeding, but none of them were deep. She could tend to them later. She cautiously walked toward the horse. She could see now that the horse had labored breathing, but still, she couldn't see any injuries. As Sophia approached the horse, she had a bad feeling in the pit of her stomach. She looked around at the steep walls and wondered if she had made a good decision. Could she even get back up the way she had slid down? Too late now; she closed the gap between her and the horse.

"OH!" Sophia said out loud when she was finally close enough to the horse to see the problem. It wasn't a problem the horse was having; it was a baby! The horse was a mare, and she was in labor. It appeared she had slid into the ravine as she was finding a quiet place to lay down and give birth. Sophia didn't know if the horse was friendly or receptive to people, so she tested the mare's tolerance to her presence.

Squatting down, making herself seem smaller, less of a threat, Sophia got closer to the horse's head. "Shhh, don't worry, I'm here to help you. I don't know how I'm going to help, but I'm here if you need me," she said in a quiet, soothing voice.

To her surprise, the horse nickered. A spasm took hold, and the mare made a sound somewhere between a groan and a soft whinny. Sophia's heart all but broke. She found herself tearing up as she watched the horse in pain. In the recesses of her memory, she recalled a documentary she had watched about animals giving birth. Animal mothers remained calm, accepting of the labor pains, and normally delivered their babies very stoically, unless there was a problem.

"Are you having problems, momma?" Sophia asked, knowing she wouldn't get an answer. "May I touch you?" she asked, trying to keep her voice steady and soothing.

Sophia inched closer until she could reach the mare's neck. She rubbed her hand down her coarse mane, then stroked the mare's face. The mare closed her eyes as another spasm took hold. Sophia jumped back as the mare thrashed, her strong front legs coming dangerously close to striking her. Standing up now at a safe distance, Sophia walked around to the back of the horse. She could see a white birth sack beginning to protrude from the mare.

The mare groaned and seemed to be trying to push. Sophia instinctively knew that the baby should be showing if the birth was imminent. "Oh shit, what do I do?" Sophia asked out loud, putting her hands to her head in distress. She felt for her first aid kit. There were tiny scissors in there with a gauze pad in case a wound or limb had to be compression wrapped. She pulled out the scissors, reluctantly, not believing she was about to intervene in this birth process, having no idea what she was doing.

"I'm going to try and help you now. Please don't hurt me," Sophia begged as she knelt behind the horse. Carefully, she reached inside the mare, cringing from the feeling of having to force her hand next to the foal. Thankfully, the mare stayed still. She felt what she thought was a nose. She felt movement from the foal as if it was trying to break free from the sac. Using her hands, Sophia pulled the tiny white nose, then the rest of the foal's face free of the sac.

Another contraction racked the mare. Sophia could feel the mare's muscles trying to expel the baby. There was no forward progress. "I need to pull, don't I?" Sophia asked, peering around as the mare raised her head and looked back as if hoping her baby had been born. Her strength seemed to be waning. "I need to grab hold of something, but there is only a head. Wait, I remember, there needs to be a leg. The babies always have a leg sticking out when they are born!"

Sophia reached back into the mare's body, searching with her fingers to find a limb. Sure enough, she located a slender, slimy leg, a gelatinous hoof. Straightening and guiding it, she managed to get the hoof slightly protruding from the mother. It was just too slimy to pull.

Despite her best efforts, Sophia couldn't get a grip on the leg to help the baby out. As another contraction racked the mother, Sophia thought, *What can I use to help get this baby out? I have nothing*, as she looked around.

Suddenly, she had an idea. The roll of gauze in her med kit just might be the solution. She reached into her small pouch and pulled out the gauze. She wrapped the gauze as tightly as she dared around the tiny protruding limb where the hoof narrowed to the fetlock. After several wraps around the tiny fetlock, Sophia tied a knot. She prayed this would work.

On the next contraction, Sophia used the end of the gauze to pull with all her might. She was suddenly thankful for her strong muscles from training with weights. One more contraction was all she needed. Sophia now pulled with all her might. The body of the foal slid out with a gush of amniotic fluid, nearly tipping her over backward. Sophia instantly went to work ripping off the sac and clearing the mucus from the baby's nose. Suddenly, a small sound erupted from the foal—a gurgling followed by a sneeze. Then, the baby took its first breath of air. Sophia's heart melted as the tiny foal began to struggle, legs going in every direction, the newborn struggling to fill its lungs with air and free itself from the sac. The foal's instincts kicked in as oxygen filled its tiny lungs and the fight for life began.

As Sophia sat next to the new life, the mare struggled to her feet, exhausted from her ordeal. She turned to meet her new baby, nickering softly. Sophia froze in her spot as the mare turned and reached her nose down to smell her newborn. She nuzzled and licked the baby gently and continued to nicker—a new mom welcoming her baby. The sensitive nerve endings of her velvet nose inspected every inch of her newborn. Sophia thought she was being a bit rough as mom nudged her baby, shifting it, prodding it, and stimulating the baby to move. It had been only a few minutes since the baby had been delivered, and the mom was already trying to get the newborn to stand.

Reality snapped back into place for Sophia. She looked at her watch. Her plans for completing her run were ruined.

She was trapped in a ravine with a horse and her newborn baby. It seemed her struggles were not over yet. How would she get herself, a horse, and its baby out of this pit? Sophia looked around, a bit proud of herself for saving the mom and baby, but assessing what she should do next. As mom and baby did their thing, Sophia took a moment to walk around the ravine, searching for a way out.

Along one side of the ravine, a row of bushes lined a crevice. Under the bushes was a natural channel where water flowed into the ravine during heavy rain. Erosion had worn away the soil beneath the bushes. The grade was less steep. Where the soil had eroded around the boulders, there were foot and handholds. Sophia began ripping out the small shrubs with her hands, making the path upward more visible. This was it. This was the way out.

Within an hour, the baby was standing and trying to nurse. Sophia was now getting worried about making it back to her car before dark. She knew her mother would be on the verge of panic, as Sophia had told her the time frame she should be back at her car. She said she would call her mom the moment she arrived to let her know she was safe. It was now pushing the 4½-hour mark of when she should be arriving. She still had two hours before she could make it back to the car. Sophia groaned out loud at the thought of putting her mom in distress.

Making a rash decision, Sophia walked over to the mom and baby. "I know you are not going to like this, momma, but I have to do this for all of us," she said, not being able to help smiling at the baby, now a fluffy white ball as her fur had dried. She was starting to get frisky with her belly full of warm milk.

Sophia reached down and picked the baby up into her arms. Mom nickered and nudged Sophia with her head. "I need you to follow me now. I promise I will take care of your baby. There's no way this baby will make it out of the ravine. But if I can make it out with my two legs carrying your baby, I'm sure you can follow," Sophia explained as she turned and walked toward the row of bushes. Mom followed, reaching her head over Sophia's shoulder to stay as close to her baby as possible.

Sophia was thankful she was strong and in such great shape. The baby was not light. Needing at least one hand to help her climb out, Sophia shifted the baby around her shoulders in a fireman's carry. The baby struggled for a moment. Sophia held on tightly to both sets of legs around her neck until the foal settled. As soon as the baby seemed quiet, Sophia began her climb. She used one hand to settle the baby and the other to keep her balance. Behind her, she could hear the mare scrambling over the rocks. She prayed the mare wouldn't break a leg struggling to keep up.

The climb was intense. Sophia was reaching her exhaustion point but looked up and saw she only had a few more feet to go. The baby began to struggle again. "No, no, please, we are almost there," Sophia begged, as she had to stop the climb and steady the foal with both sets of her hands. As soon as the foal was quiet again, Sophia resumed her climb, finally reaching the top of the ravine. One boulder stood in the way between her and success. As she took the last step, her foot slid down into a crevice between the ground and the boulder.

Sophia felt and heard a sharp crack. Pain shot up her leg like a lightning bolt.

"Noooooo!" Sophia screamed, her voice reaching a fevered pitch. It sounded foreign to her as she fought the urge to panic. Sophia rolled onto her side and let the baby down gently onto the ground. Behind her, she could hear the frantic mother fighting for her footing up the crest of the ravine. Sophia was between her and her baby. Any second, she expected hooves to come crashing down on her body, crushing her. Sophia rolled back toward the rock. Using both hands, she pulled on her leg, trying desperately to dislodge it from the boulder's grip. As soon as her leg popped free, Sophia rolled in the opposite direction of the foal, which had already scrambled to its feet.

The second Sophia moved away from the rock, Momma popped out of the ravine, her powerful hind legs propelling her up the last few feet. As soon as all four feet were stable, she whinnied gently to her foal and nudged it away from the edge of the ravine. Everyone was out, but everything was not okay. At least not for Sophia. It was a hard pill for her to swallow. The ramifications sunk in like a giant lead weight sinking to the bottom of the ocean.

As Sophia curled into a ball, wondering why this was all happening to her and how she was going to get out of this mess, she heard voices. A father and son who had been walking along the trail had seen the commotion from the path. The white mare clambering out of the ravine had drawn their attention. They walked over for a closer inspection. Sophia couldn't speak; she could only cry. She had her arms wrapped around her shins, her leg now on fire, her head buried in her chest, the protective dam now bursting.

"Are you okay?" a man's voice asked.

"Dad, I think she's hurt," a boy's voice replied.

"Thank God I have reception up here," the man responded. "I'm calling for help.

Paloma Ortega Sánchez

New York City
United States Congresswoman

PALOMA NEVER INTENDED TO get into politics. But now that she was here, there was no going back. It was a brutal lifestyle, but there were reasons people remained in Congress until they were in their 80s. Being a member of Congress meant being indoctrinated into an elite club. It consumed you; it owned you. You became part of something greater than yourself. You assumed the role of a modern-day warrior, fighting for the very foundation of your country. Your weapons were your words. Your constituents, your army.

Some mornings, Paloma dreaded getting out of bed. She had to remind herself that the big, comfortable bed she was enjoying in this luxury suite was affordable because she was a congress member. In addition, she rented an apartment in D.C. Since Congress met monthly, most congress members had a second residence. There were a few who slept in their offices. She would not be one of the "couch caucus" members who slept on cots or air mattresses in the same space they worked. Her upscale apartment was not as luxurious as her suite, but it was big enough to entertain and not too shabby by any means.

Hitting the snooze button one last time, Paloma drifted back into a semi-state of consciousness, remembering her days as a waitress when she woke up in a tiny apartment she shared with two roommates on an uncomfortable mattress. She had to slop food onto plates for a living. That job, however demeaning, was where she discovered her true talent, the one that launched her distinguished career.

One of her greatest assets was her ability to work with people. She discovered that talent while working as a waitress. While most of the waitresses earned $50 to $75 a night in tips, Paloma would take home $200 or more. The other waitresses were often jealous of her. Instead of asking her the secret to her success, they resorted to petty, jealous gossip and made snide comments behind her back. Paloma had simply learned to work the system and relate to the customers in a way that made them want to give her a big tip.

Now, as she lay sprawled in her king-sized bed, she could appreciate her first job, the one where she developed the ability to connect with the public. That skill, being able to relate to people, earned her a position in the United States Congress.

Paloma felt the bed beside her. The place beside her was still warm. Her boyfriend had gotten up a few minutes ago. She could hear the shower running. She smiled as she thought of their upcoming trip to Puerto Rico to visit her abuela. Thanks to her grandmother, Paloma had an olive skin tone, giving her the appearance of a tan without ever having to lie in the sun. She was taking Paul with her after her session in Congress was over to meet her grandmother and to show him the incredible sights of the gorgeous island, the home of her ancestors.

Her grandmother's genes endowed her with luscious dark hair. She took pride in her exotic look, representing the important people who lived in the United States and were descendants of those who migrated from foreign lands to find freedom in this great country. It was her job now to protect those freedoms and make sure that everyone who wanted to enter this country had that opportunity. She considered herself a freedom fighter, a voice for the people—one that would preserve and protect not only the sovereign nation but also those who called it home.

The next two weeks were going to be brutal. Her main goal was to get her SAVE THE CLIMATE BILL passed. She was instrumental in writing this bill. Now, she had to get it passed. It was always a struggle these days, as there was very little working across the aisle with members of the other party. The political parties were severely divided, firmly entrenched on opposite sides of the fence. It was an almost impossible task to get a bill passed, but if Paloma didn't represent all that was possible and embody the power of perseverance, nothing did. After all, she had gone from waitressing to Congress. What greater success story could be told on behalf of tenacity and perseverance? She was willing to do whatever it took to get the job done.

Since it was the last morning she would be seeing her boyfriend before their trip, Paloma hit the "stop" button on her alarm clock and rolled out of bed. She could snooze a few more minutes or go join her boyfriend in the shower. She chose him over a few more minutes in bed.

*****

With all that Paloma had learned about her new career, it struck a nerve that citizens of the United States were vastly unaware of what their elected Congress members did for a living. Sure, they started out making a starting salary of over $174,000 a year, but they worked extremely hard for those wages.

Paloma was aware of the misconception that members of Congress only "worked" 160 days a year. Polls showed that on average, Congress members put in 70 hours a week when they were in Washington for a session. When back at home, most members spent 59 hours a week working. It was true that they could take a vacation anytime they were not in Washington, but most Congress members were workaholics and rarely took time off.

With her bags packed for Washington and her trip to Puerto Rico, Paloma waited in the lobby for her limo to the airport. She glanced around the plush lobby with the concierges in their uniforms, palms planted in huge decorative vases, and gorgeous works of art hanging from the walls. She was going to miss this place, even though she was so popular in this city she couldn't go to the grocery store without being accosted.

Currently, she had over four million followers on Instagram and Twitter. She was one of the most talked-about politicians in America. Her charm and vigor had won the hearts of the people. She took one last look around her building and took a deep breath. This home represented peace, quiet, and the ability for solitude. Her Washington apartment represented 24 hours a day of complete chaos.

Paul had called earlier for a luggage cart to transport her garment bag and large suitcase to the front door. Paloma carried her purse and her briefcase with her laptop and papers. While they waited, she wrapped her arms around Paul's neck and kissed him passionately.

"I'm gonna miss the heck out of you. Don't be upset this time when I don't answer texts or take your calls. My life is not my own when I'm 'down there.'"

"No worries, babe. I know how stressed out you get. I'll be down there in two weeks. Then, when the meetings are over, we're off on an amazing vacation. I can't wait to lie on the beach with you and take walks through the rainforest."

Paloma pressed her finger gently against Paul's lips as she reminded him, "Remember, this is technically a business trip to Puerto Rico. So... hush hush on the vacation part. There's no rush to get to DC before the weekend. I won't have any time to spend with you."

They hugged briefly. Paloma pulled away and looked into Paul's intense brown eyes. His mop of dark hair gave him a rugged look that tugged at her heartstrings. His strong jawline and five-o'clock shadow rocked her world. If only he were more ambitious. He was currently a construction foreman, which is not a bad job in a big city.

There was lots of work in NYC for a construction worker. However, she was hoping to help him start his own construction firm and launch him on to bigger and better things, just as she had done for herself. She was willing to invest time and money with the belief that as an influencer, she could help mold him into the kind of man worthy of being the partner of a congresswoman.

She smiled coyly at him and whispered in his ear, "If I have my way, we are going to be doing a lot more than laying on beaches and taking walks."

The limo arrived. The driver packed the bags brought out by the concierge into the spacious trunk. Paloma turned to leave the lobby but looked back and gave Paul a wink. He smiled, his dazzling white teeth a gorgeous contrast to his mocha complexion. As she walked out the door, she memorized all of Paul's features so she could play them back every time she missed him.

*****

On the three-hour flight to Washington, Paloma reviewed her schedule. While in her home city, NYC, Paloma wrote new bills and laws and represented her people. She conducted oversight, which involved reviewing, monitoring, and supervising federal agencies and their programs and policy implementations.

As a congresswoman, Paloma also fought for the rights of her constituents and educated the public. She had a busy schedule with phone conferences, meetings, events to attend, and of course, posting daily on her social media platforms. Her people loved hearing what she was doing and what her views were about what was going on in the world. But her three most important jobs were fundraising, fundraising, and more fundraising. That was her personal joke to her friends, but if she were being honest, it was her top priority. She had to get reelected every two years. She needed to earn money for advertising and campaigning.

In Washington during sessions, it was a whole different ball game. When not on the second floor of the Capitol building for a regular session in the 'chambers,' Paloma could be talking to the press or attending meetings and events long past midnight. She also spent countless hours in her office in the Capitol returning phone calls, sifting through thousands of emails, and trying to get work done on her bill.

The most stressful meetings in DC were with the lobbyists who represent special interest groups, businesses, unions, and non-profit organizations. They were all looking to get some type of benefit from a particular bill. Paloma was extremely popular at the moment as her "Green Bill" had the potential to impact many of these groups. There was a waiting list of lobbyists who wanted to discuss what they could do for her in return for making sure their interests came to light somewhere in her bill. She had to review each group carefully and find out which ones had the potential to contribute thousands to her campaign fund.

As she reviewed her schedule, Paloma realized she had every night booked solid. She had several dinner meetings with lobbyists. Why not have them pay for an extravagant dinner? Those were her favorite meetings. She had several 'parties' to attend which were put on by companies that were looking to bend the ear of a congress member. There were a couple of fundraisers she had to attend to support fellow congressmen. Paloma suddenly felt tired from the stress of knowing she would not be going to bed before midnight for the next two weeks.

****

After the grueling two weeks finally ended, Paloma was not in a good mood. Not only was she exhausted from so many late nights in a row, but her bill got shot down. She was going to have to make revisions for it to get passed. She was convinced that the good the bill was doing for the American people outweighed the money required to be spent for a few extraneous components. It was about making positive change, not about how much it cost. No price was too high to pay for saving the planet and making the country equitable for all.

This bill's predecessor was the American Clean Energy and Security Act, which died on the Senate floor in 2009. The idea of the original bill was to pass a massive program that would invest in clean-energy jobs and infrastructure, meant to transform not just the energy sector but the entire economy. The bill was created to decarbonize the US and create a better economy. Her bills included the same ideas. It expanded into new territory as well.

Paloma's Save the Climate Bill had a plan to fully decarbonize the country, invested trillions for renewable energy, had provisions for federal job guarantees, and the icing on the cake? It addressed and mitigated historical inequalities. It even included measures such as basic income programs and provisions for universal health care.

Simply stated, the opposers argued there was too much scope to the bill and it had to be pared down. This was going to take months of work, and Paloma was not looking forward to the task. Thank God she was able to get away from Washington, the rat race, and cool down from the marathon she just ran. Paul was arriving that Friday afternoon, and she couldn't get away fast enough for her much-anticipated vacation to Puerto Rico.

Saturday morning, her power suits, evening gowns, and high heels were packed away. She and Paul were on their way to the Washington airport via a limo. They wouldn't be boarding a commercial flight to Puerto Rico; they were hitching a ride with the congresswoman from Puerto Rico, who was flying home after the session. In-flight, they would meet and exchange ideas on the Save the Climate Bill. This would count as a business meeting. Paloma would not only fly in luxury but would also write the entire trip off as a business expense.

Paul had never been out of the country. Paloma had to help him get his first passport. He was not a worldly man, but she could change that. She kind of liked that he was naïve. She had a blank slate to work with and would enjoy exposing him to new horizons and new cultural experiences. Paul's eyes were as wide as a kid's on Christmas morning as he walked up the steps and into the Cessna Citation XLS. Luxurious seats awaited them. The Cessna Citation XLS was owned by the Puerto Rican government and was used to fly dignitaries back and forth to Washington.

"You are in for a special treat, my dear," Paloma explained as they had their choice of the nine passenger seats.

"Holy crap, you weren't kidding," Paul said, eying the rows of empty seats, trying to decide where he wanted to sit. "Let's sit here in the middle... no wait, the front row. I want to be in the front row. I suppose it's all first class," he said, laughing. "I've never traveled first class before."

"Fine, Paul. Actually, I can sit with you while we take off, but then I have to go meet with the congresswoman from Puerto Rico. The three of us would be the only passengers on the plane. This is the 'business' part of the trip. It shouldn't take more than an hour. I just want to get her opinion on what she thinks needs to be changed on my bill. I'm too tired to talk long about it. I just want to get to the beach," she said as she plopped down next to Paul into the luxurious leather, fully reclining seat.

Immediately, a flight attendant approached and asked them if they would care for a cocktail. It was only 10:00 AM. The other congresswoman had not yet arrived.

"Why the hell not," Paloma responded, glancing at her watch. "Make it a Bloody Mary, a double, please... Paul?"

Paul was grinning ear to ear as he blurted out, "Really? Is it free?"

Paloma put a hand over her face and shook her head.

"Yes, Paul. It's free. Just order what you want to drink."

"Champagne!" he said, nudging Paloma. "We are officially on vacation, right? Why don't we both have champagne?"

"I already explained to you that I have to spend an hour working. When I'm done, I will come back here and sit with you, and we will both have champagne. Is that okay with you?" she asked as if she were talking to a five-year-old.

Paloma instantly regretted speaking to Paul that way. She could see the expression on his face change from thrilled to hurt. Here she was, excited to expand the boundaries of his world. At the moment, she was simply exhausted and didn't have any patience left to deal with his childlike exuberance. She had no interest in talking about her bill for an hour. Just the thought of it left a bad taste in her mouth that she hoped to hell the Bloody Mary would cure. The last thing she wanted to hear was more negativity about her bill.

In a few minutes, they both had their drinks in hand and toasted to their upcoming adventures. Paloma kissed Paul and apologized for being on edge. He was extremely under-standing, and that was one of the reasons she loved him. He had a good heart and was a kind soul. She was glad she had decided to bring him with her to Puerto Rico.

*****

Closing her eyes, Paloma envisioned her dream vacation. Upon landing at the Luis Muñoz Marín International Airport, also known as the "San Juan Airport," a rental car would be waiting. She would step off the airplane and into the non-descript economy car. She didn't want to attract any un-wanted attention by renting anything expensive. She loved the simplicity of flying to this island. There were no customs or immigration in Puerto Rico. It was as simple as flying somewhere within the US.

Paloma's grandmother lived on the outskirts of Carolina City on the smaller hillsides winding up towards the nation-al rainforest. Carolina was dubbed "La Tierra de Gigantes," meaning land of the giants. Don Filipe Birriel was born in Carolina. He was the tallest man in the country's history. He grew to the impressive height of seven feet, eleven inches. The city has a second, more notorious nickname, "El Pueblo de Los Tumba Brazos," or arm hackers' town, because of its history of resolving conflicts by duel.

Paloma loved staying with her grandmother in her quaint little house on a hillside. After having been exposed to several hurricanes over the past few years, Paloma liked to visit once or twice a year to make sure her grandmother was doing well and that her house was maintained. It was tough for the 75-year-old to live on her own, her husband having passed away years ago.

Her grandmother's three children had moved to the US as soon as they were old enough to live on their own, including Paloma's father. While they had tried to get her 'abuela' to move to the US, she was too entrenched in her life in Puerto Rico to even think about moving to a new country. She loved being warm all year round, having a garden, fruit trees, and her chickens to collect eggs every morning. It was a peaceful and pleasant life.

Carolina was the perfect location as far as Paloma was concerned. It was less than 15 miles from where her abuela lived to the center of San Juan, a city thriving with history, culture, and nightlife. The Grande de Loíza River ran through the city, which was home to a mall, parks, museums, and restaurants. Located along the coastline, the city spread to the ocean's edge. A few miles down the beach and away from the high-rises, the palm tree forests kissed the soft, white, sandy beaches with no buildings in sight. Carolina was the perfect combination of city meets tranquility.

Paloma had planned the perfect vacation with Paul. First, they would explore Old San Juan, sip wine at cafés, visit the historic fort, and spend a night at the O:LV Fifty Five hotel. She dreamt about staying there. Now she could share this indulgence with Paul. This exquisite hotel was awarded the best design hotel in the world and the best new boutique hotel by London's Boutique Hotel Awards. Nestled between the Condado Lagoon and the beachfront, this sophisticated and posh hotel would blow Paul's mind.

Of course, she would spend a day or two at the beach and visit her grandmother. They would catch up, and Paloma would pamper her. After quality time with her abuela, Paloma would take Paul to their next adventure, exploring the largest tropical rainforest in northeastern Puerto Rico: El Yunque. It was only a short drive from her grandmother's house. She had sketched out a rough game plan that began with the El Portal Visitor Center. It had an impressive walkway that wound through the surrounding treetops. From there, they would drive to the high-altitude dwarf forest, one of the few in the world. A short hike would take them to explore ancient petroglyphs made by the area's indigenous Taíno people.

For a huge surprise, Paloma would be taking Paul to the exclusive lodging she had pulled strings to get through Congresswoman González-Colón: a reservation at a Yuquiyú Treehouse. There were only four available, and if you didn't know someone who knew someone, you couldn't get a reservation. While considered a hotel, this resort also had the four treehouses that overlooked the El Yunque rainforest.

You didn't have to climb the tree to get there, as gorgeous wooden staircases led to the treetop lodges. The polished dwellings featured kitchenettes, balconies, Wi-Fi, luxurious beds, and rainfall showers. You could even order room service with food provided by their very own tropical garden and organic farm.

Paloma would have loved to spend several nights there, but at $300 a night, she was already pushing the limits of the travel expenses she would be submitting for this trip. It was her dream to sit on the balcony at sunset with Paul, sipping cocktails and listening to the forest come alive with the nightly calls of the mystical coquí tree frogs.

For the grand finale, they would wake up the next morning and head to the La Vista Rainforest River Ride. Even though Paloma had grown up in New York City, she had always loved horses. She was dying to take this highly recommended excursion. The path went down the mountain and along the Río Espíritu Santo River. During the ride down the mountain, you could pick fruit hanging from the trees, listen to the songbirds, and enjoy spectacular views of the rainforest mountain peaks.

At lunchtime, they would rest the horses and descend on foot down some steep rock stairs to explore the spectacular river pools and drink from the spring-fed pristine mountain water. It was a dream of hers to make this trip. Paloma wished she could skip everything else and teleport there.

*****

At ten fifteen, Jennifer González-Colón had boarded the plane. She came aboard in a flurry. "Sorry I'm late!" she said, breathing heavily from having rushed from her limo. "Traffic was terrible from downtown. Guess I should have left a few minutes earlier."

"No problem," Paloma said, not caring if she was late. This was a free ride on a private plane. She could be hours late, and Paloma wouldn't have cared. She was officially on vacation, or would be as soon as she got her meeting out of the way. "How about I come and join you after we take off? I will set Paul up with a movie, and we can have our meeting."

Television sets were embedded in the back of each seat, as well as charging ports for phones and laptops and retractable tables with cup holders. In the front row, these features were built into the bulkhead. The seats had an abundance of room. Paul, as large as he was, sprawled in comfort. Paul had already been perusing the list of premium movies available, some he had not seen yet. Paloma knew he would be able to keep himself occupied by ordering drinks and watching a movie.

Shortly after takeoff, Paloma gathered her papers from her briefcase. She was amazed at how little runway the jet needed to take off. The two Pratt & Whitney Canada PW545C Turbofans that powered the aircraft meant the jet could reach a speed of over 500 miles an hour. It had a range of 2,100 miles. Flying the 1,600 miles to Puerto Rico was only half its range. The flight would take about 3 ½ hours, which was nothing to

Paloma, who sometimes took 16-hour flights on commercial airlines to South America, always flying first-class, of course.

Patting Paul on the shoulder, Paloma picked up her papers and mentally prepared herself to listen, nod, and shut out anything that came out of Jennifer's mouth. Paul had his headphones on, a beer in one hand, an array of snacks on the table in front of him, and was already engrossed in the latest "Fast and Furious" movie. He looked up at her and gave her a huge grin. She smiled back, pleased with the fact he was enjoying the trip so much already.

Right now, she had to deal with this meeting. She reluctantly walked a few rows back to where Jennifer was seated, waiting for their meeting. A crooked, half-smile creased Jennifer's face, one that said, "Bring it on." Jennifer was one of those who opposed the bill and couldn't wait to provide her input. This was the price Paloma was paying to get a private jet and a free vacation. It was time for her to pay the piper. After all, it was only an hour; how bad could it be?

Paloma put on her game face and sat next to Jennifer, intending to get the damned meeting over with as quickly as possible.

"Our country is facing its worst national debt ever, and you want to spend trillions of dollars on the environment and social issues. You can't possibly think there aren't more pressing issues facing this country. I'm not even going to bring up the border crisis and all the illegal immigrants we're paying for. We won't have the money to pay for the necessities if this bill passes," Jennifer began, skipping the niceties and chit-chat.

"Tell me, Jennifer, don't you care that the United Nations is predicting our planet will be ruined in 12 years if we don't reverse climate change? You want to worry about the price tag or saving our planet?"

"Of course, I care about our planet. What I have a problem with is the extraneous bullshit thrown into the bill that jacks up the price tag. Since when is social equality part of saving the planet? And how about your plan to spend billions of dollars on ethnic studies? You want to dump money into higher education to create an army of activists."

Paloma blinked. She stayed silent a moment before responding. "So, you don't think that investing in our future generations by educating the young to protect our planet is important? Maybe, if past generations had done this, we wouldn't be in the mess we are in now."

"I agree we need to educate our young and move forward in a positive direction," Jennifer countered, "but you want to create radicals instead of free thinkers. A ten billion price tag is not going to get a yes vote from any rational congress member."

"These topics have been discussed exhaustively on the floor. God knows this point has been drilled *ad nauseam*. I understand that this section needs to be revised. Do you have any new perspectives, something we didn't discuss during the session?" Paloma asked, reclining her seat a bit to get more comfortable, crossing her arms, and preparing to tune out whatever Jennifer had to say.

"Ok, here's one no one talked about. You want to spend three billion dollars to increase the tree canopy."

"Yes, and even you can't argue that trees are important in reducing the carbon dioxide in the air; they filter out chemicals and mitigate the greenhouse effect. Think about it, Jennifer. If we don't invest in programs like this now, it's going to be too late in a few more years," Paloma said, reciting her memorized counterpoints.

"You feel comfortable throwing billions of dollars into planting new trees when we have a record number of home-less people in our country starving every day. You don't seem to think this is important in your fight for social equality. Yet, you are ready to spend money on trees when the fact is, our tree repopulation is growing without your help."

"Wait," Paloma said, sitting forward, turning to face Jennifer, and holding her hand up. "Our U.S. landmass is not doing its part. We only contain eight percent of the world's forest. Increasing the trees in our country is an essential component in addressing climate change."

"Once again, you are spending billions of taxpayers' dollars, money we don't have, to attack an issue that is already mending itself. It's just throwing money down the drain," Jennifer argued.

"Well, I..." Paloma interrupted.

"Let me finish with some facts. Globally, there has been an increase in leaf area over the past two decades that corresponds to an area as large as the Amazon rainforest. That's a five percent increase. There are over two million square kilometers of green leaf area on our planet, more than at the beginning of the 2000s."

Paloma smiled, ready for this argument. "Those increases are mostly due to China and India increasing their forests," she spouted, getting riled even though her goal was just to listen. She sat forward in her reclined seat and leaned in closer to Jennifer. "The United States is supposed to be the greatest nation in the world. Are we going to let other countries take the lead in repopulating our planet with trees while we sit back and do nothing?" Paloma fumed, the toll of having to defend her bill finally getting the better of her.

"You might want to consider that the Food and Agriculture Organization, the FAO, reported that there are more trees in the US than there were 100 years ago," Jennifer said, pulling out a sheet of paper she had obviously prepared for this point in the discussion. "The FAO, I quote, reported that 'forest growth nationally has exceeded harvest since the 1940s. By 1997, forest growth exceeded the harvest by 42 percent and the volume of forest growth was 380 percent greater than in 1920. The East Coast has doubled its volume of wood per acre since the '50s, which was the area most heavily logged by European settlers beginning in the 1600s.'"

Paloma met Jennifer's gaze. Jennifer waved a finger and said, "Uh-uh, not done. On its own, without spending billions we can't afford, the increase in trees in the US is significantly growing because of many factors. Some of these," she said, reading from the list in front of her, "include the conservation and preservation of national parks, responsible tree growing within plantations—which have been planting more trees than they harvest—and the movement of the majority of the population from rural areas to more densely populated areas, such as cities and suburbs."

Holding her hand up this time to prevent Paloma from interrupting, she continued, "Tree planting efforts that started in the 1950s are paying off. There is more public awareness about the importance of trees and forests than ever. Six- ty-three percent of the forest land in the United States is pri- vately owned. Many landowners are leaving their land intact instead of using it for agriculture or logging," she finished, holding up the paper and intentionally dropping it.

Paloma immediately got the mic-drop reference. Her face reddened.

Continuing in this fashion for another two hours, Paloma was drawn into discussions and arguments about the bill. She had heard many of these arguments already, such as push-back against spending almost $90 million on how cli- mate change affects pregnancy, $25 million for saving desert fish, $20 million on energy diversity, and $5 billion for an EPA slush fund. When Jennifer began to delve into the argument that climate change was a natural phenomenon, Paloma called it quits.

"Look, Jennifer," Paloma interrupted. "I appreciate you tak- ing the time to give me your thoughts on these points. I'm not going to be swayed that climate change is not critical to our planet's future. There is simply too much evidence to support this. I'm not backing down on creating clean energy and removing fossil fuels. It's not going to happen," she said, looking at her watch. "I only wanted to meet for an hour. We've met for over two. We are landing in half an hour. I'm going back to sit with my boyfriend. Thank you for the meeting and this lovely transportation."

Jennifer smiled. It was still disingenuous and half crooked, this time implying, this isn't over. "I hope you got something useful out of this conversation. You aren't speaking for the majority on many of these issues. You are going to have to scale down a lot of this if you want to get anything passed."

"We will see," Paloma answered, turning and walking back to her seat, feeling a bit nauseous.

*****

Paul was into his second movie. The flight attendant was leaning over his seat, her blonde hair framing her perfectly oval face, her long lashes batting at her boyfriend. Paul had his headphones off and was helping himself to yet another beverage. He was grinning like a schoolboy. Suddenly, they both laughed over something Paul said. Paloma was sure he was plastered.

"That should be your last drink, we are landing soon," Paloma announced as she pushed her way past the flight attendant and took the seat between her and Paul.

"We should be landing in about 23 minutes," the attendant announced with a huge smile on her face. Paloma wanted to punch her in the face and remove the phony grin. She felt a headache coming on. "Please bring me sparkling water," she asked, waving her away with her hand.

"Right away," she replied, disappearing into the small kitchen behind the bulkhead.

"Well, that took longer than an hour..." Paul said, slurring his words.

"Great. I had a crappy meeting and came back to find you drunk off your ass. Thanks for that, babe. Way to make a shitty flight even shittier," Paloma said, fuming. The flight attendant returned with a glass of ice and a bottle of sparkling water. Paloma put down her tray.

"Anything else?" the attendant asked with her infuriating smile.

"No thank you. You can leave us alone until we land, please," Paloma responded, glaring at Paul, daring him to make any type of remark.

Even being drunk, he knew enough to keep his mouth shut.

*****

Unfortunately, because Paul had never flown with unlimited access to alcohol, he didn't understand that its effects were amplified when flying. Airplanes typically fly at a four percent lower pressure than normal at sea level, which slightly lowers oxygen intake. With less oxygen for fuel, you get drunk more quickly.

Paloma learned this lesson the hard way early on in her travels as a congress member getting unlimited drinks in first-class. She forced herself to be a little more understanding as she had to guide her drunk boyfriend off the plane and to the rental car.

Paul slept during the half-hour ride to her grandmother's house. She pulled into the small dirt driveway and turned off the engine. She sat for a moment, taking in the sight of her grandmother's tiny house built on the hill in front of her. The roof sagged; the shutters needed painting.

Most of the front porch was unusable due to rotting boards. It made her angry that no one else in her family seemed to be taking action to upgrade the house. Just because she was now making lots of money didn't mean she should have to bear the responsibility. But she would definitely hire someone to come do repairs. She refused to see her grandmother's home deteriorate like this.

Her grandmother cried with joy the moment she opened the door to find her granddaughter standing there. "Oh mi hermosa nieta. Estoy tan feliz de verte!"

"I'm so happy to see you too, mi abuela! He estado deseando verte."

Her grandmother laughed. "You just told me you are happy being me. You need to say, he estado deseando verte. My English is not so good but it is better than your Spanish," she said with a big smile accented by two front teeth that were missing. She hugged Paloma tightly before pulling her close, pressing her dark, withered hands to Paloma's cheeks. "So, let's talk in English because I bet your novio, how you say, boyfriend, does not speak Spanish."

It felt good to be doted on by her abuela. Of course, she was delighted to prepare Paloma's favorite dinner, bistec, beef marinated in adobo, a mix of salt, garlic, black pepper, and oregano served with rice and beans. Paul was ravenous after taking a nap until dinner time to negate the effects of his drinking. This gave time for Paloma and her abuela to catch up. Paloma told her about the outings she had planned and that they would spend the next couple of days with her. They would take her to the beach, out to dinner, and even to the mall to buy her a couple of new outfits. This pleased her grandmother to the point she cried and hugged her granddaughter all over again.

*****

The few days with her grandmother flew by. The weather was perfect: sunny, warm, and ideal for laying on the beach, swimming in the crystal-clear blue ocean, and strolling through the streets of the city. Paul and Paloma took two days to see Old San Juan, spending the night at the extravagant O:LV Fifty Five hotel.

Lavishing in the opulence of the hotel, the couple had a gourmet dinner of Caribbean lobster before retiring to the rooftop pool. They lay in the lounge chairs and drank under the stars in the soft evening breeze. There was a blanket of stars above them, highlighted by a full moon. Paloma didn't think she had ever enjoyed life more than she was at that moment. She had been right; the experience did blow Paul's mind.

Sadly, after one more night at her grandmother's house, it was time to say goodbye. Paloma contracted some local men, paying them in advance, to do specific work on her home. They were friends of her grandmother, so she felt confident they wouldn't take advantage of her. Still, she made her grandmother promise to tell her if they did all the work and did a good job.

The last two days before heading back to the airport for a commercial flight home would be their two days visiting the rainforest. They would head directly to the airport for a 5:00 PM flight back to JFK, bypassing DC to go directly home.

Early Saturday morning, her abuela cooked the couple a large breakfast using freshly collected eggs from her chickens. Paloma admired her grandmother's simple life. It was such a sharp contrast to her life in the city. It was good she came back to Puerto Rico once in a while to see her roots and appreciate her culture.

The Father and Son

"What do you see when you watch this human?" the Father asked of his son.

"I see someone who has a great passion for her beliefs."

She also cares for her people, like her grandmother," the Father replied. "She is following my words from Timothy: But if anyone does not provide for his relatives, and especially for members of his household, he has denied the faith and is worse than an unbeliever."

"She is also a great believer in taking care of the Earth, as is spoken in Genesis: The Lord God took the man and put him in the garden of Eden to work it and keep it," the son added with smile.

"The issue with this one is her pride." Father continued. "Proverbs tell us that when pride comes, disgrace follows. The humble have wisdom. Pride goes before destruction, and a haughty spirit before a fall. The attributes of a great spirit and pride cannot share a throne."

The Son added, "As it is said in Obadiah: The pride of your heart has deceived you, you who live in the clefts of the rock, in your lofty dwelling, who say in your heart, "Who will bring me down to the ground?" It will be her undoing."

"She will have the chance to be judged by the ones who know the human heart. She will be exonerated or brought to the ground, "the Father concluded.

*****

As sad as Paloma was to leave her grandmother, her heart beat a bit quicker as the car began to climb the winding road into the heart of the rainforest. The canopy of trees loomed overhead, and vines, shrubbery, and thick vegetation crowded the ground beneath. She pulled the car to the side of the road at a bridge and got out to take a picture of the waterfall gushing from the cliffs above.

The smell of the air had a rich, loamy quality. The humid air was alive with the sound of birds calling from the treetops. Vibrant shades of green, brown, and yellow, with splashes of color mixed in from the wild tropical flowers, decorated the forest. "This is why I'm trying to save this planet," she said to Paul as she spun in a circle, trying to take it all in.

Paul came over after snapping a few pictures of his own from his cell phone. He hugged Paloma and pulled her tightly against his body. He kissed her and looked into her eyes. "This has been the most amazing vacation ever. I almost want to move here. It's so incredible: the cities, the beaches, and this rainforest. I had no idea, really, that there were places this beautiful."

"And it ain't over yet, baby. I think the best is yet to come," Paloma said with an alluring smile. "Let's go to our Yuquiyú Treehouse. Wait until you see the view from above all this," she said, sweeping her hand toward the bamboo grove and river rushing down the mountainside. "It's going to give you chills."

They made a stop before the treehouse at the El Portal Visitor Center. Paloma parked the car, and the two of them made their way to the very modern-looking building that served as a rainforest museum and education center. Inside, they were greeted by Puerto Rican parrots or *Cotorras*, an endangered species with very few left in the wild, only found within the 28,000 acres of this National Forest. They toured the center and enjoyed learning about the life held within this unique ecosystem and its importance to the planet.

After paying the entrance fee, Paloma and Bill set off to hike one of the many trails through the rainforest. They decided to do the treetop walkway and then one of the longer trails, which visited the ancient petroglyphs. It was a loop that ended back at the visitor center. The park did an excellent job of using placards to identify the vegetation and animals along the route. There were thousands of species of plants and animals found within the forest, and they made a game of spotting and trying to identify all the birds and reptiles they saw along the way. After completing the loop, they sat down, exhausted, to have lunch at the visitor center's café.

They had a cozy table outside in the sunshine and ordered ham sandwiches on brioche buns and a bottle of wine. The view from the center was spectacular. The Atlantic Ocean could be seen in the distance, a blue backdrop creating a sharp contrast to the rich green foliage of the forest.

"Does this help you make sense of why I work so hard? I'm creating a bill that will help keep our planet looking this beautiful. How many people here," Paloma said, looking around at the other people eating at the café, "can say they are having lunch with someone instrumental in saving the future of our planet, actually doing something to prevent the climate change that is threatening the very existence of places like this?" She gave him a wink.

"Truly, what you are doing is noble. But I'm not sure I buy into the whole climate change thing, though…"

Paloma nearly spit out the mouthful of sandwich she had just bitten off. "WHAT?" she exclaimed, her voice louder than she intended. "What in the hell do you mean, you don't buy into it? Are you blind or stupid?" Several heads of neighboring patrons turned in their direction.

One of the reasons their relationship had worked out so well thus far was that they never discussed politics. When Paloma left her work at the end of the day, she left it on the table. She and Paul hadn't ever discussed political viewpoints. He knew the rough outline of what she did, what her job entailed. They just never talked about specific points of view.

"Um, I'm not stupid," Paul replied, obviously hurt by the comment. "You've never asked me about my opinion on the topic. We have never talked about it. I assumed I was allowed to have my own thoughts on the matter."

Paloma's face froze in an icy stare. "I have millions of followers, but I also have opposers. Can you imagine the scandal that would rain down on me if anyone, and I mean if one single person, found out that my boyfriend didn't support my views on climate change? It would be all over the internet in seconds," she said, so angry that she spit bits of her sandwich onto the table. Wiping her mouth with her sleeve, she grabbed her wine glass, finished the wine in one gulp, then poured the rest of the bottle into her glass. She picked it up, looked back at Paul, and in a much more composed voice, asked him, "Care to explain?"

"A few years ago, everyone was screaming about global warming. I didn't really have an opinion about it. I do construction. I can tell you about I-beams, trusses, and scaffolding. My area of expertise does not include what's going on with the environment. I leave that to the scientists. My boss, however, he's really into it. Every day we eat lunch together. He had his panties in such a bunch over this global warming thing, and I had to hear about it. We would sit there, every day, and he would vent and tell me all about his views. He had researched the hell out of the topic."

"So he was arguing against it?"

"At first, he believed it. He was angry about the rising temperatures and what carbon emissions were doing to the planet. He's big into hunting and has a cabin by a river. He loves the outdoors. Then, when more proof came out that the warming was due to natural shifts and not carbon, he began to change his mind. Then, the climate activists changed their wording to climate change instead of global warming because they can't prove a thing. This really sets him off; he calls them all quacks."

"And what does he think about me?" Paloma asked.

"Let's just say he's not in favor of your bill. He doesn't like how much money you are spending, and he told me all the reasons you are wrong."

Paloma sat back and sipped her wine. "And you haven't mentioned this before… why?"

"Would it have made a difference?"

"No."

"I have honored our agreement not to talk about politics. I leave that at the door when I come home every night. It's the reason our relationship works, babe. We focus on each other instead of all the noise around us."

"And your view on climate change is?"

"You want to get into this right now? You realize this will void our agreement," Paul warned.

"I think this is something important to know. This is the premise of the most important thing in my life at the moment. This isn't politics; this involves the fate of our planet. I kind of need to know where you stand on this."

"If you insist, but I don't think you are going to like my answers. I have to hear my boss talk about the facts, the actual research, every day at lunch. They don't coincide with what you are peddling."

"Peddling? PEDDLING?" Paloma yelled.

"Shhh, babe, please. If you can't discuss this without yelling, we'll have to talk about this later."

"Fine!" she replied, getting up from the table. She downed the rest of the wine. "We're getting out of here. Let's go."

*****

The mood in the car distinctly changed as they drove up to the treehouse resort. Neither spoke a word. Instead of stopping, admiring the forest, and taking pictures, they continued in silence. When they reached Yuquiyú, Paloma told Paul, "Stay in the car, I'll go check us in."

Paul checked his cell signal. He had a few bars. He sent a one-line text to his boss. "It's happening." He waited for a response.

"I told you this day was coming."

About ten minutes later, Paloma opened the door. "Grab our bags." Paul got out, walked to the trunk, and retrieved his and Paloma's suitcases. A man from the office had walked over and was talking to Paloma and pointed up a path. Up the path, four gorgeous wooden houses were perched partway up gigantic trees. They were at the top of a hill, providing a breathtaking view of the rainforest below them.

After a brief tour of the treehouse, the manager of Yuquiyú bowed politely. "If you have any questions or concerns, here is a card with my personal number, Miss Ortega–Sánchez." He handed her his card. "Enjoy the complimentary fruit and champagne on the deck, and let me know if you need any-thing."

Paul carried the bags into the bedroom, went to the bath-room, and washed his face with a cold, wet washcloth. Then, he walked to the balcony where Paloma had already taken a seat. The tiny table was adorned with a white lace tablecloth. Champagne was nestled in a glass urn filled with ice.

A beautiful blue bowl in the center of the table held fruit salad brimming with mango, melon, strawberries, and other native tropical fruit. For the next hour, the couple would have an incredible view as they ate fruit from the trees around them and sipped a very nice bottle of champagne. The hour, however, was going to be the polar opposite of happy.

The debate started with the concept of global warming. Paul relayed his knowledge of the natural cycles the earth takes with periods of heating and cooling. When Paloma argued that the earth has heated up two degrees Celsius since the industrial revolution, Paul countered with the fact that the earth has had ice ages and warm periods over the last million years. During these cycles, global temperatures changed from three to eight degrees Celsius. Hence the reason the climate activists had to change their verbiage to Climate Change.

Paul cited research conducted by the Intergovernmental Panel on Climate Change (IPCC), which is where Paloma got her sources. Their research was debunked by independent studies. According to balloon and satellite data, there was no increase in tropical warming with altitude because of increased CO2. In addition, global surface temperatures have been recording a steady cooling trend since 2001. Lastly, he pointed out that the only data from the IPCC that showed a slight increase in temperature since 2001 was missing data that was needed to complete the records and validate the results.

"And if you need any more validation," Paul continued, "warming can be explained by increased solar activity during the last four centuries, as well as simply being part of a natural and persistent warming recovery since the end of the Little Ice Age, which occurred 1300-1900 AD.

"But what about the proof of polar ice caps melting?" Paloma said, not willing to concede.

"You understand that there is a big difference between Antarctica and the Arctic, right? The Arctic is an ocean. It's covered by a thin layer of perennial sea ice and surrounded by land. Antarctica has completely different conditions. It's a continent. It's covered by a thick ice cap, surrounded by a rim of sea ice and the Southern Ocean."

"Excuse me, don't you dare treat me like I don't know what I'm talking about. I know my facts about both our ice caps," Paloma replied. "The Arctic is losing ice mass. You can't deny that."

"There is still no proof that this is not a natural progression. There has been a steady increase lately in the ice around Antarctica. If it was simply a matter of global warming, the ice would be melting everywhere."

The rest of the evening ensued with more debates. The longer it went on, the more Paloma drank, the worse she began to feel. No one on the congress floor made her feel as bad as Paul had, his words like daggers in her heart. She had no idea her boyfriend was on the opposite side of the fence when it came to climate change. This, unfortunately, would be a game changer for their relationship. There was no way around it. After everything she had done for this bastard, he was one of them, the deniers, one of the people not willing to do what it took to save the planet.

While she wanted to cancel their last outing before returning home, Paloma decided not to, for her own sake. She was the one who wanted to trail ride through a rainforest, and by God, she was not going to rob herself of that opportunity because of a falling out with Paul.

****

When they woke up the next morning, there was an icy chill between them. Paul had asked before they went to bed if she wanted him to sleep on the tiny couch in the living room. Paloma said not to bother. She was quite tipsy by bedtime, and she knew she wouldn't even know he was beside her. They had to get up early to eat breakfast and be at the stables by 9:00 AM, as there would be instructions before the ride. They ordered a quick breakfast before taking the 30-minute drive to the La Vista Stables.

Neither spoke. They had talked for hours the night before. There wasn't much left to say. That didn't mean Paloma wasn't angry. She wanted to wait for the perfect time to unload her feelings and break up with Paul. She speculated that the encounter would happen the moment they arrived back at her suite. She would break up with him and kick him out. There were lots of other attractive fish in the sea.

She would, of course, have to justify her actions to her millions of followers. She would make some vague references to their lives going in different directions. She would also threaten Paul that if he spoke a word of the reason for their breakup, she would use the army of lawyers at her disposal to sue his ass.

Paloma pulled into a dusty parking lot with several other cars already present for the Rainforest River Ride. She had dressed in jeans and hiking sneakers. Paul had on jeans as well and work boots. They were warned that the footing around the river could be slippery. Solid footwear was recommended for working around the horses and for the hike to the river.

Paloma tracked down the leader of the expedition, Carlos, who was welcoming people as they arrived. She introduced herself as Congresswoman Ortega-Sanchez from the United

States. She explained she had taken riding lessons as a kid and was very comfortable around horses. Carlos didn't seem too impressed. Paul walked up and shook hands with the man. The two men chatted for a moment, laughed over a joke Paul told, and when Carlos slapped Paul's back in a manly gesture of brotherhood, Paloma almost lost it. Not only had Paul pissed her off, but he was also stealing her limelight.

Barging between them, Paloma decided to impress Carlos by speaking Spanish. This would make Paul an outsider. "Amigo, conozco bien los caballos," Paloma blurted out, saying that she knew horses well. Thinking it out carefully, she added, "Estoy muy emocionada por este viaje." She spoke haltingly, explaining that she was excited for the ride. Then she added, "Soy una persona muy importante en los Estados Unidos, así que dame tu caballo bestia," flashing her biggest smile while trying to say that she was an important person from the US and wanted their best horse.

"Caballo bestia?" Carlos repeated with a questioning expression.

"Sí, caballo bestia," Paloma answered with authority.

"No hay problema, señora," Carlos said with a grin.

Paloma flipped her ponytail and walked toward the gathering group of riders. Carlos hung back and then walked up to Paul. "Is she your girlfriend?"

"Well, she was. I'm thinking it's going to be a long ride back to the States," Paul answered.

"Good, because she asked me for the 'caballo bestia.' I think she meant to say 'caballo mejor.'

"What's the difference?" Paul asked, curious.

"Bestia is beast; mejor is best. If the lady wants a beast, I have the perfect horse. It's up to you, mi amigo. She seems a bit full of herself. Should I give her what she asked for?

Paul doubled over with laughter. Paloma heard the laughter and looked back at the two men from her spot in the group. "Please, Carlos, give the woman what she asked for. She always gets what she asks for."

After a 30-minute orientation about how to ride the horses, the route they would be taking, and what they would see along the ride, the riders were ready to mount the horses, which were already tacked up and tied to a long fence. The horses represented a range of colors: black horses with long flowing manes, chestnuts, grays, and one perky brown and white paint.

The guide explained that these horses were called Criollo, a mixed breed whose descendants were of the Paso Fino breed. Paso Finos are gaited horses that are now popular worldwide. They were specifically bred on the island of Puerto Rico.

Paloma reiterated her request in Spanish for the "beast horse." Carlos specifically led her to the paint. "Este es tu caballo, Mujer del Congreso. Él es el caballo que pediste," the guide said, reassuring her that this was the horse she had requested. Something didn't quite seem right to Paloma. She detected a smirk from Carlos as he handed the horse's reins to her. She looked at the horse and noticed the paint coloring was flashy, clearly the prettiest of all the horses. It occurred to her that Carlos was probably just flirting with her; that happened a lot with the lobbyists in Washington. She patted the horse on its neck and ran her hand down its soft mane.

"What's his name?" she asked Carlos. "Diablo," he replied as he walked away.

One at a time, the riders mounted. The horses stood still as the riders climbed onto the mounting block and grabbed the reins and the saddle horn in their left hand, as instructed. Then they placed their left foot in the stirrup and lifted themselves gently into the saddle. The two men walked down the line of riders to make sure the stirrups were the right length, the girths were tight, and everyone was comfortable.

With the guests mounted and ready, the horses were untied by the guides. The halters were left on, and the lead ropes had been looped around the horses' necks so the horses could be tied up when the group arrived at the river.

The two men mounted their horses. Carlos shouted out, "Please stay in line," as the group started off at a brisk walk. The horses knew the trail and the routine well. They were sure-footed even though the trail was filled with ruts and rocks as it wound through the forest.

Carlos took the lead, and the other guide took up the rear. He had asked Paloma to take the spot directly behind him. Finally, she was getting some respect for being a United States Congress member. She had wanted to be close to Carlos so she could ask questions and have someone to talk to. She glanced behind her and spotted Paul way down the line of horses toward the rear. *Well, this worked out well*, she thought to herself.

The ride was geared toward beginners. Most of the ride would be walking. Sometimes, the horses would break into a trot, especially when going uphill. It was easier for them to run up a hill than walk. The first half of the ride would be all downhill.

The destination was the Rio Espiritu Santo River, where they would drink the fresh water filtered by the rainforest and have a picnic lunch. The hour-long ride was promised to be peaceful, with gorgeous views of the interior of the rainforest. Carlos had explained that he would stop at certain locations to point out vegetation and viewpoints. It was a slow descent, but the path would get steeper as they approached the river.

Within the first few minutes of starting out, Paloma became irritated with her horse. He wanted to be right up the tail of Carlos's horse. It really irritated her when he got too close. No one likes to be tailgated. Carlos's horse would pin his ears back and threaten to kick Diablo. Carlos would look back at Paloma and yell, "¡Mantén tu distancia!" which meant keep your distance.

Instead of being able to ride relaxed and enjoy the sights, Paloma had to keep constant pressure on the reins. The moment she didn't have tension, her horse would speed up and have his nose right back in the tail of the horse in front of her. Worst of all, Diablo had an annoying habit of jerking his head forward and ripping the reins out of her hands. After the first ten minutes, she was already getting blisters from pulling so hard. Worse, she had broken a nail when it got snagged in the mane.

Paloma didn't understand why the horse couldn't just walk where it was supposed to without constantly trying to crowd the horse in front of her. Losing her patience, she finally grabbed the reins in both hands and yanked them back as hard as she could, trying to take an authoritative approach and gain the horse's respect. That didn't work out well. Diablo threw his head up, then immediately responded with a buck. Taken by surprise, Paloma was unseated and thrown forward onto the horse's neck. The horn of the Western saddle gouged into her midsection. She groaned. Diablo bolted forward, crashing into the back of Carlos's horse.

The dam broke, and Paloma blew a fuse. She knew how to deal with a horse that wouldn't listen to her. She didn't have a crop in her hand, but there were lots of tree branches hanging along the trail. Leaning over, Paloma ripped a branch off the nearest tree. She quickly stripped off the leaves and small stems and now had a tool to discipline the recalcitrant horse.

She didn't have to wait long to use the makeshift crop. Diablo began to speed up. She pulled back hard on the reins. Diablo responded by jerking his head down to pull the reins from her hands. Paloma gathered both reins in one hand, grasped the crop in the other, and smacked the horse as hard as she could on the ass. This was happening as Carlos was turning around in his saddle to check on his riders. She heard him yell, "You don't want to do that!" but it was too late.

Diablo took off like a speeding bullet. Inadvertently, Paloma yanked the reins to her left to avoid a collision with the back of Carlos's horse. Diablo bolted around the lead horse and off the trail. Once out in front of the leader, Diablo didn't follow the trail. He suddenly veered up the slope and into the rainforest. Paloma screamed. She heard Carlos yelling for her to "PULL BACK." It was too late; Diablo was running out of control, and no amount of pulling was going to stop him.

*****

Carlos called back for everyone to stop their horses. The guide at the back trotted around the group to confer with Carlos. The two men conversed in Spanish while the rest of the riders peered into the forest in shock. Paul rode around everyone to find out what the men were going to do about the emerging crisis.

Engrossed in an animated discussion in Spanish, the men worked out a plan. Luis, the other guide, would take the group down the mountain and continue the ride. Carlos turned to Paul and explained the plan in English. Carlos would head out after Paloma and track where the horse had taken her. If she had fallen off, he would find her. The horse would eventually return to the barn on its own, with or without her. "Can I go with you?" Paul asked Carlos. "We did just have a falling out, but I do care what happens to her."

"Not a good idea, amigo." It may be some very rough riding up there, Carlos said, nodding up the hill, which was riddled with thick vegetation. There was no clear trail to follow. "I promise I will find her and bring her back. You go with the group and enjoy the rest of your ride."

Paul nodded and walked back to his place in line. Luis took the front position. Carlos waited until the group was reassembled and began walking down the trail again. A few of the riders glanced back nervously, but order had been restored. As soon as the group was safely away, Carlos turned his horse up the hill and broke into a canter, trying to follow the hoofprints that had dug into the soft, loamy soil of the rainforest floor.

Even as experienced as the cowboys were with horses and the rainforest, it was going to be a difficult task to track the horse. The soil in the forest was always moist and soft, so the trail would be easy to follow. Several small rivers ran through the forest. The ground was rocky around the rivers. A complication might occur if the horse wandered into a river. The rocky ground would make it difficult to track the direction the horse had taken.

Carlos hoped that Paloma had been truthful about her riding experience. Her best chance of coming out of this unscathed was if she stayed on the horse. Horses can always find their way back home. It is instinct for them to return to the stable. They never get lost. If she fell off somewhere in the forest and the horse returned without her, a massive search would have to be organized to find her.

The forest was not easy to navigate on foot if you didn't know the way. More than one hiker had gotten lost in the dense forest. Carlos regretted his decision to put Paloma on Diablo. While energetic, Diablo had never reacted this way with any other rider. He was a great lead horse. If he had to go behind another horse, the worst thing he did was act a bit antsy. He had never bolted or taken off with anyone before today. As Carlos slowed, checking the ground to see if he was still on the trail, he cursed the moment Miss Ortega-Sanchez walked onto the ranch.

The Father and Son

"The humans you have selected have strong personalities and spirits. It certainly seems that those with the strongest were drawn from the pool. It seems this horse has a strong spirit as well and does not like humans," the Son said to the Father.

The Father replied, "Horses are a product of their interactions with humans. Human parents shape the morals and values of their children. Humans also shape the behavior patterns of a horse, although the horses will always have individual personalities. The biggest difference is that any human can earn the love and trust of horses by how they interact with them. Humans are more set in their ways. Once their personalities are formed, it's very hard for them to change. Horses are much more adaptable. They are trusting creatures until you give them a reason not to trust anymore."

"You created horses to be man's companion," the Son noted, "his transportation, to toil and work for him, and to carry him through the centuries. Horses are unique creations in that they are the only creatures able to judge what lies within the hearts of men.

The father nodded in agreement. "All horses are born with the same character. If man is fearful, they will back off; if man is calm and confident, they will move forward. If man is kind, they will comply; and if man is wicked, they will rebel. The great power that each horse holds is that they are a mirror of the best and the worst of human nature. Furthermore, they know what lies in the heart of a human."

*****

As the horse cantered up the mountain, Paloma clung desperately to stay seated. Conceding that she had lost control, she leaned forward, grabbed the mane with both hands, and hung on for dear life. Tree branches, bushes, and vines threatened to tear her from the back of the horse. She had to duck and cling to avoid being ripped off Diablo's back. The horse's powerful hindquarters dug into the earth to propel them up the hill; however, the soft soil was poor footing. The horse slipped and slid, making the ride even more dangerous.

Thoughts, fears, and waves of anger rolled through Paloma's mind as the horse continued to race up the mountain. She was afraid of falling off, afraid of getting hurt, afraid of getting lost, and not finding her way back to the stable. She wondered how Paul was feeling at that moment. Was he afraid for her, or was he glad she was gone? Most of all, she felt anger. She hated Carlos for giving her this animal, and she hated the horse for his reckless and belligerent attitude. All she wanted to do was take a ride through the rainforest. This was not what she had in mind.

As the terrain began to level slightly, Diablo started to veer left. The thought occurred to Paloma that he might be trying to head back to the stable. Unfortunately, there were no paths in this part of the mountain. If the horse cut across the forest here, there was no telling what they might run into. She desperately wanted to gain control of the horse so she could have a choice in their direction. Just as she was about to collect the reins and try to stop the horse, the ground gave way beneath them.

They were crossing a drainage area. When torrential rains occurred, this was where the water naturally overflowed, a shallow ravine that channeled the excess water. The ground beneath was much softer as the floodwaters washed away the vegetation and roots. Diablo went down, Paloma with him. He fell onto his side; thankfully, his body landed uphill. Had he gone the other way, Paloma would have been crushed. It happened so quickly that Paloma didn't even have time to scream. One second they were running; in a flash, she was lying on the ground, her leg pinned between the horse and the earth.

Just as she was contemplating what to do, feeling slightly dizzy and disoriented, Diablo tried scrambling to his feet. He struggled, the ground beneath him slippery. Under the silt, a shale base provided no traction for the horse to get his feet securely beneath him. As he floundered, Paloma clung to the saddle in fear, afraid that she would be injured if she got separated from the horse. With the extra weight, Diablo had no hope of regaining his footing. The thrashing caused the two of them to start sliding down the gulley.

As they slid and gained momentum, Paloma's heart skipped a beat. She heard the sound of rushing water. That could only mean one thing: the two of them were sliding toward a river. Many of the rivers in the rainforest had cliffs and waterfalls. She was correct.

The next thing Paloma felt was the ground beneath her disappear. It was an odd sensation. It was as if the ground was a big rug that had just been pulled from under them. Sure enough, the overflow basin led to a river. They were now falling over the edge of a cliff and into the river.

Time seemed to stop as she was suspended between heaven and earth. Her hands instinctively let go of the saddle as she tried to orient herself to get her feet under her to brace for the impact. Involuntarily, she unleashed a blood-curdling scream. The gentle noises made by the creatures of the rainforest halted. The sound echoed through the silence. She prayed there would be deep water below. As her life flashed before her eyes, so did one last thought. Mejor was Spanish for "best." She had confused it with "bestia," which means "beast." She had asked for this horse. That had to be what Paul and Carlos were laughing about. That was her last thought before she hit the water.

The echoing scream reached Carlos as he galloped up the hill, following tracks. He halted his horse and turned toward the direction of the sound. He wanted to turn and go directly toward it, but it made more sense to follow the tracks in front of him. He could see gouged sections of earth where Diablo had slipped and stumbled. Making a quick decision, Carlos urged his horse forward and up, following the tracks. In a few minutes, he halted again. The sight made his stomach sink.

The story was told by the marks on the ground in front of him. Diablo had fallen. The ground was indented with the impression of a horse on its side. There were deep grooves where he tried to regain his footing. Carlos scanned the ground, hoping to see human footprints walking away. There were none. There was another deep groove, however, going back down the mountain where the horse and rider had slid. The slope increased dramatically. Carlos knew exactly where it went.

In a panic now, he reined his horse up and around the shallow and muddy ravine. He got to the other side and paralleled it down the mountain. He had to go slowly as the ground was soft and slippery. He wound his way around trees and areas that were too thick to ride through.

Soon, he heard the sound he had been anticipating, the sound of the river. Riding carefully to the edge of the cliff overlooking the river, he glanced upward, toward the ravine. What he saw horrified him. The skid marks the horse had made clearly went over the edge of the cliff. What he saw next horrified him even more. Nothing. He saw nothing, no sign of horse or rider. The river bubbled and gurgled, continuing its perpetual goal of finding its path of least resistance.

*****

Fortunately, the runoff water had dredged a deep well in the river. Each time there was flooding and volumes of water flowed down the ravine and over the cliff, the silt on the bottom of the river was displaced. Diablo hit the surface, followed closely by Paloma. The two disappeared immediately. Seconds later, Diablo popped to the surface.

Paloma was so stunned when she found herself underwater that it took her a few seconds to determine which way was up. Otherwise unharmed, she swam toward the light. She burst through the surface and took a huge gulp of air. Frantically, she looked around. She noticed she was nowhere near the cliff. The swift river had already dragged horse and rider down its path. Paloma oriented herself with the flow and scanned the horizon for Diablo. He was several yards in front of her, desperately trying to swim toward shore.

Forcing herself to swim as fast as she could, Paloma made her way toward Diablo. He was struggling to keep his head above water. She caught up with him and noticed the lead rope which had been tied around his neck was now trailing behind him. She reached out and grabbed it in one hand, using the other to tread water. Diablo continued his efforts to reach the shore. The current was strong and fast and helped propel him. He was a strong swimmer and easily towed Paloma behind him.

Suddenly, a bend in the river appeared. A bank of sand had formed where the water slowed its pace around the bend. The deep channel diverted to the outside of the curve, flowing next to the opposite bank. Diablo instinctively swam toward the nearest shore. In a few short minutes, his feet contacted the bottom. In a huge effort, he pulled himself out of the current. The water gradually grew shallower. Paloma held the lead rope with a death grip.

Finally, her feet touched the ground. It was a miracle. They both had survived falling off a cliff into a river and had now made their way to the riverbank. She was so happy tears of joy rolled down her face; her salty tears merged with the sweet water of the rainforest river.

Together, they exited the river. There was a lush green patch of grass along the bank. The constant flooding kept the dense vegetation at bay, but the grass thrived. Diablo gave a mighty shake, then immediately dropped his head and began avidly eating the grass as if trying to erase the recent memory. His legs were rubbery from the struggle. He was shivering from exhaustion.

Paloma was in shock. Unlike Diablo, she had no desire to eat. Just the opposite, she wanted to vomit. Keeping a tight grip on the lead rope, she dropped to her knees and wrapped her arms around her body in an attempt to control her shaking.

The warm sun and grass revived Diablo. He tried walking away. The jerk of the rope brought Paloma back to reality. She stood and pulled Diablo back toward her.

"Where do you think you are going, buddy?" she asked venomously. "You. YOU! This is all your fault!" she screamed. Without thinking, she stood up and punched the horse as hard as she could, her fist bouncing harmlessly off his thick neck muscles. Diablo didn't even flinch. "Shit, that hurt," she yelled. "What the heck do we do now? Thanks to you, instead of a peaceful trail ride to a river, I fell off a cliff into a river, and now I'm lost in a fucking rainforest!" she screamed.

Needing to come up with a plan of action, Paloma led Diablo over to a rock and sat down. The horse took the opportunity to graze next to her. "Why?" she asked the horse. "I'm a hundred-pound human. You're a thousand-pound horse. You could easily pull this rope out of my hand and run away. What makes you stay? Why do you submit when you could simply overpower me? Are you really that stupid?"

Diablo picked his head up to chew a mouthful of grass. He was noncommittal with his expression. His head was even with Paloma's. She could see into the pupil of his eye. His noisy chewing was rhythmic. His massive jaw worked systematically to grind the grass to a pulp. The rest of his body was as still as a statue. He no longer showed any signs he had just been through a near-death experience. Paloma leaned in closer, staring into the black orb of his eye. There were strange, ethereal shapes around the edges. The interior was like looking into a galaxy. It was mesmerizing. It seemed eternal. Then, just like that, the spell was broken. Diablo pulled his head back down and continued to fill his belly.

"If it's not too much of a bother, I think we better start figuring out how we are going to find our way out of here. I'm disoriented. I have no idea which way to go. I'm hoping that you have a better sense of direction in this forest than I do. The question is, do I walk or do I dare try to ride you, Diablo?"

Suddenly, Paloma was starving. The shock was wearing off, her adrenaline had ebbed, and hunger had set in. She was also parched. She knew the rainforest river was clean enough to drink, so she led Diablo back toward the water to get a drink. Recognizing he was being taken back to the river, Diablo stopped dead. He had no intention of going near the river. He stood solidly and wouldn't budge an inch closer. Paloma looked around and didn't see anything solid to tie the horse to. If she let him go, he might eat grass or he could run. She couldn't take that chance.

Exhausted, frustrated, hungry, and mentally at her wit's end, Paloma first screamed at Diablo. He wasn't affected in the least. With a sudden impulse, she kicked him as hard as she could in the leg. Her foot collided with his leg bone. His bone was much harder than her sneaker. He backed up a few steps, putting his ears back, and raised his head in a defensive posture. Paloma screamed again, this time in pain. She was sure she had just broken her foot.

Paloma fell to the ground in pain. She inadvertently dropped the lead rope. Diablo backed up, turned, and raced into the forest. Paloma sobbed in pain and frustration. She crawled to the river's edge. Cupping her hands, she took drinks between her sobs. She washed her face and tried to take deep breaths to ease her panic attack. On the verge of passing out, Paloma crawled back to the soft grass, lay down, closed her eyes, and fell asleep. It was the only thing left she could do.

*****

Hours later, Paloma heard voices in the distance. She tried to hear them through the fog surrounding her brain. She wasn't sure if she was dreaming or if the voices were real. Opening her eyes partway, a hazy image of two people approaching her began to come into focus. She closed her eyes again, then lifted her head a bit and took another look. Carlos and Luis were walking toward her from the forest.

The men made a quick assessment to assure there were no critical injuries. Paloma said she would be okay, except for her foot, which she thought might be broken. She would never divulge she had hurt her foot kicking their horse and not by falling off the cliff. It throbbed.

"Diablo saved you," Carlos said. "He found his way back to the barn. We were able to follow his trail through the forest. Lucky for you, between the footprints and broken branches, we were able to find our way back to you."

Saving the details of the story for when they safely returned to the ranch, the two men lifted Paloma from the ground and braced her between them to help her walk. "Don't worry. There is a road not too far from here. It's an old fire road. We will radio to have a truck meet us there to drive you back to the ranch."

Luis pulled out his walkie-talkie to send the message. "You're going to be okay," Luis said, even though Paloma felt everything in her life was far from okay.

Justin Barone

Nine Pines, California
Equestrian

EASE OF LIFE IS all about perspective. A child growing up in a middle-class family didn't have to contend with the expectation of achieving greatness. There was no perching precariously on an invisible pedestal. Your life was your own; you could make your own decisions, and your parents didn't lay down the law when it came to your future.

A child of lesser means may not have the best of everything, but sometimes having the best of everything was not worth the pressure and ensuing complications. If he had his way, Justin would have preferred a modest upbringing where he could pursue his dreams without feeling like a salmon trying to swim upstream. That was Justin's view from where he stood, looking out the bedroom window of his father's mansion on the Barone Estate and Vineyard in Nine Pines, California.

Justin peered out of the large floor-to-ceiling windows that lined the east side of his bedroom. When he was old enough, he chose a bedroom that faced the sunrise rather than the sunset. He was an early riser and loved watching the sun come up over the horizon. The location of the sunrise depended on the season. The sun migrated as the earth's rotation changed. It turned out that by March, just in time for his birthday, the sun rose between the peaks of the hills that lay just beyond the boundary of the 46 acres Justin called home.

High up on the second floor of the mansion, Justin had an excellent view of the property. Elegant trees bordered the paved lane leading to the house. In the distance, a vibrant green vineyard lined the small river that snaked its way across the fields. Along the vineyard's perimeter grew clusters of fruit trees. Nestled off to the left was his favorite part of the picture: the incredible equestrian facility. The main barn was built to blend in with the natural beauty of the surroundings. The oak siding was meticulously trimmed with matching fascia. It was contrasted by the slate gray roof, completed in its classic appearance with an elaborate cupola. Adjoining the barn was a climate-controlled indoor riding arena.

Built into the indoor arena was an expansive and plush viewing room that served as a unique venue for holiday parties, conferences, weddings, and social events. The attendees were often treated to demos put on by dressage riders, equestrian vaulters, drill teams, and breed displays like Andalusians, Friesians, and award-winning, fancy-stepping, gaited horses.

Complete with elegant lavatories featuring Italian tiled floors, designer fixtures, padded chairs, staging areas with full-length mirrors, and changing rooms, even upscale events were accommodated at the Barone Estate. In addition to the unique equestrian feature, wine from the Barone Vineyard accompanied every event. The bottles had custom labels printed with the name and date of the gathering. Food was catered by local chefs and prepared in the professional-grade kitchen beneath the viewing room, adjacent to where the giant wine casks, filled with their latest vintage, were stored.

Behind the barn were individual paddocks, each with its own run-in shed. A large outdoor arena featured a state-of-the-art jump course designed by Olaf Peterson, a world-renowned equestrian jump builder. Off to the right were the pool, pool house, and three small homes that accommodated the staff and stable hands. From the view above, Barone Estate was picture perfect. Beneath its surface was a dark underbelly, invisible to the world. It hung like a cloud over Justin's head. The storm that had been brewing for several years was about to arrive.

*****

It was March 14th. Justin turned 21 years old at 6:24 A.M. He was officially an adult. He turned away from the sunrise and walked to his dark mahogany dresser. The mirror that hung above it had been his grandfather's. His grandfather died when he was eleven after a long battle with cancer. He loved his grandfather dearly and was deeply impacted by his death. His grandfather was the polar opposite of his father.

Lorenzo Barone owned and worked the land that Justin's father, Michael Barone, inherited. The small vineyard and fruit farm earned enough to keep the family comfortable. He had purchased the land years before the price of land in California became untenable for the common folk. He built the farm and winery from the ground up.

Grandpa Barone was an immigrant from Italy. He had worked in a vineyard in Tuscany since his early teens, alongside the vintner, absorbing every nuance of winemaking. When he turned 18, he took his savings and some money he borrowed from his parents, bought a ticket to America, and searched for land to start his own winery. After a long and arduous search, he purchased a parcel of land in Nine Pines, California. It was owned by a winery. This extra land was where they had planted supplemental vines. Eventually, the winery purchased more land adjacent to their main property and sold off this parcel.

It was the perfect scenario for Justin's grandfather. He built a small home and began his own small winery. Soon after, he fell in love with Justin's grandmother. He had hired her to help with the winemaking. Her shy and quiet demeanor and natural beauty won his heart—and so, the beginning of the California Barone family.

Wanting to be more than the proprietor of a vineyard, their only son, Michael Barone, went to college, worked his way through law school, and then quickly rose through the ranks of several law firms. By the time he was 45, he had opened his own office and owned one of the most successful law firms in Southern California. His tenacity at taking on battles with drug companies, and winning, launched him into the legal record books. He was a force to be reckoned with; everyone in the legal arena respected his talent.

At home, there had been many battles between Justin and his father regarding his future. His father wanted Justin to go to college, then law school, and take a place in his law firm. Justin had no interest in becoming a lawyer. His dream was to ride professionally in the hunter/jumper world. It was his passion, his obsession, and the only thing he wanted to do with his life. Justin had an older sister who moved to LA to become an actress. Justin was his father's last hope for passing on his legacy.

On the eve of Justin's 17th birthday, a junior in high school, his father asked to talk to him in his wood-paneled office, man to man. Justin remembered the conversation as if it were yesterday. The smell of his dad's cigar smoking in the ashtray on the desk, the clink of the ice cube in his glass of scotch, and the red glow of light from the stained-glass lamp on his desk swirled around his head as he relived the conversation from four years prior.

"Son, you have some important decisions to make. Tomorrow, you turn seventeen. You know, when I was seventeen, I had already applied to three Ivy League schools?"

"I know, Dad. You've told me that a hundred times. I'm not eligible for early application; I didn't take any AP-level courses. I'm not as smart as you were."

"Justin, this isn't about grades and getting into a good school. You can start in a community college if you want. I'm not asking you to apply to Ivy League; I'm just asking that you apply yourself in a good direction. Being successful in life is a journey, not a destination. If you dedicate yourself, you can get there, fill my shoes someday."

"But Dad, you know I don't want to be a lawyer?"

"Son, what are you going to do with your life? You can't play around with horses and be successful. That's not a career. If you just took some initiative to learn what I do, I think you would love it. I know I do, and you know the saying: the apple doesn't fall far from the tree."

Justin had been prepared for this day. His mother had always been the impetus for his love of horses. She knew that he was more akin to her spirit, someone who would never be happy working behind a desk. She had been as happy as a clam building a horse farm and overseeing their winery.

Delores Barone was a native Californian with a strong will of her own and a love of nature. She and Michael met in college. They were soul mates. They were both strong-willed and independent, but somehow, they were perfect for each other. They both had their passions: hers, horses and farming; his, perfecting his law career.

Their relationship worked. She capitalized on her husband's growing wealth, which gave her the freedom to oversee the vineyard and stay close to her horses. They worked together to build a state-of-the-art equestrian facility. Her greatest love was working with the horses. It kept her grounded, with her roots deeply embedded in the outdoors. It was a love she shared with her son.

As Justin became more obsessed with the competitive side of jumping and hinted that he might like to pursue it as a career, his mother warned him. "One day, your father is going to talk with you. He wants you to follow in his footsteps. He wants you to become a lawyer and one day, take over his law firm. I know your father. He's going to be relentless. That's what makes him such a good lawyer," she said with a sad smile.

The Father and Son

"It is true that horses have a significant impact on many people in society," the Son said. "This young man is passionate about them. He is facing the wrath of his father to fight to keep them in his life. He is proof that there are those who still care, who love and cherish these animals."

The Father replied, "It was written in 1 John 2:16, '*For all that is in the world—the desires of the flesh and the desires of the eyes and pride in possessions—is not from the Father but is from the world.*' Man has taken the gift of the horse and is using them for profit. He desires them as a possession, something to be bought, sold, and owned as a status symbol. It remains to be seen if this human has love for horses or is using them to avoid following in the footsteps of his father."

"You created horses for the use of man, as You have all creatures on Earth," the Son said. "Man has evolved. They no longer have the need to use horses for travel, for moving goods, or for war. It makes sense for man to use the horse in a different manner as the world changed."

"Using them for a different purpose is acceptable," the Father said. "However, when humans consider horses only as possessions, mistreat them, and lose sight of what they have contributed to their evolution, then man will be condemned. Horses were given as a gift to be treasured. They work tirelessly, they continue to give until they can give no more; they are the last bastions of patience, loyalty, and trust.

"When man loses all sight of that, it is the beginning of the end. The majority have already lost their connection with the nature around them. When the last thread of respect has been severed, if the majority have no respect for what they have been given, it will be the time for a reset, a new beginning for this planet."

*****

The memory of the last meeting with his father when he was 17 years old faded. The clock was ticking. Soon it would be time for Justin to head downstairs and go through the motions of having breakfast and chatting with his parents as if it were a normal day. This day was anything but normal. It was time for a repeat performance.

Justin replayed the night of that fateful conversation with his father, trying to recall how he had convinced his father to give him a chance. He was going to have to use the same tactics when he faced his father again in his study, just as he had when he was seventeen.

While his arguments during that first meeting had been well researched, the economic impact of the equestrian world had not impressed his father. Justin predicted this would be the case. He loved his father, but he also knew that wealth brought a great desire to maintain a certain standard of living. With his sister out of the picture, waitressing in a restaurant in Hollywood, waiting for a big break that had a slim chance of happening, it was up to Justin to carry the family torch.

Using facts his father couldn't deny, Justin had established that there was significant money being funneled into the economy from the horse industry. The next task was to convince his father that he could bring in an income that would rival the salary of a lawyer. He recalled how sweaty his palms were when he prepared for his final argument. He remembered wondering if this was how his father felt every time he stood in front of a jury in a court of law, and if it was, being a lawyer was not going to be his cup of tea.

*****

The morning started out well. His mother and father were all smiles. They hugged their son and wished him a happy 21st birthday. The cook, Hilda, appeared with his favorite breakfast: crepes filled with banana and Nutella, powdered sugar sprinkled on top. Justin had his first taste of crepes when he was ten from a street cart in France.

When he came home from that trip, he asked Hilda if she could make crepes, and she did. Hilda knew they topped the list of his favorite breakfasts. This morning, the crepes were accompanied by fresh fruit, crispy bacon, savory sausage, pomegranate mimosas, and one small crème brûlée with a candle for the birthday boy.

Justin had insisted there be no party. His father had offered to host a bash, but Justin vehemently declined. He was not feeling good about the landmark birthday, having failed to meet the goals that decided his future path. The last thing he felt like doing was celebrating.

After breakfast, his father gave him a knowing look and nodded his head toward the study. Justin nodded. No words were needed. Both men slid their chairs back and excused themselves from the table. He glanced at his mother, looking for some sign of support. Sylvia sipped her coffee. She didn't meet his gaze.

The office was exactly the same as it was four years ago. This time, Michael pulled a chair up adjacent to his own. Instead of facing his father across the desk, they were meeting face-to-face. It was never too early for his father to smoke one of his Cubans, so he pulled one out of the humidor behind his desk before sitting down. He offered one to Justin by holding it up in his direction. Justin shook his head. His father knew he didn't smoke.

"Being that you were only seventeen, I was a bit lenient on our agreement. While your proposal looked good on paper, I know in reality things don't work out exactly the way you plan, ever. If that were the case, the world wouldn't need lawyers," he said with a grin before lighting his cigar and taking deep puffs.

"The agreement, as you recall, was while you were embarking on your professional horse career, you took online college courses to get a business degree, which would benefit you for running your own business as well as preparing you for the when…" Michael paused, "…I mean if your horse endeavors didn't pan out. I thought that part of the agreement was ingenious, really."

"I have about two months left and a thesis to write," Justin said. "If all goes well, I should graduate with a 3.8 or higher." He had worked his ass off in a three-year program to attain a Bachelor's Degree in Business Administration. He had to take AP courses as a senior in high school to qualify. Fortunately, he was able to devote nights and time between shows and lessons to work on his computer wherever he was.

He spent a lot of time in the living compartment of his horse trailer at horse shows, knocking out papers, taking exams, and studying.

He had to admit that what he learned was very useful for dealing with contacts within the equestrian world in his start-up business. He was also able to use his encounters as part of his research and assignments. It allowed him to create and implement a business plan. His professors were impressed with his real-world application. While most of the other students researched topics, Justin was living them.

"The second part of our agreement was that you built a client base. You had to have students, a lesson program, and clients that you brought to horse shows."

"I currently have seven students that I train and that are competing in the National Desert Circuit and the National Sunshine Series. If all goes well, we will be heading to Florida to the Ocala World Equestrian Center for a show."

"The last part of the agreement was that you sell all the horses you purchased in Europe by your 21st birthday. What about your horse sales?" his dad asked, knowing full well that his mother had filled in every detail of what had transpired. "In order for me to accept this career you chose, the deal was that you had to have sold ALL the horses you imported by your 21st birthday. I know you only came home with three instead of five as you intended. That greatly reduced your potential profit. You had to have all three sold to fulfill our bargain."

"Dad," Justin pleaded, "I'm so close. There is one last show next month at Thermal. If my horse does well, I have a buyer for my last horse."

"I lent you the money to start this business, the money that you would have used to go to a good university. There is no wiggle room or negotiations on this, Justin," his father said, pulling a paper out of the top drawer of his desk. "I have your signature on the agreement that we drew up together. It's a binding contract. If you failed to meet the conditions of our agreement, you would repay me every cent of my investment, and you agreed to go to law school."

Justin stood up and looked his father in the eye. He took a deep breath. He felt like he was seventeen again, a shy, timid son, facing his formidable father. He worked so hard to accomplish his goals. He had made so much progress and developed a good reputation among seasoned professionals. The problem was that there were a lot of bad seeds in the hunter-jumper world. That was one factor he could not have predicted that would come between him and his ability to achieve his goals. The next words he spoke were going to be the most important of his life. They would determine the direction of his future.

The Father and Son

"Can a man truly be honorable and have a good heart if he knowingly chooses to walk into a world known for its dishonesty and false deeds?" the Son asked.

The Father replied, "Psalms tell us, 'Blessed is the man who walks not in the counsel of the wicked, nor stands in the way of sinners, nor sits in the seat of scoffers.' There are many lessons that warn man about the perils of keeping company with those who are evil. Sodom and Gomorrah are examples of what happens when all good has perished."

"Yet, you also tell men to go forth and be good examples," the Son said. "Matthew states, 'In the same way, let your light shine before others, so that they may see your good works and give glory to your Father who is in heaven.'

"If this human has a good heart, perhaps he can be the instrument of change in the competitive world of horses. Timothy tells man, 'Let no one despise you for your youth, but set the believers an example in speech, in conduct, in love, in faith, in purity.' Has Justin not lived by this oath?"

The Father paused. "It remains to be seen what quality is brought forth in this human. Will his love for horses dictate his actions, or will his desire to succeed and prove his worth to his father overshadow what is best for his horses?"

*****

One part of the process that Justin was not prepared for was the paperwork and regulations involved with shipping horses internationally. He had researched the cost of putting a horse on a plane to LA from Europe. His experience with Karen painted the complete picture of this complicated process. There were no refunds if a horse didn't work out. Once they were on that plane, they were your problem.

Most people who buy horses in Europe enlist the service of a broker who assists with the sales and oversees transporting the horse into the United States. The price of a broker is usually 10% of the cost of the horse.

When it was time for Justin to buy horses on his own, it was clear he would need a broker. There were so many rules and regulations to follow that there was no way he could be proficient in all the protocols after one visit to Europe. Besides booking the airline, there were tons of documents and forms that had to be completed. Multiple tests had to be run by a veterinarian and the proof of results was documented. A vet was usually paid to accompany the horses on the trip to ensure the horses had no medical emergencies during the flight.

Once the horses were in the U.S., they had to be quarantined for several days to ensure they didn't carry any infectious diseases. Lastly, it was necessary to communicate with the government agencies in the U.S. to facilitate the clearance of the shipment and schedule the arrival with the quarantine procedures. If any of the documentation didn't meet the import and export regulations, the horse could be sent back.

When Justin returned on his own a year later, he had his ducks in a row and money in hand. What he couldn't have anticipated was the unusual shortage of horses for sale that season.

"There was no way for me to know that there were several large operations that beat me to the punch that year," Justin explained to his father. "Jumping prospects were very limited. I was lucky to come home with three horses."

"From what I hear from your mother, one of them turned out to be a bad actor."

"He has so much potential, Dad. He could break records in the jumper classes. He's the kind of horse that could win the Grand Prix. He needs a really good rider, a strong rider, which is usually a man. The problem is that he hates men. Someone abused him along the line. I saw his potential. I knew it was a gamble, but I took the shot."

"The other two horses you brought back were sold. You took a chance, son, instead of going with a sure thing. It may not have been a good choice considering what was riding on the outcome, no pun intended. Piece of fatherly advice? Only take a significant risk when you can afford to lose. Consider this a life lesson."

This was the moment when Justin was faced with a difficult decision. Did he tell his father the truth about what went on behind the scenes of the horse industry, the truth about why he chose to buy this horse? Would telling his father these facts persuade him even more that the show jumping world was not a good profession? Or would he gain his father's admiration and respect, selling the point that he could make a difference and represent the good people?

Justin recalled his father specifically saying, "only take a risk when you can't afford to lose." What if you had everything to lose? Truth be told, he had already lost. Could he, for the second time, argue his case with facts in a way that would convince his father to extend their agreement for one more month? He made his decision.

*****

"I'm going to be straight with you, Dad," Justin said, standing up and stepping closer to his father. He wanted to appear strong and confident, and it made him feel taller when he stood next to his dad. He never saw a lawyer presenting his closing argument from his seat. To win a case, you had to face your jury, look them in the eye, and convince them you had integrity. He decided to go for it.

"When I was at the farm in Holland and very disappointed with the prospects they had, the owner came up to me and pulled me aside. She explained that she did have one more horse, but he was an unusual candidate. The six-year-old Hanoverian gelding, Apollo's Destiny, was purchased for a lot of money by the son of a wealthy Englishman, Reginald Bellingham. His son, Henry, was not a good rider. The horse was bought to carry Henry to success despite Henry's lack of talent. The truth of the matter was that Henry was overweight and pulled on the horse's mouth relentlessly. He about ripped Apollo's face off every time he lost his balance after a big jump. When Apollo showed signs of rebelling and started taking down fences, the trainer resorted to ground tactics to force the horse to jump to his potential."

"I knew this kind of thing happened," Justin continued, "but hearing it had happened to this talented horse struck a nerve. The woman went on to tell me that the trainer started by holding a bamboo pole above a practice jump.

When Apollo dragged his feet over the rail, the trainer would bash him on the coronet band with the pole, causing the horse intense pain so he would pull his feet up over the jump. He sabotaged him randomly along the course, which caused him to tuck up higher over every fence."

"Unfortunately," Justin continued, "the story gets worse. Apollo has a strong spirit. Soon, he learned to live with the pain, jumped the courses he was made to, but still dragged his feet over the rails, knocking them down. The trainer bumped it up a notch. He pounded nails into the rails facing up. If Apollo dragged his back legs over the rails, he was pierced by the nails. This was the straw that broke the camel's back. After a few times of being sliced open by the nails, Apollo rebelled. He bucked the fat bastard off. Worst of all, he learned to hate humans, specifically men."

"The last thing she confided in me was that Bellingham had drugged the horse to try and sell him. When they put him on the market, they thought if they could drug him into submission, he might be compliant enough for someone to put an offer on him. Even drugged, he resisted every male that tried him out. He was too strong for any of the women to handle. The Bellinghams gave up and sent him to the sale barn in Holland to rot or until he mellowed enough to be ridden again. They wanted him out of England."

"And this is the horse you brought home?" his father asked incredulously.

"I asked if I could meet Apollo. She said she would get someone to tack him up. I told her, 'No, I want to meet him alone, in his stall.'"

"When I approached the stall, he immediately turned and faced the back corner, his ears back, his tail tucked. I grabbed a handful of grain and stood there talking softly to him for about five minutes before he turned and approached me hesitantly."

"I looked into his eyes, Dad. What I saw chilled me to the bone. This gorgeous animal was in pain, not just physical. You could see he hated being in that stall; he hated his life. Even at rest, you could see the whites of his eyes as he stared at me, waiting to be stuck with a needle, abused in some way.

At this point, it was not theatrics. Justin teared up. "I felt a kinship with this animal, Dad. Not being a horse person, you wouldn't understand. This horse was being forced into a life he didn't deserve. He was being mistreated and abused. He was an amazingly talented horse that fell into the wrong hands and was suffering because of that fate. Without even trying to ride him, I knew I had to rescue him. It was rash; it was stupid. I followed my heart."

At this point, Justin's father got up out of his chair. He did something he hadn't done since Justin's grandfather passed away. He hugged his son.

*****

Michael was still incredulous that Justin brought Apollo home. He asked Justin how he had managed to get him back into the show ring. Justin described that as soon as Apollo arrived at the farm, he put the horse out into the pasture and simply showed him love every day for several months. He brushed him, fed him treats, and gave him the best pasture with the greenest grass.

He told the story that one day, he went out, and Apollo was lying in the sunshine. He was sprawled out on the soft grass. His eyes were closed; he was cat napping, soaking up the warm rays. Justin quietly walked up to him, knelt, and stroked his neck. Apollo was startled and began to get up. Justin shushed him, rubbed his face, and told him it was okay, to relax. Apollo looked at Justin for a minute, then took a deep breath and laid his head back down on the ground with a deep sigh.

Justin sat down on the grass next to the horse's massive head and stroked his face. He rubbed his velvet ears, massaged his temples, and spoke soft and reassuring words. When the horse remained at ease, totally comfortable in Justin's presence, Justin knew he had won Apollo's trust. It was time to ride him.

Justin and his father sat back down, both feeling slightly awkward at the unusual display of affection. "Let's have a glass of whiskey, son. I know it's not even noon, but I want to hear more about Apollo." Michael spun his chair around to the small fridge next to his humidor. He pulled two ice cubes out of the freezer and popped them into Waterford Crystal glasses. The familiar clink in the glass precluded the smooth amber liquid Michael poured into the glasses from the decanter filled with Jameson on his desk.

Handing a glass to Justin, Michael raised his glass to a toast. "A deal is a deal, Justin, no matter how heartwarming the story. However, being a lawyer, I understand the need for extensions in extenuating circumstances. I'm impressed with you, Justin. You've handled yourself well. It sounds as if nothing came easy for you. You didn't come to me and make excuses. You didn't give up. You made a difficult decision knowing the chips were going to fall where they may. Convince me why I should give you one more month to sell this horse."

*****

Justin not only convinced his dad to give him the extension but also asked him to come to watch the show. This was a stretch because Michael's firm occupied a huge portion of his life. Michael didn't promise Justin he would be there; he simply said he would try.

The last opportunity for Justin to sell Apollo was the LA June Classic at the Los Angeles Equestrian Center. The prospective client, Clive Jovanovich, would be competing in the Jumper Level 4 division. Apollo qualified for level 4 classes, ridden by Justin. Clive had qualified using his own horses, which were aging. He was looking for new blood. With both horse and rider eligible to compete, the deal was that Clive would ride Apollo at the event. If he placed in the top five of the class, he agreed to purchase Apollo for $550,000.

Justin was asking twice as much for Apollo as the other two horses he brought back from Europe. One reason was that this horse had the talent to be great. The second reason was he wanted only the best to take ownership of Apollo. Unfortunately, those with money and success were not necessarily the "best" when it came to the treatment of their horses.

Clive was 35 years old, 5'9", and weighed around 150 lbs. He was desperately trying for a spot on the United States Equestrian Team (USET) to represent the United States in the next Olympics. To do that, he had to get some major wins under his belt. He had to climb to the top of the ranking list to be a candidate.

He came from money. Clive's family had a farm in New Jersey near the USET training facility in Gladstone, the heart of horse country. Clive had been riding and competing since he was five years old. All he ever wanted was to ride in the Olympics. He relocated to California to attend the shows on the West Coast and to hunt for jumper prospects. He wanted a made horse, ready to compete.

While Justin was young and unknown as a trainer, when Clive saw Justin jumping Apollo at a show that spring in Thermal, he knew he had to have that horse. Apollo's speed, agility, and ability to soar over the widest oxers with ease were incredible. Justin cut corners and made it over fences that blew the other competition away. Clive thought Justin was female the first time he saw him go over a course. When he approached him after his amazing round, he was surprised to see he was male. He had the soft hands and gracefulness of a woman. Men were usually ganglier and harsher in their movements.

Clive approached Justin after his class and inquired if Apollo was for sale. Justin's answer was, "to the right person." At the end of the show day, Justin and Clive met at the barn.

Clive wanted to meet Apollo in person. He loved his conformation, his size, basically everything about him. Justin had Apollo's registration papers in hand along with his assessment from the Hanoverian Association with top ratings. Clive ran his hand over Apollo's hindquarters and found the H brand that marked him as approved. Clive wanted to school him over some fences, but Justin was scheduled to leave that afternoon to make another show all the way up at Woodside. There wasn't time.

The two traded contact information. As both had busy schedules, they would stay in touch and plan for Clive to try out Apollo. Justin desperately wanted to fit the trial in before June so the sale could be completed by the deadline he had made with his father. As luck would have it, there was not enough time in either of their schedules to make that happen. Justin had to fulfill his commitments to his seven students who were booked at shows. Entries had to be sent to the shows well in advance, and the fees and paperwork for every show were extensive. The show in LA was the first possible opportunity.

As they shook hands, Justin had a bad feeling in the pit of his stomach. He had reformed Apollo, gained his trust, and had him jumping like a pro again. What would happen when someone else took him out on the course? And the fact that he had fallen in love with this animal? That was collateral damage. He had to sell the horse if he wanted to continue being a trainer. He didn't even want to think about having to go to law school. His heart was tearing into pieces at the thought of having to give up this horse. He had never built a stronger bond with any horse than he had with Apollo.

*****

The day of the show arrived. Justin was a nervous wreck. There was no sign of his father; he was still a 'maybe' for showing up. Justin had five horses in the shed row. His tack room was decked out with dark blue and white curtains, his stable's colors, along with a banner bearing the name "Barone Estate Equestrians." Fancy monogrammed tack trunks lined the entryway. A carpet was laid out by the grooms with chairs, tables, and a canopy. Everything was perfectly arranged. Appearances were everything in the world of show jumping.

Most of the horses were settled, quietly munching their sweet-smelling hay. Apollo was a wreck. He paced nervously in his stall. Justin could only attribute his change in attitude to the fact that Justin was a nervous wreck. Horses picked up on their owner's state of mind. He felt guilty as hell that he was influencing Apollo. After all, buying and selling horses was what people did. It was a fact of life. As long as he sent Apollo to someone kind, like a professional trying out for the Olympics, he could justify giving him up. He didn't want to sell him; he had to or he would be going to law school.

Justin glanced at his watch. In ten minutes, the rate race would begin. He had three riders in an upcoming class. As soon as that class was finished, he would come back to the barn and meet Clive at Apollo's stall. They would tack him up, and Justin would take Apollo over a few practice jumps. Clive would get on and do a bit of schooling under Justin's supervision. If all went well, the new duo would compete that afternoon in the most important class of Justin's life. He prayed Apollo would calm down by then.

Walking over to Apollo's stall, Justin pulled a horse treat out of his pocket. He always carried them. "Look, buddy; calm down. You were born for this. I see great things in the future. I would feel honored to help you get there," he said, trying to feed the horse the treat. Apollo grabbed the treat nervously from Justin's hand. He banged the door with his hoof, a habit Justin had not seen since he first brought him home. Justin shook his head in frustration and turned to make sure his students were tacking up their horses for their group warm-up.

As Justin walked away with his students leading their horses, Michael Barone and his wife were walking down the aisle between the stables looking for the dark blue and white banner of Barone Estate Equestrians. Michael was eager to surprise Justin and meet the superstar, Apollo.

"I see it up ahead," Sylvia said, pointing to the tack room. Potted plants with flowers were placed underneath the banner. This was Michael's first time at a big show. He was surprised at the professionalism, the obvious rivalry for each stable to have the best presentation.

Suddenly, Sylvia paused. She grabbed Michael's arm. They both stopped. Michael looked at his wife. "What's the matter?"

"Two people just walked into Apollo's stall. Three horses are gone," she said, noticing the unlatched doors, "which means Justin is out schooling with his students. No one is allowed in another competitor's stall. People do bad things to other riders' horses to take them out of the competition. I know everyone who works for Justin and his students. I don't recognize those people."

"I want you to trust me, Sylvia," Michael said, thinking quickly. "Walk past the stalls and wait at the end of the barn around the corner. Give me five minutes, and I will meet you there. If there is anything nefarious going on, I will uncover it. This may be my first horse show, but it's not my first rodeo, if you know what I mean," he said with a wink.

"But...,"

"No buts, no argument. I'm playing this safe. I promise. We don't have time to argue. Please, go," he said, giving her a gentle nudge forward.

Sylvia looked over her shoulder with a worried expression as she walked forward without Michael, trying to look unobtrusive and uninterested in the Barone stalls. When she was a few feet ahead, Michael followed. As Sylvia passed the stall with Apollo, Michael ducked into the tack room adjacent to the stall. A tack trunk placed against the bordering wall was just what he needed. He pulled out his cell phone and hit the video record button. Quietly stepping on the trunk, he was able to aim the edge of the phone with the camera lens over the divider. With his ear to the boards, he could clearly hear the conversation taking place in the stall next to him.

"We need to do this quick, Clive," a woman hissed. "If this backfires, my ass is on the line. My career is over, as well as yours. I'm bringing you down with me."

"No one is here. Everyone will be away for at least an hour. Let me get the halter on this horse, and then you be ready with the shot." There were some scuffling sounds as Clive cornered the nervous horse and slipped on his halter.

"Remember, give him just enough that he's calm and compliant. I still need him to be somewhat sharp. I don't want anything to go wrong with this round. This is my one shot to get this horse. I need a win, and I need to own Apollo. Sometimes, you need a little extra advantage. That's all we're doing here."

"I'm a licensed vet, Clive. I know exactly what we're doing and how terribly illegal it is. You did pay off the show steward to make sure Apollo doesn't get drug-tested, right? If an unknown horse like Apollo does very well in a big class, he may get tested. I know it's supposed to be random. But if one of your competitors is skeptical about your placing, they can easily put money into someone's pocket to drug test your horse, as easily as you just paid to not have him tested."

More scuffling sounds occurred as Apollo reacted to the sight of an unknown person with a needle and syringe. "Get this beast under control, Clive. I'm not going to risk getting hurt over this," the vet whined.

Suddenly, there was a loud thump and a banging as something large collided with the wooden boards of the stall. The whole wall shook. Michael couldn't resist any longer. He pulled himself up tall and peered over the top of the wall. Clive had Apollo pinned against the back wall. He had grasped the horse's sensitive ear and was twisting it. The horse had his head lowered in submission, obviously in so much pain that he forgot all about the shot. "Hurry, do it now," Clive ordered.

"DON'T YOU DARE!" Michael yelled over the wall. He still had his camera recording everything, but now he could see for himself what was going on. Everyone froze. "Let that horse go. I'm Justin's father, also an attorney. We are going to have a few words. Come meet me in this tack room."

Not being able to contain her curiosity, Sylvia peeked around the corner at the end of the barn. When she saw the two people come out of Apollo's stall and into the tack room where Michael had to be hiding, she bolted down the aisle. Breathless, she popped inside. Three people faced each other. Everyone had questions.

"Look, before you get yourself in a tizzy, I'm looking to buy Apollo from Justin. I'm riding him later today. I'm an Olympic candidate, and I'm simply giving him something to help calm his nerves; that's it. I'm not one of those people that go in and drug my competitor's horses," Clive explained, his face bright red, sweat dripping from his face.

"And I'm just doing what he paid me to do," the vet said, pointing a finger at Clive, defending her part in the scheme.

"I call bullshit," Sylvia interjected. "Michael, what these people just did is highly illegal. They will both be fined and possibly banned from ever being on show grounds again if this comes to light."

"Wait, wait," Clive interjected. "Let's not be too rash. How about a little deal here? What if I sign over a check right now for the full price of the horse? You said you are a lawyer. If we skip the vet checks and all the formalities, I will sign a paper right here for the sale of the horse and hand you a check. You can let this slide. We enter our class, and I purchase the horse regardless of how we do today. Half a million is a lot of money for this horse. I'm willing to pay that to make all of this go away," Clive said, walking up to Michael and looking him straight in the eye.

Michael folded his arms, met Clive's gaze, but refrained from answering. Clive squirmed a bit. He looked at Sylvia, trying to reason with her. "Surely this works out for everyone, right? No more stress, just a win-win." The vet stayed silent, her back against the wall, a terrified expression on her face, her black medical bag clutched tightly to her chest.

"This is what we're going to do," Michael said, quickly forming a plan. "You're going to give me your names and phone numbers. I'm going to put them in my contacts. Sylvia and I are going to wait here for Justin's return. We're going to have a chat with Justin. He's going to decide whether or not he sells this horse to you. I want you to know that he has a lot riding on this sale. If he sells the horse to you, he continues his career as a horse trainer. If he decides not to sell the horse to an unethical asshole such as yourself, he not only forfeits the half a million, but he has to end his riding career and go to law school."

Not sure how to respond to that, Michael and the vet exchanged uneasy glances. Michael pulled out his phone and clicked the "new contact" button.

"Do you have to mention the sedative?" Clive asked hopefully. "You could just surprise him with a check. Tell him his horse is so great I decided to buy him on the spot!"

"Not a chance, pal," Michael answered after getting both their phone numbers entered into his phone. "Now get the hell out of here before I change my mind."

*****

"Our son has done pretty well for himself, hasn't he?" Michael asked Sylvia. "A rider trying to qualify for the Olympics wants to buy his horse, a horse that he took a huge risk buying. It's obvious he has good instincts. He is talented; he loves what he does. Can I ask you a question?" he said, turning to his wife and putting his arms around her neck. "What makes someone with so little ethics a candidate for the Olympics?"

"Anyone who gets enough points on a national ranking list can be a candidate for the Olympic team," Sylvia explained. "It takes good horses, talent, and a lot of travel and dedication to make it to the top of that list. You have to travel internationally and transport horses overseas. It's quite complicated. You also have to have some pretty heavy financial backing."

"Tell me, Sylvia. In your honest opinion, does our son have the kind of talent it takes to pursue a goal like that? The average rider on the United States Equestrian Team is 38, you know," proud of himself for remembering that fact from his conversation with Justin when he was seventeen.

Sylvia threw her head back and laughed. "Wow, what a transformation. You spend five minutes at your first horse show, and you want to know if your son has what it takes to get to the Olympics. The reason I never encouraged or pushed Justin was that I thought you would never be on board with him pursuing a riding career. I knew you wanted him to be a lawyer and take over your firm. I simply encouraged him to do what he loved until the day came when he had to leave it behind and grow up. I never let him know how good he was, how much talent he had. I thought it would make leaving so much more difficult."

Michael looked into his wife's eyes. They were watering. Her emotion made it clear that she loved both her husband and son. It had to rip her apart inside to have to separate herself from both situations. She didn't take sides; she stayed neutral, a difficult task for a mother.

As they looked into one another's eyes, Justin popped through the entrance of the tack room. He wore a huge smile. He ran up and put his arms around his mother and father. "Wow, both of you at one of my shows! How special is this?"

"Hi, son," Michael said, returning his son's embrace.

"I just checked in on Apollo. He seems a lot calmer than he was this morning. He was uncharacteristically agitated. I guess he felt how nervous I was about this sale. I changed my attitude while we were out schooling, which went very well, by the way. My kids are ready and the horses look great. I also came to peace with the fact that selling horses is what I do. I love Apollo, but if he makes it to the Olympics, that will put me on the map as a trainer."

Glancing first at Sylvia and then at his son, Michael asked Justin, "What if you didn't sell Apollo? Do you think the two of you could work your way up the ranking list and make it to the Olympics? He has the potential. What about you, Justin? Do you have the potential?"

Justin was speechless. He looked at his mom. She was smiling. He was pretty sure this wasn't a joke. His dad wore his characteristic neutral expression, though his eyes were sparkling. "I've never even considered the possibility. I would have to buy and sell a lot of horses to make the kind of money you need to do that. The time I'd need to import horses, train them, and sell them, I don't have time for both. And the chances of finding the talent Apollo has for such a reasonable price—well, he's one in a million."

"What if," Michael began, "you rode in that class this afternoon, you know, the one that guy Clive was supposed to ride in? You come in the top five, and I hand you a check for $550,000, purchasing Apollo for Barone Estate Equestrians? Perhaps Barone Estate could sponsor your campaign?"

Justin had no idea what to say. His head was spinning, and his world had entirely turned upside down. "But what about Clive? We had a deal."

"Clive stopped by and we had a chat. It seems he may have changed his mind about Apollo, not because he doesn't think he's a great horse, but because Apollo doesn't seem to like him very much. You know how he feels about big guys," Michael said to Justin with a knowing nod.

In the span of a few minutes, Justin's world turned 180 degrees. Instead of watching his horse compete, he would be jumping the round of his life. What was it with his dad making life-changing, mind-blowing bargains? Justin wasn't sure why this was all happening or if it was happening at all. Maybe this was all a dream? All he knew was he had to make a rider change for the upcoming class. Justin Barone would be competing on Apollo, and he couldn't remember a time in his life when he felt happier or more excited.

Justin was about to turn and walk toward the show office when he saw two men with official-looking badges approaching. Justin had a feeling this was all too good to be true. When show stewards hunted you down, it was never good news. Some rule had been broken, or someone was turning him in for a violation. Justin had no clue what he had done wrong. So far, he had done everything by the book.

Eduardo Fernandez

San Antonio de Areco, Argentina
Lawyer, Gaucho

As Eduardo sat behind the desk at his law office, he couldn't keep his thoughts on the task at hand. He looked at the stack of papers in front of him and sighed. He had dozens of potential cases to look through, but his mind kept drifting. Eduardo was the first person in the Fernandez family to go to college and graduate with a law degree. His father and his family were extremely proud of his accomplishments. All his life, he had dreamt of being a lawyer, of having a prosperous and distinguished career. Now that he was a lawyer, all he could think of was a way out.

Eduardo's father was a gaucho. Gauchos were respected and honored within the culture of Argentina; however, it was not a distinguished career, nor was it necessarily lucrative. It was more of a time-honored occupation that emerged from the very roots that built the nation.

The first compatriots of the American cowboy, gauchos emerged during the Argentine War of Independence in 1818.

Groups of rural horsemen banded together. Using their horses and knowledge of the terrain, they acted as scouts, fought in ambushes, and gathered intel in support of the patriots. These men were instrumental in helping to end the war. Thus began the legacy of the breed of men known as gauchos.

When the war was over, many of the gauchos migrated to the fertile lowlands and became cattle farmers. They developed a unique brand of riding attire that included bombachas, the traditional baggy riding trousers, ponchos for staying warm during the winter, and large-brimmed hats for protection from the sun. Tucked under their belts were a *facón* (long knife) and a leather whip and lasso. These items were carried at all times. The main diet of a gaucho was beef, maté, and wine. They were rugged men, born to ride, herd cattle, and protect their country. When Eduardo was not at his law desk, he donned his gaucho attire and assisted his father in his cattle business.

Eduardo's life was diverse in many ways. While he was immersed in his law practice, his weekends were spent on the plains of Argentina herding cattle. His one hobby that floated his boat was his avid interest in Argentine history. There was a thin line between his decision to become a lawyer and a history professor.

Lawyers made a lot more money. Studying history was something he could pursue for fun. He chose to become a lawyer. It provided a financially comfortable lifestyle. His greatest passion was delving into the history of his country, uncovering hidden gems, and linking bits and pieces of abstract information to help paint a colorful mural of his nation's past.

Eduardo's unofficial knowledge of history earned him respect within his community. The extensive library he had collected over the years included rare copies of manuscripts, letters dating back to the War of Independence, diaries of Spanish explorers, and firsthand accounts of Argentina's past. He was frequently asked to be a guest speaker and give presentations on his knowledge of certain subjects. His main area of expertise was his knowledge of the Argentine breed of horse originating from the Conquistadors, known as the Criollo.

*****

The first dwelling on the Fernandez Ranch, located in San Antonio de Areco, was a small wooden building that stood for over 100 years. It was once the home of Eduardo's great-grandfather, a one-room building with a fireplace and wooden floors. It was one of the first established gaucho towns in the Pampas region of Argentina. Isaias Fernandez, Eduardo's grandfather, inherited the ranch and reaped the benefits of a growing and lucrative cattle industry.

When Isaias reached adulthood, he moved out of the small house and built a large family home in town. Eduardo's father, Ihan, now owned the home and ran the ranch, which he hoped would be run by his youngest son, Eduardo. While Eduardo supported his father when he could, he suspected the legacy of the Fernandez gaucho family was about to end.

Rising over the horizon, the warm glow of the sun filtered through the grimy windows of the ranch house. Ihan handed his son the traditional varnished gourd filled with hot water and a mash of floating maté leaves. A metal bombilla straw stuck out of the top with a built-in filter.

Maté, Argentina's national beverage, is made from the leaves of a species of holly. Its healing properties are touted as the reason for rural Argentinians' low cancer and illness rate. The tradition of passing around the gourd and sharing maté was the secret to health and longevity, as well as a time-honored social custom among gauchos.

Eduardo shook his head at his father and handed him back the gourd. "You keep trying, don't you, father? I can't stand that stuff. Ever since my all-nighters studying for law school, I discovered the secret of coffee. It tastes better, has more caffeine, and, well, doesn't taste like a combination of dirt and alfalfa."

"Eduardo, my son. You don't drink maté, you won't take over my ranch, and you have turned your back on your family traditions."

"Escúchame una cosita," Eduardo told his father, using the common Argentine phrase to get someone to 'listen.' "You have another son, Maico. I don't see him out here on weekends helping you with the cattle. At least I'm here when I'm able."

"¡Viste!" (Don't you see?), Ihan replied. "You have potential. Your brother has gone off and runs a hotel of all things. He never learned to ride a horse well; he can't rope a cow. He does not carry the spirit of the gaucho. You, Eduardo, are my only hope. What am I supposed to do with this land, this business that was built by your great-grandfather?"

"All good things must come to an end, father. Sell the land, buy a big house by the ocean. You and your mother can retire there and enjoy your golden years. There are much worse fates, father."

Eduardo walked over to the dust-covered window and cleared a small patch with his sleeve. He looked out over the grassy fields at the herd of 50 cattle grazing contentedly. Today would be a day to round up the calves and brand them. It would be a long day, as each calf had to be roped, brought down, and tied, then branded with the Fernandez family symbol.

Five more men would be joining them, friends of his father and cattlemen as well. They had learned long ago to band together and help one another. This was especially important now, when their legacy and livelihoods were in jeopardy. The small cattle farmers of the western Argentine Pampas were being threatened to the point of extinction.

Walking over with a steaming cup of coffee, Ihan handed it to Eduardo and gazed out the window beside his son. Eduardo knew his father kept a tin of coffee just for him. He always had to ask for it, though. His father always tried handing him the gourd and kept the hope alive that one day his son would resume the tradition of drinking maté.

A puff of dust rose from the dirt road that led to the ranch house. "Mira," Ihan said, pointing to the figures riding up the road. Five men rode abreast. Their well-bred Criollo horses cantered almost in perfect stride. "Mis amigos, what would I do without them?" he said, shaking his head and grabbing his hat from the peg alongside the door.

"I'll be out in a minute, as soon as I finish my coffee," Eduardo told his father as he disappeared out the door without looking back. The door closed. Eduardo felt the pains of regret; yet, he was aware of the reality of the changing dynamics. His father's farm was not long for this world.

There was nothing Eduardo could do to stop it—not even being a lawyer. Swirling around Eduardo's head was a maelstrom of thoughts. His father's future, his future, and the new law of the land were colliding. He wasn't sure where exactly he would fit in when the dust settled.

He looked out the window as the riders dismounted and tied their horses to the hitching rail. The men gathered in a group. Eduardo's father pointed back toward the house. The men nodded. A discussion broke out, most likely about the day's plans of building a fire, a strategy being developed for who would catch the calves, and who would brand.

One of the men turned toward his horse and retrieved a saddlebag. He threw the large bag over his shoulder. Eduardo could take an educated guess at its contents. At the end of the day, the fire used for branding would serve another purpose. There would be a celebration for a job well done.

No good day on any ranch would end without a traditional asada. A grate would be settled over the hot coals. Hunks of meat would be cooked: asada de tira, the classic strip roast, and ribs. The heavily salted meat would be charred and eaten on rolls baked fresh that morning. A jug of red wine would be consumed as the gauchos recapped the day.

Eduardo smiled at the thought of sitting around the fire with his father's friends. He could already smell the sweet aroma of the roasting beef. His stomach growled in anticipation. It was a far cry from the stuffy lawyers he dined with in suits and ties at bougie restaurants in the city of Buenos Aires, 70 miles southeast where he lived and worked.

The Father and Son

"One more example of men creating the extinction of their roots," the Son remarked.

The Father nodded solemnly. "Hence, another argument for my decision. It seems that the greed of men is greater than their respect for why this Earth was created. On this Earth is every resource man needs to thrive. He can eat from the fruit of the land, live in harmony with nature, and raise his children to do the same. Gone is the appreciation for the basics. The desire of the few, the powerful, and the leaders of corporations is overtaking the Earth. They have enough already, but they always want more."

"How will judging one small sampling of the human race be enough to determine if man is worthy to remain on this Earth?" the Son asked.

"While it is disheartening to see the decline of man's respect for nature," the Father replied, "he has proven himself in the past; he has provoked change during times when a change was desperately needed. Single, strong individuals like Mother Teresa, Rosa Parks, Martin Luther King, Mahatma Gandhi, Nelson Mandela, and Alexander Hamilton are examples of how humans can make a positive difference in the world."

"With so many people working against the good," the Son questioned, "how will this small sample of people indicate if man is truly worthy to be saved? You are only drawing from a pool of motivated and passionate people."

"I gave you examples of how one person can make a difference," the Father answered. "Even if the mass majority are not contributing to the good, one single strong individual is stronger than thousands of weak, uncaring humans. Think about David and Goliath turning the tides of an empire. If more than half of the humans whom I have chosen show passion and are ready to fight for this world, it might mean there are enough who care to save this world."

*****

As Eduardo finished his coffee, rinsed his mug, and placed it back in the cabinet, he heard the crunch of tires pulling up to the house. His body stiffened. There was no good reason a car would be driving up to the ranch. His instincts were usually pretty good when trouble was threatening, and right now, they were bristling like a porcupine.

When Eduardo stepped out the front door, six gauchos surrounded two men in business suits. The men most likely had firearms beneath their coats. He knew for sure that there were six *facóns* hidden beneath the ponchos of his father and his friends. Eduardo immediately rushed into their midst and took the role of mediator.

"Why, may I ask, are you trespassing on Fernandez property?"

The two men in suits were tall, very muscular, and prepared for confrontation. They spoke fluent Spanish, but their skin tone and their strange accents hinted they were from North America. One of the men stepped forward and extended a hand toward Eduardo. Eduardo crossed his arms and stared at the man, waiting for an answer to his question.

"We represent the U.S. Department of Agriculture. We have come to make an offer on this property. We are interested in using this land for farming and are prepared to make an offer far above what you would get from anyone who lives around here, including your government," he stated in fluent Spanish.

The group of men immediately responded by unsheathing their knives and slowly moving as a pack toward the two men. Eduardo turned to face them and held up his hand, silently asking them to stop in their tracks. Like angry wolves, they remained at bay; they did not pass Eduardo, but the tension was thick enough to slice with their *facóns*.

"¡Salir!" Eduardo instructed the men. "I will handle this," he said, gesturing to the two intruders to follow him into the house. He needed to separate the two groups as quickly as possible. He could feel the icy stares of the gauchos following them to the door. When the door to the house closed behind them, Eduardo turned and looked out the window. The group slowly made their way back to their horses and mounted, heading off brusquely to take care of the cattle. Eduardo breathed a sigh of relief. He nodded toward the rustic table surrounded by chairs. "Take a seat."

Over the past few years, Eduardo had been following the facts. His law firm had even represented cattle farmers who were losing their land to the Argentinian government. It was a battle they never won. There were rumors that the U.S. was moving in to capitalize on the crops the fertile Pampas lands were producing. Proof had just arrived.

Eduardo watched as little by little, the U.S. moved in and the government of Argentina profited. They made it harder and harder for the small farmer to survive by raising taxes and instituting price controls on beef. The small farmer now found it difficult to make a profit. The way of the gaucho was being extinguished, replaced by crops, and the land was polluted by pesticides. The prized beef was now being raised artificially and tainted with toxic substances. This was another reason Eduardo had no desire to take over his father's ranch. He knew in his heart it was a losing battle.

He faced the two men across the table. Eduardo knew they were here to make a deal with his father. They would be at the farms of the other men to make offers in a matter of days. Eduardo took a moment to consider his words very carefully. He was happy at this moment that he had chosen to be a lawyer. He was able to protect his father and friends, temporarily. There would be no death, no bloodshed today. His goal was to be a buffer and protect the parties involved while fate played its course. It was all he could do.

"My name is Eduardo Fernandez. This is my family farm. I am also a lawyer. I represent the Fernandez Ranch as well as the ranches that surround this property. There are five ranch owners here today whom I also represent. I'm quite sure if you are here today you will be knocking on their doors as well. I am here to tell you not to do it. They will try and kill you."

After an hour of animated conversation, an agreement was made that all offers by the U.S. Department of Agriculture would be presented to the six ranches through Eduardo. Eduardo suggested a meeting at his office in Buenos Aires. He would bring the local land maps and review each of the offers. He would make a presentation to the ranchers and provide answers to the offers.

The two agents agreed. Even though it made his skin crawl, Eduardo shook hands with the men before showing them to the door.

With a heavy heart, Eduardo watched the car drive down the road, spewing swirling clouds of dust in its wake. The mounted men had all paused to watch the car leave. Times were changing. This might be the last time Eduardo rode with his father, herding cattle. The gauchos would settle down after a hard day's work over the open fire and feast on the beef raised on the Pampas plains. The men would drink red wine and tell the same stories he had heard as a child, intermixed with tales of the day. Eduardo would savor every second, as he knew, in his heart, that he was witnessing the end of an era.

In less than a month from the date of the U.S. Agriculture agents' arrival, Eduardo's father had signed the agreement for the sale of his property. Two of his five amigos had signed as well. The other three would only be able to hold out for so long. Ihan was devastated.

The reality of the situation finally hit Eduardo. He knew his life would never be the same. While he didn't choose the life of a cattle-farming gaucho, he never expected that his family would be unwillingly severed from the roots of its heritage and the land established by his forefathers sold to a foreign country.

The negotiations and subsequent results took their toll on Eduardo. He developed a new feeling toward law, one of hatred. While the law provided constructs to protect, it also provided avenues for those greedy enough to take from others legally. As his father signed the agreement, tears ran down his cheeks. Even though Eduardo had brokered the best possible deal for his father and made him more money than he would have ever seen in his life as a cattle rancher, it made him sick to his stomach.

"Father, the cattle are also taken care of as I have arranged to have them taken to the farms of your friends. I hope you don't mind that I sold them for less than market value. I know your friends have always been there for you, and it's the least we can do to support them as they make a stand. Who knows, maybe their farms will prevail," Eduardo added, without any conviction.

"What about my horses?" his father asked, turning to look at Eduardo, the tears still flowing freely. "Mis caballos siguen siendo importantes," Ihan confessed, relaying that the horses were a meaningful and important part of his life, even without the farm.

"I have a plan," Eduardo told his father, walking closer to him, putting his hands on his shoulders, and looking him in the eyes. "Being a lawyer is not what I thought it would be. It is a great living, but it doesn't make me happy. Do you know what does make me happy, father?"

"No, I thought running the ranch might, but you are the one who sold it."

"I sold it because I know what is coming. We can't stop the tide of progress. It is taking our cattle-farming lands. I cannot prevent that. But you do know that my heart lies with our country's roots. You know my passion for our country's history. The path I have followed thus far in my life is leading me in an inevitable direction. I have done what I was destined to do, but now my life must change directions."

Eduardo's father looked at him with a raised brow. "What do you mean, change direction? You don't want the farm, and you have become a very good lawyer. What more can you want?"

"Come, father. Let's get out of this office and let me take you out to lunch. I will tell you my plans."

Despite the somber mood, Eduardo's father was still able to joke. "Are you kidding me? You have seen the size of the check I'm getting. I will take you out to lunch, my son."

*****

The Criollo breed extends from southern Brazil to Uruguay, Argentina, and Chile. This unique breed shares bloodlines with Peruvian Pasos and the Venezuelan Llanero, horses that inhabit the islands of Ecuador. Due to the indiscriminate breeding of the native Criollos with Andalusians and Percherons brought over by other cultures, the pure Criollo breed was close to extinction by the early twentieth century.

In some areas of Buenos Aires, it was all but impossible to find a pure Criollo. During Eduardo's study of the history of the Criollo breed and its importance to the gaucho culture, he developed a deep love and respect for the breed and its history. He had no idea that one day, this love would change the course of his life.

Criollos had been a constant part of Eduardo's life. They were workhorses that were calm, well-mannered, and adept at running beside a herd of cows. They were agile enough to cut a single cow from the herd, yet would stand still and wait patiently as a gaucho dismounted to tie up a calf. Like most young Argentine men, Eduardo spent his share of time on the polo field. Polo is to Argentines as football and baseball are to Americans.

For generations, gauchos have played polo for fun after work on any flat field on their farm. Anyone who wanted to take it a step further joined a polo team and played competitively on the weekends. While Criollos don't have the speed for highly competitive polo, it was learned centuries ago that breeding a Thoroughbred with a Criollo created a pony that was fast, rugged, smart, and able to make quick starts, stops, and turns. As polo evolved into the Sport of Kings, most of the best polo players and ponies in the world came from Argentina.

As Eduardo's love of studying history unraveled the birth of his nation, it also revealed the evolution of the native breed of the Argentine Criollo. Eduardo found it fascinating. In the beginning, the first set of Spanish conquistadors came across feral herds of horses in the Pampas region known as baguales.

The forefathers of the baguales were Spanish horses that had been abandoned or had escaped from early immigrants. Many travelers reported seeing herds of wild baguales numbering in the thousands roaming the Pampas. Native tribesmen soon discovered the benefits of taming these horses and quickly became expert horsemen who would later be known as gauchos.

In time, the Spanish settled in the Pampas. They depended on horses to move across the vast territory. As settlers moved into the land occupied by natives, they brought
change to the Pampas. Fences, livestock, and the introduction of new breeds began influencing the feral herds.

When the British invaded the region in the early 1800s,
they brought with them the Thoroughbred. Next, the French
imported their Percherons. The baguales were crossed with
Thoroughbreds to make them lighter, more elegant, and
faster. Baguales were crossed with Percherons to create
larger and heavier animals more suitable for pulling carts and
plowing fields. As a result, by the end of the 19th century, the
baguales, now identified as the Criollo breed, were threatened with extinction.

Fortunately, in 1917, the Sociedad Rural de Argentina was
formed specifically to preserve the "Creole" breed of Argentine horse. After much research, a herd of 200 purebred
Criollo mares was located within a native Indian tribe in
a southern province. This herd became the foundation for
the restoration of the breed, which was first known as the
Argentinean but was later changed to the Argentine Criollo.

With continued research about Argentina and the Criollo, Eduardo discovered a unique talent associated with the
breed. He noted that the Criollo was known worldwide for its
remarkable stamina and endurance. This reputation began
in 1925 when A.F. Tschiffely rode two Criollo geldings 10,000
miles from Buenos Aires to Washington, D.C., to honor the
breed. Both horses not only made the trip but stayed healthy
and sound; they both lived to the ripe old age of 30.

Recognizing this accomplishment, the Criollo Breeders Association decided to implement an endurance ride to test the stamina of a purebred Criollo. The 465-mile ride (750 km) must be performed in 14 days. The horses must carry a minimum weight of 250 pounds of rider and tack. The rider is not allowed to bring food for the horse. The horse must get all its sustenance from the land surrounding the trail. If a horse passes the test, it is considered quality breeding stock.

The history and knowledge of the Criollo breed had been stored away in Eduardo's mind. Now that his family's ranch was about to be demolished, his desire to be a lawyer had waned. The future of the carefully bred Fernandez Criollo ranch horses was uncertain. Eduardo had a plan.

*****

Instead of mourning over their loss, the two men decided to celebrate the good that was left in their lives. They had their health, their family, and ten of the best-bred Criollo ranch horses in the Pampas. The horses would remain in a neighbor's pasture on the edge of town, where Ihan could still ride and tend to them until their fate was decided.

Eduardo had a plan for the three of them, but before he revealed it, he wanted to enjoy a meal with his father. He would be sure to give him plenty of wine before he shared his idea. There was no better place on Earth that Eduardo could bring his father to cheer him up than Fogo de Chão, a famous Brazilian steakhouse.

The name Fogo de Chão means "ground fire." The affluent chain of steakhouses uses the traditional gaucho method of roasting meats over an open fire. They offer a "full *chur-rasco* experience" which includes continuous servings of fire-roasted beef, lamb, pork, chicken, and other meats until you feel full enough to burst. Men in authentic gaucho attire are the servants who walk around with platters of various types of meat.

Customers have red and green cups in front of their plates. As long as the green cup is on top, the servers will keep offering slices of meat carved right off the freshly roasted slabs. When the red cup is on top, only then will the offerings cease. Also included in the meal is an extensive buffet with salad materials, olives, cheeses, and dessert items. Eduardo's father, upon experiencing Fogo for the first time, looked around and exclaimed, "This is enough to make a grown man cry!" Needless to say, coming here was the best tonic for what Eduardo had planned to tell his father. He would keep the meat and the wine coming.

Almost two hours had passed. Eduardo and his father ate, drank, and reminisced. It was one of the most pleasant afternoons Eduardo had spent with his father in a very long time. Both men were filled to the brim. As their food settled, they enjoyed the traditional drink of the Argentine working man, Amargo Obrero. Amargo is a dark brown bitter characterized by its herbal, almost licorice flavor. It was created in 1887 as a response to the sweet drinks of the upper classes and was often enjoyed after an asado. Eduardo toasted his father and figured this was as good as it was going to get as far as timing, so he leaned in so his father could clearly hear him in the din of the restaurant.

"Father, I have come to a decision. I'm selling my home and I will buy from you three of our best horses."

"Are you going to run off into the highlands and become a full-time gaucho?" his father asked with a curious sideways glance.

"No, father. I'm giving up on being a lawyer, and in a way, I am becoming a gaucho. But not in the way you think. You know that my true love is history. I have studied it since I was a boy. I became a lawyer because I thought I would prefer money over doing what makes me happy. I know now that I was wrong to make that choice. Becoming a lawyer had a purpose in my life. That purpose has been fulfilled. I probably saved men from dying, and I got you the most possible money for your land. That alone made my short career invaluable. However, I have decided to sell everything I own and do what makes me happy."

His father's expression didn't change as he listened to his son. He merely nodded and said, "Go on."

"You remember how Tschiffely rode two Criollo geldings 10,000 miles from Buenos Aires to Washington, D.C., to honor the breed that has served the gauchos and helped develop our country?"

His father nodded. "It took him two years of his life if I remember correctly. You want to be gone for two years?"

"Father, I want to take it a step further. I want to retrace the old route, all the way from South America to Africa. I want to ride approximately 25,000 miles and set a world record. It will put the Criollo horse in the record books. They will never be forgotten again, left on the verge of extinction. What more noble calling could I have in this life? I'm spending my life behind a desk, doing paperwork; how is that something to be proud of?"

"Do you know how long this ride will take you? How will you pay for it? You have bodies of water you will have to cross, which will cost a lot of money. You aren't expecting me to fund this crazy idea, are you?"

"As for time, I know it will take years, maybe five or six. As for money, I will spend what I have. When I run out, I will rely on the kindness of strangers. Surely, there will be those following my trip who will want to help me see it to its completion. It will be a journey of faith, Father."

Ihan rose from his chair. He stared down at Eduardo. While he was in his 70s, he was still a towering presence. He was fit from working with cows. His complexion was hardened from time beneath the sun. The scowl on his face foretold what he thought of the idea.

"No. You will not take this dangerous journey. It is foolish and unnecessary. I have just lost my ranch, my livelihood, the land that I worked a lifetime to protect. Now you want to take away my son! I forbid you to take this journey." Ihan threw his napkin on the table, turned, and walked away.

Eduardo looked around for a waiter. Spotting one, he raised his hand to get his attention and called out, "I need a double shot of tequila, please. In fact, why don't you go ahead and bring the whole bottle."

The Father and Son

"It seems this man understands the importance of the horse," the Son observed. "He knows how instrumental the horse has been in man's history and is challenging his father to preserve that heritage. This man will surely be chosen by the horse in favor of mankind."

"We are seeing the change a man makes when he realizes he has made a mistake," the Father replied. "Remember that he chose the life of a lawyer over preserving the ranch built by his ancestors."

"Man has free will," the Son countered. "Perhaps he thought he could serve a good purpose as a lawyer, protect the innocent, and advance the righteous when they are facing impossible odds. Some lawyers have good intentions to help people, amidst those who knowingly defend the guilty. It is certainly an example of a profession where people can use their talents for good or for evil. He has indeed changed his mind, but could it not be for a noble reason?"

"We will let those designed for that purpose decide," the Father said. "Could his decision be based on glory for himself, or is he truly humble in his desire to honor the Criollo breed? Will he be using the horses simply for transportation and his own glory? His words do not prove his motive or what intentions are in his heart."

*****

In three months, Eduardo sold his apartment, folded up his law career, and convinced his father to sell him three of his favorite horses. His father was not happy about it, but Eduardo wore him down. He pointed out that when he wrote a book about the journey upon its completion, the Fernandez family would be immortalized. Their horses and the journey would become a part of history. This had enough appeal to his father to concede.

Chaja, Graciella, and Calchalero were all under 10 years of age. They had good experience, were sound, reliable, and had good attitudes. These horses needed to be unflappable to undertake the journey. Riding out of South America would entail riding 2,300 miles across the Pampas, through the hot valleys of Bolivia, Ecuador, and Peru. Next came the forests that climbed to altitudes of nearly 14,000 feet. Eduardo would have to travel across Peru, Ecuador, and Colombia before crossing the Panama Canal into Central America. In Central America, Eduardo would have to cross through five countries before reaching the border of the United States.

There were three major concerns that Eduardo faced. The first was that each time he crossed a border into a new country, he had to have the proper paperwork to enter that country. The second was that some highways and bridges didn't allow horses. He would have to find alternative routes where he could to avoid them. Some of the bridges were inevitable.

On those occasions, he would have to rely on the kindness of strangers, fellow horsemen, to use their trailer to transport him and his three caballos over those bridges. The third concern would not affect him until he reached the United States. Eduardo had never learned to speak English.

He would have to cross that personal bridge alone when he came to it.

The one resource Eduardo did have, and that he had already contacted, was the Long Riders' Guild.

Established in 1994, the Long Riders Guild was the world's first international association of equestrian explorers and long-distance travelers by horseback. The guild has members in forty-eight countries. They wholeheartedly agreed to support Eduardo and use their resources to assist him on his journey. Their philosophy: "In the midst of space-age, high-speed technology, a band of humans has slowed down the earth and sky sweeping past them by seeing the world from the back of a horse. They are called Long Riders." The guild has the largest collection of information on horse journeys in the world. They were eager to add Eduardo to their list.

One of the missions of the guild was to ensure the safety of the horses during the journeys. Eduardo was provided guidance on the best equipment for the ride. As one horse would always be ridden and two led with packs and supplies, care had to be taken that the horses didn't get sores. They gave advice on the number of miles a day Eduardo could safely ride and how many days of rest should be incorporated into his schedule.

Most importantly, they helped with the paperwork he would need for the border crossings. He needed to have current documentation from veterinarians that certified the horses had all their immunizations and were disease-free. Some of the countries would require equine inspections by vets before being allowed to pass through. The guild was extremely helpful in providing as much information and forewarnings as possible to prevent complications in an extremely complicated adventure.

When the day finally arrived for Eduardo to depart, he was as prepared as best he could be. He was thrilled that he had just received word that his journey had the official blessing of the Minister of Argentina. The only thing he couldn't prepare for was how distraught his parents were when he checked his girth one last time, mounted Calchalero, gathered the two lead ropes of Chaja and Graciella, and turned to wave goodbye.

He got a good idea of what his funeral would be like. His parents were hugging, tears streaming down their faces, inconsolable with grief. Eduardo would not be returning at any point before the completion of his journey. His parents were sure either they would be dead, or he would die along the journey, and they would never be reunited again. His brother, friends, and a horde of gauchos looked on, most of them teary-eyed.

Eduardo reached into his backpack and pulled out something he had been saving for his departure. It was an Argentine flag. Draping it over his shoulders, he turned in his saddle and addressed the group. The message he shouted was simple: "FOR ARGENTINA AND FOR THE CRIOLLOS!"

$$\star\star\star\star\star$$

Days blended as Eduardo made the long journey across the Pampas. He developed a rhythm where he rose early, stopped for about two hours for lunch, and let the horses graze. He took the opportunity to nap.

During the second half of the day, he kept a lookout for safe places to spend the night. He preferred somewhere that had grass for the horses and trees to tie them to for the night. If he was lucky, there would be dry sticks and timber to make a small fire for a hot meal and a flat area to pitch his tiny tent. He did carry a sack of grain for the horses and treated them to high-protein pellets for their dinner. His protein was dried beef.

Water was another essential item for horses and their rider. Whenever they saw water, everyone drank. Eduardo filled one jug, which would be a small portion for three horses, and a bottle for himself. Food and water were the main travel concerns across large expanses of land. Every so often, he would come across a ranch.

Eduardo was quickly climbing to the status of an Argentine hero in the horse world. Many had heard the news of his journey and welcomed him and his horses. He was able to refill his food supplies and spend a day or two resting. Sometimes, he was even treated to a hot shower and a washing machine for his clothes. He always slept near his horses, though, making sure they were safe and comfortable.

Each horse took a turn carrying Eduardo. He quickly determined that his favorite mount was Calchalero. The horses had unique personalities, and while Calchalero was not the most well-behaved, he had the most character. As Eduardo had no one else to talk to during the long days alone in the saddle, he often had conversations with his horses.

Calchalero had a bad habit of getting into trouble. He frequently untied his rope at night, having learned how to pull the tail of a quick-release knot. Eduardo had to change his style of tying up the horses. He had to be able to free them quickly in an emergency, yet tie a knot that was Calchalero-proof.

"Calchalero, my boy, this journey is hard enough without you making things more difficult. You went too far at that last farmhouse." As Eduardo spoke, Calchalero gave Eduardo his full attention and turned his ears backward, listening to the tone of his voice.

"You unlatched that gate and let all the farmer's cows loose. People will not want us to stay with them."

His response was a head bob and a loud sneeze. Suddenly, Calchalero stopped dead in his tracks and gave a tremendous shake. Eduardo had just taken his bottle of water out of the holder and was enjoying a drink. The reflexive shaking of a horse is rather unsettling for the rider. Small children have been known to tumble off a horse when they shake. Eduardo simply cursed as his water sprayed out of the canteen and doused him.

"I swear you did that on purpose!" Eduardo yelled. "See? This is what I'm talking about. You are a troublemaker. You are a bully!" His words were harsh, but deep down, his love for his horse was immense.

*****

Eduardo was fortunate and crossed 2,300 miles across the Pampas without any major issues. There were a few sores caused by the packs and a stone bruise on Graciella's front hoof that caused a few days of delay until it healed. At one point, crossing a wet field, his horses almost got stuck in a bog. They sank to their bellies. Eduardo had to dismount and pull them to safety. They escaped unharmed, but all of them and his equipment were covered in mud. Little did he know, that was the easy part of the journey. Things were about to get a lot tougher.

Charging his cell phone was Eduardo's biggest hindrance to communicating with friends and family about the progress of his journey. In addition, there were many times he was completely out of cell range. When his phone was charged and he had cell service, after contacting his parents, he sent updates to the Guild. His progress was posted on their website. This allowed people following him to be aware of his location and potentially look out for his arrival for those wanting to offer lodging and supplies. His posts were often in the form of small, informative snippets.

February 22nd – Arrived at Puno on the shores of Lake Titicaca, Peru. At Desaguaderos, the horses had to pass veterinary inspections before leaving Argentina for Bolivia.

April 29th – I am in Peru. I arrived last night at about 9 P.M., and since there was nobody around in authority, it was by pure chance that a distant cousin, Francisco Melendes Fernandez, met me. I was able to breeze through the check-in to this country. I was supposed to have arrived around 5 P.M., but I took a wrong turn. I am expecting to stay here for five days, enough time for the horses' wounds to heal – wounds from the stones on the very difficult and dangerous mule trails.

The conditions of the trails became worse and worse as Eduardo rode deep into Peru. Fortunately, the people of Peru were very supportive of his journey. Eduardo had sympathy for the toll the journey was taking on his horses, but he knew he had to push on anyway. Conditions would improve dramatically when he finally made it to the United States. No one in his family, including himself, had ever traveled to the U.S. He was looking forward to traveling through a country that was not riddled with crime, poverty, and harsh living conditions.

*****

May 15th – I was lucky enough to meet some muleteers and ride with them for fifty miles. They were traveling with 56 horses and 3 mules. The experience of living with them in the mountains is one I will never forget – completely unique. One was mute, one was lame, and one only had one arm. In spite of their sinister appearance, they immediately offered me hospitality, as have all the Peruvians, and invited me to follow them.

July 18th – I'm in Ecuador. They have named me the Equine Ambassador. The horses are well, in spite of a few sores on their backs caused by the heat. The sores have to be aerated every hour on the journey and, if possible, bathed. I'm staying in Santa Rosa until the 29th, the village's feast day. They are going to give me their flag as a witness to my passing through, but no money – nothing. It's their choice...

September 1st – I have arrived in Colombia. It's a dangerous time here. I was detained in prison overnight for not having the right paperwork. My brother had to fax verification for them to release me from jail. It was terrifying. I was afraid my horses would be stolen while I was incarcerated. There is a civil war going on.

September 15th – The countryside is more welcoming, even though the political situation is horrible. The people are kind, even if they are all armed to the teeth because of attacks and livestock theft that they suffer. Last night, we heard someone trying to force the big door open to the barn in which I'm staying. It's reinforced with metal plates. I now carry a machete with me at all times. When people meet me on the street, they step out of my way.

October 5th – The most dangerous part of travel in Colombia is coming into a small village on a Sunday. The people have been drinking since the morning and spend the afternoons on the road, motionless. I cannot understand what they say, and they become aggressive. Their faces often bear traces of whip marks or kicks from the horses. I was held up by two men with guns. They took my cash. I managed to keep my cell phone hidden; otherwise, they would have taken that too. I'm happy to have escaped with my life.

*****

Then it happened. The Guild and Eduardo's family received the news that Eduardo and his horses met with a devastating accident. It was everyone's worst nightmare. Followers around the world held their collective breath.

*****

October 28th – I'm in the hospital after having had an accident. On a narrow mule track, the soil gave way beneath our feet, and we fell 30 yards down a 70° slope. Calchalero rolled on top of me. I have broken ribs and a broken collarbone. Chaja and Gracielle are seriously injured. I was able to call for help on my phone. It saved my life. It is going to take weeks for us to recover. I'm not sure Chaja and Gracielle will be able to continue.

*****

By October 27th, Eduardo had completed almost ¼ of his journey by the time he was deep into Colombia. His horses were haggard. He simply wanted to complete as many miles a day as possible to get out of the country. Despite the dangers of criminals and thieves, his fame in South America continued to grow. One of his supporters, a man who owned thousands of acres of land in Colombia, a doctor, and a horse enthusiast, had arranged for a boat to take Eduardo and his three horses from Colombia to Panama. It was an all-expense-paid passage. He just had to reach Octavia on the northwest coast.

Eduardo had stopped to rest and get supplies at the tiny town of Antado for the last leg of his trip in South America. There were no roads in this part of the country; he would be trekking across the wilderness. He planned on taking a week to travel the 200 miles to reach Octavia. The benchmark of completing his ride through South America was going to give him a great sense of accomplishment. It would fuel his passion to continue.

Central America was going to have its challenges with the dangerous countries he had to pass through, but once he reached Mexico, America was in sight. The most difficult part of the journey would be behind him.

As he tacked up his horses the morning of his departure, he was approached by a man asking him questions about his plans. He had heard of Eduardo.

"Amigo, do you have money for me? I bet lots of people will give you money along the way."

Eduardo vividly recalled being held up by two men on the road. He pulled out his wallet and opened it. There was not a single paper bill. "I have been robbed recently. I have no money for you, and no money for me." He did have a small stash tucked into a secret compartment in one of his saddle bags.

"That's a shame," the man said, clicking his tongue and shaking his head.

Wanting to change the topic, Eduardo asked, "I'm trying to get out of here and go north. What's the quickest route?"

"You see that hill over there?"

Eduardo nodded. He could faintly make out a winding path leading up the side of a steep hill just outside the town.

"If you go up that trail and down the other side, you will find a nice trail leading north. It's a mule track. All the locals take it."

There was a road with cars that went out of town and weaved around the hills. It was narrow and had no shoulders. It would be difficult to keep himself and the two other horses safely to the side of the road. In Columbia, there was no respect for people traveling on horses. On some of the roads he had traveled along, the cars came dangerously close to hitting his horses. He warily eyed the steep trail but decided it was better than the alternative. Not realizing the danger he was about to face, he decided to take it.

Mounting Calchalero, he took the lead ropes of the other two horses and headed out of town and toward the hill. When he finally reached it, the path was so narrow and steep that Eduardo had to untie the ropes to Chaja and Gracielle. He prayed that they would behave themselves and follow. He felt sure they would.

They had traveled over 10,000 miles together thus far. The horses didn't like being separated even for a minute. On the rare occasions when he found a blacksmith to replace his horses' shoes, he had to have all three horses stand next to each other while the work was being done. Not one of them would stand still and cooperate with the blacksmith if the other two were out of eyesight. That had its benefits and its disadvantages. Today, it was an advantage.

As the horses picked their footing carefully along the nar-row trail, pebbles and rocks became displaced and rolled down the hillside. It made Eduardo dizzy to watch them plummet down the hill. It was unnerving even for him, with all his experience on horses and mountain trails. Eduardo willed himself to look forward, not down, and trust his sure-footed horses.

Finally, they made it to the apex. They rounded the corner at the top of the hill and started to descend down the backside.

Suddenly, Eduardo felt Calchalero stumble. He thought his horse had tripped. That was not the case. The ground under his front feet gave way. Eduardo's heart dropped into his stomach as his worst nightmare was coming true. The trail disappeared in front of them. The footing beneath them crumbled. All hell broke loose.

Calchalero tried desperately to stay on the path as it disappeared beneath his feet. He lurched sideways. Eduardo clung to him out of sheer reflex. Calchalero quickly lost the battle with gravity. He fell down the hill onto his side, trapping Eduardo beneath him. Then he rolled. Fortunately, momentum took over and he rolled over the top of Eduardo, crushing him beneath him, but they were separated quickly. Calchalero slid past Eduardo and down the hill with the avalanche of dirt and rocks.

In his peripheral vision, Eduardo watched in horror as the trail continued to disintegrate beneath the other two horses. Floundering, they were swept together down the hillside. He felt the pain from the 1,200 pounds of horse that steamrolled his body. Worse was the pain of seeing his horses sliding and rolling down the rocky hillside.

At the bottom of the hill, Chaja lay on his side. Gracielle was sitting on top of him like a dog. Both horses were bloody, their sides heaving. At least they were both still alive. Eduardo searched for Calchalero. He had made it to his feet and was standing, every inch of his body shaking from the trauma.

Trapped beneath some large rocks, Eduardo managed to get his right hand into his inside coat pocket. His fingers found his phone. He pulled it out. He had his brother's number programmed. All he had to manage was to hit number one and send. The phone rang a few times. Eduardo could barely speak when he heard his brother's voice on the other end.

"Listen carefully, Maico."

"Are you in trouble again, Eduardo?" Maico joked. Eduardo had called many times when he was in a crisis situation. He called right after he was almost sucked into the bog, once when a giant snake fell out of a tree and barely missed taking him off his horse. He called when intruders were trying to break into the barn he was staying in, and right after he was robbed by two men with a gun.

"It's bad this time, Maico. I'm hurt," Eduardo managed to say, his breath limited to short gasps. "My horses are hurt. I'm trapped under rocks..." he uttered breathily, his energy and voice fading due to the exploding pain in his body.

"Dear God, Eduardo. Where are you?" Maico yelled into the phone, now in panic mode.

"I'm just outside the town of Antado, Columbia. They have a small police department," he managed to get out, having to pause to take deep breaths in order not to pass out before he got out the information. "Call them and tell them I'm on the donkey trail leading out of town." More deep breaths; the world was starting to fade. "Tell them we all fell down the cliff; we are all injured..." Then, the world went dark.

Destiny Khumalo

Cape Town, South Africa
Medical Doctor

TANJA AND REINER KHUMALO were professors at the University of Namibia (UNAM) when they met. Tanja had her Ph.D. and decided to be a professor rather than open a medical practice. She graduated at the top of her class in med school. Reiner was a geologist. His love of studying the earth and all its geological phenomena made him a popular and enthusiastic educator of future geologists. With Africa being a hotbed of gem and uranium mining, he had no lack of students lining up for his classes.

The couple met on campus as colleagues and began their courtship dance. Falling hopelessly in love, after a six-month courtship, they got married and immediately started a family. The problem was that life outside of campus, in the home they could afford on UNAM salaries, was not what they had envisioned for raising their children.

Windhoek, the campus location for UNAM, was prestigious and beautiful. Within a short drive of the campus were exclusive neighborhoods. Also within a short distance from the campus were areas of extreme poverty. While Tanja and Reiner owned a townhouse in a safe community, now that they had two children, life in the city was no longer desirable. There was no way they could afford a house in one of the affluent communities that had safe neighborhoods and access to excellent private schools.

The social, economic, political, and cultural center of Namibia, Windhoek was a thriving metropolis. Nearly every Namibian national enterprise, governmental body, and educational and cultural institution was headquartered there. However, poverty and unemployment in Namibia were the reasons for its high crime rate. 43% of Namibia's population lived in poverty, much of it extreme. There was a fair amount of opportunistic crime such as pickpocketing, purse-snatching, vehicle theft, and break-ins. More severe crimes were not as common but were certainly a viable threat.

Both parents had the dream of having property for their children to roam, safe places to play outside, and access for their children to enjoy nature without being in danger from criminals. While Tanja and Reiner were fond of the city and its culture, they both knew that their priorities had changed since their single days as college professors. As their twins played on the floor of their crowded living room, Tanja decided it was time to have "the talk." The twins were turning five soon, and they had to expand their living quarters.

Tanja turned, arms crossed, and looked out the picture window of the balcony that overlooked the neighborhood of their three-bedroom townhouse. The golden morning light shining through the window silhouetted her frame. The fabric of her brightly colored gown brushed the hardwood floor. It was a Saturday. Tanja often wore the traditional garments of the Herero tribe on the weekends. When she was in her professor role, she wore smart business attire. On weekends, she cherished the time to preserve the culture of her native roots. One of the ways she could do that was to wear traditional clothing—colorful long dresses and a headscarf, an adaptation of the Victorian German settlers who influenced her ancestors.

Reiner's parents had been members of the Ovambo tribe, which comprised 50% of the natives in Namibia. He didn't have to worry about donning the traditional clothing of his tribe. They wore very little.

Both husband and wife were unique in that their parents decided to leave their tribes, find employment in the city, and send their children to school to get an education. Education within their villages meant learning how to be a good wife and nurture babies, weave baskets, and prepare food if you were female. If you were male, your role was to father children to keep the village thriving, keep a roof over the family's head, and provide food.

For the Herero tribe, their primary food consisted of the milk and meat of large herds of cattle, sheep, and goats, which grazed the tree-studded grasslands. The Ovambo tribe equally relied on husbandry, supplemented by fishing, hunting, and gathering. Cattle were of particular importance for marriage payments as well as for milk and butter. Millet and were often cultivated by the Ovambo people.

Neither Tanja nor Reiner had to worry about hunting, gathering, or living within the social confines of their tribes. Their parents had decided to leave the simplicity of their native lives and introduce their children to the civilized world of education and modern jobs. The walls that surrounded them meant greater comfort and convenience than the huts in which they were born. The fences surrounding the community in which they now lived were meant to keep them safe from predators - the two-legged kind that might rob or kill them. Life was no longer simple. They were no longer walking down the same path their ancestors had followed for thousands of years.

Tanja gazed out the window. Her view included the other townhouses, pavement, and a wall topped with barbed wire surrounding the perimeter of the complex. Living in Namibia offered opportunities for her children to stay in touch with the culture of their ancestors. She also had relatives living in the local village they could visit.

The city of Windhoek embraced the heritage of the indigenous people. There were celebrations and festivals to appreciate the diverse tribes of Namibia. However, looking out at the concrete walls and barriers, Tanja thought that if this was the best they could do, this was not where she wanted her children to grow up. Besides, there were growing complications with the tribes that Tanja felt were battles she didn't want her own children to face.

With her husband's blessing, Tanja made the decision. Their family would move to somewhere her children would have no borders, no fences, and where life was simple and safe. Finding a home and new jobs wasn't easy, but move they did to Cape Town.

*****

Destiny seemed like an undignified name for a physician, or so she thought. What were her parents thinking? They named her Destiny and her twin brother Justice. For being so close in their genetic makeup, and having been raised by the same two parents, she often wondered how they had grown so far apart.

She remembered moving to their house in Hout Bay when she and her brother were seven. Even as young children, they realized the differences between their townhouse in the city and their new house, perched on a hillside, surrounded by trees, with a view overlooking the ocean bay. They were in awe of their new surroundings. She and her brother thought they had died and gone to heaven.

The terrain surrounding Cape Town was filled with lush, green vegetation. While there were green trees in Namibia, much of the terrain was arid, brown, and thorny. If they wanted to roll around in green grass, they had to go into the city to a park. There, they could play in fountains and walk barefoot in the grass. Now, they could walk barefoot in their own front yard. From their hillside view of the ocean, they looked down on the many moods of the sea as it gently lapped the sand-lined coast.

Besides having a lush, green lawn, their new house had three bedrooms and a suite in the basement with its own entrance and kitchen. She and her brother would have their very own rooms. They were promised they could pick the color of the paint for the walls and their own furnishings. They could play outside to their hearts' content, no fences needed, with the stunning view of the valley beneath them and the vibrant blue ocean hugging the shore of the fishing village below.

Their house was situated on three acres of land. The best part was that the property backed up to Table Mountain National Park. Shortly after they settled in, Destiny had a memory of her dad saying he was giving up geology and going into botany. She had to ask him, "What is botany?" Her father explained that it was the study of plants.

"I love studying rocks, gems, and minerals, but the plants here are very special," he explained. "We live next to a very unique national park. Africa is an amazing continent, but something quite special grows right here behind your house. It's called fynbos vegetation."

"Fynbos?" Justice chimed in with a growing interest in the conversation. "What's that?"

"We live in what's called the Cape Floral Region, floral meaning flowers. This park behind us has one of the richest floral regions in the world. What's even more special is that 70% of the flowers are endemic. Endemic means a species that only grows naturally within an area."

"But what about that other word, the 'fine' something..." Destiny asked, impatient for the answer.

"I'm getting there. I had to explain why fynbos is so special. These plants don't grow naturally anywhere else in the world. Just like you will only find giraffes in Africa and polar bears in the Arctic, you will only find fynbos in this area of South Africa."

"Oh," both kids chimed in at the same time. They looked at each other and laughed hysterically.

"I have a question," Tanja interjected. "What does the term native mean? Isn't it the same as endemic, something that grows naturally somewhere?"

"Good question. Native means that something occurs naturally in a specific location. It could have originated in a different part of the world and has eventually spread somewhere else through humans or animals. Endemic means there is only one place where something is found naturally."

Continuing to answer the original question, Reiner explained, "Now I can tell you about fynbos."

Destiny and her brother listened. Her father was captivating when he spoke. He was a natural-born teacher and drew his students in with his animated expressions and dynamic way of speaking. She still remembered the details of his mini-lecture.

First, he defined the word fynbos (fine-bose), which meant "fine-leaved plants." These plants only grew on the southern tip of Africa. They included many plant species, including some trees and shrubs. Fynbos only grew along a 200-kilometer stretch along the coast from Clanwilliam to Port Elizabeth. Many of the species were in danger of extinction. There were over 8,700 species, 1,700 of which currently were in danger. That was why the park above them was so important. It was protecting these plants.

"So, these are like the dinosaurs?" Justice asked. "They are all going to die?"

"What's hurting them, Daddy?" Destiny wanted to know.

First, her dad explained that every country has a national flower. South Africa's was the protea, which was a type of fynbos, as was the daisy. Other types of fynbos were used for health and medicine. Some of the medicines treated infections and inflammation; others were used for skin care. Other species of fynbos, like rooibos, were made into a very healthy tea.

Then, her father went on to explain that there were tall, rigid reeds called restios that were once used to make shelters by South Africans. They were still used today for making thatched roofs. But one of the fynbos' most important purposes was helping the water cycle. Fynbos grows in the water-rich mountain tops, but they don't need much water. They help keep the soil from eroding with their roots, but they allow the water to flow into the rivers and reservoirs. Out of every five glasses of water, one of them made its way into the drinking water because of fynbos.

"But what's making them extinct? You haven't gotten to that part," Destiny noted, always the impatient one.

"Most of the land is owned by individual people. The people who live on these tracts of land are not taking care of the fynbos. Another reason is very interesting..." Reiner teased by theatrically lowering his voice to a whisper. The kids leaned closer, their eyes wide.

"You do know how seeds are normally spread, by birds, insects, and animals, right?" Both kids nodded enthusiastically. "Well, some of the seeds of fynbos are spread that way, but most of the fynbos plants need fire to BURN their seeds," he yelled, making them both jump back and shriek.

Destiny recalled not believing her father, thinking he was kidding. "No way, if something burns, it dies!"

"Not the fynbos plants. The seeds are stored in fire-safe cones. They can only be released by being burned. The heat releases the seeds. Some of the plants need to be reseeded every six or so years; others can last up to 45 years. But without fire, the plant weakens and gets taken over by weeds or trees. Humans tend to put out fires, so the plants don't burn like they need to."

"My new job will be to help work with landowners, getting them to protect the fynbos growing on their property. We will also be planting new seedlings that we start in green-houses."

"Wow, that's a cool job, Daddy," Destiny said, then looked at her mom. "Are you still going to be a college professor?"

"No, honey. In order to afford this new house, I have to go to work in a hospital as a doctor. I will be making much more money than I used to, but it means I will be gone more. Sometimes, I'll be away for a couple of days at a time."

Destiny remembered the sick feeling in the pit of her stomach when her mom told her about her new career. Little did she know that this career change meant not only that her mother would be away a lot more, but it was also the beginning of a huge change in their family dynamics; not a change for the better.

The Father and Son

"It is true that family and family values shape the minds of children," the Son began. "Perhaps it is not always the fault of humans that they are directed in one way or another. Perhaps this cascade of people growing away from nature, from what they have been given, is not their fault."

"It is always the choice of the human to choose their path," the Father replied. "The parents of Destiny have followed different paths for two very different reasons. The father could have taken a job that made more money, but he chose the one to protect the endangered vegetation. The mother chose to go into a profession to help people, but one that would take her away from her home and make her less influential in raising her children. Mothers have an important role in instilling values."

"Fathers can fulfill that role as well," the Son countered. "Fathers are strong, important figures in the lives of their children."

"This is true," the Father agreed. "But nurturing, caring, compassion, tenderness, and empathy are the strongest traits spread by the female soul. Does it not say in Proverbs, 'Strength and dignity are her clothing, and she laughs at the time to come. She opens her mouth with wisdom, and the teaching of kindness is on her tongue. She looks well to the ways of her household and does not eat the bread of idleness. Her children rise up and call her blessed; her husband also, and he praises her: "Many women have done excellently, but you surpass them all."

"It is true that despite the lessons taught by the mother and father," the Son reflected, "a child will eventually have to choose which values they hold dear."

*****

The memories of her childhood home evaporated. Reality came crashing back. It was 2:00 AM. Destiny drove to the back of the hospital. She had just gotten off her shift in the emergency room. The anonymous text message told her to park behind the hospital in the first open space next to the handicapped parking. There were not many streetlights in this lot. Being the dead of night, not one other car was in the lot reserved for overflow parking. Her headlights cut a swath of bright light that guided her into the vacant space.

Having arrived a few minutes early, Destiny would have to wait. The clock on her dashboard read 2:08. She was supposed to meet her contact at 2:15. She turned off the engine and waited in the dark. Her heart beat unevenly in her chest.

There was no going back from what she was about to do. She had made her decision, and she was going to follow through, even though she was jeopardizing everything she had worked for: her college degree, her Ph.D., and her position at a prestigious hospital in Cape Town. Her greatest fear was getting caught and disappointing her family.

Destiny struggled not to overthink what she had to lose and what she had to gain. She had already made her decision. Instead, she thought about her past.

She had a lot to be thankful for. Destiny retained the family home she had grown up in from the age of seven. She and her brother had an amazing childhood. There were downsides, though. Their father became the primary caregiver as their mother worked shifts in the ER and was often gone for three or four days at a time, sleeping at the hospital.

By the time her mother got home, she often slept for an entire day. By the time she got caught up on housework and other chores, she had little time to spend with her kids. The money was good; her income paid for the kids to have the best of everything.

Their father took them for long hikes and camping trips in Table Mountain National Park. It became their playground. They learned all about the flora and fauna from their father. The twins kept journals and wrote down everything they learned about the plants and animals. It was their idea, and of course, Dad was thrilled that his children showed such an interest in the wildlife.

Destiny was more interested in the plants, while Justice was thrilled with the diverse animal life they spotted on their adventures. When they got home, they would take their notes and sketches and identify what they had seen. They had fun researching facts and filling in the information. It was an educational, ongoing project. Her wildlife diary was among her most prized possessions.

It seemed they were destined to be opposites of one another. When it came time to graduate high school, Justice decided he wanted to be a veterinarian. Destiny was determined to follow in her mother's footsteps and become a doctor.

Justice flew through an advanced degree program and graduated in seven years with his veterinary license. He was married and had three kids by the time he was thirty. Destiny struggled through the eight-year medical program. Dating took a back burner, and she wasn't interested in getting married or having kids. She had always read stories about how close twins were in their interests, in staying close to one another, yet she and her brother had gone in opposite directions.

Their parents had moved into a retirement community in the heart of Cape Town. They left the home to Destiny but helped Justice with buying his home in Noordhoek, a more distant suburb of Cape Town nestled on the coastline. Justice fell in love with Noordhoek when they were taken there as kids for horseback riding lessons.

Noordhoek was well-known for its serene rural atmosphere with leafy lanes as well as spectacular ocean and mountain views. It was a popular destination for lovers of the great outdoors, especially for those who loved hiking, fishing, boating, and cycling. It was also a mecca for horse farms. Like its hometown, it was located adjacent to Table Mountain National Park.

Justice developed a great love for horses. Destiny enjoyed riding on the beach, cantering along the bright white sand, and watching the waves wash up and spray around the horses' feet. She loved the rush of speed, the wind in her face, and the sand flying past at a dizzying rate. Beyond that, she didn't have any great love for horses or riding. She found riding in the ring boring and was less than thrilled with trail riding along the mountains. It was mostly walking and spending long hours in the saddle, which caused her to be sore for days afterward. Justice didn't care what he was doing, as long as it was on the back of a horse.

She glanced at the clock again, comforted by thoughts of her past. It took her mind off the fact that she was entering new territory in her life, making decisions that were going to have a permanent impact on her future. The clock now read 2:15. The night was eerily silent. A knock on the passenger side window nearly put her into shock.

The sound of tugging on the locked door handle spurred her back to reality. Destiny hit the unlock button with shaking hands. The door opened, and a figure in black settled into the passenger seat, pulling the door closed. Trying to control her breathing, she looked at the man sitting next to her, wearing a black knit hat and black mask. She couldn't make out any of his features in the dark car. Without looking at her, he handed her the bag. She took it and put it underneath her seat.

By the time she looked back up, the car door was shutting, and the stranger disappeared into the night.

*****

It all began when Destiny traveled back to Namibia for the annual tribal festival. She hadn't been able to attend in several years. She was greatly looking forward to it. Sadly, she had to attend the event alone. Her mom had a conflict, and her brother had no interest in hanging out with relatives from the Herero Tribe.

Destiny was more aligned with keeping in touch with her family and her heritage. Justice was too preoccupied with life on his farm and making emergency visits to the clients of his rapidly growing veterinary business. Destiny was able to get coverage for her ER shift that week and was enjoying one of her first vacations since she began working at the private hospital in Cape Town.

The reunion was taking place in one of the few remaining Herero villages outside Windhoek. One of her favorite tribal traditions was the holy sacred fire, which was kept burning continually. The fire played an important role in ceremonies like weddings and was a place for prayers. It was an integral part of ancestral worship and Destiny's favorite part of Herero culture.

Another aspect she felt deeply drawn to, probably due to the influence of her mother, was the distinct dress of the Herero women. She fondly remembered looking through her mother's closet at all her brightly colored dresses and wishing she were big enough to try them on. Her fondest birthday memory was when she turned ten; her mother surprised her with her very own traditional dress and tribal headpiece.

Herero women wore horn-shaped hats made from rolled cloth. The horns stretch out horizontally and were meant to pay homage to the importance of cattle farming to their people. The Herero dress was adopted from the Victorian era and inspired by the German missionaries and colonists' wives who came to the continent of Africa.

As soon as Destiny graduated from med school, she returned to her village and purchased several dresses to put into her own closet. She would not be like her brother and ignore her heritage. She was going to preserve and embrace it. Her brother constantly pointed out that they were also half Ovambo. Destiny felt no attraction to that culture. She preferred the colorful costumes to running around topless like the Ovambo women. She was dying to wear her dress and hat among the other women at the festival.

At the beginning of the festival, a speaker described the history of the Herero tribes to the non-Herero spectators. He spoke of the semi-nomadic beginnings where the tribes thrived on the rich grasslands. Then, in the 1830s, the native Afrikaners, the Nama, and Orlam tribes drove the Herero off the main grasslands. The tribes settled in the southernmost part of Namibia, where they still reside today.

Destiny mingled with her relatives and the other tribe members. She watched in awe as they performed cere-monies, dances, and elaborate prayers over the sacred fire. No one asked about her life as a doctor in the big city of Cape Town. Today was about celebrating the traditions of the tribe. There was no place for talk of those who had left their villages for the modern world. Destiny wondered what her life would be like if she had chosen to return to the village rather than pursue a career as a doctor, but her thoughts were interrupted by a tap on the shoulder.

Isra was a handsome tribal Herero man. He was technically her second cousin. It was common for women to marry within the family, and Isra did make Destiny feel a little weak in the knees. He was in his early twenties and searching for a bride. There was a bit of an age difference, but with the lack of eligible women in the tribe, it made little difference to Isra. While Destiny had no intention of developing a relationship with a tribal Herero bachelor, she couldn't help being a bit coy and flirtatious, especially as she donned her gorgeous traditional dress with matching horns.

What she wasn't expecting was when Isra linked arms with her and led her off into the darkness, beyond the reach of the eternal flame's glow, which was their initial topic of conversation. Isra continued with a short rant about the opening ceremonies.

"Education about our tribe should not only be about good history. If we are to survive, we need to remember all of history and learn from it. There was no mention of our nation's growing poverty and of the fact that we are still fighting for justice from the war of extermination of our people by the Germans."

Destiny was a bit taken aback. "I know a bit about apartheid and how South Africa had brutal segregation policies around 1950. I didn't know Germans had anything to do with the extermination of our tribe."

"There are those who are still fighting for reparation. What the German colonists did to our people was a precursor to the Holocaust. Because of the past and being forced from our lands and making it a capital crime for the Herero people to own cattle, our way of life was outlawed. We were told we would be killed if we were found with livestock," he said with anger in his voice. "They took away everything we used to live on. We have never fully recovered."

Destiny felt sadness. She was always on the fringe of the Herero culture. She looked into it from the view of an outsider. She admired the connection they felt to their tribe, to one another, to their land. She never saw the pain, the poverty, the struggles they encountered daily. Her mother had never educated her on the plight of the Herero. She had only focused on their culture and traditions.

Isra continued. "The Herero did try to fight back but were beaten savagely by the colonists. The horrific abuse became worse when a German general issued an extermination order. Soldiers forced the Herero people into the desert. They poisoned their drinking water and confined thousands to concentration camps. Sixty-five thousand Herero lost their lives to starvation, disease, and dehydration. Our population was reduced to the low ten-thousands. Because of the violence, many of the Herero fled the country."

Tears leaked from Destiny's eyes as she imagined the horrors. Even with his skin matching the shades of the darkness around him, Destiny could see the pain etched on Isra's face.

"If not for the genocide, the Herero would be a thriving community. We would own large tracts of land. They stole the roots of our being. We were reduced to a small minority in our own country. Meanwhile, the white German descendants thrive. There are those of us who are fighting to take back what is ours."

"What can you do now, after so many years?"

"First, we want the land back that was taken from us. Second, we want Germany to take responsibility for its genocide. We want reparations paid to the descendants of the victims. Our poverty is generational, and unless we get help breaking that chain with aid from the Germans who caused this, the Herero will remain in poverty."

"It sounds like a difficult battle, Isra. Are there many people on your side, you know, fighting for these reparations?"

"We have a lawsuit pending under the Alien Tort Statute that allows foreigners to sue the perpetrators of human rights violations. The Herero are officially challenging Germany in a U.S. federal court. The wheels of justice turn slowly. We do have a plan to put pressure on the government of Germany. I'm asking for your help. I would like to recruit you as one of our warriors. We are fighting a battle, Destiny, a battle you would be able to help us with."

Destiny sat quietly for a moment, digesting everything she had just learned. She felt anger for what had happened to her tribe. She felt sad that she knew so little about their current struggles. There was a growing feeling, the small ember of a flame being fanned, that perhaps this was her opportunity to become part of the Herero tribe. If there was some way to help her people, was it not her duty to try? Could it, in fact, be her 'destiny'? The thought gave her chills that ran down her spine despite the warm, humid air.

"I'm listening," she said to Isra after her moment of contemplation. What she didn't expect was that Isra was serious about becoming a warrior. People die in battles, and what Isra was about to ask her to do was murder.

*****

The plan to put pressure on the government of Germany that would force them to concede to their demands was to systematically take out Germans living in South Africa. They had to be cunning in how they implemented this plan. Currently, there are around 100,000 Germans living in Cape

Town. Twice that number traveled each summer to the city for vacations and to enjoy the beaches.

Other countries in South Africa also had large numbers of Germans living or visiting. If enough Germans started disappearing or dying while in South Africa, the Herero people might be taken more seriously in their demands for reparations. They were inviting war with Germany, but it was the only way to save their dwindling culture.

Isra explained how their cause was gaining strength. People of Herero descent were gaining traction in developing a movement to wage war on the Germans. Prominent and wealthy Germans were being targeted all over South Africa. Through underground networks and connections, certain notable people would be taken out.

There were several plans on how this would be accomplished. Some would mysteriously disappear. Others would be killed in seemingly random car crashes. A large number would sustain an injury that would force them to seek medical help at an emergency room in a hospital. Those who entered would suddenly develop complications and die. That was where Destiny would become involved.

Destiny was shocked. She had so many questions. She was unprepared for her life to be turned upside down. Isra assured her that the plan was already being implemented by doctors of Herero descent in hospitals all over South Africa. It was simple, really. South Africa had a huge problem with counterfeit drugs. They were being produced in China and Japan and were filtering into the South African medical system at an alarming rate.

Many of the knock-off drugs were dangerous. South Africans were dying at an alarming rate from the pills they thought they were taking to cure themselves. Isra explained that it was easy for their movement to intercept the illegal drug dealers and steal their shipments. They already had a supply of the illegal drugs and had given them to doctors who were warriors for their cause. He asked her to look on the bright side of what they were doing. The Herero were taking the bad drugs off the market so they didn't end up killing the innocent people from their country, the ones that needed the real medication that cured malaria and halted the diseases to which they were prone.

Isra went on to explain how the system worked. Destiny would be given a disposable cell phone. She would get a text with a patient's name that would be coming into the ER in a certain time period. As soon as she received it, she would destroy the phone. All she had to do was issue medicine for that patient. She was to flush the real medication down the sink and give the patient counterfeit pills. Since it was so prevalent for illegal drugs to be peppered into the hospital system, no one would suspect the death was anything other than an unfortunate occurrence from the epidemic that plagued the system. There was no way to trace the drugs to her.

There was no way she could have prepared for what happened next. Destiny truly believed in the cause she was supporting. Her tribe had been slaughtered by the thousands. The people who caused those murders had a chance to make restitution. They chose not to. The choice was to fight back or slowly watch the Herero race be wiped from the planet.

The Germans had taken everything away that the tribe need-ed to survive. War was justified. Wars were not always fought with guns and missiles. Destiny was sure she was on the right side of this battle.

*****

Less than two weeks later, her first text came through. A man named Christoph Brehm would be coming into the ER by ambulance in a few hours. No more information was provided. The fact that he was coming meant that he was probably someone important in the German political world. He most likely had an expensive vacation home near the beach in Cape Town.

Through a series of convoluted events designed to throw any investigations off the trail, Christoph would have an accident that appeared to be random. The injuries would probably be minor but cause enough concern to take a trip to the ER to get checked out.

Mr. Brehm arrived around 7:15 in the evening. Several doctors were working in the ER. Patients were seen by whoever was available at the moment. When Brehm arrived, he entered the ER clearly in distress but not in any imminent danger. His wife and young daughter accompanied him. He had a bloody bandage wrapped around his arm. Blood was seeping from a deep slash across his forearm.

After getting checked in, Christoph sat in the waiting room to be seen. His daughter played on the floor around the chairs, and his wife had picked up a magazine. Christoph was pale. He sat staring at nothing as he waited. He had been given a pack of ice to put over the top of the bandage to help stem the bleeding. He was instructed to keep his arm elevated. He seemed to be deep in thought.

Christoph and his family had gone out to eat an early dinner. His daughter, only four, would need to be home in time for her bedtime at 8:00. When they left the restaurant, Eve, his wife, held their daughter's hand. Elsa always held her mother's hand. He led the way out and was opening the glass door just as a group of four Africans was entering. The next few seconds were a blur.

It was playing like a movie in his mind. Christoph was recalling the incident. It began with him bumbling to get the door open while the men tried to bustle through from the outside. Then, there was a crash. The glass shattered. One of the men yelled. The others bumped into him, causing chaos. Christoph felt a shooting pain across his forearm. The man who initially yelled held up his bleeding hand and screamed, "What did you do?"

Staff appeared out of thin air. Blood started soaking the torn sleeve of Christoph's white shirt. Someone pressed a cloth napkin to his arm. Another waiter was attending to the cut on the other man's hand. Profuse apologies from the restaurant's manager followed. Both men were asked if they needed an ambulance. The African man and his buddies immediately said "no" and turned and left, putting on a show of how irate they were for the inconvenience.

Two busboys were busy sweeping up the glass and taping a sheet of plastic over the door when Christoph and his wife determined the cut was not that bad. The bleeding had been stemmed, and Eve could take him to the local hospital. He would definitely need stitches.

As Destiny glanced at the package in her hands, she realized this was Christoph's death warrant. Looking at his wife and young daughter, Eve was not sure she could go through with the plan. She had taken an oath to never cause intentional harm to another human being. She had dedicated her life to saving others, not killing them.

On the other hand, she had given her word that she would follow through on this mission. A lot had gone into setting it up. If she didn't complete her task, she might be putting herself in danger. She knew too much. What would stop the people who were risking their lives for this cause from silencing her?

She took a deep breath and called into the waiting room, "Mr. Brehm?"

A nurse cleaned and disinfected the wound while Destiny gathered the tools to stitch the laceration. It was a straight clean cut, as if it had been sliced by a piece of glass or by a sharp knife. Destiny was pretty sure she knew which it had been. She had asked Christoph how the wound occurred, and he gave a confused account about trying to open the door, colliding with men who were entering, hearing the glass shatter, and simultaneously feeling a sharp pain in his arm. Destiny took notes on his chart. Their eyes met for a brief moment. She quickly looked away.

When the stitching was completed, her attending nurse bandaged Christoph's forearm. He was instructed to keep the wound dry for the next couple of days, to change the dressing once a day, and come back in a week to get the stitches removed.

"Oh, and one more thing," Destiny added. "Just to be on the safe side, I'm prescribing some antibiotics. We don't want that wound to get infected. Give me a minute while I print out the label and instructions. The nurse will bring them to you."

The medication would be switched with the pills given to her by the man in the car. She had no idea what was in them. Destiny felt sick to her stomach as her hand clutched the pills in her pocket, the ones she would replace with the real prescription. She walked to the hospital pharmacy to get the prescription filled.

On her way back down the hall with the white bag containing the prescription inside, she ducked into an empty exam room. She dumped the real antibiotics down the sink and replaced them with the counterfeits. She took the empty vial and the burner cell phone into her pocket and placed them in a brown paper bag. She walked over to the hazardous medical waste bin, placed the bag in it, and closed the lid. It was filled with bloody bandages and empty syringes. No one would be going through that trash.

All she had to do now was hand the nurse the bag and go find her next patient. Destiny felt sick to her stomach. She now deeply regretted her decision to get involved, to agree to be an accomplice to murder. She had been so swept up in the idea of rectifying the wrongs caused to her people that she didn't understand what it would feel like to be responsible for taking the life of another human being. Perhaps he wouldn't take the medicine. Many people threw it away when they got home. Maybe it would just make him sick and he wouldn't die. There were still many uncertainties that could play out.

Destiny knew she couldn't be a part of this anymore, but she had nowhere to turn. Her parents would be mortified, her colleagues would turn her into the police. Most of her closest friends were doctors. Anyone from her tribe might be connected to the cause. She had to find a way out.

She had no one she could talk to about this except her brother. While they didn't talk to each other that often and only saw one another on holidays or special occasions, he was still her twin. They had a deep connection and complete trust in one another. She felt an illness coming on. That's what she was going to tell the head of the ER department. She needed to go home early and would need the next day off as well. There were substitutes available who got paid for occasions such as this. She had never taken a sick day, so no one would suspect she was faking because she was in a state of panic.

*****

When she finally got to her apartment at midnight, two hours earlier than her shift officially ended, Destiny wanted to call her brother immediately. She figured Justice wouldn't appreciate being woken up; he was a dad, after all. He had to wake up early and help take care of three kids. Destiny liked having her life to herself, with no one relying on her for anything. But in times like this, when she needed someone to talk to, she realized the downside of living alone.

Opening a bottle of red wine, grown in the Cape Town vineyards, she breathed in the sweet aroma wafting from the bottle after she popped the cork and poured herself a hefty glass. She threw the cork in the rubbish bin. She knew there wouldn't be any wine left to cork with the way she was feeling. The further removed from the situation, the easier it was to breathe. She could convince herself that if she hadn't performed the task, someone else would have. She was a cog in the wheel of a machine set in motion. Unfortunately, while she had carefully weighed the pros and cons, she couldn't predict the feelings that would emerge after she carried out her mission.

Death was not a big deal. She watched people die daily in the emergency room. She admitted that there were times when she and other doctors didn't try as hard to save a life: a repeat drug overdose offender, a murderer with a gunshot wound responsible for the deaths of others - situations where humanity would be better off without those people taking up valuable hospital space. They did do what was required; they just didn't go above and beyond.

She remembered one incident during her first year in the ER. A four-hundred-pound man with diabetes and a bad heart was in the ER again. Hc was complaining of chest pains. He came in two or three times a month with the same complaint. He would spend the night in the hospital, get all the tests done, then get sent home the next day.

Every doctor told him the same thing: "Go home and lose some weight. You will feel better." This particular night, no one wanted to deal with him. The nurse put him in a room and laid him down on the bed, assuring him someone would be right with him.

Every time his chart was picked up, the doctor would shuffle it to the bottom of the pile. Four hours after he had been put in the room, the nurse walked in to check on him and found him dead on the floor. He had tried to get up to get help, but he didn't make it. Destiny was the one who pronounced him dead and filled out the paperwork. She remembered thinking that he must be important to someone. Someone would surely grieve when they found out he had passed. However, no one would ever know that he had been neglected.

*****

It was Friday morning. Destiny woke up at 6:00 AM and felt slightly dizzy. She had finished the bottle of wine and fallen into bed exhausted. She didn't even take off her scrubs. She looked at the clock and damned it. She had to give Justice at least until 7:00 before she rocked his world with her story. She got up and took a much-needed long, hot shower.

Precisely at 7:00, she dialed her brother's number. He answered right away, most likely thinking it was an emergency call at that hour from one of his clients.

"Justice. It's me. I need to talk to you about something very important," her words spilled out.

"Take it easy. Are Mom and Dad okay?"

"They're fine. It's me that has the problem. I have something very serious going on in my life right now, and I have no one else to talk to."

"You aren't pregnant, are you? Because if you are...,"

"Shut up and listen. I'm not pregnant. I can't even remember when my last date was. This is more serious than I'm afraid. Can I come over and talk to you? I don't really want to talk about this over the phone."

"Geeze, this does sound serious. I have patients until 4:00. Then, our family is going on vacation this weekend. We are going camping on Table Mountain. Want to come with us?"

"No, Justice, but thank you. Can we meet for lunch? You must take a lunch break."

Justice paused for a moment. "Let me look at my schedule." After a quick glance at his calendar, he decided he could make the time. "Meet me at 12:30 at the café in town. You know the one. Don't be late."

He hung up. Destiny knew the café he meant. They always had lunch there after their Saturday morning horseback riding lessons when they were kids.

Destiny spent the rest of the morning pacing nervously around her apartment. She rehearsed exactly what she was going to say to her brother. First, she had to fill him in on all the details of what had happened to the Herero tribe. If Destiny hadn't known about it, Justice certainly would be clueless. She had to get him to feel empathy for the tribe before she filled him with the other details. She was coating the pill with honey, trying to make it a bit easier to swallow.

Leaving earlier than she needed to, Destiny drove out of Cape Town. It would take 40 minutes to reach the Foodbarn Deli in Noordhoek. She arrived half an hour before their meeting time so she could be sure to get a seat outside, out of earshot of any other customers. They had a "barefoot" outdoor patio where they loved to eat as kids.

When Destiny entered the Foodbarn, the tantalizing aroma of fresh bread and coffee suffused the air. She took a deep breath and was transported back in time. She could picture her and her brother in their britches and boots, filthy from their lesson, running into the deli, ravenous.

An attractive young waitress greeted her. Destiny explained she was waiting for her brother and would love to sit outside on the patio. The friendly teenager guided Destiny outside. "Could I have that table at the end, please?" she asked, pointing to the lone table on the far side of the patio.

"Sure," the perky waitress responded with a beaming smile. "Go ahead and have a seat, and I'll bring you some water and a menu while you wait for your brother." Destiny sent a text to her brother, "I'm waiting for you at the end table on the patio."

Some things never changed. When she saw her brother, she was quite sure that when she hugged him, he would be carrying the scent of a horse on his hands and clothing. When he wasn't working on horses as a veterinarian, he was out playing on his own horses. He was an avid collector of a breed of South African horse known as Boerperd, commonly known as the Cape Farm Horse. The Boerperd is the oldest and most distinctive of all the South African breeds, and Justice was one of their biggest advocates.

The very first of their ancestors came over from Indonesia. They were a cross between Arabs and Barbs. Over time, more Arabs were bred into them to improve their quality. The breed became known as the Cape Horse, with a distinctively soft, thick, curly mane.

Over the years, the Boerperd was crossed with Thoroughbreds to further improve the breed. The qualities that emerged were hardy horses that could survive on small portions of food and were very comfortable to ride. These horses were known for their endurance and strong spirit as well as their kind and gentle hearts. In Justice's opinion, there was not a more beautiful horse on the planet.

Like most species, the Boerperd had its battles for survival. During the Anglo-Boer War, a huge number of Boerperds were killed. Some breeders used Thoroughbreds, Clydesdales, and Hackneys to replenish their herds. Other traditionalists took their time and only used purebreds to re-propagate the breed. Six different lines of Boerperd emerged from the results of the Anglo-Boer War. In 1948, the Boerperd Breeders Society was formed to resurrect the original breed.

By the 1970s, breeders had banded together to continually improve the breed, while traditionalists fought to preserve the existing breed. In the 1980s, two distinct groups formed. The SA Boerperd was established to protect the original and purebred Boerperd. The Kaapse Boerperd group continued to refine the breed, but they were not allowed to take away any of the original qualities. Justice was on the board of the SA Boerperd group and was known throughout South Africa as one of the leading experts on Boerperds and a staunch supporter of the original bloodlines.

Destiny found it unusual that Justice was going camping with his family on Table Mountain. Most weekends, he was off at a polocrosse event. When she and Justin achieved proficiency in their riding lessons, their parents decided to let them branch out and choose other activities. Destiny joined a soccer club and ran track and field, but Justice was only interested in horses.

Their parents finally broke down and let Justice start playing polocrosse. They leased a horse for him to call his own, a concession to buying one for him. Justin immersed himself in the world of polocrosse. He had exceptional talent and soon became an asset for local polocrosse teams that needed a young rider to be a ringer in tournaments. He earned respect within the equestrian community for his skill as a polocrosse player as well as for being an excellent horseman.

The first horse he bought for himself was a Boerperd. Since then, he wouldn't consider owning any other breed. While he treated all breeds of horses as an equine vet, his farm only contained purebred Boerperds, all of which were trained for polocrosse. Justice had risen through the ranks in South Africa and had earned a position on the South African Polocrosse team competing in the upcoming Polocrosse World Championships. He spent most weekends at tournaments with his teammates.

Just as Destiny was lost in thought about Justice and his quest for a world championship, a stinky hand landed on her shoulder. She was startled but did not need to turn around to see who it was. The musky scent of horses told her all she needed to know.

*****

After a long hug and feeling their strong connection, Justice and Destiny took a seat at the outdoor table on the patio where they had spent many Saturday lunches as children. The only thing missing was their father.

The twins caught up briefly on what was going on in their lives. The waitress interrupted their conversation to take their order. They ordered the same thing. The Foodbarn had its own bakery. Their croissants were buttery, soft, and flaky and made the most excellent BLT sandwiches. They both loved them as kids and ordered them now, not only for old times' sake but because they were mouth-wateringly delicious. They agreed to share a basket of chips and got iced tea, as Justice had to go back to work.

"It's time to tell me why we're here," Justice announced. "Obviously, this is important, so spill the beans."

Destiny didn't know where to begin. "Did you know the Herero tribe suffered from a genocide in the early 1900s?"

"Yes," Justice answered, much to Destiny's surprise. "I never knew about that. Mom said nothing to us growing up."

"I took a course on South African culture in college. I had to fulfill my electives. It covered the annihilation of the Herero tribe. What about it? That can't possibly be what you need to talk to me about. If it is, I'm going to label you as the biggest drama queen ever," he said with a laugh.

"It's not funny, Justice. I just learned about it when I went back to the Herero tribal festival. Isra pulled me aside and asked me to help out with something having to do with the tribe getting restitution."

"Oh God, this can't be good. I'm not a fan of that upstart Isra. He spells trouble, if you ask me," Justice said, suddenly serious and very concerned. "What did you agree to do, Destiny? I hope you didn't agree to anything stupid, anything that would be breaking the law. You are a doctor now. You can't afford to put your career in jeopardy."

The food arrived. The conversation was interrupted. The waitress placed their food down and asked if they needed anything. They both said, "No, thank you." She noticed the serious looks on their faces and replied, "Enjoy your lunch; I will leave you two alone. Just give me a wave if you need anything."

Destiny had lost her appetite at this point. She took a bite of her warm croissant filled with crispy bacon and red, ripe tomatoes. The sandwich had no taste to her, so she put it back on her plate and turned to her brother.

The time had come to tell him everything. She probably had a half hour before he needed to leave, so she condensed the story and briefed him on the basics. He didn't take it well.

"How in the hell could you have agreed to that!" he yelled at her. She immediately shushed him and told him to lower his voice.

"Look, I made a mistake. I don't know how to fix this. I came here for your help, not for you to condemn me. I have nowhere else to turn!" she replied, trying to keep her voice low, close to tears now.

"I have no idea how we are going to get you out of this situation. You know you can't ever be a part of this again. We can only pray that this man doesn't die. That's your only hope. Wait a second..." Justice paused, suddenly having an epiphany. "I know exactly what you are going to do. You are going to call the hospital and tell them you want to check up on your patient. You're going to get that man's number and call him. Tell him not to take that medication. Explain that there have been some bad batches of medicine and he shouldn't take any chances. Tell him to throw out the rest of the pills and go to the hospital for new ones."

"I would have to call in a new prescription for him. I hope that doesn't raise any suspicions at the hospital. And what happens when he doesn't get sick and die?"

"All I can tell you is what is going to happen if he gets sick and dies. You are going to be a murderer. That's not who you are. This is your way out of this, Destiny. Make the call. Now."

Destiny's hands were shaking as she made the call to the desk in the ER. She asked the nurse at the desk to give her Christoph's phone number. She said she just wanted to call and check on her patient. Her agitation grew worse when she dialed Christoph's number. He answered. Sure enough, he was feeling sick. He thought maybe he was coming down with the flu. Destiny breathed a sigh of relief that he wasn't a lot worse.

She instructed Christoph to stop the medication immediately. Destiny advised him to drink lots of water, and if the wound didn't seem to show any signs of infection, to not worry about taking the medication. She warned he could be having an allergic reaction to the antibiotics and to just keep an eye on things. Lastly, she instructed him to call her personally if he didn't feel better in a couple of days.

Christoph was appreciative of Destiny's call and thanked her for caring enough to call and check on him. What he didn't know was that she had just saved his life.

Hopeful for the first time that things might be able to be turned around, Destiny was about to thank her brother when his cell phone rang. He answered and was upset, again.

"What do you mean you can't take care of my farm this weekend? We have planned this trip with my kids for months. I can't let them down. I'm gone almost every weekend and booked solid for the next few months with games. Who else am I going to get on this short notice to take care of my horses? Wait... never mind. Go take care of your mother. It turns out I do know someone, someone who owes me big and is capable of taking care of the horses for the weekend," Justin said with a smile, turning to look at his sister.

*****

Destiny resisted with all her might, but Justice had her in a bind. He had just saved her ass, and he was asking for payback. True, she wasn't out of the woods yet. But Justice promised they would figure things out together as soon as he got back.

The plan was for her to drive back to her apartment and pack for the weekend. Justice would finish his calls and meet her at his farm at 5:00 PM. The wife and kids would be packed in the truck with the camping gear. He would give her the written instructions for the horses.

Everything was prepared for his regular farm sitter. All she had to do was feed twice a day, turn the horses out during the day, and clean a few stalls. It was the least she could do.

Fortunately, Destiny was not scheduled to work that weekend. She didn't have to request any more time off after leaving early and taking a sick day. She still had to worry about what would happen if Christoph didn't fall ill and die. At least she wouldn't be at her apartment, so that would buy her a little time to figure things out.

*****

Five o'clock on the dot, Destiny arrived at her brother's house. As promised, the family was in the car, all packed and ready for their camping trip. Of course, they all jumped out when she arrived. Justice's wife, Alicia, hugged her as the three kids grabbed her around the waist and thighs, bubbling with excitement at seeing their aunt, their father's twin.

"We keep hoping you come to visit with the news that you are getting married and are going to have some cousins for these kids," Alicia joked.

"Sorry, no news on that front. But I promise to take good care of your farm while you're away. I hope you all have a wonderful weekend camping. Be safe. I can hear all about your trip when you get back, and we can catch up on everything."

"Thanks, sis," Justice replied. "That would be great. Stay out of trouble till then, will ya? We will be back first thing Sunday morning."

"Can't make any promises, but I will certainly try," Destiny said, half kidding. A gnawing feeling in the pit of her stomach warned her that she wasn't out of the woods yet.

Destiny waved, the truck kicking up dust as it drove down the driveway. She was envious of her brother. He had the ideal life: a wife, kids, a career, and the opportunity to do what he loved the most. She sighed and took a deep breath as she headed off to the stable with the printed directions in hand. She would pin them to the corkboard in the feed room and take stock of what her routine would be for the next two days. She didn't even like horses, and here she was spending the weekend taking care of them when her life was in complete chaos. The only silver lining was that at least Christoph was still alive. Justice had saved her from being an accomplice to murder. She had to be thankful for that.

Falling into a distantly familiar routine, Destiny led the six horses into their stalls. She had their feed portions already in the buckets. The list of supplements her brother fed the horses was impressive. Each horse had a specific formula based on its age and level of training. They got more supplements than most people she knew. However, his horses' coats were sleek and shiny. They had incredible muscle tone and were obviously in top shape.

When the last stall door was closed, Destiny sat against the wall in the barn aisle, her head in her hands, mentally exhausted. As the horses finished slurping the last bit of oats from the bottom of their buckets, they began munching hay. The quiet sound of chewing had a calming effect. The aroma of fresh pine shavings, mingling with the sweet smell of the hay, was an elixir that calmed her frazzled nerves. She had to admit that there weren't many experiences as tranquil and rewarding as a barn full of content horses. It seemed strange to her that being in proximity to them had a calming effect.

Her day was almost done. Still on the list of chores was collecting the eggs from the chicken coop and shutting the chickens inside, as just about every wild animal loved to eat chickens. She would have to be up early on Saturday morning to feed the horses their breakfast, lead them outside and into their paddocks, and then clean the stalls.

Destiny poured dry cat food into a bowl. Two barn cats came running up at the sound. They were the resident mouse population controllers. The last animal she had to care for was the beloved family Australian Shepherd, Alfie. Alfie was always busy wandering around the perimeter of the farm. He took his job of protecting the farm and family very seriously.

Alfie knew a softy when he saw one. Destiny knew from previous experiences staying at her brother's house that the moment she hopped into bed, Alfie would be curled up next to her. All the other family members had established that he was not allowed in bed with them. Alfie took advantage of the naivety and kindness of visitors like Destiny and languished in the opportunity to sleep in a human-warmed bed.

When the last rays of light finally disappeared over the horizon, shutting her world down to night mode, Destiny finished the last of the bottle of wine her brother had left out for her. He had quite a collection of South African wines. He was an avid wine collector and had memberships with all the local wineries.

Growing grapes was big business locally. Many of Justice's clients were grape farmers who owned horses. There were over 2,000 farms in South Africa that grew grapes for wine production and over 500 wineries. South Africa ranked seventh in the world for wine production. To those living there, it was a matter of national pride.

After a quick bite to eat, a mac and cheese casserole Alicia had left for her in the well-stocked fridge, Destiny headed off to the guest room in the modest rancher her brother had built for their family. She was exhausted, mentally and physically. As soon as she crawled between the crisp white sheets, out of nowhere, Alfie appeared and turned three times before nestling himself against her body. She groaned but patted him with resignation. It would take an act of God and more energy than she had to win the battle of keeping him out of her bed.

Drifting off into a fitful sleep, Destiny immediately began dreaming. In her dream, she was in the dark corner of a stall using a pitchfork to scoop the manure into the wheelbarrow stationed in the barn aisle. A figure appeared at the entrance of the stall door, dark, silhouetted by the light filtering in from behind.

"Why didn't you do it?" a man's voice asked.

"I did, I did give it to him," she responded, now terrified by the man's presence. "I did what you asked!"

"He's not dead. The medicine would have killed him. You are lying," the voice stated as the man began to slowly close the distance between them. "You should have followed through, Destiny. Now, I can't let you live."

Destiny raised her pitchfork between them defensively. The man continued to close the gap. Suddenly, he kicked the fork out of her hands. A long blade in the man's hand glinted in the dim light. Destiny shrank into the corner of the stall, cowering from the man who walked closer and closer. As quick as a flash of lightning, the man slashed his knife into her side. The pain was intense as the blade pierced her flesh. Destiny screamed.

She sat up, trying to silence the scream escaping her lips in the waking world. Pain radiated from her side, where the phantom knife had struck. Alfie had already launched himself off the bed and turned to watch her with a guarded expression. Destiny put her hand to her side and felt a scratch. She turned on the light next to the bed. There were red streaks of a dog's nails across her side. Apparently, she had startled Alfie with her nightmare, and he had jumped out of bed, using her as a springboard. That pain spurred the attack in her dream. Her sides heaving, Destiny turned and put her feet on the floor, trying to calm her pounding heart and frazzled nerves.

"It's okay, Alfie," she said encouragingly to the scared dog. She patted the bed next to her. "You can come back now. I won't scream anymore, I promise."

Alfie jumped back onto the bed and waited for her to climb back under the covers. As soon as she did, he circled three times and nestled next to her. She embraced the dog's warm, soft body. With silent tears, she cried herself back to sleep.

The Father and Son

"It seems that this human has a passion for helping people and was tempted to cause harm to another human in an attempt to do good," the Son began thoughtfully. "War is justified to fight evil. Ecclesiastes tells us there is a time to love, a time to hate; a time for war, and a time for peace. Man is warned in Proverbs to fight evil: 'Like a muddied spring or a polluted fountain is a righteous man who gives way before the wicked.' David asks for help in Psalms: 'Blessed be the Lord, my rock, who trains my hands for war, and my fingers for battle.'"

"It can be confusing for man to make the distinction between good and evil," the Father replied. "When it is time to fight, and what justifies going to war against other humans. This human has not asked for any guidance for her actions. She has chosen a side based on her emotions. She handed down judgment to a man who is innocent of the crimes of his ancestor."

"She did regret her decision and made restitution for what she has done," the Son countered. "Does this not speak to what is in her heart? Man is known to make mistakes, and as long as he asks for forgiveness and is truly repentant, his sins will be forgiven."

"Is she sorry because she was going to take the life of another human being?" the Father asked. "Or is she regretting her decision to become involved in an ongoing war where she will be taking the lives of many others? Even humans without faith can regret harming others."

"The horse has yet to play out his part," the Son said, shifting the focus. "This story is still unfolding. The ones I have sent for this purpose have yet to make their judgment. A horse can hear a human heartbeat from four feet away. They hear intention. They feel what is in the mind of humans. They are tellers of the self and mirrors to their souls."

*****

The next day flew by quickly. After the morning chores were finished, Destiny took the dog and went for a long walk into the hills behind Justice's farm. She took comfort in the dog scouting the ground around her. He would dash from one scent to the other, checking it out and then returning to keep an eye on Destiny. If she didn't work such long hours and wasn't gone for days at a time, she would surely get herself a canine companion. The two walked for miles on the trails leading up into the hills.

When the two returned, she knew it was time for the horses' supper as they all crowded around the gates waiting to be led into the barn. They had internal alarm clocks and were used to a routine. Yelling at them to calm down as they pawed at the gate, Destiny hurried to carefully measure the food and supplements into their respective buckets.

When all the horses were in their stalls, grain and hay supplied, water buckets cleaned and filled, she collected the eggs, closed in the chickens, and wandered back into the house. It had been a quiet day and a much-needed break from the chaos in her life. She couldn't wait for tomorrow—when Justice would arrive back home and they could brainstorm the best way to eradicate herself from this messy situation.

Just as she opened the fridge to pick food to throw together for dinner, her phone rang. Nervously glancing at the number, she breathed a sigh of relief to see it was her mother calling. "Hi, Mom. What's up?"

Her mom knew she was at Justice's watching the farm for the weekend. Knowing her lack of love for horses, she was probably checking up to see that she was fulfilling her promise to take good care of Justice's treasured herd.

There was a bustle and some arguing before her dad took over the phone. "Where are you?" her dad asked, seemingly out of breath.

"Dad, what's the matter?" Destiny asked, a horrible feeling growing inside her at the sound of her father's distressed voice.

"I asked, where are you?"

"I'm at Justice's house. Why? What on earth is going on, Dad?"

"Three Herero men just showed up at our house. They asked to talk to your mother. Two of them forced me to stay outside. One went into the house and asked your mother a bunch of questions about you."

"Let me speak to Mom, Dad. I need to know what she told them!" Destiny begged, her voice frantic.

Shuffling noises. "Destiny. What did you do? Why were Herero men looking for you? Tell me. What have you done?" she sobbed into the phone.

"Before I say anything else, I need you to listen, Mom. Tell me exactly what the men asked you. Tell me why they said they were there. This is very important, Mom, don't leave out a single detail."

Her mother haltingly recalled the details, still shaken. Three men came to the door. Two men grabbed her father and took him back outside. The man that stayed inside grabbed her by the arm and sat her forcefully down in a kitchen chair. He pulled a chair up backward and sat very close to her face, his face inches from her own.

"He asked where you were, and I told him most likely at the hospital or at your apartment. I told him I hadn't spoken to you in a couple of days. He mentioned that you had a conversation with your cousin Isra and asked if I knew about it. I told him I knew you went to the ceremony, but I didn't have any conversation with you about what happened there."

"Did you say anything about me being at Justice's house?"

"No, Destiny. I knew these men didn't have good motives for finding you. I didn't give them any hint where you were. It isn't going to take much investigating for them to figure out where you are. It's not like you have any social life or go anywhere very often. They are going to figure it out very quickly!"

More shuffling sounds. Her father grabbed the phone from her mother. "Listen, Destiny. I don't know what you are mixed up in, but we need to call the police. I'm calling them. Stay put. They should be there soon."

"NO! DAD! You can't do that... Look, I can't explain everything right now. I need you to trust me and let me work this out. If you call the police, it's going to make things worse."

"What did you get yourself into, Destiny, that you can't go to the police for help?"

It pained Destiny to hear her father so distressed, so worried about her, and not be able to help. "Listen, Dad. You and Mom need to calm down. Justice and I will call you Sunday afternoon when he gets back. He knows what's going on and has agreed to help. The less you and Mom know, the better. I promise this is going to be okay. I'm sorry you were involved, but it's going to be over soon and I will tell you everything. Nothing bad has happened yet. Promise me, Dad, you will just relax until we call you back. Please!"

Her dad asked a few more questions. Her mom piped up in the background with a few more. All Destiny could tell them was not to worry. She would be in touch on Sunday night. She told them she had to go now, and everything was going to be alright. It was the first time in her life she intentionally lied to her parents. She had no idea if anything was going to be okay, ever again.

*****

Darkness settled in, a thick blanket that smothered Destiny. She longed for sunrise and the sound of Justice's truck driving down the lane. There was one long driveway onto the farm, lined on each side by horse pasture fences. There was only one way in and out.

Destiny sat on the front porch. She knew her brother had a few guns in a cabinet in his office. The cabinet was locked, and she had no idea where the key was or any knowledge of how to use the guns if she found the key. She sat with the dog at her feet, a blanket wrapped around her despite the warm air, and a knife in her hand. Her worst fear was someone entering the house and surprising her in bed. She had every intention of sleeping in the chair on the porch until the morning. The dog would alert her if anyone approached the house.

Her car was parked facing down the lane. Destiny thought about leaving the farm and going to a hotel. She abandoned that idea for two reasons. One, the men might not find her at Justice's, so she might as well stay put. Secondly, she wasn't going to leave the horses and the farm with no one to take care of them. She prayed Justice would return before the men tracked her down. She had no doubt he would protect her. She couldn't call Justice; there was no cell service where he was camping.

A low rumbling came from Alfie. He lay facing the driveway, his head inches above his front legs, his fur bristling around his neck. Destiny had to check if she was dreaming or if this was reality. She threw the blanket on the chair and stood, the knife in her hand. Unfortunately, it wasn't a dream. She could hear a car coming down the driveway, no lights on, in the black, moonless night. Her worst fears were coming true.

With a plan of action already in place, Destiny forced Alphie inside the house then bolted for the barn. It was no use getting in the car. It was a single lane, and she would meet whoever was coming down the driveway head-on.

There was only one way off the property without getting caught. Having thought about this scenario in the unlikely event it happened, Destiny had placed a saddle and bridle on a saddle rack in the aisle of the barn. Grabbing them in the dark, she placed the saddle on the first stall door. She rushed into the stall and bridled the horse from memory. The horses in the barn, sensing unusual activity in the dead of night, shuffled and whinnied softly to one another.

The saddle was a bit more difficult. The horse was agitated and kept moving away from her as she tried to get the saddle on his back. She finally got the saddle in place and reached under the horse's belly to grab the girth. The horse stepped quickly away, causing the saddle to fall to the floor of the stall.

"Stop it!" Destiny whispered loudly. "You really need to cooperate, buddy. This is important!"

She picked up the saddle, which she knew was probably very expensive, and tried again. She got the saddle on, then pushed the horse sideways until he was up against the wall. Then, she reached under and grabbed the girth. The horse tried backing up, but Destiny yanked on the reins, which were wrapped around her left arm. "No, you don't, buster. Stand. Stand still," she threatened. The horse stood as she tightened the girth.

Peeking around the corner, she could see the faint outlines of a sedan parked near the house. She was sure she could make out moving figures walking up the front porch. She could hear Alfie barking furiously inside the house.

Destiny opened the stall door and led the horse into the barn aisle. There was a mounting block waiting. She had already adjusted her stirrups during the setup, so all she had to do was tighten the girth. She pulled the stirrup irons down their leather straps and mounted lightly from the block. The horse danced beneath her. She pulled on the reins sharply until he stopped. She took a deep breath and rode him down the barn aisle and out the back entrance of the barn.

During her walk that afternoon, Destiny had scoped out trails that led away from the farm. It was going to be difficult to find them in the pitch black. As soon as the horse was a few feet from the barn, he decided he didn't want to leave the rest of the herd. He halted. Destiny kicked him lightly at first. "Come on, buddy, I need you to help me out here. Please, we need to leave, now."

The horse didn't want to cooperate. The herd instinct was strong. His instinct told him not to leave the safety of the barn and the other horses in the dark of night. Destiny kicked him harder this time. He started backing up. Just then, the barn lights flashed on. The barn was lit up like a beacon. Destiny panicked. She yanked on the reins, pulling the horse to one side to get him unbalanced, then kicked him fiercely, urging him forward. The horse was startled by her intensity and bolted forward. They were just outside the perimeter of light extending from the barn. She cantered off toward the path that was etched in her memory from her walk earlier that day.

*****

Justice's pickup truck rolled down the driveway. Three happy kids tumbled out of the back door. One tired mother and father emerged from the front. Alfie ran up to them, wagging his tail, ecstatic his family was home. Justice ruffled the hair on his head. Alfie smiled back.

Taking a look around, Justice noticed Destiny's car parked facing the drive. There was no sign of her. He thought for sure she would be out to greet them the moment they arrived home. He had done a lot of thinking over the weekend, way more than he wanted to about her situation. He had some semblance of a plan he thought might work.

Alicia came over and put a hand on his shoulder. "Everything okay? You look worried."

"I'm just wondering where my sister is; my twin senses are tingling. Why don't you take the kids to the house? I'm going to go to the barn and check that everything is okay. Destiny is most likely in the kitchen, cooking us up a huge homecoming meal."

"Kids, grab some of the bags on your way back in the house. We have a lot of gear to stow. Camping is not all fun and games, you know. There's going to be a lot of unpacking to do," he warned. Groans came from each of the dirty, exhausted kids. Alicia smiled, kissed him on the cheek, and went to help with unloading the truck.

Justice strolled to the barn. He noticed things were out of place before he even entered. There was an empty saddle rack and mounting block in the middle of the aisle. Destiny would never have gone out riding without permission, nor would she even have the desire. As he got closer, he noticed the horses' heads peering curiously from their stalls. The smell of dirty stalls, the pungent scent of urine, invaded his nostrils. His horses were agitated, nickering softly to one another. One stall door was open, and the horse inside was missing. It was the stall of his prized horse, the polocrosse horse of his dreams, the horse that was going to help him and his team take home the polocrosse world championships.

As Justice's mind raced, taking stock of the clues that surrounded him, shouts came from the house. Justice raced outside. His wife was calling from the porch, motioning for him. He ran to the front porch. Alicia had tears rolling down her face. She held a blanket in one hand and a large carving knife in the other.

"Destiny isn't inside the house. The door was ajar. I found a blanket and this knife on the porch..."

Ivan Novak

Vodnjan, Istrian Peninsula, Croatia
Olive Grower

Ivan was searching for inspiration. He was at a crossroads in his life. It had been a year since his father passed away. To ease his pain, Ivan immersed himself in the family business. He took over the role his father had played for decades. His dreams, however, lay in an opposite direction.

On the first anniversary of his father's death, Ivan sat at the base of the oldest olive tree in Croatia. Ivan figured that if there was any place to connect with his father's spirit, it would be at the base of this tree. His father had lived and breathed olives.

In 1962, experts claimed the tree was older than Jesus. They dated it at over 2,500 years old. Government protection was placed on the tree, and a fence was built around it. It became a little-known side trip for those fascinated by the history of olive growing in Croatia. As he sat on the earth, his back against the massive trunk, Ivan willed the tree to reveal the truths it must have entwined within its roots, deep beneath the earth. Anything that had survived for over 2,500 years had to be wise.

Ivan shook his head and smiled. He thought about the American couple that had taken a tour and visited his tasting room. They were from California and were traveling through Italy and Croatia - self-proclaimed olive experts. They bragged about the olive trees in Napa that dated back to the 1800s and how Napa had some of the finest oil in the United States. What they considered old was just a speck on the timeline of recent history.

Picking a blade of grass, Ivan bit down on it and closed his eyes, letting the tree support him physically and emotionally. There was something ethereal, grounding, about its presence. What had this tree seen throughout its life? Had Jesus or one of his disciples picked a branch from this tree? It was mind-boggling to think anything could have survived for thousands of years and still be living, breathing, growing.

The question, the dilemma Ivan was facing had to do with his own roots, his family tree. He was trying to get an answer in some form or another. Did he have to follow the path of his ancestors, or could he veer from that route? While his father was alive, there was no talk of Ivan being anything other than an olive grower. Secretly, Ivan had other ideas of what he wanted to do with his life. It had nothing to do with olives.

With his father gone, this was his chance to follow his own dreams. He just needed to know if breaking the family tradition would set the universe spiraling out of control. Would his father roll over in his grave and return to haunt him? Ivan's soul ached.

"Papa," Ivan spoke into the quiet silence beneath the massive tree, "is it okay for me to leave? I was born a different man than you, than your father, and all generations of olive growers before me. I have a different calling, Papa. I know you can feel that now. You are part of this tree, the earth beneath me. Nothing lasts forever, Papa. I want to follow my own path, go in a new direction, but I need to know you are okay with this." Ivan bowed his head, his eyes still closed.

Out of nowhere, the wind suddenly picked up. A strong gust blew through the branches, shaking them with vigor. Ivan opened his eyes in disbelief. He knew this was a sign even before a single unripe olive fell from the ancient branches above and landed next to him. The wind buffeted his hair as he reached down and plucked the olive from the ground. Dust devils swirled around him as he threw his head back and laughed.

"Thank you, Papa; I love you."

*****

It wasn't difficult to find a buyer for his orchard. Besides Istria's history of producing the world's finest olive oil, the rolling green hills, the gentle landscape, and the captivating countryside made it one of the most beautiful and desirable places to live in Croatia.

The Romans began cultivating oil on the Istrian peninsula. Ancient terracotta amphorae on display in the cellar of Pula's Roman amphitheater were testimony to the history of pressing olives for their precious oil. The amphorae were once used to transport and store oil.

While Croatia only represented a drop in the bucket compared to Spain's oil production, no olive oil compared in quality to that produced in Istria. The family-run olive oil makers didn't think of quantity; only quality mattered. Their products were so revered that they referred to their oil as "liquid gold."

Ivan's father had won several international awards for his extra virgin oil. In 2018, out of the 40 Croatian oils at the New York International Olive Oil Competition, 29 were from Istria. His father's oil won best overall.

What made the olive oil from Croatia stand out from the rest was its rich fruity green notes and a pungent, peppery finish that tickled the back of the throat when tasted. His father explained to him when he was a small boy that the peppery finish was a sign that the oil was high in polyphenols. "Poly what?" his curious young self asked.

"Polyphenols are chemical compounds that are very healthy for you. They are antioxidants that keep you healthy and strong," his father said. "We pick our olives earlier than other olive growers, just as soon as they start to turn purple. This means they are filled with polyphenols. Then, we press them within 24 hours of being picked. That's what makes our olive oil the best in the world," his father explained, his eyes sparkling with pride.

Much like a winery, Ivan's father ran a booming olive business. Tourists visited his olive groves and were educated on how the oil was produced. When the tour ended, the visitors filed into the tasting room. The room was cozy, adorned with captivating, handmade furniture constructed from olive wood.

There was a lighted display case with a single wooden spoon carved from a branch of the oldest olive tree in Croatia. Long before the tree was protected by the government, Ivan's father had gathered a fallen branch. The local olive growers knew the history of this tree. They visited the tree to find inner peace and show reverence for their hallowed traditions. He carefully carved several items from that branch, one of them being the spoon in the display. It was worth a fortune.

Not only did the visitors enjoy the tasting experience, they often left not only with bottles of precious olive oil but with items made of olive wood. Many fell in love with the olive wood furniture and carvings after Ivan's father spoke of its biblical importance. The beautiful creamy color was marbled with brown and black streaked spider webbing. Staring at a piece, you could discern the intricacy of the wood. You could feel its history. You had no doubt of the part it played, its importance even as far back as the time of Christ. Cutting boards, small tables, chairs, wooden vases—all made from aged olive wood—were scooped up by the captivated audience.

Ivan put the plan in place for his new life. He had never been comfortable leading tours and talking to strangers, but he was confident now that he had his father's blessing. He breathed a long, pent-up sigh of relief with mixed emotions before making the call to the agent to list the Novak Olive Farm for sale.

The land, the orchard, the sprawling home, and, of course, the equipment and tasting room all went as a package deal.

Within six months of the olive dropping beside him, as he prayed to his father for guidance, Ivan signed the contract for the sale of his home and his business. He had no wife, no children, and a few cousins to whom he would send a portion of his money, but in essence, he was alone in the world. He was just fine with that. The day he left, he took with him only a few items: a duffle bag filled with clothes, a book bag with his favorite sailing books, his laptop, and the sacred wooden spoon.

The Father and Son

"This is going to present a challenge for the equines," the Son observed. "This man has very little history of interacting with people. He is an empty palette, leaving little trace of what he has created over his lifetime. How can a man be judged when he has lived such a sheltered life?"

"For where your treasure is, there your heart will be also," the Father quoted from Matthew 6:21. "This man has obediently followed the passion of his father, and his father before him. He has humbly and dutifully followed the path of his ancestors. Is it right for him to live the remainder of his life serving the passion of those who are now gone, or should he seek his own treasure?"

"It is true his passion is not for olive growing," the Son replied. "However, the life he is now choosing is one of solitude and the unknown. It was not the will of his father. Will he be able to prove his worthiness when he has no interaction with other humans? You said through Jeremiah, 'For I know the plans I have for you, declares the Lord, plans for welfare and not for evil, to give you a future and a hope.' What hope is there for this olive grower's son to have success in this new life, one that he has no experience or knowledge of?"

"Ah, my son, this is true," the Father acknowledged. "However, Corinthians states the importance of faith. This man is taking a leap of faith. 'Now faith is the assurance of things hoped for, the conviction of things not seen.' This man is the epitome of faith, leaving behind the path of wealth for the unknown. He has not been a leader, however, simply a follower. What remains to be seen and to be judged is what his character is when faced with adversity, for surely there will be adversity on this new path he has chosen. Does he love and respect the gifts of the Earth, and will this love help save humanity?"

*****

Some of the most vivid childhood memories for Ivan were those rare times when his father brought him to the sea. A friend of his father's taught him how to sail along Croatia's coast. His father loved sailing, but his passion was strictly recreational. As a child, Ivan cherished those outings.

The seeds of love for the ocean and sailing had been planted deep in Ivan's soul. As his father's olive groves gained in popularity and prestige, and he began traveling to olive oil competitions around the world, Ivan's visits to the sea halted. His father no longer had free weekends to bring his son sailing. His thriving business consumed all his waking hours.

Ivan would lie in bed at night and dream of his times with his father on the sailboat. As the boat flew across the water driven by the wind, Ivan would stare in amazement at the water beneath him.

The vast expanse of the ocean was like a beacon. It called him to explore. Ivan would say to his father, "Can we get a sailboat, Papa? I want to be a sailor when I grow up!"

"No, son, sailing is not our life. Yes, it's fun and a great hobby, but you come from a legacy of olive growers. Sailing is something you can do one day after you retire. Your job will be to grow olives and make the best olive oil in the world."

On the day his father died, as he looked upon his worn and wrinkled face, lying still and pallid in the coffin, he thought to himself, "You never retired, Papa. You worked hard until the day you died."

*****

At the age of 16, Ivan began learning in secret about his sailing obsession. Driver's licenses are not issued in Croatia until 18. He had obtained a license with a special permit for driving his father's truck for the olive farm. Ivan was confined to a 50-kilometer radius, but it was all he needed was to get into town.

Having his father's truck at his disposal allowed Ivan the freedom to visit the town and the local library, where he began checking out books. His goal was to learn everything there was to know about sailing. Ivan would take a trip into town for supplies and return with a book bag full of sailing books. This was a well-kept secret, as he knew his father wouldn't approve.

By the time he was in his 20s, Ivan had read every classic sailing novel as well as every modern-day nautical manual from such sailing greats as Joshua Slocum, Jimmy Cornell, and Bernard Moitessier. *The Old Man and the Sea* and *Kon-Tiki* were two of his favorite classics. He read them so many times he could recite entire sections from memory. Through books, Ivan lived the first passages of the Vikings as they discovered new continents. He viscerally felt every struggle and every joy of the modern-day single-handers who bravely circumnavigated the planet.

It was the books on solo sailing around the world that stole his heart and fed his fantasies. *Dove, The Long Way,* and *Sailing Alone* were the fodder that fueled his dreams, the dreams he had to keep hidden and deeply buried from the members of his family. Now there was no one left from whom he had to hide his true passion.

His mother had been the first to pass. As an only child, that left him and his father to carry on the family business. Ivan often wished his father had given him brothers and sisters so the burden of the olive-growing tradition would not fall solely on his shoulders. However, when his mother almost died giving birth to him, all chances of her bearing more children were erased.

Completely devastated by the premature death of his mother in her fifties, his father immersed himself even further into his business. It was then he collected a large branch that had fallen from the ancient olive tree during a storm and carved the wooden spoon. It was the beginning of his new craft—creating things from olive wood. Ivan knew it was his father's way of giving life to things that had passed, as he wished he could have done for his wife, having left the earth before he was ready to be without her.

The time had finally arrived for Ivan to live his dreams. He hopped into the rusty truck and threw his duffle bag and backpack on the bench seat next to him. The door closed with a squealing groan. It was the same truck he had driven as a 16-year-old. Ivan carefully preserved the truck over the years as a matter of sentiment. It would be the last item to sell before he boarded his boat. He started the truck, which wheezed and protested, then drove down the driveway of the Novak olive legacy without looking back.

As he pulled out of the driveway of his family home for the last time, he was sweating profusely and felt slightly sick to his stomach. What had been done couldn't be undone. He had given up everything he knew, ended the family legacy, and was abandoning the dreams generations of his ancestors had so carefully built. Did this make him a bad person? Was he condemning himself to hell? Was it even possible for a person who had never learned to sail, at 51 years old, to solo circumnavigate the globe?

*****

To distract himself from the growing anxiety of leaving his former life behind, Ivan focused on the plan he had been preparing since he was a teenager. He started a journal when he was 18. In that journal, he charted out his plan for sailing around the world. He listed every detail, every fact, and every piece of knowledge he gleaned from his avid reading of sailors past and present. He was arguably one of the leading sailing experts on the planet who had never owned or captained a sailboat.

Through the books he read, Ivan sailed on ocean-crossing passages, struggled through violent storms, and sweated through weeks of being becalmed in the Horse Latitudes. He knew how to fix and maintain a marine diesel engine. He knew the intricacies of operating a water maker. He could name every line, halyard, and fitting on the deck of a boat, and he knew the purpose and function of each one. Studying the greatest sailors, Ivan understood the tactics of storm sailing and how to heave to when the wind and waves became overwhelming. He knew the most important mantra for sailors: have a spare part for everything. It wasn't a matter of "if" something was going to break; it was "when."

Ivan had even gone so far as to subscribe to weather routing services for mariners. He would listen for hours to the recommendations for sailing through the Adriatic and other parts of the Mediterranean. He would listen in on the questions asked by sailors on the HAM radio he installed in his bedroom. Having also taken online courses in meteorology, which he told his father was to further his knowledge of the weather to help plan for irrigation needs for the olive trees, Ivan could often answer the questions posed by inexperienced sailors who were out there sailing but didn't have a clue about weather patterns.

From provisioning to boat care, tides, currents, and Trade Wind routes, Ivan was a sponge. He absorbed information and tied together the bits and pieces that seemed important to both legends and modern-day sailors. He developed a plan of action to embark on the journey of his dreams. He was anxious to begin checking the items on the list he had developed and refined for the last three decades.

1. Choose a marina.

Ivan's choice of marinas to move into and call home changed over the last 30 years. At first, he thought about the marina closest to where he had visited the sea as a child. He loved that stretch of the coast of Croatia.

As Ivan's knowledge of sailing filled in, he realized it would be best to have certain geographical features around the marina where he would learn to sail. Within the last few years, a brand new, state-of-the-art marina had been built on the southern coast of the Bay of Kaštela, the Kaštela Marina.

Kaštela Bay was protected by Hozjak Hill to the north, the Marjan peninsula to the southeast, and Čiovo to the southwest. This incredible geographical location provided protection even in the worst weather, so the sailing practice could commence without impediments, yet it provided access to the Adriatic, the gateway to the Mediterranean Sea.

As Ivan got his feet wet and was ready to venture out on his own, he could use the islands around the marina and the neighboring Dalmatian Islands to make short ventures to practice navigation and hone his skills.

The marina even had apartments for rent. Ivan had already sent in his deposit and secured an apartment with a six-month lease. It was ambitious to think he could find his boat, learn to sail, and be ocean-bound in six short months.

For a complete novice, this would be unthinkable. For someone who had studied everything there was to know about sailing, Ivan felt this was doable.

The final reason Ivan chose the Kastela Marina was that it was close to an airport. It also offered bus and ferry connections to every European country. This was a necessity for the next step on his list.

2. Purchase a Contessa 32.

The moment he finished *Cape Horn to Starboard* by John Kretschmer, Ivan knew he had found the boat he wanted to single hand around the world.

This epic adventure involved John and one or two other crewmates trying to break the world record for the smallest American yacht sailing a 14,000-mile historic passage. The route would follow the track of the clipper ships that sailed from New York and around Cape Horn to San Francisco in the 19th century. Sailing the "wrong way," the clipper ships' average time to complete the voyage was 120 days. Gigi was the smallest American sailing vessel to complete this voyage in 161 days.

Gigi, a Contessa 32, was built in Britain by Jeremy Rodgers as a fast, sleek, and ocean-safe boat. What sealed the deal on Ivan's decision was the disastrous 1979 Fastnet Race off the coast of Ireland, a classic and prestigious race established in 1925 and still held annually. During the race in 1979, a horrible, unpredictable storm hit in which 15 sailors lost their lives. All 14 Contessa 32s in the race survived the storm. The boat was built to roll and turn back upright.

Upon researching the boat, Ivan found that Contessa 32 owners often mentioned the forgiving nature of the boat, the responsive helm, and excellent windward performance. They touted the Contessa as having a sea kindly motion. According to John Kretschmer, she was a "wet" boat affectionately known as "a submarine with sails."

Ivan needed a boat that was kind, forgiving, and one that would save his ass when things got rough. The Contessa 32 fit that bill.

3. Enroll in sailing school.

Once again, the Kastela Marina had exactly what Ivan required: a sailing school with highly reputable instructors. Ivan had enough of a bankroll that he could enroll in the sailing school while taking weekly private lessons.

He planned to begin on whatever boats were available in the marina for lessons. Once he found and purchased his Contessa 32, he would begin his private lessons on her. If he found and purchased his boat within three months, that would give him three months of intense sailing time before he began his trade route voyage.

Ivan felt this was not only doable but reasonable. He had read about a man named Dan Stroud, who had never previously sailed, and who on May 24, 2020, completed a two-year, nine-month circumnavigation. Dan only sailed for one year before his circumnavigation and had not been reading and researching sailing for 30 years. Ivan felt it reasonable to cut his hands-on sailing time in half.

4. Complete a non-stop trial sail from Kaštela Bay around Sardinia and Croatia and back.

Studying Dan Stroud's plan, who circled the UK for his trial run, Ivan would sail around the boot of Italy and the islands of Sardinia and Corsica and back, a distance of 2,500 nautical miles. He would gain some experience with overnight passages and hopefully complete the non-stop journey in three weeks. The longest passage he would have circumnavigating would be at least four weeks without landfall as he crossed the Pacific from Panama to Fiji.

A few hours after leaving his driveway, Ivan pulled into the apartments at Marina Kastela. He parked in a space by the office. The truck hissed and wheezed a bit as he turned the ignition key, like a tired old man after a long, hot walk. Ivan sat still and took in the enormity of his arrival at this place, at this time. This truly was the moment he realized that he was about to live his dream. It was the first day of the rest of his life.

*****

Settling into his new apartment was easy. It was furnished. All he had to unpack was a duffle bag full of clothes and his books. He had looked up the closest grocery store, and it was conveniently located only a mile away. His stomach was growling, but he was too excited to think about grocery shopping.

Ivan opened his laptop and pulled up the search he had done for Contessa 32s for sale. Currently, there were a dozen in the UK and three for sale in the United States. He was hoping to buy his boat in the UK. He would be able to put it on a trailer and have it shipped directly to his marina.

Sketching out a plan, Ivan narrowed down his choices to six Contessas that were outfitted for cruising and built in the last ten years. He lined them up in order of his top pick first; the other five were listed next. If fate had a hand in this venture, he wouldn't need to see the other four. He sent a quick email off to the broker asking for an appointment in the next two days. He felt good about this boat, "Aldea." Her description covered every item he desired for his boat.

"A rare opportunity to acquire a nearly new Contessa 32 in excellent condition. Aldea was first launched in late 2016 and since then has been lightly used and professionally maintained. Her owner has just completed a further refurbishment at the Jeremy Rogers yard in Lymington, including new sails and new electronics, where she now lies ready for viewing."

It was a 20-hour drive by car to see Aldea. Ivan was not sure his old truck was up for that trip; not only that, he was much too impatient to wait. He performed a quick search for airline tickets. Sure enough, there was a morning flight he could catch to Bournemouth. The airport was only 12 miles from the marina. He could find a hotel and be ready for his appointment to see the boat the following day. He just needed the boat broker to respond to his email before he booked the ticket.

He couldn't stand the wait. Ivan picked up his cell phone and called the agent directly. He was on the fast track to boat buying and sailing. He was like a boulder tumbling down a mountain, gaining momentum, and nothing was going to stand in his way. Five minutes later, the appointment was confirmed. Ivan had a huge smile on his face as he booked his plane ticket and hotel. He couldn't believe how perfectly everything was falling into place. He looked toward the heavens with a tear of joy in his eye and gave a nod to his papa.

*****

Planning, determination, execution—those were the three qualities that facilitated the perfect transition from life as an olive farmer to a competent sailor. Ivan's list had been followed precisely. He was able to buy Aldea, ship her to the marina, and learn to sail her in six months. His dream had officially launched, and the hours ticked away until he cast off the dock lines and began his circumnavigation.

Ivan took to sailing, as Algernon Charles Swinburne might say, as fast as the gin's grip on a wayfarer. He kept the stories from his books playing in his mind like a movie. As he grasped the helm and adjusted the sails, the spirits of authors past and present guided his movements. He had memorized the descriptions of the actions so well that it was as if he were a character in a movie made from books. The motions were innate and instinctive, and his brilliance in such a short time blew away his seasoned instructors.

The biggest challenge had been gathering the necessary equipment, both the technology and hardware for crossing oceans. While the boat was updated and outfitted, Ivan had to buy a generator to produce electricity to keep the batteries charged. He had a wind vane and solar panels installed. The boat came with an autopilot, but he also had a self-steering vane installed. This was an energy-free option for self-steering as a backup, even if all power failed.

The last task before departure had been provisioning. Since he was on a 32-ft. boat by himself, he had an easy time buying canned and packaged foods that would last him months, if not an entire year. He would buy fresh food at each port he visited and eat fresh when he could. For the long passages or extended time between ports with grocery stores, he was well-prepared.

As for water, he could carry 30 gallons in his water tank, and he could make water at four gallons an hour from seawater with his water maker. Along with his granola bars, bags of rice, beans, dried meals, wine, beer, and a few bottles of vodka, Ivan purchased 15 jars of olives from his family's former vineyard and had them shipped to the marina. Along with his wooden spoon, it was the only evidence of his former life as an olive grower.

There was quite a hub of excitement at the marina for Ivan's departure. He had become a local celebrity; "Olive Grower Turned Sailor" was the talk of the Bay of Kaštela. Ivan had not welcomed the attention. His instructors and the sailing school had broadcast his accomplishments, so pleased that he had chosen them as the link he needed to complete the chain of his journey.

Even the weather cooperated the morning of Ivan's departure. He purposefully didn't reveal the day and time of his departure, despite the prodding of the marina and media to be there when he cast off the lines. He had avoided answering reporters' questions like, "Aren't you going to be lonely sailing by yourself?" "Why don't you have a shipmate?" "What made you leave one of the most successful olive farms in Croatia to sail around the world?"

Ivan couldn't explain his obsession. He couldn't say why he never bonded with other people. He had no attraction to females or males, for that matter. He was simply happy in his own skin, being alone, pursuing his dreams that were spurred as a young child sailing on the ocean with his father.

*****

Before the sun even hinted at peeking above the horizon, Ivan climbed out of his bunk, closed all the hatches, turned on the switches for his electronics, and started Aldea's engine. He cast off the dock lines and quietly motored away from his slip. Once out of the harbor, he turned into the wind. He pulled out the mainsail and chose both his jenny and staysail to accompany her. A steady 14 knots were blowing as he turned 90 degrees to the wind for the perfect beam reach.

With a course set on autopilot down the Adriatic to the bottom of the boot of Italy, Ivan took a deep breath and thought about his father. His papa had to be approving right now. Everything he had planned had gone along perfectly. There was only one negative thought nagging at the back of his mind. Sailors normally had someone on land with whom they filed a float plan. A float plan provided a time and destination that, if exceeded, would prompt a call for help.

Since Ivan had no one, he was relying on his EPIRB unit, an Emergency Position Indicating Radio Beacon. The EPIRB could signal a rescue service via satellite if he found himself in distress. He also had a marine radio, which he could use to issue an SOS if anyone was in range, and an AIS signal that could detect the location of his boat.

His most important piece of emergency equipment was his life raft. It inflated upon impact with the water and had enough food and water to sustain him for a week, as well as flares, a med kit, and other emergency supplies. This was far more technology and resources than the sailors of the past had as they crossed oceans. Ivan thought it was all expensive and redundant and that if all went well, they were things he would never need to use.

*****

With each leg of his journey, Ivan's confidence increased. Having successfully navigated out of the Mediterranean, once Ivan passed Gibraltar, he was in his first new ocean, the Atlantic. The coast of Africa loomed portside as he sailed through the Straits of Gibraltar. He would take a quick stop to buy fuel, refill his water tanks, and provision in the Canary Islands.

It was about a 20-day sail from the Canaries to the Virgin Islands, which he departed for in early November. He was eager to make his first passage across an ocean with no land in sight. This was his first major benchmark as a solo sailor. He left slightly earlier than recommended, as the official end of the hurricane season in the Caribbean was November 1st. There was a good chance there would still be strong winds and maybe storms, but hopefully no hurricanes.

Halfway through the 3,100-mile passage, the weather started to deteriorate. Ivan felt the change in the air pressure. The winds whipped the waves into a white-capped frenzy, the waves started to build, and large, bluish-gray clouds appeared like giant bruises on the horizon. Checking his radar, he saw a wave of red closing in on him, signaling nasty weather was coming his way.

Ivan worked quickly to reef his sails. He pulled in his mainsail until it was the size of a bedsheet. He pulled out his staysail, a small and sturdy sail that would keep him moving without being overpowered. The wind increased, as did the size of the waves. Within an hour, the waves were an impressive 18 to 20 feet. The wind gauge vacillated from 35 to 45 knots. Ivan was experiencing his first gale.

The wind sounded like a freight train passing by, the waves towered in front of him, then crashed relentlessly on his bow. Aldea took the hits like a pro. This was what she was built for and when she shone. She dipped down and took the wave hits, popping back up and shaking the water off like a Labrador Retriever. Ivan's heart beat faster, yet he was thrilled with how his boat was performing. He felt exhilaration rather than fear, as he was living and surviving in conditions sailors had been experiencing for thousands of years.

His first sight of an island brought joy to his heart and energy to his soul. He had managed fine in the rough weather; his boat was stable and seaworthy even in rough conditions. He had managed just fine taking short naps during the night and longer periods of sleep during the daylight hours. All his preparation had paid off. He knew in his heart he would make it around the world.

*****

Hours turned into days, days into weeks, weeks into months. Ivan sailed a steady course, spending a week or two at sea, landing in a port, refilling his supplies, sleeping heavily for a few days to energize his internal battery, then moving on. He had never felt more alive or more pleased with life.

Ivan missed his mother and father, but he treasured the experience he was living and the dream he was fulfilling. Sometimes, when the skies were crystal blue, the sea flat, and the wind steady, Ivan would literally pinch himself to make sure he wasn't dreaming.

Since there had been no major boat part breakages or failures up to this point in his voyage, Ivan was meeting his schedule. His latest conquest was successfully navigating through the Panama Canal. The passage was not only expensive but required the purchase of special fenders as well as hired guides to help with the lines. He decided to forego stopping at the Galapagos Islands as the paperwork and logistics were complicated and the fees immense. It would cost him weeks and thousands of dollars to see its beauty. He decided to push on, straight to Fiji. This would be his longest stretch without seeing land, a total of 7,100 miles.

Ivan studied each country before his arrival. He used charts downloaded on his electronic chart plotter and paper charts, as well as the books he brought with him to guide him through each country. He strived to give himself a basic education of each country's history and culture before arrival. There was also a process of knowing where to check in, supplying the proper paperwork and fees, and getting his passport stamped.

Fiji was halfway through Ivan's journey around the world. It was another huge benchmark. Ivan read that Fiji comprises some 540 islets and 300 islands, of which about 100 are inhabited. The main islands are Viti Levu and Vanua Levu. The big islands are mountainous and volcanic in origin, rising abruptly from densely populated coasts to forested central mountains. The smaller islands are also volcanic, and all are ringed by rocky shoals and coral reefs. Ivan plotted his course for Viti Levu.

The Fiji Islands had a fascinating history. The first settlers arrived from Melanesia some 3,500 years ago. The first Europeans to sight the islands were the Dutch in the 17th century. In 1789, Capt. William Bligh spotted them. He returned in 1792 to explore the mystical islands. Traders and the first missionaries arrived in 1835. European settlers began arriving in the 1860s. Goosebumps raised on Ivan's arms when he realized he was retracing the voyage of sailors from the 1700s.

What Ivan didn't read about were the devastating wrecks that littered the surrounding islands. With a lack of advanced knowledge regarding storms, ships bringing cargo and supplies to Fiji found themselves blown onto the dangerous reefs surrounding the smaller, outlying islands. Little did he know he was about to experience the intensity of the storms generated in the Pacific and follow in the rocky wake of his sailing ancestors.

As the weeks progressed, most of the passage was pleasant. The trade winds were strong but steady. The days grew monotonous with no change in weather or scenery. For the first time in his life, Ivan was lonely. It was an unfamiliar feeling, being void of any human contact for such an extended time.

Then, like an ethereal dream, just after daybreak at the beginning of his fourth week of the passage, a large dark object appeared on the horizon, then another, then another. A plume of water shot up into the sky, followed by others, creating the effect of a fountain shooting water intermittently from a city square. Ivan was sailing toward a pod of humpback whales.

He wasn't sure if he should change course or let the whales avoid him. He didn't think they would damage his boat, although he had read Moby Dick at least three times; he knew they had the potential. Quickly, he pulled in his sails and decided to drift for a bit. The pod turned slightly, the large barnacled backs surfacing every so often, expelling air and water with a palpable woosh.

Aldea was drifting gently toward the pod as they approached. Ivan walked to the bow to get a front-row view. Two of the whales seemed to be going toward the starboard side to investigate, while three others picked the port side. Ivan unconsciously clenched the metal rail as he stared out at the massive creatures. They dwarfed his boat. He had no experience dealing with whales and had no idea what to expect. He had seen many dolphins playing in his bow wake, but this was a whole new barrel of olives.

The whales suddenly disappeared in unison. All Ivan could see were the ripples they left behind. No dark shapes loomed beneath the surface. Ivan leaned over and peered into the depths of the sea, which he knew stretched miles beneath him. Nothing stirred. He thought they had gone.

Then, in the blink of an eye, 60 tons and 50 feet of whale exploded from the water inches from his boat. He felt like a toy boat in a bathtub next to the monolith that heaved itself out of the water and into the air. The entire pod had regrouped and was leaping from the water and broaching in unison, spraying water in giant waves toward the tiny boat. Ivan didn't know whether to laugh or cry. He was terrified and mesmerized at the same time.

Drenched with spray, Ivan let out a loud and boisterous laugh. Fear turned into delight as he quickly realized the whales meant no harm; they were simply enjoying life. They broached and sang to one another in eerie and varying tones of bass instruments. Ivan clutched the rail as his boat rocked in the wake of the broaching pod. A few tail slaps and sideways leaps later, all seemed to quiet down.

For the finale, as a gesture of goodwill, one single whale rose gently, nose first, from the sea very close to the boat it dwarfed. He raised his head level with Ivan and rotated slightly to be eye to eye with the human creature. For one brief moment, Ivan was staring into the very soul of the universe. He could sense the intelligence, the kindness, the ancient wisdom of the massive creature floating effortlessly beside him. The whale's eye was the size of Ivan's body. That one moment redefined everything he knew about life. He was not alone in the world or at sea.

The Father and Son

"This man has faced nature, embraced it, and has true love in his heart for the world around him," the Son said. "He left a life of unwilling burden to see the Earth, feel the sea, and embrace its creatures. He is living the words of Galatians: 'It is for freedom that Christ has set us free. Stand firm, then, and do not let yourselves be burdened again by a yoke of slavery.'"

"We can see this in the actions of this man," the Father replied. "He has given up his material possessions to take this journey of faith. Matthew states, 'For where your treasure is, there your heart will be also.' He has found more happiness in the simplicity of living in nature than many rich men will ever find in their abundance of useless possessions."

"The equine will surely see into his heart that he cherishes the Earth and her gifts," the Son continued. "He has stared into the eye of a whale and seen eternity—an experience shared by only a handful of humans."

"Equines are not gods; they are our creations," the Father cautioned. "They do know what is in the hearts of men. However, this man's weakness lies in dealing with others. The final judgment made by the equine will depend on his interaction with that equine. Will the equine see him as good and loving, or will there be confusion due to his lack of ability to connect with these creatures? That is the question that remains to be answered."

*****

Ivan's mood changed from sullen to energetic with the brief visit from the whales. It was the mental push he needed to get him over the mental hump and headed back on course. Hours after the whales departed, the wind began to build. Ivan suspected an unpredicted front was rolling through. Little did he know how strong it would grow.

Three days later, Ivan was exhausted. He had little sleep, not because he was afraid of sleeping at night in the Pacific. There were no other boats to encounter. Aldea rocked and rolled and protested at the barrage of waves. Ivan knew this was what she was built for; the proof was from the Fastnet disaster, but that didn't make the storm any more tolerable. It seemed relentless. It was growing stronger.

Much to his surprise, when Ivan checked his electronic charts, he had progressed many more miles than he thought possible. His boat was averaging 9 to 10 knots. He saw the gauge hit 11.2 rolling down a wave. The wind was gusting into the 50-knot range. As a result, he had covered double the miles he would have traveled at five and six knots.

The worst part for him was not the wind and the waves. He could always heave to if he felt he was in danger. By turning into the wind and back-winding the main on one side and the staysail on the other, the boat would stay pointed into the wind. He would drift off course for a while, but the waves would roll under him gently, and the force of the wind against his boat would be diminished as he drifted in the same direction the wind was blowing.

It was a safe tactic when you had plenty of sea room. However, due to the increase in speed, he was now in the vicinity of the outlying islands of Fiji. Suddenly, and without warning, a giant rogue wave struck the boat broadside. The effect was immediate. Fortunately, Ivan was below when Aldea rolled.

His world turned upside down. Everything that had been secured suddenly took flight as the boat rolled. She paused for a pregnant moment, just long enough for gravity to pull every dislodged object to the ceiling of the upturned boat. Then, as quickly as it upended, the boat popped back upright like a bobbing cork. Ivan's world was not only turned upside down, bouncing around inside the rolling boat, with objects striking him from every direction, but his body took a beating. He felt blood oozing from his forehead. He felt dizzy and struggled not to pass out.

The boat lurched and struggled to find momentum with the wind and the waves again. It lurched and rocked violently but slowly began to sail, which eased the rolling motion. Thankfully, the hatch had been closed when she rolled. Very little seawater added to the chaos below. Ivan grabbed a dish towel in the dark and pressed it to his bleeding forehead. The dim red nightlights that shone through the cabin cast a foreboding light on the interior of the boat, which lay in complete and utter disarray.

Ivan felt he was at a crucial moment. He was scared for the first time during his voyage. He could press his EPIRB, but he knew rescue would be impossible in this wind and waves and in the dark. He could heave to, but he had no idea if he was near any of the small reef-surrounded islands. The next giant wave hit and rolled the boat again. This time he knew what to expect and gripped the handholds with all his might. Shortly after the third wave hit and rolled the boat, he was almost used to the motion but decided it was time to heave to.

Grasping the hatch cover, Ivan slid it aside and bolted up to the helm. He turned off the struggling autopilot and grabbed the wheel. He could see nothing on the dark, inky, torrential rain-filled horizon. Glancing at the wind gauge for the wind direction, Ivan turned the boat into the wind. She rolled violently to one side as she struggled through the oncoming wave. Ivan prayed he would not roll while unsecured in the cockpit. An eruption of flapping sails sounded as the mainsail crossed the threshold of the wind. The boom pounded with force across the boat and then made contact with the wind again after tacking. Meanwhile, the staysail remained stubbornly on the opposite side of the boat, exactly where it needed to be.

The effect was dramatic, like a silent scream. The sound of the wailing wind instantly ceased. Aldea immediately found the status quo with the wind and began a rhythmic dance with the waves, a gentle ebb and flow. Ivan breathed a sigh of relief as his entire world morphed from hell to heaven. It was miraculous, really.

Tired, shaken, and slightly woozy from the bash on his head, Ivan did the only thing he could imagine doing now. He went down below and waded through pots, pans, books, and couch cushions to his bunk. He lay down and instantly fell into a deep sleep.

*****

Horses were first brought to Tonga by Captain Cook on his third voyage to Fiji. They did not survive. Varying accounts of their fate are speculative. Precisely when and by whom the horse was established in Fiji cannot be clearly identified from secondary sources.

Original missionary archives have been studied and have established what seems to be the first mention of a horse, early in 1847, lent to John Thomas by a French trader who had settled in Fiji in 1846. Horses became essential to the missionaries for traveling to their chapels on their circuits. They were eventually adopted by the natives for personal use and agricultural transport. Although little is written about this, they were also used for food.

Had Ivan read about a ship loaded with horses that crashed on Cobia Island, part of the northern island chain of Fiji, he would have understood how he was lying on a beach, drifting in and out of consciousness, staring at an emaciated and dying horse. While there were no human survivors from the ship carrying horses destined for the main islands of Fiji, some of the horses were able to make it to shore and establish a home on the island. It wasn't a healthy herd and had dwindled over the centuries due to inbreeding and lack of nutrition. No humans had discovered their existence until now.

Ivan thought perhaps he was dead and this was the after-life. He was crusted with sand, the sun was shining, he was on solid ground, and there was a hazy outline of an animal in the periphery of his vision. As his foggy vision cleared, his first thought was of Aldea. The previous night came flooding back in segments.

He was dead asleep when his boat contacted the reef off Cobia Island, the same reef the ship carrying horses crashed into in the mid-1800s. Perhaps the wind and waves had been identical, and they too had heaved to, waiting for the storm to abate. Unlike his fellow human predecessors, when Ivan's ship crashed into the reef and began taking on water, he was able to crawl his way onto the deck and deploy his life raft.

Unfortunately, because of the surf pounding on the reef, Ivan was not able to climb into the life raft. His boat was already breaking apart. All he could do was jump into the water beside it and hang on to it for dear life. He clung to it and waited to be washed over the reef. He remembered losing his grip on the life raft as it surged over the reef. That was the last detail he could recall. Everything he owned in the world was now gone. His voyage had ended, and all he had left was his life.

Besides the pain pounding from his head wound, he felt immense thirst. It was a painful burning like he had never felt. He managed to sit up and braced for the throb in his skull he knew would follow. He waited for it to abate. Ivan looked around and saw the shadow of a horse peering at him from behind a coconut tree. It made no sense. Taking stock of his surroundings, he noticed that he was in the dead center of a moon-shaped sandy cove. He would have thought it beautiful if not for the dire circumstances.

First, he shaded his eyes from the bright sunlight and peered down the beach to his right. Nothing caught his attention. Straining his sore neck, he turned and looked to his left. A bright red object immediately came into focus. There was his life raft, washed up on the beach, totally intact. He wept with joy at the prospect of quenching his thirst.

Ivan stumbled down the beach like a drunk man. He reached the enclosed life raft and peered inside. There was his food and water supply, enough for a week, as well as a flashlight, a med kit, a solar blanket, and a fishing line. He dove inside and grabbed the first bottle of water he could reach.

*****

Well before the evening of the first day, the storm had passed. Ivan dragged the life raft up to the tree line. He ate a few bites of food and did his best not to consume too much water. There was a painkiller in his med kit, which he took, as well as the disinfectant and band-aids for the wound on his forehead. His greatest pain was seeing his boat washed up on the reef.

The sails were torn to shreds and she lay on her side. Aldea lay low in the water against the reef. Ivan knew she was filled with water from the gaping wound in her hull. He planned to take the life raft out at dawn the next morning when he had regained some of his strength. Hopefully, the water would be calm and no waves would be washing over the reef. This would allow him to do some salvaging.

Meanwhile, the horse was an ominous presence. On one hand, if a horse had survived here, there must be fresh water. The horse was skin and bones, its ribs protruding from its sides. It was in much worse shape than he. For now, he had to ignore the horse. It was no threat, and there was certainly no way he could offer it any help. Tomorrow was a new day. He had to wait to see what it would bring.

After a fitful night's sleep in his life raft, Ivan woke when the first rays of the sun stretched their fingers over the horizon. He eagerly looked toward the reef. It was as still as a millpond. The water flowed gently over the rocks. It was the calm after the storm. Naked as a jaybird, Ivan dragged the life raft down to the water, empty of all its contents. He had prepared a long thick branch to use as a pole to get out to the reef. He could have swum the raft out, but the pole worked well as the depth of the shallow bay never got over six feet.

A well of emotion flooded over him as he neared his boat. His beautiful boat, his new life, was completely devastated. Clearing the rocks of the reef, Ivan approached the tilted deck of his boat. He could see the water gently lapping inside the cabin. Various objects floated in the water. He had a huge job ahead of him.

Tying the raft to what was left of his boat, Ivan went to work. He climbed the deck and descended into the flooded cabin. He had to salvage whatever he could find. He had no idea if or when he would be rescued from the island. Suddenly, he thought of the EPIRB. He quickly waded over to the bulkhead wall where it had been mounted. A gray veil of grief descended over him as he saw the empty bracket. It was gone. All his electronics were dead. He was on his own.

*****

A month passed on Cobia Island. Ivan had seen the movie Castaway and knew he looked very similar to Tom Hanks at this point. Long hair, shaggy beard, ribs showing, even though Ivan had been able to salvage quite a bit from his boat.

One large compartment on the upside of the boat was still filled with food, most of it undamaged. He cut away the torn sails and brought them back to make a nice tent dwelling inside the palm tree forest. He had learned how to catch fish, cook, and eat the shellfish he collected on the rocks around the reef. He had followed the horse to a freshwater stream. His daily life was focused on survival.

Another boon was that he was able to recover most of his books. They had miraculously remained on the bookshelf, though they were salty and waterlogged. He rinsed them carefully in fresh water, opened their spines, and dried them in the sunshine. Most were still readable. It was his only entertainment.

His relationship with the horse evolved quite a bit. Ivan unraveled a bit of the mystery of the single horse on the island. He found many piles of bones and horse corpses on the island. The edible vegetation for the horses had finally run out. The last horse was barely surviving on new bits of growth here and there. It seemed to be young, even though it looked a hundred years old. It most likely required less food than the adults, which explained why it was still alive.

As Ivan trekked to the stream each day, he noticed the horse followed at a distance. It probably missed contact with other living creatures, as horses are herd animals. It was still very fearful of the human creature that showed up on the island. Ivan noticed that branches of the green vegetation were void at the base of the bushes and trees. They were quite abundant above a certain height. The horses had starved because they could no longer reach the leaves they needed to stay alive.

That gave Ivan an idea. Having rescued the tools from his tool cabinet, he had a pair of shears. They were strong for cutting the metal shrouds in case the mast ever broke. Cutting the shrouds quickly would prevent further damage to the boat, but industrial-sized shears were required. He had saved his massive shears. On his way to the stream, Ivan piled rocks beneath a tree with leaves. He was able to reach the lower branches, clipped them, and let them fall to the ground.

He could see the horse peering from behind the trees, eagerly waiting for Ivan to move away so it could fill its empty belly. Ivan continued to the stream and watched the horse advance until he was a safe distance away. Once he felt safe, the horse began devouring the leaves.

Later that night, Ivan noticed the horse lying on the beach. It was the first time he had seen the horse lying down. The horse seemed to be in pain. He kept glancing back at his side as if it were the source of pain. Ivan immediately felt bad for putting too much food in front of a starving horse. He hoped the horse would be alive in the morning. If he was not, Ivan knew what he had to do with the horse meat. It would be salted to keep himself alive.

*****

Six months passed. Both horse and man survived. The bond between the horse and the man had solidified. They only had each other for company, and they had learned to adapt. It started out slowly, the horse coming closer to each tree Ivan cut the branches from, until one day, the horse was close enough to eat a branch Ivan extended to him.

Eventually, the horse accepted a light touch to the nose. Ivan noticed the horse's ribs no longer showed, and his barrel had begun to round out. His coat seemed less dull, and there was a slight sparkle to what once were dull and pallid eyes. The horse not only learned to accept rubs and hugs from Ivan, but he also became his shadow. Wherever Ivan went, the horse would follow in his footsteps.

The horse's health greatly improved when Ivan began supplementing his diet with coconut meat and even fish. The oil from the coconut and fish helped his coat to shine. Ivan rubbed the horse down with a boat brush until a hint of dapples reflected in the sunlight. Ivan had transformed a bag of bones into a beautiful young stallion. In return, the horse was the first companion, the first real friend Ivan had made during his life. The horse gave him purpose and made him feel loved.

The two fell into a routine of walking and running on the beach together. Every day they visited the stream to drink and bathe. The vegetation had filled back in, so Ivan did not have to cut branches to feed the horse anymore. They coexisted as partners. There was one huge difference between the man and his horse. The island was the horse's home, where he was born, even though its herd was gone. Ivan still planned to leave the island and thought daily about how to make that happen.

Remembering the movie Castaway, Ivan used stones to make a huge SOS on the beach. He thought about trying to make a large raft out of what he had salvaged to float to another island. He could even make a small sail from the remnant sailcloth he had gathered. He had constructed a giant red flag on a long stick so he could run up and down the beach waving it in case he ever spotted a passing boat. He had the proverbial flare fire ready to ignite if he saw a plane passing overhead. He also had one flare.

While he was as prepared as he could be for signaling for help at the first sign of a human, Ivan had been consumed with getting the horse healthy again. It had been his priority. Now, the horse was healthy again, and Ivan had a decision to make. There was safety on the island. He had fire, water, food, and shelter. The question was, was this where he wanted to live out the rest of his days? Was it time to strike out on his own on a raft and try to make it to the main island? To say he was struggling with the idea was an understatement.

He didn't know exactly where this island was located or which direction to strike out in. There were no other islands in sight. He could make a prediction based on the wind direction from the night of the storm and his last known location. He could guess at the general direction he thought the main islands were, but if he was wrong, the results could be disastrous.

Then, one day, the decision was taken out of his hands. He and his horse were playing on the beach. They had made a game where they chased each other, kind of like tag. They were both breathing heavily when "horse" perked his ears up and looked toward the sea. There was a dot on the horizon. As Ivan strained to see what it was, transfixed by the small dot, it seemed to grow a little larger. Soon the outline took the form of a ship, and it was growing closer.

Ivan raced to light the signal fire. The boat was much too far away to see the red flag on the pole. He needed to get the fire hot and smoky. He would use palm branches to fan it and send the smoke up in puffs, hopefully signaling for attention. In minutes, the flames were glowing, the dry fodder crackling, and white smoke began to puff up from the center. His heart was pounding, and he was sweating profusely. He realized he was naked and ran to find some clothes.

As he ran into his hut, which was neatly arranged into a living area, he spotted one lone item on his makeshift table. It was the wooden spoon carved by his father, the most precious retrieval from his mortally wounded vessel. Ivan paused. His father had carved that spoon to give life to something that had died. He carved it in memory of his mother, who had passed away wishing he could have given her life. He picked up the spoon and smiled as the face of the horse pressed inside the tent, curious as to why his friend had left.

At that moment, Ivan realized he had brought this horse back to life. He was responsible for saving this animal. This horse had also saved him. Grabbing shorts and a shirt, Ivan put them on and pushed back out of the tent and past the curious horse. With a heavy heart, he ran to the signal fire with his flare in hand.

The Conclusions

Reginald Dupuis

Paris, France
CEO Omega Drug Company

ALTHOUGH THERE WERE ABRASIONS from the rope tightening around the horse's neck, there was no permanent damage done. The boy patted his horse, hugged him, and opened the stall door. The horse wandered through and back out to his pasture as if nothing eventful had ever happened.

The man and the boy turned without a word and started walking out of the barn. Reginald ran to catch up to them as they walked past the parked car and back toward the house. It was clear they wanted nothing to do with him; they just wanted him to go away. The man and his son were not happy that Reginald had tried to steal their horse and had kicked down the door to their home. Reginald worried they were heading to the house to call the police.

Reginald called after them, trying to explain that he was an important CEO of Omega Drug Company and that his train had broken down not far away. He was simply trying to get transportation to the airport to catch a plane to Paris for the most important meeting of his life. The man and his son didn't even turn to acknowledge he had spoken to them.

Since his explanation wasn't having the desired effect, Reginald resorted to the language he knew would get through to the father. He ran up, tapped the man on his shoulder, and pulled out his money clip. Reginald always traveled with a money clip containing at least 1,000 euros of pocket change. He was willing to part with it to make the nightmare go away and get his ride to the airport.

Reginald looked at his watch. If he could bypass Dijon and get to the airport in 20 minutes, this day could still be salvaged. The man had a car; he had cash. This scenario was possible and a much better deal than having to ride a horse to the main road, hitch a ride to Dijon, then find a ride to the airport. If only the man had been home 30 minutes ago, all the unpleasantness could have been avoided. Reginald rolled his head around in a circle in each direction, a gesture he used to release tension in his neck when things got rough.

"Here's the deal," Reginald explained, striding next to and then stepping in front of the father, fanning through the wad of bills. "If you can get me to the airport in 20 minutes, you can have all my cash."

The man stepped around him, continuing toward the house. Up ahead, the broken door lay askew on the porch, holding on to the house by a single hinge.

"And what about our broken door?" the boy chimed in. "Who's going to fix that?"

"There is over a thousand euros here," Reginald said, almost pleading. "I'm sure this is enough to pay for your time, your gas, and a new door."

No response.

"Look!" Reginald almost screamed, unable to control his temper any longer. "I've now got 18 minutes to get to the damn airport. I will send you $10,000 if you just get in the car and drive me to the airport. You can renovate this entire shithole for ten grand."

The boy and the father paused, then looked at one another. The father spoke. "Excuse me if I don't trust you. You broke down my door and almost killed my horse. After you leave here, there is no guarantee you will ever make good on your deal. I don't want anything to do with you."

The trio arrived at the porch. Reginald bolted up the steps ahead of them and grabbed his duffle bag and briefcase. "What do you want from me? I have nothing I can give you other than this cash."

"What's in the briefcase?" the boy asked with curiosity. "I bet you have a fancy phone. I sure would like a fancy phone," the boy said with a smile.

Dad patted him on the head and ruffled his hair.

Reginald pulled his phone out of his pocket and contemplated it for a second. There was no way he could give up his phone.

"How about a computer? I think I'd like a computer even more than a phone," the boy said with a smile. "Then I could play games like my friends in town!"

"I do have a very nice computer, but you can't have it."

The father crossed his arms and looked at his son. "I guess you have about 16 minutes to decide if a computer and 1,000 Euros are worth a trip to the airport for this 'meeting of your life.'"

"Merde," Reginald muttered under his breath, finally realizing he was feeling panic tiptoeing up to this shitshow. He unzipped his backpack and pulled out his state-of-the-art, very expensive laptop. It was his only bargaining chip at this point. He smiled as he handed it to the man and said, "Take the damn thing. It's yours. But you better get me to the airport in the next 15 minutes."

He handed it to the man with a fake smile, knowing they would never be able to get into the computer without the password. Reginald knew it would take a computer genius to crack his code. He highly doubted if anyone was fitting that description in the town of Dijon. He would simply hire someone to come back to this home and take it back.

The dust swirled around the car as it sped down the dirt tracks of the driveway. The grass and flowers waved wildly in the wake of the car. Reginald had gotten into the front on the passenger side. Dad had nodded to his son to climb in the back. The boy was clutching his new computer; a smile creased his face.

Pushing the limits of the car, they sped down the paved road. Fortunately, the paved road was straight as it ran along a small drainage ditch that kept the road high and dry in the rainy season. Since the valley was low and close to the river, precautions had to be taken for it not to flood. For the first time in hours, Reginald allowed himself to relax. He was going to make it, despite the major hitches. He was desperately looking forward to that shower and his whiskey.

Unfortunately, the brief respite halted abruptly when the father suddenly stopped the car in the middle of the quiet road. Not another car or house was in sight.

"Oh, and one more thing…" the dad announced. "We will need the password to your computer. You can give it to me, or the deal is off. I will give you back the computer, and you can get out." Looking at his watch, the man announced, "You have sixty seconds to cough it up. Open the computer, son."

All the color drained from Reginald's face. No one had ever gotten the best of Reginald. He was way too smart for that.

"Forty seconds," the dad continued in a sing-song, mocking tone.

Reginald needed to think. What were the ramifications of turning over all the sensitive information on that computer to this farmer? Would he even have any idea what any of it meant? As soon as he got to the airport, he could put a team in place to get here and retrieve the computer. Everything on his computer was backed up, so all they had to do was retrieve or destroy the laptop. How much damage could this man do in that time?

"Fifteen seconds."

"Okay! 2022#OMEGA, all caps," Reginald recited. He had created the password himself and changed it often. He could hear the boy typing with agonizing slowness.

"Time. Are you in, son?"

"Yes, father."

The man put the car back in gear. The tires squealed as the car was spurred forward to get to the airport on time. Reginald seethed. He was already planning revenge. Fifteen minutes later, Reginald was delivered to the door of the small airport. Reginald handed the wad of cash over to the man. He took it with a smile and said, "Merci!"

Reginald briefly thought about reaching over to the seat and grabbing the laptop from the boy. He decided against a confrontation here. There would be one soon enough, and it would not end well for the farmer. He would make sure of that. He slammed the car door and rushed into the terminal to find the fastest way to Paris, no matter what the cost.

The car pulled away from the entrance to the airport and pulled to the side of the road once they were out of view. The man reached behind him and took the laptop from the boy, who had been holding it patiently on his lap. He pulled out his cell phone and dialed a number. A man on the other end answered on the first ring. "We have the laptop. He was as predictable as you promised. Except he did almost kill my son's horse. Other than that, everything progressed perfectly."

The man listened for a moment to a set of instructions. "Will this be enough?" The voice on the other end of the line assured him it would. "Good. I hope Interpol will be welcomed when they show up to arrest him at his big meeting."

As the car pulled away from the curb, a puff of smoke could be seen in the distance. The train that had to make an emergency stop along the river miraculously fixed itself and was on its way again, with just an hour's delay.

*****

Reginald boarded the commuter plane headed for Paris. There was no first class, so he paid extra for the entire exit row—both seats. He didn't want to look at another human being right now. He would be arriving in Paris in an hour and a half. If it hadn't been for handing over his laptop, he could have chalked the entire day up to an unfortunate adventure, one that he overcame despite the odds.

Waiting to board the plane, Reginald made a phone call and gave explicit instructions on how the acquisition of his stolen computer would proceed. He had used this team for other cleanup jobs and knew they were competent. They would get the job done. "And if there are a few bruises to the man's face, I won't complain," Reginald added before he hung up.

He was tired—oh so tired. Shortly after the plane took off, Reginald reclined his seat. He was overwhelmed by sleepiness, almost as if he had been drugged. He hadn't eaten or had anything to drink since he left the train, except for a bottle of water from the airport vending machine, so he knew that wasn't the case. He was still thirsty, but the desire to sleep was greater. He immediately drifted off into the strangest dream ever.

*****

When he became conscious inside his dream, it was vibrant and lifelike. Never had he had a dream this vivid. There were colors and smells, and he could feel a gentle breeze against his skin. Reginald rubbed his arms, and that's when he noticed he was dressed in white linen.

He followed the marble stone path forward that he was on and found two men sitting in chairs on a raised platform, surrounded by intricately carved marble pillars. Chairs were really not a good description; thrones were a better word. The arms seemed to be carved of white stone resembling ivory, with exotic patterns and designs. The backs of the thrones were high and laced with lush green vines. There were bright red velvety-looking cushions on which the two men sat. They were both dressed in white linen. The men looked royal, but Reginald was confused because they certainly didn't appear to be kings.

One of the men spoke. "Welcome, Reginald. We have been expecting you. If you look to your left, you will see seven chairs. Please take a seat in the first chair."

This was the strangest dream he had ever had. He wanted to ask questions or even defy the order, but he didn't have the will to refuse. As directed, he looked left. There was a giant field of green grass—the softest and most vibrantly green grass he had ever seen—and not a single weed amidst the pristine field.

The air seemed to be the perfect temperature, and the breeze kept his skin delightfully cool. Trees lined the back of the field. It was a full-fledged forest. The trees were arranged perfectly, as if they had been planted in staggered rows to leave just the right amount of room between each one. The chairs where in a straight line facing the marble platform. Reginald approached and tried to sit in the middle chair but found that when he sat down, he was in the first chair where he was instructed to sit.

This is the oddest dream I've ever had. I must have suffered more trauma than I thought today, he mused.

One of the men responded, "This isn't a dream. It's judgment day. Six others will be arriving shortly. You and the other six humans have been chosen to represent mankind."

Reginald froze, letting the reality of what the man just said sink in. Was this truly a dream? How else would he know my thoughts?

"No, this isn't a dream; it is reality," the other man on the throne responded. "We feel mankind has strayed too far from the gifts of the Earth that he has been provided. It may be time to reset the clock. There may not be enough of you that are good for your race to be salvaged. You are destroying the Earth and all that has been given to you through nature."

Reginald was ready to argue that he loved nature and could describe every beautiful nuance of South-Central France. He could plead a good case. He was just about to speak when his thoughts were interrupted.

"We are the Father and the Son, but we will not be the ones judging the seven representatives of the human race."

This confused Reginald. If not God and His Son, who would be judging?

The voice continued. "Each of the seven humans appearing here today encountered an equine, the species of animals that have been present since the modern evolution of mankind. They were placed on the Earth to help you, guide you, and, if it ever came to this point, to judge you."

Fear and terror crossed the threshold of Reginald's emotions for the first time in his life. His brief encounter with the horse came flooding into his mind like a tidal wave: the kick to his side, pounding the horse with a shovel, and watching as it nearly strangled to death from the rope he tied around its neck. Reginald began to weep. For the first time in his life, he felt regret and sorrow. His only hope was that the rest of the human representatives were far better humans than he.

Sofia Santiago

Olhão, Portugal
Marathon Runner

SOFIA WAS MET ON the trail by a team of EMTs. The man who found her had been instructed not to move her. He provided their GPS location from his phone and was given an ETA on when help would arrive. As soon as Sophia relaxed and knew help was on the way, she asked to borrow the man's phone to call her mother. She was now officially overdue. She knew her mom would be frantic with worry.

Her mother saw a strange number calling her cell phone and answered with trepidation. "H-hhhello?" she said hesitantly.

"It's okay, Momma. It's me, Sophia. I ran into a little snag and I'm going to be a bit late," Sophia announced, trying to ease the news gently to her mother. "In fact, I had a little accident and I need you to meet me at the hospital."

There was great disappointment all around that Sofia would not be competing in the upcoming Comrades race.

Portugal would have to wait to have its first competitor in the prestigious long-distance race.

Compentensia Deportes canceled their sponsorship when they heard the news that Sophia had been injured. Talk about adding insult to injury. Sofia was devastated. Things had been going so perfectly. She had a very difficult time accepting that, because of an act of kindness, she had dashed her own dreams.

As Sophia lay in the hospital, still groggy after the surgery on her ankle and feeling very sorry for herself, a familiar face popped into view at the door. Her mother had been in the waiting room for the entire day. Sophia finally convinced her to leave to go home and get some sleep.

There were two other visitors soon after, one big and one little. It was the man who had rescued her and his son. When the four EMTs arrived on the hill, they found the man and his son waiting patiently with her. The man had helped her lay down and supported her with their backpacks—one under her head and the smaller boy's pack under her leg to raise and support her ankle.

The man had stayed with Sophia as she was placed on the stretcher and painstakingly transported to the ambulance. He waited quietly in the halls of the hospital and eavesdropped on Sophia's diagnosis and the surgery that would follow. He knew that she was going to need pins put in her ankle to strengthen the bone that had broken. He knew Sophia's chances of ever being a long-distance marathon runner again were very slim.

Her room was filled with bouquets from family, friends, and fans who had been following her incredible running career.

What she didn't know was that while she hadn't met the man who rescued her, he was very aware of her. Ever since she had won the marathon in Lagos, he had been following her training and rooting for her. The largest bouquet in the room was from him.

Benjamin Alves and his son Luis poked their heads into the room. "Hi. We just wanted to check in and make sure you are okay," Ben said shyly. Luis peered under his arm and nodded in agreement. "May we come in?"

Sophia had to smile. "Of course. You two rescued me. How could I deny you anything?"

Ben entered the room. Luis hid with just his face peeking in. "You can come in too, little man. You were part of my rescue team."

Luis entered, carrying with him a tray of homemade sweets. There was an assortment of cakes, muffins, cookies, and homemade desserts on the tray. He walked up to Sophia's bed and held them out to her. "These are for you. We thought you might like some sweets to cheer you up!"

Before she could get a word of thanks out, Luis ran up to the biggest bouquet in the room. "Do you like these? I helped my dad pick them out. He said the yellow flowers reminded him of your smile when you are happy. Do these make you smile?"

Ben grabbed his son by the shoulders and pulled him close. It was apparent he was very uncomfortable with his son's outburst. "We just wanted to show our support for your courage in training for the Comrades race. We have been following your path for quite some time."

Sophia didn't know what to say. Standing here in front of her was one of her fans. He had rescued her and was now showing up to follow up on her progress. It simply melted her heart.

"I'm so happy you are fans of my efforts," Sophia responded, still teary and emotional from her recent rollercoaster of events. "I'm afraid I have let down everyone, including the entire country of Portugal. I don't know if I will ever be able to race again!"

******

In the mass of swirling, chaotic life upon our planet, Sophia had to ask herself if we collided with one another through fate or destiny, or was it all by accident? The look Ben had on his face when he entered her hospital room told her that his visit was more than a coincidence.

Ben had been a runner himself and had aspired to compete in the Comrades race. His knees had other ideas. He transferred his hopes and dreams to a woman he had never met. Fate had her own ideas as to how and why he and Sophia had met.

When he was 18, he married his teenage sweetheart. They gave birth a year later to their beautiful baby boy. One day, crossing the street to the market, a truck came around the corner and struck his wife. She was killed instantly. That left him heartbroken and the single parent of their baby boy. Luis was too young to remember his mother.

Ben turned to long-distance running to ease the pain. He overcame the physical pain of long-distance running, cleared his mind of all his emotional pain, and focused on the here and now. He trained hard and wanted to achieve the ultimate accomplishment in long-distance running by qualifying for the Comrades ultra-marathon. His mother helped raise Luis as Ben trained. Unfortunately, the wear and tear on his body, physically and emotionally, took its toll. Ben didn't have what it took to compete at that distance. He was never able to complete a 25-mile qualifying marathon without succumbing to pain.

When he read the headlines about the unknown phenom winning the Lagos Marathon and her dreams of racing in the Comrades race, he avidly followed her progress. He was her strongest silent supporter. When he came upon her on the trail, shaken and injured, he immediately knew who she was. His heart rejoiced at their surreptitious meeting, then instantly broke the moment he suspected she had shattered her ankle.

To compensate for his injuries, Ben became a sports physical therapist. He wanted to help other athletes accomplish their goals. He obtained his license at the university in Lagos and became a certified sports physical therapist. He entered the room at the hospital vowing to help Sophia, whatever the cost was to him personally, so she could achieve her dreams. If anyone could get Sophia on the path to running long distances again, it was him. What he didn't account for was falling hopelessly in love with her.

Sophia felt sleepy. The surgery, the pain medication, and the trauma of the last few days were taking their toll. Ben saw her eyes fluttering and stood beside her bed. "I can see how tired you are. We will leave now and visit later. I left my card on the tray with the sweets. I do physical therapy for athletes. Call me if you need anything, or even if you don't," he said with a wink. "I'm offering my services to help you recover."

Smiling, Sophia reached up and took his hand. It was warm, soft, the hands of a healer. She could feel his positive energy. "Thank you, Ben. You have truly been sent to me as a gift..." the last words she spoke before drifting off into a deep sleep.

*****

The first part of the dream that shocked her was that she was walking on her broken ankle, pain-free. The next shock was how beautiful the surroundings were and how real the dream felt. Sophia followed the path before her and saw, in the near distance, two men sitting on thrones. She knew instantly she was in the presence of God.

Trembling, Sophia's first thoughts were that she had died. She wasn't ready to go yet. She wanted another chance to make her mark in the world as a runner. Even with the setback, she was ready to do whatever it took to heal and race again. It seemed that while she traded the chance to compete this year in the Comrades Race, she might have met the man of her dreams. Could it be that through tragedy she had been brought together with the love of her life?

As she approached the men, she felt love emanating from them. Her fear turned into awe. She was standing in the presence of God and His only begotten Son. She still didn't know if this was a dream until God spoke.

"Welcome, Sophia. This is not a dream, but you have not passed into the great beyond. You are here because you have been chosen to represent mankind. Man has strayed far from his purpose of being created. That purpose was to love one another and all the gifts given to him on Earth. It seems that man has strayed from this purpose."

Sophia gasped. "I'm not worthy," she said, tearing up. "How could I possibly have been chosen? I am no one special," she pleaded.

"Every human being born into your world is special," the Son replied. "Life is a precious gift. What each person chooses to do with that gift is a personal decision. You have been chosen for your passion and dedication to what you love."

Sophia didn't know how to respond. She felt honored and terrified all at the same time. She asked another question, fearfully, "Have I been good enough?"

"We will not be judging," God answered, much to Sophia's surprise. "Long ago, we gave man the gifts of equines. They have been with man through the ages, carrying him and his burdens, and helping him build the civilized world from homesteads to empires. They are the guardians of the Earth and will be judging seven of you. We designed them to know what is in the hearts of men. If enough humans are deemed by the equines to have good hearts and souls, mankind will continue. If they find more are lacking a connection to Earth's gifts and no longer have love for these gifts in their hearts, it will be time to wipe the slate clean and begin anew."

On one hand, Sophia was terrified for the fate of the human race. On the other hand, she was very pleased her last decision on Earth was to rescue a pregnant mare and her foal.

She followed the directions to sit in the second chair in the beautiful field facing the throne. A man sat in the first chair. It was then she noticed she was dressed in white linen like the man. She assumed he was the first of the seven chosen. Even though the fate of the world was at stake, the breathtaking scenery exhilarated every fiber of her being.

She had a feeling she was being given a rare glimpse of heaven as she took her seat and glanced at the man beside her. He didn't acknowledge her and certainly did not look happy. Sophia took a wild guess that his last encounter with an equine didn't go well. She prayed the remaining five humans would bode well for the fate of mankind.

Paloma Ortega Sánchez

New York City
United States Congresswoman

CARLOS AND LUIS DROVE down the dirt path that had hairpin turns winding through the rainforest. What they were driving on didn't constitute a road, really; it was more like a goat path. Every bump caused pain in Paloma's throbbing foot.

"Can't you try to avoid the bumps and pits?" Paloma finally yelled. "I'm injured here. You are causing me more pain!"

Carlos brought the truck to a halt and looked at her, sitting on the bench seat between him and Luis. "Would you like me to drop you off here and you can walk back? Because this road is only wide enough to allow us a narrow path down this mountain. Feel free to walk if you think I'm doing a poor job driving."

Paloma's mouth opened and closed like a fish out of water. "Of course, I can't walk," she seethed. "Can you at least drive slower over the rough parts? Can you have a little consideration for my injury?"

Carlos put the car back into gear and continued slowly down the slope. Sophia crossed her arms, satisfied she had won the argument. After all, she was a United States Congresswoman and deserved respect.

When the truck arrived at the barn, the horses were all back in their stalls. Several poked their heads out of the open top door, having finished their dinner, and were resting contentedly. Sophia looked for Diablo, the evil beast that he was, but didn't see him.

She scanned the barn area and saw Paul, seated on a bench, obviously waiting for her. Paloma needed him for a little while longer. She wouldn't sever her ties with him and kick him out of her life until she got home safely.

Paul walked up to the truck when it parked. Luis got out first and extended his arm to help Paloma out. As soon as she stepped out of the truck, Paul hugged her. "I'm so glad you are safe. I was so worried about you."

"I do have an injury; I might have broken my foot."

"Let me take a look at it," Paul offered.

Paloma laughed. "Yeah, a construction worker is going to tell me if my foot is broken. No thanks. Take me to an emergency room now," she ordered.

Paul pulled out his phone and, with the help of Carlos, pulled up the directions to the nearest urgent care center. It was 45 minutes away in the direction of the city. Paul shook hands with the two men. "I'm so sorry for everything that happened. Thank you for rescuing her," he said. "I hope we haven't totally ruined your day."

As Paul helped Paloma into the passenger seat of the rental car, Carlos commented, "I feel sorry for that man. I know he is about to get dumped by her, but the fact that he wasted any of his life with her is a crime."

They both laughed.

*****

Paloma's foot was sprained, not broken. She was given a boot and crutches after the x-rays confirmed the results. Paul drove her back to her grandmother's house for their last night in Puerto Rico before heading to the airport the following morning.

Paul would be taking a commercial flight directly back to NYC. Paloma would be given a courtesy transport on Jennifer González-Colón's private jet, the same one she took to Puerto Rico. True, it was a waste of fuel to be the only passenger going to DC on the jet, but Paloma had important matters to contend with, like pushing the Great Green Deal.

After a tearful goodbye to her grandmother, Paloma limped to the rental car with her crutches, leaving Paul to carry all the bags to the car. She waited for him to load the car and then open the door for her.

"Remember, keep an eye on the men I paid to come to fix your house. Make sure they do good work or they will have me to contend with!"

"Te amo!" her grandmother replied, wiping away her tears and waving a checkered dishcloth.

Once they turned in the rental car and got a cab back to the airport, Paloma and Paul had to go their separate ways. Paul would be entering the airport's main terminal to catch his flight back to New York. Paloma would be continuing to the private section of the airport where her jet awaited outside the hangar.

The taxi driver waited while Paul pulled out his suitcase. Paloma remained in the car and would be delivered to the gangplank of the jet. There was an awkward silence as Paul stood at the open car door facing Paloma. Suddenly, she blurted out, "I think we both know that things didn't work out well for us this trip. I think we have irreconcilable differences, so it's best you get your things out of my apartment before I return in two weeks."

Paul nodded. "You know the biggest difference between us?" He didn't wait for her answer. "You are a self-righteous hypocrite who is urging us to pass the Great Green Deal while taking a private jet back to DC. You have no business being in Congress because you are not well educated and, frankly, are not that intelligent. You push your agenda and think your looks and your prowess with other idiots on social media will help you succeed with plans that have no basis in facts or reality."

Paloma's face turned beet red as she tried to respond. "Nope," he stopped her, raising his hand in front of her face. "I'm going to finish. Another huge difference between you and me is that I create and build things. I'm successful because of hard work, educated planning, and integrity. You build nothing from bullshit based on whatever advances your changing agenda and puts money into the corrupt wheels that turn our nation. Here's a tip: go back to bartending. You were much better at that."

With that, he slammed the door and walked away.

Thirty minutes later, Paloma's flight was taking off for Washington. She was exhausted and had downed a glass of wine and two painkillers before the plane even left the ground. The single flight attendant tried to get her to raise her seat upright and put on her seatbelt for takeoff. When she couldn't rouse her, she looked around at the empty plane and shrugged. Who was she to ruffle the feathers of a congresswoman? She walked forward to her rumble seat and fastened her seatbelt.

*****

There was a distinct difference between a normal dream and what Paloma was currently experiencing. She had an intuitive feeling that the sights, sounds, and feelings were far too real for this to be a dream. Her surroundings were breathtakingly beautiful. She struggled to take it all in. She pinched herself. It hurt. That's when she noticed she was wearing strange white clothes.

Paloma also noticed that her ankle no longer hurt. That was a good thing. She continued walking down the marble pathway and spotted the two men sitting in fancy chairs under marble pillars. *I swear on my mother's grave I think I'm in heaven*, she suddenly thought, very confused. She felt compelled to approach the two men. Could her plane have crashed? Was she dead? *Wait. There's only one God; why are there two men on thrones?*

"Welcome, Paloma," the Father said.

"We are the Father and the Son," the Son explained. "You are not dead; you are here because you have been chosen to represent mankind."

Paloma swelled with pride. "Well, I am one of the most important people in the United States, so I guess that makes sense. What do I need to do? What is my task? I'm your humble servant," Paloma said with a bow.

"Actually," the Father explained, "it's not what you need to do; it's what you have done. You have been chosen to decide if mankind is worthy to continue living on the planet..."

Paloma laughed and held up her hand. "You can stop right there. I, as I live and breathe, am working tirelessly to pass the Save The Climate Bill to save our planet. I'm sure you are aware of that, of course," she said with a grin. "I have done more to try and save our planet than just about anyone in our country. Surely, I will pass this judgment test."

"Unfortunately, Paloma," the Father continued patiently, "we are not the ones judging you. The criteria are not lobbying to pass bills that will line the pockets of the rich and corrupt while doing little to improve the planet."

The smile quickly faded from Paloma's face. "What are the criteria, then?"

"You are being judged for the goodness in your heart and the honest connection to the gifts bestowed upon you on Earth. Man has strayed from honoring the gifts he was given. We have placed those in your midst who will decide if man has strayed too far or if he is worthy to continue life on planet Earth."

Paloma looked around, trying to discern who these beings were and if there were any around her at the moment. She only saw two people, like her, sitting in a row of seven chairs. "I'm confused," she said. "Who exactly will be doing the judging? Is it those people? Because I don't know either of them."

God chuckled. "No, Paloma. It is not other humans. The beings we placed on the planet have been around since the rise of the human species: the equines. You will be judged by the one you came in contact with. He has been blessed with the gift to see into the human heart. He will deem if you are worthy.

Every ounce of good feeling drained from Paloma quicker than sand pouring through the funnel of an hourglass. "Wait a minute," she blurted out. "You are going to have a horse that ran away with me, jumped off a cliff into a river, and was responsible for me spraining my ankle, judge me? This is ludicrous! If I'm going to be judged, it should be on my contributions to humanity, not by some stupid animal!"

God and the Son looked at one another. They shook their heads at the same time. Paloma found herself walking unwillingly to the third chair in the row of seats lining the gorgeous green meadow, which she completely ignored. She tried to protest but found that she was now mute. She felt angry, humiliated, duped... She unwillingly took the seat between a pretty girl with a pleasant smile on her face and a white male who looked utterly depressed.

Justin Barone

Nine Pines, California
Equestrian

THE BARONE FAMILY TRANSITIONED from a semi-lucrative equestrian training program to Justin becoming a possible candidate for the Olympics in show jumping in one afternoon. With Justin's talent and Apollo's ability to jump, they had the potential to be a winning team. All they needed now was to compete against the best to see how they ranked. Justin was on his way with his father's blessing to start those wheels in motion, when the show stewards appeared; the enforcers, the horse police. They were every competitor's worst nightmare.

Justin and his father watched as the show stewards approached. He knew Justin didn't have a clue what had transpired in the stall with his horse. If anyone caught wind that Apollo was going to be given a sedative and that stewards were paid not to drug test him after the class, Justin's pristine reputation would be ruined along with any hope of him becoming an Olympic candidate. In the blink of an eye, all their dreams were on the edge of a cliff. The next few moments would determine if those dreams would fall or take flight.

Michael was trying to shield Justin from the truth. Perhaps he needed to know the details so he could defend himself. Suddenly, he had a better idea. He had taken the video of Apollo attempting to be drugged and of Clive admitting he had paid stewards not to drug test his horse. Michael had left the video running when he put the camera back in his breast pocket and asked to speak to the dastardly duo. He did that on purpose to get an audio recording of the conversation. He knew Clive would behave differently if he knew the conversation was being taped. He had thought like a lawyer, and it paid off in spades.

He watched the terrified expression on Justin's face as he realized the two men in dark blue suits and large United States Equestrian Federation (USEF) patches in the shape of a shield had their sights honed in on him. At the last second, Michael stepped in between Justin and the men. He shook hands with the two men and introduced himself as Michael Barone. He informed them that he was a lawyer and represented Barone Equestrian Estates. "I have something very interesting I think you need to see."

"Justin, go make your class changes. I know exactly how to handle this."

The look on Justin's face was something between confusion and terror. Michael had done nothing to help Justin along in his career thus far. The boy had become a man and was making his mark in the world as an honest, trustworthy, kind, and responsible human being. There was nothing that could make a father prouder. It was time for Michael to stop denying what his son was born to do and be an asset instead of a hindrance. He had every intention of doing just that.

"Come with me, gentlemen," he said, gesturing toward the couches in front of the tack room. "If you have any questions for Justin when I am finished with what I have to say, he will be back in a few minutes. He has an important class change to make." Wanting to spare his wife from the confrontation, he told her, "Delores, why don't you go brush Apollo."

*****

The two stewards seemed hesitant to let Justin out of their sight. Michael stood solid and gestured again toward the couches. "Please, gentlemen, have a seat. The way I see it, you should not be concerned with my son right now, but with your own careers."

This caused a reaction. The countenances on the men's faces turned from neutral to hostile. They glared at Michael, not used to being threatened by an outsider. Everyone knew everyone else of any prestige in this business, and Michael Barone was a nobody as far as they were concerned. He carried no clout in their world. Unfortunately, he was a lawyer, and he had threatened them. It was the only reason they were not tracking down Justin and granting Michael an audience.

"What is this all about?" one of the stewards asked impatiently. Michael had taken a seat, leaned back, and looked relaxed in one of the comfy chairs. The stewards remained on the edge of the adjacent couch and sat bolt upright in a defensive posture.

"Gentlemen, we have a situation."

In just a few minutes, Michael used his most polished lawyerly jargon to lay out the facts. He began by describing how his son had adhered to every ethical standard in the book. He had risen to his present level with integrity and hard work. Next, Michael explained that he understood there were competitors in this sport who didn't conduct themselves with integrity, which is the reason the stewards had their jobs.

"We don't need lectures on what we do for a living," one of the men interrupted. "Either tell us what you know or stop wasting our time."

"If you will allow me to continue, I'm building my case."

Michael pulled out his cell phone, held up a finger, then clicked on the video. He scrolled to the section where Clive and the vet were in the stall with Apollo, trying to sedate him. He hit the play button and turned the screen toward the men.

"I have on video one of your competitors trying to drug my son's horse while he was at the schooling ring with his students. This man is trying to earn a spot on the United States Equestrian team and he wants my son's horse to do that. Not only do I have one of your top competitors and your veterinarian performing highly illegal actions, but I also have a confession on video that a steward was paid off not to drug test this horse after his class."

This caused an immediate reaction from the two men, which Michael immediately squelched. "You are going to listen to what I have to say," he responded, raising his hand to stop their protests. "I own one of the top law firms in Southern California. I take on drug companies and win for a living. Your organization is peanuts compared to what I'm used to dealing with. So, here's how this is going to work."

After revealing a bit more of the video so the men knew he wasn't bluffing, Michael held all the cards. He was willing to work with the two men to minimize the damage from this unfortunate affair. As it stood, if the evidence he had was submitted, they would be losing a very wealthy and prominent Olympic competitor, one of their veterinarians, and whichever steward had taken a bribe. Michael promised that he would personally oversee that each indiscretion was brought before USEF and litigated in an outside court in addition to the USEF violations.

Rats have survived for so long because they know when to keep quiet and when to squeal. Michael felt positive he had two sitting in front of him because these men didn't say a word. Michael agreed to keep his video evidence to himself under the condition that Clive would be questioned due to an anonymous tip reporting they saw him entering the stall of another competitor's horse with the veterinarian. After all, he was trying to rig things in his favor to legally buy the horse, but what he did and how he did it was highly illegal and unethical.

He wanted the shit scared out of Clive and the veterinarian so they would never consider another illegal action. As for the steward who took the bribe, he had no evidence of who it was. He was going to leave it up to them to sort that out.

His last statement was to inform them that, as of today, he was taking over ownership of Apollo. That meant he would be running the campaign for Justin through USEF quali-fying events. Michael assured the two men that he would be keeping a close eye on any spontaneous and unethical actions by the stewards. If there was even a hint of unethical enforcement of their duties, he would submit the video and have them all investigated.

Neither man said a word when Michael announced he was finished and they could leave. As timing would have it, Justin was returning from making his class change. His face had an expression of deep concern as the two men stood up without giving him a second glance. Both sets of eyes were glued to the ground in front of them as they walked away.

"I really don't understand what is going on right now, Father," Justin confessed. "Did I do something wrong? I've been very careful to do everything by the book!"

"No, Justin, you did everything right. There was some plotting going on behind your back that is probably best left there. It doesn't benefit anyone for you to know the details. Keep your nose clean, play by the rules, and you will have my complete support for your campaign."

Justin couldn't help but hug his dad. Just then, Justin's mother came walking up to witness her husband and son hugging. "Who would have thought that we would have a family hug fest at a horse show?" she said with a laugh and wrapped her arms around both men.

Justin was curious and wanted to probe his dad to find out what on earth was going on behind his back. Then, he thought better of it. He knew how resolute his father could be, and if he said Justin didn't need to know, extracting information would be like trying to break into a steel trap.

"All the changes are in, and in a couple of hours, I will be riding my horse in the biggest class of my life. The stress is killing me; I think I need to go lie down on the cot in the tack room. I'm mentally and physically exhausted. Can you two promise to wake me up in exactly one hour?" Justin asked, glancing at his watch. They both nodded.

"Awesome. You can have a seat out here, and if you look in the mini-fridge against the barn over there, you will find some cheese and very good Barone wine," he said with a wink before disappearing into the tack room and drawing the curtain shut.

As he lay down on the cot, he was a bit worried about how utterly exhausted he felt. He chalked it up to the physical and mental stresses of the day, to training his students and all the worries that brought, and to his father showing up and offering to buy his horse and help his campaign for the Olympics. The real drain was when the USEF stewards mysteriously popped up out of the blue. It was a rollercoaster of a day. Justin fell into a deep sleep the moment his head hit the pillow, which opened immediately with a very vivid dream.

*****

Justin was blown away by the vividness of his dream. *It had to be a dream, right?* He noticed that he was dressed in loose, brilliantly white cotton clothing. It was a stark contrast to his tight-fitting breeches and boots, which he wore almost every day. He glanced around in amazement at the marble path lined with rich green grass.

Up ahead, Justin was shocked to see two men sitting in throne-like chairs lined by tall marble pillars. They reminded him of Greek gods. He knew instinctively that he was in the presence of divine beings. The question burning in his mind was, *am I dead, or is this a dream?*

His heart beat faster as he approached the men. It seemed intuitive to follow the path toward them. They offered an answer to his question.

"No, Justin," answered the Father, addressing his unspoken fear. "You are not dead; you are very much alive."

The Son filled in the details of who they were and that he had been chosen to represent mankind. Each human would be judged by an equine who could see into the heart of that human. The equine would determine if he or she was connected to the Earth and her gifts; a loving human worthy of being saved.

Justin became concerned. He bought, trained, and sold horses as a commodity. Surely this didn't make him unappreciative of their amazing qualities. He knew the show jumping world was fraught with unethical morons who used horses to climb the social ladder of the horse world. He was different. He loved his horses. Then it occurred to him that maybe his horses didn't see it that way. Maybe being bought and sold made them feel unappreciated and unloved.

As he fretted, he also wondered which horse would be judging him. He had imported three horses this past year. His question was answered.

"Apollo was the horse assigned to you. He will be the equine that looks into your heart and decides if you are worthy."

Apollo had been rescued by Justin and rehabilitated through love and kindness. Then, Justin tried to sell him to another person when he was the only one who had shown him kindness and cared for him. Did Apollo even know that Justin was keeping him? Would he think him evil for putting him back into the arena where he had been abused by other riders?

The Father spoke reassuringly to Justin. "There is no sense worrying about the past. What is done is done. We have three more candidates who will be arriving. Focus on your good intentions, what you have done right, and the love you feel for your horse."

With those words echoing in his mind, Justin turned to see the three others sitting in the row of seven chairs on the edge of the most beautiful field he had ever seen. He looked out into the forest behind them and wondered how this was all going to play out. The others seemed lost in their thoughts. Justin took the fourth seat and joined them.

Eduardo Fernandez

San Antonio de Areco, Argentina
Argentinian Long Rider

HE HAD NO MEMORY of being rescued. Eduardo suffered from broken ribs, cuts, and bruises. Losing consciousness was a blessing. He didn't feel the pain of being untangled from under the boulders and rolled onto a stretcher. He didn't have to watch as two of his horses had to be assisted by six strong men to walk into the trailer. Calchalero limped in behind them on his own.

Hours later, after a blurry recognition of bright lights, hearing the hum of machines performing scans and taking pictures, Eduardo slipped into a deep place, assisted by heavy doses of pain medications and muscle relaxers. He was standing in a field; tall green grass undulated in a gentle breeze. He lifted his face to the sky. The warm sun kissed his face. All three of his horses stood around him, facing him, each at an equal distance away. He wondered why they didn't have their noses buried deep in the lush grass, filling their bellies.

Calchalero had his tack on, his bridle, and a saddle. Gra-cielle and Chaja were bare of any tack. Eduardo walked over to Calchalero and rubbed his hand down his face. He walked to his side, put his foot in the stirrup, and mounted. Gracielle and Chaja turned and walked away. They didn't look back to-ward their herd mate. Calchalero didn't whinny to his friends as they left. He stood as still as a stone, waiting for Eduardo to direct him.

Eduardo was about to ride after them when suddenly, they disappeared. In their place, two men were sitting in chairs. Eduardo rode up to the two men, sitting in the chairs, in the middle of a field of green grass. He asked them, "Where am I?"

One of the men answered, "You are at a crossroads."

"Crossroads to where?" Eduardo asked, looking around and not seeing any roads.

"Where is it you want to go?" the other man asked.

"I want to continue my journey to retrace the route my ancestors rode with their horses."

"This journey has been difficult for you, and there will be many more hardships to come."

"I'm prepared to handle them," Eduardo answered.

"What about your horses?" two voices asked in unison. "The care you have taken, is it enough?"

Then, the entire scene disappeared, as quickly as it had appeared. Like a puff of smoke, the dream was erased from Eduardo's memory.

After two months of rehab for himself and Calchalero, Eduardo and two new Criollo horses walked up a ramp onto a large flat boat that would take them across the bay to

Panama. Gracielle and Chaja healed, but they were not sound enough to continue the rigorous journey. They were shipped back to Ihan, where Eduardo's father would take care of them.

A woman from Texas, who was also a long rider, had two purebred Criollo horses. She donated them to Eduardo so he could continue his journey. Calchalero took the separation hard. He missed his herd mates and resisted making friends with his two new companions. It took several weeks before he accepted them as his herd. There wasn't the bond between them that there was with the original trio, but they tolerated each other.

Once the horses were safely in their onboard stalls, munching hay contentedly, Eduardo walked outside to the rail of the ship. He gazed out at the horizon, searching for the distant coast of Panama. It would be hours before it came into sight. Eduardo sighed. He realized this was a pivotal moment. He had certainly faced hardships and successfully overcome each one. There was a groundswell of support for him from the horse community. He briefly thought about giving up after losing two of his horses and being severely injured. Giving up meant failure. He was completing this dream not only for himself but for all the people supporting him, living vicariously.

Dozens of cards, letters, and donations poured into the hospital where he was recovering. He thought about the heartfelt notes written to him by his supporters. There was no way he was going to give up as long as he had his health and horses to ride. He had both of those.

The one thought that kept nagging him, however, was that he had the free will to choose to make this journey. His horses didn't. It was a fact that horses had been making long journeys since the dawn of modern man. Wasn't this the reason they were put on Earth? They were beasts of burden, built to travel and carry men. Eduardo didn't know how this debate started in his mind. He had always shown great compassion to his horses and treated them the best way he knew how. Was it enough?

Eduardo found peace and comfort traveling with his horses by boat. The ocean was kind, and the boat moved smoothly through the water. The gentle rocking of the boat was soothing. Eduardo checked on his horses several times. They seemed much more comfortable than when they traveled by horse trailer.

Not yet 100% recovered from all his injuries, Eduardo was not pushing himself too hard. He would keep his travel days short and work back into full travel mode when he and the horses were in shape. The boat had bunk rooms where passengers could sleep on overnight passages. Feeling quite tired from his morning excursion, Eduardo found a room with an empty bed and crawled into it. He fell asleep instantly.

*****

Eduardo wasn't surprised when he found himself inside a very vivid dream. He walked down a marble walkway and saw two men sitting on ornate thrones surrounded by intricately carved marble pillars. The men looked vaguely familiar. He had a comforting feeling that this was a dream he had previously experienced.

He approached the men without hesitation. "Welcome, Eduardo," said the Father. "You are correct that we have visited together in the past. This time, it is different. This is not a dream."

Fear was not something Eduardo was accustomed to feeling, but something akin to it began forming in his mind. If this wasn't a dream, was he dead?

The Son answered without him verbalizing the question, "No, this is not a dream, and you are not dead. This is something different."

Eduardo shifted uncomfortably as it was explained to him that he had been chosen to represent humanity. As he looked down at his feet in wonder, he then noticed he was barefoot. He was wearing strange white, loose-fitting clothing. He was dressed the same as the men on the thrones. The memory came flooding back of the dream he had when these two men appeared.

"You came to me before, after my accident," Eduardo recalled. "You talked to me about my dreams and goals and asked if it was the same for my horses. When my horses were not capable of continuing, I sent them home to relax in a pasture and heal. Does that not show that I have compassion and care for my horses?"

"There is no doubt that horses have been an important part of your life. You have asked them to make a journey for your desire, not theirs. We created horses to be the watchers of men and to serve them. What remains to be seen is how Calchalero views this journey. Equines have served men for centuries. We have left it up to Calchalero to decide if you are driven solely by personal reasons on this quest. As a watchdog of men, he will know what is in your heart and if your love for nature and her gifts is part of your passion."

Eduardo departed the presence of the men to take his seat in one of the two remaining chairs. He saw before him two men and two women. All were silent, lost in thought. Eduardo glanced around the vibrant green meadow and at the giant, perfectly planted forest beyond. His heart fluttered at the beauty. Even though he was fearful, not knowing if he was worthy, he felt honored to be representing mankind and to be in this place, at this moment. Humbly, he took his seat.

Destiny Khumalo

Cape Town, South Africa
Medical Doctor

GALLOPING OFF INTO THE dark on an unwilling horse was not an easy task. Destiny hadn't been on a horse in years. She was terrified of falling off. This was nothing like cantering down a stretch of beach on a beautiful, sunny day. She tried to let her eyes pick out obstacles to steer clear of as she put as much distance between her and the barn as possible. She knew the eyes of her horse saw far better than human vision in the dark of night.

She found the path she was looking for and slowed the horse down. The anxious horse still wanted to race back to the barn. It took all her strength and willpower to keep him heading away from his herd. The path went up a rocky hill. She had to slow the horse to keep him from injuring himself on the rocks. At one point, he made a quick turn to unseat her and make his break back to the barn. She tugged hard on the reins and kicked him. He reared up slightly, then continued forward. Destiny thought her heart was going to beat right out of her chest, but she won the battle.

Destiny knew the men couldn't keep up with her on foot. Her goal was to get as far away from the farm as possible and wait until the morning light. They would be gone by then, not knowing when Justice was due back home. The trail split at the top of the hill. The last section of the trail became very narrow, with a steep slope on each side. She was going to have to take that section carefully, but once the hill plateaued at the top, she would turn right and have a much smoother, flat path to put distance between her and the Herero men.

Slowing down to a walk, she reached the narrow section of the trail. Destiny had a temporary panic attack and dismounted. She figured it was better to lead the horse across this part. One step to the left or right would result in a fall down the rocky hill. That would be bad, for both of them.

She carefully stepped over the rocks and pulled the horse behind her with the reins. She could hear his metal shoes sliding off the rocks. At one point, a spark flew from the contact between the stone and the metal shoe. She turned to check if the horse was okay. The reins slackened. The horse took his chance and pulled away. He turned nimbly on the narrow trail, but his back foot slipped.

In the black of the night, Destiny's horror show went from bad to worse. She heard more than saw the commotion of the horse trying to gain his footing. She heard rocks sliding and the sounds of struggling by the desperate animal. Then, the sounds of the horse receding into the dark. The sounds were followed by men's voices, yelling at the base of the trail.

Panicked by the thoughts of her brother's horse dying a horrible death, and from her own life in extreme jeopardy, Destiny turned and ran up the hill as fast as her legs would allow.

*****

It was Justice's turn to panic. Giving orders for his wife to go back in the house, Justice raced back to the barn. He scanned the paddocks with the faint hope Goose would be in the paddock and his sister was out wandering the property. With no sign of him in any of the paddocks or the pasture, he took off on the trails leading away from the farm.

It was the only logical place for Destiny to have fled. The clues indicated that someone had arrived from the Herero tribe to question her, or with more nefarious plans in mind. She had gotten on Goose and fled. It was most likely in the dark. The rough terrain would have been almost impossible to navigate. Justice's heart sank not only for his sister but for Goose.

He ran to the base of the hill and looked up the trail. He could barely see the top of the hill. Justice started a slow jog. He was in excellent shape and could probably make it to the top without stopping. Three-quarters of the way up, his heart stopped. The trail was shredded with deep grooves. The grooves, on this narrow section, continued over the edge of the left side of the trail.

Justice peered down the hillside. He immediately squatted and began sliding down the slope. Rocks cut and bruised his hands as he tried to control his descent. As he slid, small rocks and boulders tumbled as they became dislodged. By the time he reached the bottom, a small rockslide preceded his arrival.

The dust cleared. Goose, trembling but standing on his own, was trapped a few feet away between rocks and brush. His broken reins were caught between two boulders. The saddle was still in place but shredded. Dried blood encrusted several areas of his body. He whinnied at Justice, straining his neck around as far as he could to see his human. The whites of his eyes showed his fear and pain. Justice broke down as he made his way to his friend. He threw his arms around his horse's neck and sobbed. His horse was still alive, but he had no idea about the severity of his injuries. Regarding his sister, he realized as he glanced back up the hill that he had no idea if she was dead or alive.

That's when he heard a moan. He knew it was his sister. At least she was alive. She wasn't far away. Goose became agitated the moment Justice began moving away. "Don't worry, buddy. I will be right back for you."

He found her crumpled a few meters away in a heap between some boulders. She was curled in a protective ball. "Destiny! It's me. Please tell me you're okay?" Justice shouted as he worked his way toward her.

Destiny felt the knot on her forehead and sticky dried blood. Her head was pounding. She felt nauseous. She tried sitting up to answer Justice, but immediately thought better of it and stayed lying down.

"I slid down the hill looking for Goose in the dark. I hit my head. I think I have a concussion. I feel very nauseous, but other than that," she said, as she took note of her other body parts, "I don't think I have any other serious injuries. "Goose! Where is he? Is he okay? I was looking for him; the men had left…"

"Goose is just over there. His reins are stuck, but he is standing up and seems to be fine. I need to get the two of you out of here and home."

Justice worked his way over the boulders and knelt next to her. "Boy, it looks like you two had a rough night."

*****

Justice used his cell phone to call for an ambulance. He sat with his sister and directed a rescue team with a stretcher to their location. As he waited, he wandered between his sister and his horse. He did a brief exam and determined that Goose had some superficial wounds but otherwise seemed to be sound.

Destiny wanted to try to get up and walk out of the boulder field, but Justice would not hear of it. She had been unconscious for quite a while, and he knew a head injury was nothing to mess around with.

In less than an hour, his sister was being carried off on a stretcher by the rescue team to an ambulance waiting on the path leading back to the farm. Justice led Goose out of the rocks, and the two walked home.

After his horses and family were taken care of, Justice drove to the hospital where his sister had been admitted. He had called their parents. They were waiting at the hospital when she arrived by ambulance.

The ER doctor who attended her was her colleague. He stitched up her head and performed a series of tests for a concussion. "You have a nasty bump on your head. We are taking you down for a CT scan. How did you get it, Destiny?"

Woozy and having difficulty focusing, she tried to fill in the gaps. "I went for a ride when things went very bad. My brother's horse slid down a hill. I was leading him at the time. I guess I went down the hill to look for him and slipped and fell myself. I must have hit my head on a rock."

Destiny left out the part about being chased by men who wanted to hurt her by fleeing in the dark of the night.

"You're lucky you only hurt your head. Let's get some shots of your skull and see what kind of damage you did," he told her as a nurse showed up to wheel her down to the room with the scanning equipment. "I'm going to go talk to your brother and parents who are in the waiting room. We will see you in a bit." He squeezed her hand as the nurse rolled her away.

As soon as the doctor appeared in the waiting room, Justin and his parents rose from the couch and bombarded him with questions. He held up his hand. "She is going to be fine. I stitched her up and we are getting a CT scan. She has a concussion, but she is conscious and responding normally for someone with a head injury. As soon as I have the results, I will let you know. My guess is with a few days' rest she'll be fine."

The doctor headed to the lab room and watched as Destiny was transferred by two orderlies onto the bed of the CT scan machine. She was still too dizzy to move on her own. The medication she was given was also kicking in. Destiny gave a thumbs up to the doctor in the viewing room as the machine buzzed to life and she was sent into the tube. Destiny knew they were looking to see if there was any bleeding inside her skull, which was the worst-case scenario. Hopefully, there was none. After a night or two of observation, they would let her go home. She had a lot to straighten out in her life.

As her body moved deep into the belly of the machine, she heard the voice of the tech asking her to lie very still. Then the buzz, whir, and clicking sounds began, indicating the machine was doing its scan. The medication helped her relax and fall into a deep sleep. It wasn't long before she found herself in the dream world.

*****

It was a relief to find herself in such a beautiful place after the trauma of the last two days. Destiny spun around, in no pain, feeling the cool breeze on her face as she inhaled the fresh, sweet air. She noticed she was not dressed in a hospital robe but in soft, bright white, comfortable clothing. She was in one of the most beautiful places she had ever seen.

In a state of euphoria, Destiny found herself wandering down a marble pathway. Suddenly, she noticed two men sitting on beautiful thrones surrounded by marble pillars. She felt she might be wrong about being in a beautiful dream. Perhaps her injury was worse than she thought. Maybe this was the afterlife, and she had died in the CT machine?

"No, Destiny," said the Father. "You did not die. This is not a dream."

Destiny froze in fear as she listened to the same introduction given to the five people before her. She was blown away by the fact she was chosen to represent mankind. This was a heavy burden; one she didn't feel worthy to carry. When it came to the part about being judged by an equine, her heart sank. She had been responsible for her brother's horse falling down a hill and getting injured. She had forced him to carry her in the dead of night. She began to cry.

"Horses understand they are beasts of burden, Destiny. They have willingly accepted this role in the lives of humans. You will be judged for what was in your heart, not for the outcome of the accident."

"That is what I'm afraid of," Destiny said under her breath as she recalled almost being an accomplice to a man's murder. She followed the directions to sit in the second-to-last chair in the row of seven. The other people all sat like statues, lost in their thoughts. Destiny didn't have long to wait before the final candidate arrived and to find out whether the fate of humanity would fail because of her actions.

Ivan Novak

Vodnjan, Istrian Peninsula, Croatia
Sailor

As much as Ivan wanted to stay and protect his equine companion, he had to put his priorities first and get off the island. He rushed back to the signal fire with a tarp. He shaded his eyes, checking the ship's progress, and knew that if the ship was looking with binoculars, they would see the smoke.

Ivan had studied Morse code. Few people bothered to learn the code, but most sailors were familiar with the dashes and dots associated with the SOS distress signal. Having previously fashioned two posts in the sand next to the rescue fire, Ivan tied the tarp to the two posts and then walked around to the other side of the fire. Using the tarp to gather and then release the smoke, he began a steady stream of puffs: three small, three big, three small. He put all his effort into repeating the process.

An hour later, Ivan could see the ship had veered toward the bay. It was a sailing ship. His best guess was that it was a ketch as it had two masts and three sails. As far as size, he speculated it was in the 40-to-50-foot range. It was a common size and type of ship for people who circumnavigated and made the jump across the Pacific Ocean. He couldn't even begin to guess why they had ventured toward his island. He implemented phase two. First, he set off the flare; then he began running up and down the beach with his red flag.

Horse watched with interest. It was clear he was picking up on Ivan's excitement. Unknown to Ivan, his horse was aware of his heart rate. As Ivan raced back and forth, Horse kept pace with him. His giant heart beat slower than his human counterpart, the magnetic pull so strong that it had the ability to calm Ivan and soothe his nerves.

Nothing was going to slow down Ivan's heart rate, however, as he raced to the final phase of his plan. He put down the flag and ran to drag his life raft to the water. He grabbed his pole and prepared to make his way out to the reef. He didn't want the ship to think it could enter the harbor and meet the same fate as his own boat, of which all traces had long since been washed away by stormy waves.

Horse wedged himself between Ivan and his raft. It was as if he knew Ivan was leaving him. When Ivan went fishing and collected shellfish from the reef in his raft, Horse was never worried. He waited patiently for him to return. Ivan could tell Horse sensed this was different. Horse pushed Ivan with his nose and nickered softly, almost mournfully.

"I've got to go, buddy," he explained, barely able to keep his emotions in check. Ivan rubbed his favorite spot behind his ears, but Horse stared, not tilting his head in pleasure like he normally did. He knew.

"Maybe there's a way to come back for you. I will do everything I can, I promise. You see, there is just no way to get a boat close enough to this island to rescue you. You surely can't swim over the reef and onto a boat. It's just not possible."

Ivan threw his arms around Horse's neck. Horse tucked his head over Ivan's shoulders as if he were hugging back. Ivan cried into the soft, lustrous mane he had so carefully brushed every day until it was long, silken, and beautiful. He knew he couldn't linger, that he couldn't take any chances of missing this boat. He pulled back, tears streaming down his cheeks, and took Horse's head in his hands. "I love you, Horse," he said, his voice cracking with emotion. "I think you saved my life as much as I saved yours. I'm so sorry I can't make you understand. I hope you can forgive me."

*****

Six men were aboard the 49 ft. ketch. The ship was conducting a dedicated survey of the dolphin population of the Marquesas Islands in French Polynesia. Three observers were on duty at all times. The observation included visual searching and acoustic sampling with a towed hydrophone. The goal was to log 1,400 miles around all the islands, as well as in the open sea between the islands. The boat moved on zigzag tracks dictated by sea and wind conditions.

It wasn't luck that brought them close to Cobia Island; it was part of their research. Spotting the puffs of smoke signaling SOS and then the flare was lucky, as the white smoke against the vast sky had been difficult to spot. One man on watch thought for sure he saw something strange coming from the beach of the island. Since the island was uninhabited, he got out the binoculars to take a closer look.

Spotting the flare and then a lone man running up and down the beach waving a red flag, he knew they had found a castaway. Turning the ship toward the island, the captain kept a careful eye on the depth gauge, as he knew these islands were surrounded by dangerous reefs. When the ship got as close to the island as the captain dared, they dropped anchor and launched the dinghy.

Ivan had poled his way over the reef and was using a makeshift paddle to row toward the ship. He was riddled with anxiety. It had been so long since he'd had contact with humans that he was nervous about even speaking. He was sure that his disappearance at sea had resulted in news reports in the sailing world. He wondered if a year later anyone remembered his name. He looked like a Neanderthal with his long hair and thick beard.

Worst of all, he kept glancing back at the beach. Horse was running up and down the beach, working himself into a lather. He had deep regrets about leaving his simple life with Horse and going back to the world of people. Horse could survive on his own now, but Ivan felt deep in his heart that his horse would die of loneliness if he didn't return.

The dinghy intercepted the raft as it covered the distance to the reef in minutes. The two crew members welcomed Ivan. Ivan briefly explained how he had survived a shipwreck on the reef. He had been living alone on the island, hoping to be rescued, for almost a year. The men prepared to help Ivan transfer from the raft to the dinghy.

"Wait," Ivan said before stepping into the dinghy. "I need to get one thing." He had only one possession from his past that he wanted to take with him from the island. He reached inside the raft and pulled out a wooden spoon. "Now I'm ready."

It only took a few minutes to reach the ship. The men had taken a handheld radio with them and had already informed the captain that they successfully picked up the passenger and were heading back to the boat. The life raft was left floating to hopefully wash back up on the shore of the island.

Ivan was introduced to each of the crew members; thankfully, everyone spoke some English. He was asked lots of questions and answered them all as best he could. Then came an easy question. The captain asked if he was ready for a hot shower and a welcome meal before they pulled up anchor and set out for the main island. Even though it was out of their way, the captain would take Ivan to the main island before they continued their research.

Despite the thrill of being rescued, Ivan wanted to borrow binoculars to get one last glimpse of Horse before he left. Unfortunately, it would break his heart into pieces, and he wouldn't be able to explain his feelings to these strangers. He accepted the hot shower and the wonderful meal they cooked in honor of his rescue. Then they led him to the private V-berth where he could sleep on a soft bed while they got underway.

Ivan put his head on a soft pillow for the first time in a year. He pulled the sheet up around him and curled into a ball. He was so tired that even the thoughts of Horse running up and down the beach frantically searching for him couldn't keep him awake. He drifted off into a deep sleep.

*****

Although Ivan didn't consider himself religious, he was very spiritual. He held a deep connection to the spiritual realm. He believed in an afterlife and that good men went to be with their creator. He firmly believed his father was with him now and perhaps even had a hand in directing the sailboat to his little island. When he found himself on the marble path in the most beautiful world he had ever seen, he felt sure he was in heaven. Destiny.

The first thing Ivan noticed was the white clothing he was wearing. It confirmed for him that he had died and was in heaven. This pleased him. He was confused as to why he died shortly after being rescued. It didn't matter. He could be with his family again and didn't have to restart a new life on land. He wasn't afraid in the least. He was relieved.

Ivan looked around, expecting to be welcomed by his parents. Instead, he saw two men sitting on heavenly thrones, surrounded by majestic pillars. He assumed these were the biblical pearly gates through which he would have to pass.

"We are pleased to meet you, Ivan," the Son announced. He was the first human to be greeted with a smile. His enthusiasm was infectious. "This may sound satiric, but I regret to inform you that you are not deceased."

"What? Not dead? Is this just a very vivid dream?" Ivan asked, incredulously.

The Father replied with a chuckle, "Ivan, you are not dead and this is not a dream. I'm afraid this is a somber occasion for which you have been called."

Ivan was briefed that he had been chosen to represent mankind for judgment by the equines. He was filled in on the details that seven had been chosen from all walks of life and various regions of the Earth.

When Ivan tried to argue that he was merely an olive grower's son, the Father answered, "You may be the son of an olive grower, but your passion for sailing is what made you noteworthy. You are a sailor, Ivan."

Ivan shook his head and glanced down at his feet. He had indeed fulfilled his dream. Yet, when he realized he was being judged by Horse, all the good feelings evaporated. In his mind, he saw Horse running frantically up and down the beach as the man he had grown to love abandoned him. He knew this could go either way. Either Horse would see he had a kind and generous heart for saving him and bringing him back to life, or he would judge him as heartless for making him healthy and whole again only to then abandon him to the fate of living out the rest of his life alone.

The Father and Son had no words of consolation for Ivan as the fate of humanity was not going to be their decision. Mankind had made its choices. Man's time-honored servants, who were designed for this specific purpose, would be deciding their fate. The failsafe button had been pushed; the time had come to decide if man was worthy to continue living on the Earth or if it was time to wipe the slate clean.

Walking to the seventh and final chair in the row, Ivan's heart was heavy. He made no eye contact with his fellow humans. His greatest fear was not that mankind would be deemed unworthy to inhabit the planet any longer. Perhaps it was time for the world to be reborn. There was a lot wrong with humanity, and things only seemed to be getting worse.

What scared Ivan the most, what frightened him to the very core of his existence, was that he would be the one to tip the scales to the negative side. What if he was the fourth of the seven humans who were not chosen as being worthy? He would be responsible for the destruction of all mankind and for destroying every single life on planet Earth. It was a heavy burden for any man to bear.

*****

Seven chairs were filled by the men and women chosen to represent humanity. Their passions made them strong people. If the majority of these seven individuals had love in their hearts, appreciated the gifts of the Earth, and had a true connection to the planet and not just to their desires, humanity would be saved.

If four out of the seven people were deemed to have only self-interests, no appreciation for the gifts bestowed upon humans, and didn't have a strong connection to the Earth and her bounty, the humans who had been given thousands of years to evolve and grow would be wiped clean. Like a puff of smoke, all humans would fade away: their souls would be released.

The Father and Son knew this day would come. When humanity reached a certain level of apathy and self-serving desires, equines would be the ones to judge their fate. Their strength, their loyalty, and their desire to give of themselves to assist man were beyond contestation. They had carried man, fought with him in wars, served as ambassadors of peace, plowed his fields, and helped sow his crops... they had been by man's side for thousands of years. The history of mankind was carried on the backs of horses, and yet there were few humans left who even acknowledged their existence.

Equines were endowed with the ability to know what lies in the human heart. They could feel every heartbeat of a human standing next to them from a distance of four feet away. They knew when he was angry, when he was sad, when he was scared, and when he was happy. They sensed if there was love in his heart, hatred, or apathy. No matter what was inside the human heart, equines still served and gave completely of themselves. It was time for them to reveal what lay in the hearts of the seven humans chosen to represent humanity.

The Father and the Son rose from their thrones and approached the Seven. Each human was lost in introspection, struck dumb by the fact that the fate of the human race now rested on his or her shoulders. It was a burden almost too much for any of them to bear.

The two figures, dressed in white, appeared very large next to the humans in the chairs. Their presence drew furtive glances from the humans who were filled with awe and fear. All they could do was wait for the verdict. The Father and the Son stood before them and spoke what weighed on their hearts.

"If only humanity had been more intuitive, more appreciative of the gifts bestowed upon them," the Father began solemnly, "today's proceedings might not have been necessary. Regrettably, even though I granted you the greatest gifts, second only to sending my Son to bear the burden of your sins, mankind has evolved to a point where those very gifts have been disregarded. The faithful companion that has stood by humanity's side for centuries, aiding and supporting, has been forgotten, its contributions to humanity overlooked."

The Son interjected, "There were those who tried to awaken humanity to the importance of these celestial gifts. Parelli, for one, recognized the strength of the equine heart when he wrote, 'A horse doesn't care how much you know until he knows how much you care. Put your hand on your horse and your heart in your hand.'"

Continuing, he added, "Some of your fellow humans possessed the intuition to appreciate the divine connection between these gifts and mankind. Joni Mitchell eloquently captured it when she wrote, 'In their eyes shine stars of wisdom and courage to guide men to the heavens.' She comprehended the profound bond between horses and heaven."

The Father chimed in, "Even the Arabs, in their wisdom, devised proverbs that underlined the celestial connection between heaven and horses. 'The wind of heaven is that which blows between a horse's ears,' they declared."

"Monica Dickens posed this thought," the Son continued, "'You and your horse. His strength and beauty. Your knowledge and patience and determination and understanding and love. That's what forges the extraordinary partnership that leaves you wondering, what can heaven offer any better than what I have here on earth?'"

"There were individuals who comprehended the pivotal role horses played in your society and in nurturing the human soul," the Son pointed out. "Toni Robinson, for instance, recognized this when she wrote, 'Horses change lives. They bestow confidence and self-esteem upon our youth. They provide peace and tranquility to troubled souls; they give us hope.'"

"And now," the Father continued, "we shall summon forth those equines with whom you interacted—the ones destined to be the judges of what lies within the hearts of select men and women. Despite your fear and apprehension, I hope you feel honored to represent the human race."

Judgment of 'The Seven'

FOR THE FIRST TIME, there was an interaction between the seven individuals in the chairs. No words were spoken. They glanced furtively at one another and became restless knowing the time of judgment was at hand. They wanted to study the expressions on the faces of those around them. Were the expressions hopeful? Were they fearful? Did they give some hint as to how they felt they were going to be judged?

Those who felt good about their encounters were happy for themselves but still fearful for the fate of humanity. Were there enough of them to make a difference? Those who had doubts and concerns about their encounters looked to see if there were hopeful faces in their midst. Were there enough to be given a second chance?

Suddenly, there was a loud single note from a horn. The sound was pure, ethereal, and emanated from the sky above them. They all looked up. Floating in the sky was an angel dressed in white robes flowing in an unseen breeze. She was surrounded by an aura of light. She was not adorned with white-feathered angelic wings or a halo, yet all who saw her knew she was an angel. In her hands was the golden instrument. She lowered it from her lips. She looked down at the humans with a sad expression, then simply disappeared as quickly as she had arrived.

The Seven looked around them, specifically toward the perfect rows of trees lining the forest. They all sensed the forest was an important part of their experience. They were not wrong.

Seven horses emerged from the forest, walking in a straight line. Each person spotted the horse they knew would be judging him or her. They came in the order of their respective humans seated in the seven chairs. The horses were non-committal in their gait; their heads were neither held high nor low. They walked in unison as if being guided by an unseen rider. They walked steadily through the perfect green grass toward the humans and their creators.

There was a mix of emotions flowing through The Seven. Those that had strong bonds with their horses teared up. Those who shared brief experiences with their equines felt if they had only known how important their encounter had been, the outcome may have been vastly different. They all fanned the flames of hope that during their encounter there was enough good in their hearts that the horses would judge them kindly and fairly.

As the horses drew closer, it was obvious that these creatures were special. They exuded beauty not seen in the light of the Earth. In heaven, they were transformed into ethereal creatures. Their coats gleamed in the golden rays of sun that shone from the sky above. Their manes and tails were long and flowing. Dapples shone like starlight, the hues and colors of each horse were so enhanced that each spectrum of color shone with dazzling brilliance.

It dawned equally and abundantly on The Seven that these were creatures of God. Each recalled with trepidation images of how they had seen horses treated on Earth.

A single horse, ribs threatening to burst from its sunken sides, tied in a dusty field by a single rope around its neck, with nothing to eat and not a drop of water in sight. A team of exhausted and sweaty horses pulling a steel plow through a field on a 100-degree day, straining every muscle to make the teeth of the plow bite into and soften the earth. A horse being ridden over jumps relentlessly until lather foamed from under the girth and the horse's sides heaved with exhaustion.

Then there were the horses running around a track, the small rider beating it over and over with a crop, whipping every last bit of power and strength to cross the finish line first. Horses pulling carts in the cities, working for hours in the heat and traffic, smog-filled air filling their lungs.

Worst of all were those who had images of groups of horses being packed into a large trailer in the dark behind an auction. Shoved into the trailer, they were packed in like sardines for the long ride with no food and water to a factory where their flesh would be used for dog food.

The Seven wept at their beauty, the beauty that had been hidden from them. They all knew that mankind had failed these creatures. They had been used, abused, and credit for their accomplishments had long been forgotten by most of humanity.

Worst of all, they knew that most humans knew little about them and failed to find any connection to them. Many people feared the large animals even though they had been domesticated for over 10,000 years. Men had become usurpers, climbing to the top of the food chain. Once they were at the top and could control their destiny by machines and technology, respect and reverence for the greatness of these creatures had all but evaporated. This was not true of all humans but of many. This was the last thought of each of The Seven as the trail of horses arrived.

The Father and his Son had sadness in their eyes and in their hearts. They shared an unspoken thought. These humans, a small random sampling of mankind, understood humanity's lack of respect for the equines. They wept for the failure of their fellow humans. What chance did they have of being spared by the creatures that collectively knew how their species had been treated in the last few decades?

The Seven horses moved as a unified force, forming a line before the humans who remained seated in their chairs. Each person's face bore an expression of deep distress, haunted by reflections on how humanity had treated these majestic creatures. The memory of the goodness, kindness, and love once extended to these horses had seemingly faded into oblivion.

The Father spoke. "Go to your horse. If you need to apologize, do so. If you have good and loving memories to share, do so. You are not here to judge the rest of humanity. You are responsible for your actions and will be judged by these equines accordingly. Remove the negative thoughts in your mind and focus on the positive."

With that command, each person rose from their chair and went to meet his or her horse.

Since heaven is timeless, there was no telling the length of time for the visits with the equines. There was no hurry for the judgment to be passed. The Father and His Son listened to the thoughts and words conveyed between each person and horse.

Clusters of horses and humans spread around the lush, green field. Each pair was absorbed with one another, oblivious to the others around them. Apollo lay sprawled in the soft green grass. Justin lay beside him, his arms wrapped around his neck, his face buried in his mane. He was whispering, "I love you, Apollo. Please forgive me for even thinking of selling you to another person."

Paloma stood facing Diablo. Her eyes were focused on him. Her hands were placed on each side of Diablo's face. She was conveying her thoughts to him, explaining her actions on the day they had their encounter. "I know it was wrong to treat you that way. I get so wrapped up in trying to control everything in my life. It's my job, and sometimes I take that too seriously. I feel like I have to control every aspect of my life. You weren't very helpful," she pointed out. "You didn't have to run away with me, so I can't help feeling this is partially your fault," she lectured.

Not far from Paloma, Reginald and Jacque stood face to face. Reginald had a lot to convey. He was babbling about how he was a man who got things done and how he was a very successful man due to his ability to think critically and problem-solve. Reginald ranted on, explaining to his horse that it was just an unfortunate accident that caused their desperate situation. Jacque appeared disinterested.

Destiny was on her knees, her face in her hands, sobbing. Goose stood in front of her, his head lowered inches from hers. He was so close that each time he breathed out, his breath rustled her hair. "I'm sorry, I'm so sorry. I should have never ridden you away from the barn in the dark. If I had any idea you were going to be hurt, I would have never, ever done that! I'm so sorry, Goose."

Calchalero and Eduardo were so comfortable with one another that Calchalero lay in the grass on his side. He lazily took mouthfuls of the lush green grass and chewed contentedly. Eduardo sat in the grass next to him and leaned against Calchalero's shoulder, a blade of grass sticking out from his mouth. Eduardo basked in the beauty around him. "Who would have ever thought we'd end up in heaven together, huh, buddy? Seems like we rode right up to heaven. You know, I won't hold it against you if you judge me unworthy. I did try to ride you around the world. But we undertook the journey as partners, you know? We were a team retracing your routes so your breed could get the respect they deserve for their accomplishments." Calchalero's head bobbed up and down, seemingly agreeing.

Sophia had no idea how to talk to her horse. The brilliant white mare had a kind eye. They seemed to sparkle from their inky black depths. Sophia asked if she could touch her, and the mare responded by placing her head over Sophia's shoulder. Sophia teared up and threw her arms around the horse's neck. She buried her face in her thick, soft mane and cried. She didn't know why she was crying. She had no agenda in helping the mare give birth and get out of the ravine; she simply knew it was the right thing to do. Sophia felt the mare appreciated what she had done. The woman and mare embraced. No words were needed.

Ivan and Horse faced off. Ivan pointed at the horse with his index finger. "I was going to come back for you. I wasn't going to leave you there forever. I had to get off the island so I could rescue us both!" Horse turned; his back end now faced Ivan. Horse's tail swished with agitation. "Do you not remember that I rescued you? I brushed you every day, fed you, played with you on the beach of that deserted island? If I hadn't nursed you back to health, you would have died!" Ivan began to cry, burying his face in his hands. "It broke my heart having to leave you. There was no way I could make you understand. You were the first real friend I ever had. I love you," Ivan sobbed. Horse turned around slowly, his head lowered, he walked up to Ivan. He pushed him gently with his nose. Ivan threw his arms around Horse's neck and wept.

*****

The trumpet sounded again. Horses and humans looked toward the sky. All movement paused in a pregnant moment of silent anticipation. The same angel appeared and gave the signal that judgment was about to begin. All creatures, now bound as one, knew the meaning of the sound. The horse and humans disentwined from their one-on-one interactions. Each human stood or straightened, and every horse moved closer to its human partner. In pairs, they approached the Father and the Son.

The Father and Son

"TAKE YOUR SEATS, PLEASE," the Father instructed.

The humans silently returned to their seats. The horses followed, their heads hung low, and took their positions behind each human. The looks on the humans' faces ranged from peaceful to panicked. Some seemed to have found comfort; others let their emotions feed off their fears. They glanced at one another and back to the Father as he prepared to speak to them. The tension in the heavenly air was thick enough to slice with a sword.

"The time has come, my children," the Father announced. "I will call each horse forward. I will ask if he accepts or rejects you as a worthy human." No one spoke or asked any questions. They simply sat still, waiting for their verdict, wearing masks of nervous anticipation.

The Father and Son stood side by side. This was a tense time for them as well. The humanity they had created, watched over, and assisted through the ages would either be saved or erased. They loved their children enough to know that sometimes starting over was better than wandering down the wrong path. Should they be judged not worthy, each soul would begin anew. All that had been created, all that had transpired, would be erased. Man would begin again on a clean planet with a clean slate.

Yet, there was beauty in evolution as well. Man had such intelligence and inspiration that wonderful inventions and creative enterprises had turned the world into a globe of wonders. It took centuries for those arrivals. As long as humans could merge those changes with the beauty of the Earth and still respect her gifts, life could continue. The time had come for the equines to make that decision. This was the first time since the creation of humanity that God and his Son didn't know the outcome.

For the third time, the angel blew her horn. The sound was long, a cry reverberating through the heavens. Soon, the sky was filled with heavenly beings. Angelic shapes, wisps of white, and slivers of cloud-like forms merged, mixed, and filled the sky above the humans. There was an eerie quality about the gathering, an unsettled feeling felt viscerally by all souls. The humans looked up to the sky above, then back to the Father and Son, silently waiting for answers.

"Our host of heavenly angels has come to watch the judgment. This gathering is unprecedented. They too have stock in the outcome as they all have loved ones on Earth and in Heaven. If man is found worthy, Heaven and Earth will continue as they have for thousands of years. If man is judged not worthy to continue, there will be many changes for all of us."

The Father looked up to the sky. "BE STILL," he commanded in a way that was felt rather than heard. The shapes and vague figures above swirled energetically for a moment, then merged. The sky became quiet, a still blanket of white. The humans stared up in awe, then turned back toward the Father and his Son.

*****

"Reginald, please rise." Reginald felt weak in the knees and wasn't sure he could stand. But he did, shakily. He was wringing his hands as his horse passed him and approached the Father and the Son.

Jacque walked up and stood before the Father with his head bowed low, almost touching the ground. The Father placed his hand on Jacque's crown, between his ears, nestling it softly amidst his forelock. "What say you? Do you find your humans appreciative of the gifts of the Earth? You know what is in his heart. Dear one, please tell us, is Reginald worthy?"

The Father closed his eyes for a moment, then raised his hand. Jacque raised his head, turned slowly, and walked back to his place behind the chair.

"Reginald, you have been judged. Your equine has seen into your heart. He finds no appreciation for life other than your own. He feels you are greedy, you feed upon the weak, and your only goal is to enhance your wealth and your own life."

Reginald sank down into his seat and squirmed in his chair. He wrapped his arms around his body and embraced himself tightly. He wept silently, knowing the verdict was true.

*****

"Sophia, please rise." Sophia took a deep, shuddering breath, rose from her chair, and stood tall. She had a look of neutrality as her horse approached the Father.

"Beautiful white mare," he said as he placed his hand on the crown of her head. His hand became lost in the lustrous, bushy white forelock nestled between her perky white ears. She met his gaze. "Please tell me, what say you? Do you find your human appreciative of the gifts of the Earth?"

Father stood still with his eyes closed and absorbed the verdict without expression. He lifted his hand and the mare turned and walked to her spot behind Sophia's chair.

Sophia stood confidently, waiting for her verdict. If there was doubt, she didn't let it show. Her posture suggested she felt good about her efforts to save the mare and about the values in her heart.

"Sophia," the Father announced. "You have been found worthy." Instantly, there were sounds like rumbling thunder in the sky above. The humans were shocked and cringed in their seats. Father smiled. "Sorry, that is the celebration from above. You have many souls rooting for you right now," he said with a sad smile. "Let us hope there are more among you who are worthy."

Sophia sat with a relieved look on her face, but not with a smile. She knew she was only one. The world needed three more good souls to save the human race.

*****

Paloma was next. "Paloma, please rise." Paloma wore a sour expression. It seemed she was about to protest. Father raised his hand. "This is not your time to speak, Paloma. Your actions have been judged. It is time to hear the verdict."

Diablo walked without hesitation to the Father. Diablo shook his head and snorted as the Father placed his hand gently on the horse's head. "Please tell me, Diablo, what say you? Do you find your human appreciative of the gifts of the Earth?"

Father closed his eyes. It was not long before Diablo turned and walked to his place behind Paloma's chair. Paloma followed him with her eyes and glared at him. There was no love loss between the two.

"Paloma, you are a child of God," Father began, "but you have strayed far from what is important to humanity. Diablo has seen into your heart and tells me that not only do you not appreciate the gifts of the Earth, but you use others to achieve your agendas."

Paloma's mouth opened, but no words came out. She seethed in anger but remained speechless.

"I'm sorry, my child, but you have been found unworthy."

Paloma didn't shed a tear. She sat back down rigidly and stared straight ahead. Her fiery Latino roots were deep. Even in the face of disaster, she would remain stoic.

*****

Eduardo was called next. He rose from his seat when asked to rise. He watched Calchalero as he walked up to take his place before the Father. His expression was neutral, that of acceptance. His fate was out of his hands, but his bond with his horse was strong.

With the respect shown to the other equines, the Father placed his hand gently between Calchalero's ears. "Calchalero, please tell me, what say you? Do you find your human appreciative of the gifts of the Earth?"

Father closed his eyes. There seemed to be a long pause. Father nodded. Calchalero walked back to his place behind Eduardo's chair. Eduardo's expression changed, not appearing neutral anymore. His brow creased as he waited for his verdict.

"Eduardo," Father began, "it appears you have used your horses as beasts of burden. You have used them to herd your cows, and you have undertaken a long journey that has caused harm to your horses."

Eduardo cast his eyes down, wondering if his motives were self-driven. He had asked a lot of his horses, but he also valued them greatly and always strived to take good care of them. Was that enough?

The phrase "Was it enough" echoed in his head. He had heard it before. A memory appeared like he was watching a scene from a movie. The Father and the Son had warned him after his accident about taking into consideration his horses and their needs. The memory returned to Eduardo in a flash that shocked him to his core. Fear creased the brow of the seasoned gaucho.

"Calchalero has decided," the Father stated. "He told me that your bond with your horses and your respect for them is immense. You do push their limits and make them work hard, but he does understand he must serve you." There was a collective breath expelled by angels and humans as the Father announced, "He has deemed you worthy. You respect nature and her gifts, and you have a good heart."

Thunder boomed across the heavens for a second time. Eduardo let out a huge sigh of relief. Three humans remained to be judged. There was still hope for humanity.

*****

Justin waited for his turn. He was next. He almost jumped out of his chair when the Father announced his name. "Justin, please rise." Nervous, Justin inhaled deeply and rose from the chair. Apollo walked forward and took his place before the Father.

Father placed his hand on the large horse's head. Apollo was the tallest of all the horses. "Please tell me, Apollo, what say you? Do you find your human appreciative of the gifts of the Earth?"

Father closed his eyes and nodded several times before removing his hand from between Apollo's ears. "You may return," the Father instructed Apollo.

Justin glanced nervously at the horse as he returned to his spot behind his chair. His heart involuntarily beat faster. He felt breathless at the sight of the beautiful animal. As incredible as Apollo was back on Earth, in this enhanced form, Justin was completely in awe of Apollo's magnificence. For a brief second, he forgot his fear as he was transfixed by his beauty. Then, Father broke the spell.

"Apollo has made it clear that men have abused him," the Father began. "Justin, you rescued Apollo. It was only through love that you helped him recover mentally and physically from the abuse he suffered from men. However," Justin froze at the word "however," "you almost sold him back into the world of evil men."

Justin's heart sank at the mention of the sale. Had he doomed the fate of humanity with his unthinkable action? He had tried to justify it even though, in his heart, he knew it was the wrong thing to do.

"Fortunately, your father came to your rescue and gave you the means to keep Apollo. This action saved you, as Apollo felt you did love him and desperately wanted to keep him. It was your will, hard work, perseverance, and love for your horse that turned the tide. You have been deemed worthy."

Thunder roared from the heavens above. The humans clutched the sides of their chairs. Justin almost passed out from relief, fearful he might collapse from the ground shaking beneath him. He sat quickly, wiping the tears of joy from his eyes.

There were only two humans left to be judged. The fate of humanity could go in either direction, as all seven humans and the hordes of angels above were well aware.

*****

Second to last, Destiny was sweating bullets. The fate of humanity rested with her and the man seated beside her. It was down to him and her. Her countenance did not exude confidence that she would be chosen worthy. After the rumblings from heaven ceased, Destiny was asked to stand. "Destiny, please rise."

Goose walked forward and took his place in front of the Father. The Father placed his hand on Goose's forelock to hear his thoughts. "Please tell me, Goose, what say you? Do you find your human appreciative of the gifts of the Earth?"

The Father closed his eyes and listened in silence. He nodded. His expression remained neutral, yet when his eyes opened, there was sadness in them. He dropped his hand slowly from Goose's forehead. The horse walked back to his place, his head down low.

No one watching had a warm, fuzzy feeling about Goose's decision.

"Destiny," the Father began, "you have chosen the profession of a medical doctor to help people. That is noble. But somewhere along the line, you have lost sight of your purpose. You have been complicit in attempting to harm others, even though you are a good person. You have lost your way."

Ashamed and afraid, Destiny dropped her head and began to cry. The outcome of this decision had been foreshadowed. There would be no thunder from heaven for her.

"I'm sorry, Destiny. You plotted to hurt humans, which ultimately caused harm to Goose. The goodness in you was veiled to Goose because of the evil with which you were intertwined. For this, the decision has been made that you are not worthy. You have lost sight of the true gifts of the Earth."

*****

No rumble of thunder emanated from the heavens to herald the joy of another human having passed the test that would save mankind. Ivan trembled at the thought. His worst fear was coming to fruition. He was going to be the deciding factor in whether mankind was given another chance or destroyed.

The mere thought paralyzed him with fear. He trembled, head bowed as he waited to be addressed. "Rise, Ivan," the Father commanded. Ivan rose and waited for Horse to approach the Father.

"Horse," Father called. "Please come forward." Horse didn't budge. "HORSE," the Father repeated, using the name given to him by Ivan on the island. Ivan turned and looked behind him. This time it was Horse trembling with fear.

All seven humans watched the interaction between Horse and the Father in stunned silence. Whatever was happening was not part of the script. Equines were the chosen servants of the Father, created to watch over men. They were obedient and compliant. This reaction took everyone by surprise.

God and the Son looked at one another. They exchanged silent thoughts. The Son walked over to Horse. All eyes locked on the scene unfolding before them. The Son placed his hand on Horse's neck and said, "Come, it's time for you to make your judgment."

Reluctantly, Horse began to walk forward, following the Son. Halfway to the Father, Horse caused humans and angels to catch their breath. Without warning, Horse's front legs folded. His body lowered to the ground; his hindquarters followed. Horse plopped unceremoniously to the ground, then rolled onto his side, his front legs tucked in tightly. He closed his eyes and lowered his head to the ground. He was protesting. He was refusing to make a judgment on Ivan.

The Father came forward and knelt next to Horse. He placed his hand on the crown of Horse's forehead. He closed his eyes and was silent. Every human and every angel held their breath.

Finally, the Father rose. Horse remained still, lying with his legs folded under his body, his nose touching the ground, his eyes closed. He appeared to be asleep.

Father and Son conferred in their silent, collective thoughts. Father approached the Seven. "It seems we have a conflict. Horse has refused to make a judgment. The weight of the burden has stricken him silent. He refuses to be the deciding factor for mankind."

The humans were shocked; the sky above them rumbled from the unexpected turn of events.

"This cannot end in a tie. A decision must be made," the Son announced. "We will go now with the horses back into the forest. When we return, a decision will have been made."

In the blink of an eye, the Father, the Son, and all the horses were gone. It was like a jump cut in a movie. One moment, they were all there together. The next moment, they were gone. Seven humans sat in their chairs, dumbfounded, except for Ivan. He remained standing. He was shaking and sobbing.

*****

In a daze, one by one, the humans stood up and looked around. There were no Gods or horses in sight. Ever so slowly, they began to mingle, to talk quietly amongst themselves. Several laid a comforting hand on Ivan's shoulder and spoke soft words of encouragement.

The main question they had on their mind was why Horse refused to pass judgment. Only Ivan might have the answer. The group closed in around Ivan, desperate to hear his story.

Ivan began by introducing himself as an olive farmer. Then he said, "No, I am a sailor. I used to be an olive farmer. I sold my farm to solo sail around the world."

His fellow men were in awe of this man. He had never sailed as an adult, yet he took a bold leap of faith to circumnavigate the Earth. This raised a multitude of questions.

"How did you meet Horse?" "What was the encounter like?" "Did you part on good terms?" The questions flew fast and furious.

Ivan looked around. "Let's all sit in the grass," he said, looking longingly at the green field. It looked so peaceful and pleasant. "I don't know how much time we have. I will tell you the story."

The group moved as one. They entered the field and sat in a circle. The world around them seemed peaceful even though the fate of humanity lay in the balance. If they just heard the story, maybe they would have a better clue as to how all this would end.

He began with his dream to sail and the decision he had to make to leave behind the legacy his father had created. Ivan recalled that after his father passed away, he wanted to follow his own dream. He described his plan to buy the boat, learn to sail, and depart on his voyage in the six months following the sale of his olive farm.

No one interrupted. Ivan explained the route he took, the places he visited, and how he naturally took to sailing, being alone, becoming one with the sea. By the time he reached the Pacific Ocean, he had sailed almost halfway around the world. It was there that the storm hit; his boat rolled over three times before he managed to get the sails set to ride out the storm.

Ivan described the wreck on the reef and waking up on the beach, seeing the shadow of a horse peering at him from behind a palm tree. He told the story of how he used his life raft to salvage what he could from his sunken ship. He explained that his chance of being rescued was slim as he was on one small island in a chain of hundreds of uninhabited islands.

The six humans were enraptured by his tale. Ivan described how he solved the mystery of why the horses on the island had died and how he nursed the last remaining horse back to health. For almost a year, Horse was his best friend, the first real friend he had ever had.

"Why would he not choose you to be worthy?" Justin finally asked. "You did everything to save him; why is he refusing to save mankind?"

"It seems we have hope," Destiny interjected. "You are obviously a good person. You were kind and loved Horse. How
can that decision not go in your favor?"

"I haven't finished the story," Ivan answered, not able to
meet the gaze of the others. "One day, as Horse and I were
playing on the beach, we spotted a boat on the horizon. A
ship finally came close to the island. It was a research vessel.
I had prepared for the event that a ship might ever venture
close to our island. I lit my signal fire. They spotted the smoke
and saw me.

Ivan described how the ship anchored beyond the reef. "I
had to decide whether to save myself or stay with Horse. I
suspected he would die of loneliness if I left him, but there
was no way to get him over the reef and onto the boat with
me. I used my life raft and paddled out past the reef, where
I was rescued."

"You left him?" Paloma asked. "How could you do that?"

"I had to take the opportunity to be rescued," Ivan responded, visibly upset. I was in a quandary. I knew I couldn't explain
to Horse that I was leaving and that I would do my best to
come back and find a way to rescue him, too. On the other
hand, the island was his home. It was where he was born,
where his herd had lived for hundreds of years. I didn't know
if that's where he wanted to live out the rest of his days. It
was the hardest decision I ever had to make," he said, burying
his head in his hands and sobbing at the memory. "I planned
to try and find a way to come back and rescue him. I had no
way to tell him that."

*****

There was silence among the humans. Each was lost in his or her thoughts. They sat in the grass and admired the beauty around them as they contemplated the situation as well as their emotions. Time was not a construct. It was a thread woven into the existence of the place that was simply part of the fabric of reality. It didn't tug in any particular direction. It had no impact or feeling of passing. There was no past, present, or future; they existed in the 'now.'

When God and his Son reappeared, the group rose to their feet. They looked back at their chairs and wondered if that was where they should be.

"No need to return your chairs. All has been resolved," the Father spoke. "Sit, my children, relax, and we will explain the conclusion of this event."

The humans looked at one another. They had bonded. Instead of seven separate individuals, they were now a tight-knit group. They had come to know one another. Their shared experience of representing mankind and the fate of the world had drawn their spirits together.

Instead of sitting, the group instinctively drew closer together. They were going to hear their fate together, not sitting alone, separated from one another. Without saying a word, the seven reached out and took one another's hands. They formed a line of solidarity. Whatever their fate was, they were prepared, the last vestiges of man, holding on to one another for support.

God and his Son smiled at their reaction. "It is good you have found strength in one another. If humanity had learned this lesson long ago, the world would be a different place."

It was Reginald who spoke. "Tell us our fate, then; we are ready."

"Horse was torn because he loved his human. He refused to make a judgment on Ivan because he grieved when Ivan left. He didn't know he would try to come back. He couldn't make a judgment because his heart was broken."

"Did you tell him?" Ivan asked. "Did you let him know that I was planning on trying to come back for him?"

"No," God answered, sorrow in his voice. "Horse disobeyed me and refused to complete his task. His input was not given. That left the decision back to us. Because Horse disobeyed a commandment, our plans have been altered."

The humans stiffened involuntarily, then shuffled nervously, glancing at one another, fearing the worst about the fate of humanity.

"You're going to wipe us out, aren't you?" Sophia asked, fear in her voice.

"My children," the Father replied, trying to comfort the terrified humans. "We have decided that we will give humans more time. Mankind is going to be granted one more chance to appreciate Earth and her gifts."

There was a collective sigh. Some smiled; others wiped away the tears of joy and relief that had been waiting behind their eyes. Everyone except for one human. Justin. He had a feeling there was a caveat to this decision. "What about the horses?" he asked, bravely stepping forward. "How do they feel about this?" His voice was thick with emotion and suspicion.

The Father and the Son looked at one another. The silence that ensued as the humans were taken aback by Justin's response left a gaping hole in the happy moment. All motion paused as they waited for the response.

The Son spoke, filling the humans in on the decision made in the forest. "We have decided that instead of wiping the slate clean of humans, we will be relieving horses of their duty as the watchers of men. They have performed their duty for thousands of years."

"What do you mean?" Eduardo asked, looking very uncomfortable with the statement.

"Horses have been so far removed from their original purpose that it seems it's time to call them all home. It's not fair to them anymore, as we can see the effects, the toll that was extracted from the burden we have placed on them," the Son answered. "We will decide the fate of humanity in the future."

"But that's not fair!" Justin shouted. "They are my life! You gave them to us as a gift, and now you want to take that gift away?"

There was a flurry of activity. The group surrounded Justin. The Seven came together and formed a pack. They hugged, Justin at the center. "If you'll please excuse us?" Destiny asked, turning from the group to address the Father and the Son, "We need a minute. Alone."

The group of humans moved away. The Father and the Son looked at one another and smiled. "Do they really think we can't hear them, that we don't know every thought in their minds?"

$$*****$$

As soon as the group felt they were out of earshot of the Father and the Son, they sat back in a circle on the soft, fragrant grass. As they glanced around them, they noticed the blanket of white souls in the heavens above, trying to be unobtrusive, undulating restlessly. They too had been waiting for the final decision and hopefully a reason to celebrate.

"Do you think they can hear us?" Paloma asked, pointing upward.

Speaking softly, Justin led the discussion. "I don't know about you guys, but I think that removing horses from the planet is a very bad idea. I know they have served us for centuries and may be tired of serving us, but they are the reason humanity has survived and thrived. We still need them."

"What happens if we lose them?" Eduardo asked with concern. "I know many people have lost connection with them, but what if that can be brought back? I know my life is better with them in it. I feel comfort, safety, and empowerment with them by my side. One moment of riding my horse was better than all my moments combined being a lawyer," he pointed out.

Reginald chimed in, "I know that I was one of the people who failed. I didn't recognize and appreciate the gifts of the Earth. I see now, through your eyes, the power, the strength that horses are, the gifts they have given and continue to give humanity."

The group took turns, each sharing his or her thoughts about the potential horses had to make the world a better

place. They all felt it was important for the younger generation of people to experience horses and for their parents to
encourage them.

They talked about the lessons learned from horses about
hard work, patience, and loyalty. They agreed that horses
brought us closer to the values that were important in life.
As mankind strayed farther from their appreciation of horses, they also strayed from the values that made humanity
better. To do away with horses was the first step in erasing
hope for mankind. A silent decision was made by the Seven.
When someone finally uttered it out loud, they all nodded in
agreement. The group rose, hugged one another, and walked
to face the Father and the Son.

"We have come to speak our peace," Justin said, the unofficial leader of the group.

The Father and the Son looked knowingly at one another.
"Go ahead," said the Father.

Justin shuffled his feet and looked down at them. The
burden he was carrying was almost too great for him. The
others put their hands out to touch him, lending him the
courage to speak. Justin took a deep breath, raised his eyes
to the deities, and spoke.

"We would like you to reconsider your decision to take
your gift of horses away from humans," Justin began, his
voice breaking with emotion. "You gave us this gift, and
maybe we haven't recognized its value, but you also gave
us hope and the ability to believe in miracles. We would
like another chance. We think humanity will come to see
horses as the gifts they are. If you take them from us, we feel
strongly that humanity will continue to deteriorate."

"We have made our decision," the Father said. "It is humans or horses that have to go."

"Humans," Eduardo interjected without pause. "Take us. We don't want to live in a world without those you sent to help us, guide us, and make us better."

The Seven turned toward the Father and the Son as one, and nodded in agreement.

"You are all in agreement that you are willing to erase humanity rather than live without the equines?" the Father asked, rubbing his chin and glancing at the Son.

"Yes," the Seven replied in unison.

Suddenly, the ground began to shake. The Seven grabbed one another for balance, frightened at the sudden eruption. Their collective thought was that this was the end of their lives as humans. Then, with a sudden burst of light, the angel with the horn appeared above them. A single note echoed powerfully through the heavens. The Seven grouped as one and hugged tightly, not understanding what was happening. The white blanket of souls covering the heavens erupted, broke apart, and began to celebrate. The ground shuddered beneath the humans.

"My children," the Father announced. "We chose wisely from the pool of humanity. You have passed the test. As a group, you decided to honor the gifts of the Earth over your own lives. It was a brutal test, but you have passed. Humanity and horses have been saved."

*****

With the threat of extinction over, the Seven embraced as a group. Their emotions poured forth as the reality set in. As one, they had managed to save humanity and the equines. Sins of their past had been erased. They had all been deemed worthy.

Time was not a factor as the spirits of those they loved and who had passed before came to greet *the* Seven.

Ivan embraced the spirit of his father, who told him how proud he was of him for his strength and for following his dreams. His father also told him that there would be a groundswell of support after his rescue. There would be those who would help him find a way to rescue his horse off the island. They could have a long and happy life together if that was the path he chose. Ivan cried tears of joy.

Reginald met with his mother and father. They were disappointed with him and the importance he had placed on power and money. Reginald saw the error of his ways and promised things would be different now that he had seen the light. Reginald vowed he would use his gifts to make a positive difference in the world instead of seeking money and power for himself.

Justin met his grandparents. They were proud of the courage he had shown, for the dedication to horses, despite having to battle the will of his father to succeed. They were pleased with the fact the family had built the small vineyard they had started into a beautiful estate. Most of all, they wished him well as he would be representing his country in the Olympics with the full support of his family.

Paloma met her grandfather. He was not happy that she had succumbed to the power and corruption found in her government position over finding her roots, giving back to her culture, and being a person that positively contributed to life. She nodded and cried as she took the criticism and vowed that when she returned, things would be different. She even promised to give up politics and move back to Puerto Rico so she could spend more time with her grandmother.

Eduardo had a visit from his favorite uncle, the brother of his father. He made Eduardo promise that after his journey to retrace the roots of his horse was over, he would reunite with his family. Family was more important than any journey. There was work to be done in his country of Argentina, for the farmland and for the livestock. Eduardo needed to make that a priority. His country needed his services. Eduardo promised he would do his best to make that happen.

Sophia met her grandparents on her father's side. They took immense pride in her ambition to become a world-class marathon runner, her unwavering dedication, and her commitment to chasing her dreams. Her grandmother told her that it wasn't an accident that she found the horse that day. And the man that saved her? He was going to help her achieve her goal of racing in the ultra-marathon. He was also going to be an excellent father to their children, she said with a wink.

Destiny was greeted by a relative from the Herero Tribe. It was a great aunt on her mother's side. She explained that Destiny's battle was not with getting retribution for the persecution of the Herero tribe. It was to make a positive difference in the lives of people living in the present. She told her to support her brother and be there to celebrate his success with his horses. Be a healer. Promote the gifts of the planet, like horses and nature, and make them a part of who you are. Heal the inside of the people around you as well as the world around you. Destiny agreed to try.

*****

As suddenly as they had appeared, the spirits returned to the heavens, wisps of evaporating mist. The Father and the Son stood before The Seven. The celestial celebration had come to an end.

"You have done well, my children," the Father relayed. "You have given the human race more time. Decades will pass before we will assess if positive changes have been made."

The Son continued, "You will be returned to Earth. We hope that you find your way toward the positive changes you have been shown. Because of your passion, you all can make a difference in your world. You will not remember anything that has transpired here, but the seeds of change have been planted in your hearts. Let them grow. Sow them in everyone you meet.

"Understand this," the Father announced. "You cannot force someone to hear a message they are not ready to receive, but never underestimate the power of planting a seed. If you sow enough seeds, seven of you can make a difference."

With that, The Seven vanished. Each human would wake up from a very deep sleep with a strange feeling that his or her world had changed.

*****

"Do you think it will be enough?" the Son asked the Father. "I hope so, my son; I truly hope so."